Boundless Dreams

DIANE GREENWOOD MUIR

Cover Design Photography: Maxim M. Muir

ISBN-13: 978-1977616739
ISBN-10: 1977616739

Don't miss any books in Diane Greenwood Muir's

Bellingwood Series

Diane publishes a new book in this series
on the 25th of March, June, September, and December.
Short stories are published in between those dates
and vignettes are written and published each month
in the newsletter.

Journals
(Paperback only)
Find Joy – A Gratitude Journal
Books are Life – A Reading Journal
Capture Your Memories – A Journal

Re-told Bible Stories
(Kindle only)
Abiding Love - the story of Ruth
Abiding Grace - the story of the Prodigal Son

You can find a list of all published works
at nammynools.com

CONTENTS

ACKNOWLEDGMENTS

While I write fictional stories set in Bellingwood, there are many things in the real world that feel overwhelming. Tonight, as I write this, Florida is in the middle of Hurricane Irma. Hurricane Harvey is long gone, but the devastation left in its wake is enormous. Fires rage throughout the Pacific Northwest, major earthquakes have rattled Mexico and southern Asia is devastated by floods.

In the midst of these awful tragedies, glimmers of hope and beacons of light shine forth. People come through and show us their very best as they care for each other. Those glorious stories of goodness, both told and untold, are what push us forward.

Those stories of hope are why I write these books. It's easy to look for the negative and find the bad in people. We have to work much harder to recognize goodness and even greatness. If only for a short time, I want you to show what I see in the world and what I bring to life in Bellingwood. No matter what, hope can be found. I'm so grateful that it is part of my life.

I am thankful for those who help bring these books to publication. There is so much that goes on before a book gets to you and these people mean the world to me for the things they freely offer. Thank you to: Diane Wendt, Carol Greenwood, Alice Stewart, Eileen Adickes, Fran Neff, Max Muir, Linda Baker, Linda Watson, Nancy Quist, Rebecca Bauman, and Judy Tew.

My gratitude for you, my readers, is unending. You are a real community of friends for me and when I need encouragement, you are right there - ready to offer it. When I need a little insanity, you're also there. The Bellingwood page on Facebook is more than just a page to find out about these books. It is a growing community of wonderful people. Spend time with us at facebook.com/pollygiller.

.

CHAPTER ONE

"I'm glad you're home," Polly said and nodded toward the cats and dog. "So are they."

"Thank you so much for watching our animals," Andy said. She bent to pick up one of the black cats. Polly couldn't tell which was Chaz and which was Addam, but as long as Andy could tell them apart, that's all that mattered.

Len's aging golden retriever flopped his tail on the ground and stretched out in the beam of sunshine he'd claimed. Dusty was a wonderful dog. Rebecca begged to take him home every evening, but Len had insisted he'd be happier in his own house. The old dog had grown fond of Andy's cats and they kept each other company.

Andy and Len had returned late last night after a short vacation to Estes Park. Since Andy worked nearly full-time at the library this summer while Joss Mikkels learned how to manage five children, Len was ready to drag his wife away from Bellingwood as soon as Joss returned to the library. The spur of the moment decision gave Andy no time to get anyone in place to care for her animals so Polly had volunteered.

Polly went out the sliding glass doors onto Andy's deck and down the steps, looking up toward the Bell House. They'd finished Polly's back fence two weeks ago and Henry added a gate at the southeast corner for access to … well … the cemetery. From there, it was a quick walk along the pathways down to Andy's house.

The path home took Polly past a couple who were standing over a tombstone. She smiled and nodded as she approached them. This was always so awkward. Sometimes people wanted to be left alone in their grief. Others wanted to tell stories of people whose graves they were visiting, while still others acted as if they wanted to talk about anything other than death and how it had impacted them. In a couple of weeks, Polly had met them all.

The man turned and put his hand out. "I'm Reuben Greene. Do you live near here?"

Polly shook his hand. "Hi, I'm Polly Giller." When he released her hand, she pointed at the Bell House. "My family and I live there."

At that, the woman looked up. "In the old Springer House?"

"Yes, do you know it?" Polly asked.

The woman shrugged and smiled. "Just old ghost stories from when I was a kid."

Polly put her hand out. "I don't know you. Are you from around here?"

"Not for a very long time," the woman said. She took Polly's hand in both of hers and held it gently. "I'm Judy." She glanced at the tombstone. "Once upon a time I was a Grady, but for the last forty-two years, I've been a Greene. It suits me much better."

"Are you staying with family in town?" Polly asked, curious as to why these two had chosen to stop her to talk.

Reuben put his hand on his wife's back. "Her sister lives in Bellingwood, but we're staying at the hotel on the highway for now."

"I can't believe that someone fixed that place up," Judy said. "It was a run-down junk of a place when I lived here. I figured it would have been long gone, but now it's gorgeous. Things have changed in the last forty-five years." She smiled up at her husband. "Almost fifty, I guess."

"My husband and I renovated the hotel," Polly said.

Judy pointed at the house. "And that place, too?"

Polly chuckled. "I guess we have the bug. Henry is a contractor. I met him when I bought the old high school."

"You're the one!" she said. "I couldn't believe what I was seeing when we came into town. And that beautiful garden out front, too. You also have horses. Isn't that barn standing where the old gym was?"

"The gym was gone by the time I arrived," Polly said. "We had a fun barn-raising. I knew I wanted animals, and one day I discovered four big Percheron horses needing to be rescued. The next thing I knew, they were in my brand-new barn."

The woman creased her forehead as she peered at Polly. "Are you from Bellingwood? I don't recognize your name."

"No. My family lived in Story City. I moved out to Boston to go to college and returned to Iowa about five years ago."

"We're thinking of doing the same thing," Reuben said. "All those years living in San Francisco and I'm plumb wore out." He chuckled when his wife poked him. "She reminds me that I'm not a hick. I'm worn out. Is that better?" He winked at Polly. "I have an excuse. I grew up in the hollers of Kentucky, so it's okay if I'm a hick."

"You're thinking about moving back to Iowa?" Polly asked.

Judy took a deep breath before speaking. "We're looking around the country. I wanted to see if Bellingwood was still the uptight little town that I ran from so many years ago." She smiled. "I don't know why we're telling you this. You only just met us. We're generally quite a bit more circumspect in our conversations with strangers."

"It's what happens when you leave the big city and end up in central Iowa," Polly said. "You can hardly help yourself. Are you staying in town long?"

"For a short time," Reuben acknowledged. "Judy hasn't seen her sister in ... what's it been, honey, ten years?"

"When Mother died." Judy pointed at the tombstone. "Twelve years ago. July, 2005. Hot summer day. We stood right here and I wished for a fan to blow up my ..." she stopped, flinching as she giggled. "I'm sorry. That was rude. I have a tendency to say things I shouldn't. You don't know me well enough yet."

"Your sister lives here in town?"

"Out on a farm," Judy said, pointing toward the southwest. "Sandy Morrison."

Polly smiled. "I know Sandy. She and her husband ..."

"Bob," Judy interrupted.

"I first met them a couple of years ago when they were hosts for a group of boys that come to town from Chicago every summer. They had two boys stay with them again this summer."

"Sandy would do that," Judy said. "She likes to be involved, especially when there are kids that might need some love." She rolled her eyes. "Even though she's the youngest of us, she always thinks we need her to take care of us, too. Twelve years since I've seen her and she was furious that I wasn't staying at their house. I don't need a mother hen nagging at me to get up in the mornings. I'm sixty-six years old. I know when I want to get up."

"Now, now," Reuben said, patting his wife's back. "That was one time and she was upset because your mother had just died."

"Who wakes their guests up at four thirty in the morning?" Judy asked, her hands on her hips.

"We should let you get back to your family," Reuben said. "Judy wanted to visit the graves. We thought we'd get that out of the way first."

"If you have a free evening," Polly said, surprised at what was about to come out of her mouth, but she went ahead anyway. "I'd like to invite you to dinner. My family is unconventional, but I'm sure you'd enjoy spending time with them."

Judy looked up at her husband, who nodded. She smiled at Polly. "We'd love that. We're having dinner at Sandy's tonight, and Wednesday we're planning to have dinner in Ames with an old friend of Reuben's. We're free tomorrow evening."

"How about six thirty," Polly said.

"That's quite friendly of you," Judy replied. "I'd like it very much. We'll let you go. I apologize for talking your ear off, but you are quite easy to talk to."

"You too. It's been nice to meet you both." Polly put her hand out and shook theirs again. "I look forward to dinner tomorrow night. Is there anything you don't eat?"

The two shook their heads.

"We eat it all," Reuben said. "Can we bring dessert?"

"I'll take care of it. Just come and be sure to wear comfortable clothes. We might eat outside."

Instead of heading straight for the house, Polly turned north on the next path. She'd seen something when she had walked down to Andy's house and wanted to check it out. The groundskeeper wouldn't be back until Friday and it looked as if someone had left an old red wagon in the trees at the back edge of the cemetery. In her wildest dreams, Polly never imagined that she would be keeping an eye on a cemetery, but here she was.

Henry was very careful not to tease her about the fact that she felt so comfortable living next to these dead bodies. Polly tried to remind him that there was a line of bushes and small trees separating their house from the actual cemetery, but that didn't change anything. He still got a kick out of it. She hated to admit how peaceful she found the place.

Charlie Heller had been in charge of the grounds for as long as anyone could remember and took great pride in keeping the cemetery beautiful. His shed at the northeast corner of the lot was neat and tidy. He'd given it a fresh coat of white paint this spring and just last week Henry had chased him off the roof when he caught the old man trying to replace shingles.

She glanced back to see if the Greenes were still there, but the cemetery was empty. She couldn't wait to get to know them better. Her first impression was that they were a wonderful pair of old hippies. They certainly dressed the part. Polly hated to admit her own assumptions and prejudices, but if they'd spent their lives in San Francisco, that increased the probability that they'd been part of that life. She did some quick math in her head. If Judy was sixty-six, she graduated from high school in the late sixties. It sounded like the woman left Bellingwood right away, too. Polly wondered where she'd gone from here.

Giving her head a quick shake, Polly stopped and looked into the bushes and trees separating the cemetery from the beanfield. She was sure she'd seen the sun glint off something metallic. She pushed back the branches of a bush and walked through, coming out on the other side. There was no fence between Jim Bevins' field and the cemetery. Polly was finally used to seeing these open fields in Iowa. When she'd left, there was no such thing, but farmers were always looking for ways to increase their yield, and stripping fences away was one step they often took.

This was the same field where she'd chased young Amy Hewitt last May. She hadn't heard much about what happened to the girl after that. The trial wasn't scheduled yet and as far as Polly knew, the poor girl was tucked away in a hospital. The rumors around the Hewitt fire had spun out of control for several weeks following the event. It was finally settling down, as was the traffic that had increased in the neighborhood. Between the fire and the murder of poor Barney Loeffler at Jim Bridger's house next door, people had been driving through every evening to gawk and ask neighbors what they knew.

Al and Pat Lynch were in pure heaven. There was always someone in their yard asking questions. Al had purchased a set of cedar Adirondack chairs for his front lawn and took his place out there early in the morning, ready to tell what he knew to anyone who would listen. He'd even gotten some new clothes and Polly had counted at least three new ball caps.

She looked down the row of bushes and frowned. It must have been nothing. She turned to walk toward the Bell House, walking carefully along the edge of the field. Then she saw it. Someone had dumped a rusty old wheelbarrow, breaking down a few of the bushes. They'd tried to cover it with branches, but had done a lousy job of it.

She got closer to the wheelbarrow and then backed up. This couldn't be. Not here. Not now. Turning away from the wheelbarrow, Polly took a deep breath and then moved in. It had been turned upside down, and she hated the idea that she might disturb the scene, but before she called Aaron, she had to be sure.

This was when she needed crime scene gloves, but how in the world was she supposed to know that she'd stumble across something like this on a random Monday morning in her own back yard?

Polly stopped, took out her phone and shot pictures all around the wheelbarrow, then after turning away again for another deep breath, leaned over and took an edge, attempting to lift it. One hand wasn't going to do this — it was heavy. How in the world had they gotten it back here without anyone noticing? Bracing herself, she put both hands on the edge and lifted, glancing underneath. She let the wheelbarrow fall back into place. The smell assured her the poor man was dead, as did his glassy stare and unnatural pose. Polly did her best to stay off the bean field and walked away while swiping to place a call.

"What are you about to do to my week?" Aaron asked, when he finally answered.

"Give you something to do. I know you're bored," Polly replied.

"Where are you and what did you find?"

"Aaron, I think they're starting to just bring them to me."

"You're at home?" He sounded incredulous.

"Close enough. I'm on the other side of the cemetery in Jim Bevins' beanfield — twenty or thirty yards from my place."

"That's pretty close. What made you go looking for it?"

"I saw the glint of an old wheelbarrow. It's upside down and they tried to camouflage it with tree branches." She looked back and shook her head. "Are you sending Tab to me?"

He chuckled. "She's already on her way. She was in my office when you called. Best way to come through the cemetery?"

Polly looked around. "Charlie's not going to like that, but I don't know that Jim would be any happier to have you come through his beanfield."

"I'll give Charlie a call," Aaron said. "Let him know we're

going to be messing up his grounds. He can yell at me and then he'll figure out how to clean up after us. He knows I'll send my people back to help if necessary.

"Thanks," she said. "I don't want to be in trouble with him."

"I understand that. Can you show Tab how to find the body?"

"No problem. I'll go back through into the cemetery and look for her. The road turns not far from where I am."

"Then I know exactly where it is," he said. "You didn't recognize the person under the wheelbarrow, did you?"

"No," Polly said with a small laugh. "I didn't take a long enough look for that."

After he hung up, Polly pushed her way back through the bushes and took another breath. No, that smell wasn't going away any time soon.

She'd walked through the cemetery several times this summer and glanced at names on the headstones, trying to associate them with people she knew. There were a lot of family names that she recognized. Right now, the last thing Polly wanted to do was think about the amount of death that was surrounding her. Thank goodness her part in this very familiar ritual was nearly over. Once Tab Hudson arrived, Polly would answer a few questions, point them in the right direction, and escape to the relative sanity of her own home.

Things were getting better there. Okay, that was relative, too. They continued to make progress on the interior of the house. Hayden and Heath should move into their rooms upstairs this week. All that was left was to paint the walls, hang curtains, and secure rods in the closet. They were so close.

Stephanie and Kayla Armstrong were still living with them. The apartment building had been damaged by the fire to a greater extent than anyone realized. The owners hoped to have it finished before school started, but that was only three weeks away and no one held out much hope. Stephanie was heartsick at their continued intrusion in Polly and Henry's life, but the house was big enough for everyone and it only took a little extra work to keep people sane and happy.

They'd emptied the library and Rebecca's old bedroom for Stephanie and Kayla. It was all back in the foyer.

As the girls' belongings came in to the Bell House, they started the process of cleaning out as much smoke damage as they could. Stephanie left her sofa and chairs to be trashed by the apartment owners. She would buy new furniture. The beds were in better shape, but had required work to get the rest of the smell out. At least the girls were in their own beds and their own rooms. With Hayden and Heath upstairs, they'd be able to completely take over the bathroom off the room Stephanie was staying in.

She wandered back to the corner of the cemetery when she saw the sheriff's vehicle come in. Waving, Polly waited for Tab to park and get out of her car.

"What did you find?" Tab asked.

"You know what I found."

"I suppose that *was* a silly question." Tab laughed out loud. "I'm sorry. What were you doing out here anyway?"

Polly pointed at Andy's house. "Just coming back from seeing Andy."

"That's right. You told us you were doing that last night at Pizzazz. I didn't put it all together. Okay, where is this?"

"Just there," Polly said, pointing. "You can see the metal of the wheelbarrow. It's all rusted and they covered it with branches, but you can still kind of see it."

"I know I always ask this, but you're sure he's dead?"

Polly lifted her nose and sniffed. "Can't you tell?"

"I wasn't paying attention," Tab said, sniffing the air. "I'd best put my detective persona on. Are you sticking around?"

"Not if you don't need me." Polly waggled her phone. "I took pictures before I went in and disturbed the scene by lifting the wheelbarrow. Do you want me to email these to you?"

"It never hurts," Tab said. "We'll talk later?"

"You know we will."

CHAPTER TWO

Drawing the gate open to her back yard, Polly was greeted by two little boys, two happy dogs, and two curious girls — Rebecca and Kayla.

"Was that the cops?" Rebecca asked.

Polly nodded. "Yeah. The sheriff's department. Tab is there."

"If you called the sheriff, that means …" Rebecca turned her head toward the far end of the yard. "Did you really? Right back there?"

"What?" Elijah asked. "Why is the sheriff here?" He trotted alongside Polly as she walked toward the house.

"Duh," Kayla said. "She found a dead person."

"Duh," Elijah mocked. "It's a cemetery. There's lotsa dead people out there."

Rebecca laughed an uncomfortable laugh. "No, 'Jah, she means that Polly found someone who wasn't buried. You know, like she does?"

He had beat Polly to the side door and ran up to the top step, putting him that much more level with her face. "Back there?" he asked, pointing.

Polly reached forward and scooped him off the step and into her arms. She gave him a strong hug and put him back down on the sidewalk. "Yes, back there."

"I bet if we go upstairs, we can see them working," he said, running back up the steps. He opened the door and started to walk through.

"Be polite," Polly said, touching his arm.

He stopped in his tracks, backed up and held the door for her. "Oh yeah."

"Thank you." She smiled down at him and rubbed his shoulder.

The little boy beamed at the attention and waited until everyone was inside to close it.

Noah hadn't said a word the entire walk back to the house. Once they were inside, Polly took his hand. "You okay?"

"Did you really see another dead person?"

"Yes I did."

"And you weren't scared?"

The other three kids hovered around Polly. She nodded to the back steps leading upstairs. "Go on. If Heath and Hayden are okay with it, you can watch from their rooms, but you don't get to play in my room, okay?"

They tore through the kitchen and Polly sighed a deep breath. There was no slowing them down some days.

"Do you want to talk about this?" she asked Noah.

He looked toward the stairway and down at her hand.

Polly laughed. "Go ahead. If you want to talk about it later, we can." She released him and he ran to catch up to his brother and the girls.

She was headed for the dining room when the back doorbell rang. That should be Andrew. He had to mow his yard as well as his neighbor's and since it was so beastly hot this summer, he chose to get up early in order to finish before the day became unbearable. Neither Jason nor Sylvie wanted to shuffle him around this summer, so he'd taken to riding his bike. That had made it much easier for Polly and Henry's decision to purchase a bike for Rebecca. She complained about it at first, but once she discovered that it was either ride or stay home, she rode. Kayla and Rebecca had done research and found a used bike shop in Ames. Polly sat down with Stephanie to decide on a budget for the girls. Anything over that, the girls would pay on their own. Funny how they managed to stay under the prescribed budget.

"Come in," she called out, heading for the door.

She fully expected Andrew to burst in with a mouthful of questions regarding the activity in the cemetery, but she heard nothing. When she got to the back door and he hadn't come inside, she opened it and smiled at Chris Dexter from across the street.

"Hi, Chris. Come in." Polly stepped back, holding the door.

"I can't stay and I hate to ask, but could my kids come over and play in your back yard? I have to take Lucas to the doctor."

"Is he okay?" Polly gave her head a quick shake. "Send them right over. My kids are all upstairs watching the activity in the cemetery."

"Yeah," Chris said. "I want to know what that's about, but I need to run. Lucas has terrible diarrhea and I'm at my wits end. You'd think that after three kids, I'd be able to handle this, but I'm a little freaked out. Doc Mason said he'd see him right away."

"Do you need any help? The girls are here and can watch your kids if you want me to go with you."

Chris looked at Polly plaintively, then stepped back onto the stoop. "No. I'm fine. I just need to go."

"Then go. I'll walk over with you and bring the kids back." Polly let the door shut and walked out with her neighbor. As they crossed the street, Andrew rode up.

"Go on inside," Polly said to him. "I'll be back in a minute. Everyone is up in Heath's room."

"What's going on?" Andrew asked, pointing to the cemetery.

"I'll tell you later."

"When I heard the sirens, I thought someone had heard me crying," Chris said, chagrined. "Glad they weren't coming for me. What happened?"

"You go on in and send your kids out. I'll tell you everything when you come home. If Lucas is okay, come over for coffee." Polly put her hand on Chris's car. "If you need me to keep them longer, give me a call."

Chris nodded absentmindedly and picked up speed, running into her house. Within minutes, the three oldest — Jeremy, Julia and Aiden — came out of the house and stopped in front of Polly.

"Go on over and inside," Polly said. "I'll be right there. I want to make sure your mom is doing okay."

The two older kids crossed the street, but Aiden remained. "She's scared," he said, his big blue eyes looking up at her. "Lucas is so little."

Polly smiled at him and patted his head. "Yes he is. Go with your sister and brother."

He stopped at the end of the driveway, looked both ways and then ran across to his siblings in Polly's driveway. She waited a few more moments for Chris to come out with little Lucas in her arms. Polly saw that his car seat was on her side, so she opened the car door. It was stifling hot in there, so she opened the driver's door, too, hoping to get a little air movement going.

"Thank you," Chris said. She put Lucas in his seat and pulled the restraint around him, buckling it, then tugging to make sure it was secure. "I'm so sorry to ask you to do this, but I didn't know what else to do. I usually have time to schedule things."

"It's no problem at all. I have a big house, a big yard, and tons of big kids to keep everyone occupied. Are you sure you're okay with going alone?"

Chris was already in the driver's seat. "It's only a few blocks, but thank you."

Polly watched her back out and drive away, then headed home. The Dexter's kids, as well as Rose Bright, spent a lot of time playing with her kids. Most of the time they were in the back yard, but on rainy days, they often ended up playing among the boxes and extra furniture in the foyer. Hayden, Noah, and Elijah had set up the race tracks again and the kids loved running cars around that room. When she got inside the house, she looked for them, but found no one in the kitchen. She opened the door to the foyer and heard noise coming from the second floor. Stepping back into the kitchen, she buzzed Heath's room.

"Hello?" she asked.

"Yeah, we're here," Heath responded.

"Did the Dexters find you?"

He laughed as sound erupted around him. "Yeah. Everybody is here."

"Too much?"

"No. It's okay. They're vying for the windows. Apparently, the coroner arrived and is taking the body out."

"Great." Polly shook her head. Kids were always fascinated with the uglier sides of life and she never knew quite how to handle it with them. "Let me know if you need help sending them on their way."

"We can handle it, Polly," Hayden said loud enough to cut through the noise. "Don't worry."

She went on in to the dining room and dropped into a chair. She was still trying to finish curtains for Heath and Hayden's rooms. They were also working to finish the third bedroom in the main part of the second floor. The rooms above the kitchen were still in chaos. She wanted to move her sewing room up to one of those rooms, but would take the empty bedroom they finished for now; anything to get off the main level so the rooms could be used for what they were intended. Polly was tired of living in the kitchen and family room.

Clattering footsteps down the back stairs caused her to take in a deep, slow breath. The sound of little voices yelling her name caused another one. She waited, knowing they would find her.

"Polly!" Elijah yelled, rushing up to stand beside her.

"Inside voice," she said, pulling him into a hug.

"Can we play in the tunnel?"

She looked at the line of kids that trailed behind him.

"Go ahead, but I hope this isn't an attempt to leave our yard and go into the cemetery to watch the sheriff. They're busy and don't need your help. I can see the back yard from here and I don't want any of you out there until they're finished. Got it? Stay in the studio or underground."

Four little heads nodded enthusiastically and the boys ran out of the room.

This wasn't a new request. On these hot days, the kids spent a lot of time moving in and out of the tunnel. She'd told them stories of the whiskey runners from the early part of the twentieth century. Noah's infatuation with Andrew had led him to read Andrew's short story, *Hidden in the Trees*, and the boys wanted to know more about the Underground Railroad. Polly discovered she was growing into quite the story teller. As long as she had an audience, she was glad to spin a yarn.

There was always some bad guy / good guy play going on when the kids got together and it usually ended up with Noah and Aiden lying dead on the ground while Elijah and Jeremy stood over them, proud as could be. When Elva's children were here, the chaos hit an all-time high and Polly was grateful for that basement room and the tunnel that led out to what was supposed to be Rebecca's studio and the back yard.

Rebecca had yet to take possession of the studio. She was in love with her new bedroom and found multiple reasons to spend time in there. She sat on the window seat with her sketchpad in hand, looking out at the world in front of the house, drawing and sketching. Andrew was allowed in there when Kayla was around and so far, there hadn't been any breach of trust with that. All three kids were terrified of Polly's wrath should she catch them at anything untoward. She knew that wouldn't last forever, but right now, she had their attention. Besides, there were usually way too many kids around for them to get away with much. When Kayla and Stephanie finally moved out of the Bell House, Polly would have to come up with new rules, but that was a concern for another day.

Polly stood and walked over to the intercom and buzzed Rebecca's room. "You in there?"

"We're here," Kayla responded.

"Is Julia with you?"

"Yeah."

"Okay. Just checking."

She sat back down at the sewing machine. The dogs had followed the boys, and most of the cats were upstairs. Luke and Leia usually hid in Polly's bedroom when the house filled with children. Once the noise settled, the two older cats would find their way down to the dining room and perch on the cat trees in the window. They wanted to be close to Polly, but didn't want to be involved when the kids were playing. Rebecca and Kayla's kittens were much more willing to chase and play with the kids.

As Polly put her foot on the sewing machine pedal, her phone rang. She glanced at it to see if maybe it was a call she could ignore. When she didn't recognize the local number figured she should just pick up.

"Hello? This is Polly Giller."

"Ms. Giller, this is Leroy Forster. I work with Henry, you know?"

"Yes?" She scooted back from the table, holding her breath.

"They took him to the ER. He was in a wreck."

Everything went gray. She stood, but found that her legs weren't working so sat back down.

"Ms. Giller?" Leroy asked. "You there?"

"Yeah," she said breathlessly.

"He's not hurt bad. They said stitches and they want to do an x-ray of his arm. Worried it broke."

"He's not?" Polly's emotions rushed from terror to relief and then she landed on furious. He could have led with that. Knowing that it she wasn't handling things well, she steeled herself and spoke carefully. "What happened?"

"Some girl went through the stop sign across the road, and rammed into him. She didn't pay no attention and crossed the center line right into his front end. Lucky for Henry, he wasn't moving. She was texting or something, the cops said."

"Does he have his phone?"

"Nah. That's why I'm calling ya. He asked me to. Me and Ben was in my truck right behind when it happened. It was like watching a slow-motion horror show. I tried backing up so he had room to move, but she was coming for him no matter what he did. I called the 9-1-1 because we couldn't get him out. That truck is a goner. His phone is in the wreckage somewhere."

"So, the hospital in Boone?"

"Sorry. No. Webster City. We was up north a ways working on the Bloom's house. He and I was leaving there to go check the concrete at that new house we're building over by Kamrar."

"He's not badly hurt and he's going to Webster City, right?"

"Yeah. He said he'd call when he got there, but he wanted me to let you know."

"Okay, thanks, Leroy. I'm going to head up now."

"He thought you would."

She hung up and took a deep breath. No more sewing today. Polly stood up, holding the table for support. When her legs finally functioned normally, she walked through the kitchen and up the back steps. Henry's whole life was in that truck. She sighed. No. His life was in good hands; his business was in that truck. They'd deal with that later. Hopefully, they'd tow the truck to Bellingwood. Polly shook her head. Why was she even thinking about that right now?

"Hey," she said, walking into the room where Hayden and Heath were working. They were taping the windows and sills so they could start painting.

Hayden turned. "What's up?"

"Henry's fine, but he was just in a wreck. A girl hit his truck. Leroy called and they took him to Webster City. I need to go. Can you guys keep an eye on the kids. The little boys are down in the tunnel."

He walked over to her and took her arm. "Are you okay?"

"I think so. I need to get moving."

"Let Heath or me drive you."

"No, I need you here. Chris Dexter is going to come back from the doctor's office with news about her baby and she'll need to know that her other kids were safe. Tell them what's going on." Polly patted his shoulder. "I'll be fine. Don't worry. I'm a little shook up, but when Leroy finally told me that he wasn't sliced in half and his guts weren't bleeding out, I got my head back together."

"He said that?" Heath asked.

Polly chuckled. "No. That's what I imagined in my head when Leroy said they took him to the ER. It took a few sentences to find out that he needed stitches and might have a broken arm. If that's all, we'll get through it. Will you be okay with the kids?"

"We're nearly done in here. I'll check on the boys and we'll keep an eye out for Mrs. Dexter."

"Thanks." Polly left and went into her bedroom. She was dressed in a pair of shorts and an old t-shirt, not planning on doing anything out of the ordinary today. If she was about to spend several hours in a hospital while waiting with Henry, the least she could do is look like a normal wife. She pushed her door closed and went into the bathroom. For once, her hair was doing what it should, so she fluffed it and left it alone. She pulled jeans on and a plaid blouse, then sat down on the edge of her bed and put socks and shoes on.

"Polly?" Rebecca rapped on the door.

"Come in."

"What happened?" Rebecca asked. She was followed closely by Kayla and Julia.

"I'm sure he's fine, but Henry was in a wreck. I'm heading up to the Webster City hospital."

"Do you want me to come with you?" Rebecca sat down beside Polly and put her hand on Polly's thigh. "Kayla said she'd help keep an eye on the kids."

Polly took a breath and looked at her daughter, her mind racing with new information. In truth, she'd love to have Rebecca come along, but she didn't know how much pain Henry would be in. "You stay here. I'll be okay. I don't know how long we'll be at the hospital." She stood up.

"I hate to be pushy," Rebecca said, "but do you want to pack extra clothes for him? What if they had to cut something off?" She was already moving toward his dresser. Opening a drawer, she took out a t-shirt and then she moved to the next drawer down and took out another pair of jeans. "Just to be safe. If you don't need them, it's no big deal. Right?"

Polly put her arms around Rebecca and held on. "Thank you."

"You're sure you don't want me to come along so you can cry and be all gloopy?"

"I can do gloopy without you, but thank you."

"Will you call us as soon as you know something?"

"You bet. I'll call Hayden or Heath." Polly stepped back and grinned at Rebecca. "Because your phone stays on the charger today, right? Nice try, though."

"Can't blame a girl."

Polly gave her daughter another quick hug.

CHAPTER THREE

"Not to worry," the nurse said when Polly expressed concern that she was in the wrong place. The woman pulled back a curtain. "He's right in here."

"Thanks," Polly said, her eyes focused on the man lying in front of her. She heard the curtain close again and stood there, willing her feet to move forward. The left side of Henry's face was bruised and bandaged. He was going to have a heck of a black eye.

"Hi, Polly," he said quietly.

"Hi. I want to tell you that you look terrible, but that doesn't seem helpful."

He laughed and moaned. "Don't do that. I hurt all over."

"I'll bet you do. I'm so glad that you're alive. What happened?"

"This girl took out the front end of my truck. She was blazing down the road, not paying any attention to me. When I saw her go through the stop sign, I knew it was going to be bad, but my brain couldn't work fast enough to come up with an escape. The ditch was too deep, Leroy was behind me, and there was a big tractor taking up most of the road on the right. I kept waiting for her to look up, but she didn't. Not once." He tried to shift, then settled back. "That is, not until she hit me."

"Is she okay?" Polly knew that even if he hadn't been at fault, anything that happened to the other driver would weigh on him.

"Pretty banged up. She's here somewhere, too."

"Thank God you weren't moving."

"I know. Leroy called you?"

"Yeah. You might want to tell him that leading with the tragedy instead of the fact that you weren't spilling your life out onto the ground might have been nice. I nearly had a heart attack."

He tried to laugh and brought his right hand up to hold his stomach. "I told you not to do that."

"Sorry." She pointed at his face. "Have you seen someone yet?"

"No. We're going to be here a while. I need to have an x-ray on my arm. I don't think it's broken, but they want to make sure. It hurts like hell, though. Did you call Mom?"

Polly shook her head. "I'm sorry. Not yet. I barely focused enough to get here. I don't even remember most of the trip."

"Sit here beside me." Henry patted the right side of his bed and scooted his legs over. "When I saw that girl coming at me, the first thing I thought about was you. I know it sounds like a damned romantic comedy, but I didn't want to never see you again."

She dropped onto the bed and gripped his thigh. "Stop that."

Tears leaked from his eyes. "I know they say your life flashes in front of you and they aren't kidding. In a split second, I saw images of you and the kids. It couldn't be over. Not like that."

Polly took a deep breath. "I promised myself I wasn't going to cry."

"I'm crying. It's okay. That scared me today." He stretched his right arm out and Polly gently lowered herself to lie down beside him, reaching up to touch the side of his face that wasn't bruised and battered.

"I was so scared," she whispered. The tears flowed as Henry tugged her in tight against him.

A few minutes passed as they held each other.

"Excuse me."

Polly jumped off the bed, brushed her tears away, and wiped her hands down her jeans as an older nurse smiled at the two of them.

"I need to take him to x-ray. We'll be gone for a while and the doctor is going to check the gashes on his face. There will most likely be stitches. Do you want to be with us for that?"

Henry chuckled and then moaned again. "She's no good with blood. If she weren't so worried, I'm pretty certain she wouldn't be this close to me right now."

"Then why don't you take a seat in the waiting room and when we've got him cleaned back up, I'll come find you. My name is Audrey."

Polly bent down and kissed Henry's cheek, catching the edge of his lips. "No more wrecks on the way. My heart can't take it," she said.

"We'll make sure nobody else crosses his path today," Audrey said with a smile.

"Do you have the other driver here?"

"We can't say much," Audrey responded. "HIPAA, you know."

"Sure." Polly nodded and slipped past her. "Thank you. Are her parents in the waiting room?"

Audrey smiled at her. "Clever one, aren't you. Yes they are, with her little sister."

"Polly?" Henry asked, a warning tone in his voice.

"I'm not upset," she replied. "I want to make sure they're doing okay. Kids are stupid. This wasn't their fault. They're as scared as I was."

He nodded and gave her a half smile as she left him.

Polly's phone buzzed as she made her way to the waiting room. She looked at it and saw a text from Hayden.

"Is Henry okay? Why haven't you called yet? I knew I should have come with you. Did you call Marie first?"

Polly stopped and looked around. Seeing the doors that led outside, Polly headed straight for them and dialed Hayden's phone right back. She wasn't at all surprised when Rebecca answered.

"Why haven't you called yet?"

"Because I just left him."

"You left him? Why wouldn't you stay with him? They're doing terrible things to him, aren't they, and you couldn't stand the blood. Am I right?"

"You're spot on with the blood thing, but don't say another word until you let me speak." Polly waited and when Rebecca remained silent, she went on. "Henry is fine. He's pretty banged up. They're taking him in for an x-ray of his arm and then we'll make decisions about when we're coming home. They also have to clean up his face. There were bandages on it, but I'm guessing he'll need stitches."

"Make sure they check for internal injuries," Rebecca said. "Those can kill him if they aren't caught."

Polly grinned. "I'll make sure that he's healthy enough to be released before we come home. I promise."

"And you're going to call us again so we know what's happening. You can't leave me in the dark again. Promise me that."

"I'll do my best," Polly said. "If we get busy, I might not be able to make a lot of calls."

"I knew I should have come with you. You know how I get. Not knowing is the worst thing in the world for me."

"I've learned my lesson. Now let me hang up so I can call Marie and tell her what has happened."

"Fine, but you have to promise to call me back."

"I promise to do my best. I love you, Rebecca."

"Tell Henry we all love him and we're worried."

"I'll tell him. Good-bye."

Rebecca was probably right. Polly should have let her come. The poor girl couldn't bear to be out of the loop and she worried something fierce when bad things were happening to the people she loved. Not that Polly blamed her. Those months of caring for her mother and knowing there was nothing anyone could do to change the outcome had made it difficult for Rebecca to watch her family get sick.

Noah had gotten a bad case of stomach flu just after school let out and Rebecca hovered over him like a mother hen. Henry thought that the little boy had extended his illness by at least a day because he enjoyed the attention, but Rebecca had been a wreck. She'd slept in a sleeping bag in his room and was up at every sound or movement. Polly felt a little guilty for not being more motherly, but Noah didn't need two of them acting like he was about to succumb to death.

She placed the call to Marie and waited while it rang.

"Polly. Is he okay?"

"I was afraid that Leroy would get to you before I could call. I'm so sorry. Henry is going to be fine. He's banged up and looks terrible, but he'll heal."

"Thank you," Marie said with a loud sigh. "I knew you'd call when you could. Are you in Webster City?"

"Yes. Henry's having x-rays taken right now and if they're stitching up the gash on his face, I shouldn't be in the room."

Marie laughed out loud. "It would be awful if you fell and hit your head. Only one of you at a time, okay? Do you think he'll have to spend the night?"

"I don't know. We haven't gotten that far."

"What can we do to help? Are the kids okay?"

"Yeah. Hayden, Heath and Rebecca have things well in hand."

"I'll make supper for them. Bill and I will take it over and spend the evening. Even if you come home, we'll make sure your family is fed."

Polly considered protesting, but knew that Marie wanted to do something and felt completely helpless right now. "That would be wonderful, thank you. Kayla and Stephanie are still there, so Stephanie will want to help."

"Oh, sure," Marie said. "Then that's okay. I don't have to go over."

"No, no, no. That's not what I meant. Let Stephanie know how she can help you when you get there. I'd like to have you and Bill check on the kids. Rebecca's a bit of a wreck and I can't get a good feel for how Noah and Elijah are dealing with this. Henry's always the strong one."

Polly had a flash of realization. "Marie, I found a body behind the fence this morning. The kids have been watching the activity with the sheriff and now this. I know it's exciting, but they'll have questions and I'm not there to talk to them. And I'm worried about Henry's truck. His business is in there and I don't know where it will be towed. My head is spinning and all I can think about is how much pain he'll be in when the drugs wear off."

"Would you like me to take Molly over to your house this morning? I have things here to make sandwiches."

"So do I," Polly said. "And the Dexter kids are at my house because Chris had to take her baby to see Doc Mason. The family of the girl who hit Henry is in the waiting room and I need to go inside and make them understand that we aren't angry. I feel like it's going to be another one of those crazy wild couple of weeks and I'm spinning so far out of control in my head."

"You focus on Henry," Marie said. "If you need to talk to that family, you do that, but let them handle their own troubles. You have enough of your own. And I don't care how many kids are at your house. You have plenty of older kids there to give me a hand. Molly will love seeing everyone. I'll make sure they're fed and watered and Bill will make calls. Do you want the truck towed into town here?"

"I don't know," Polly said.

"Bill will know what to do. You don't need to worry about a thing."

"Henry's phone is the first thing we need to find or replace," Polly said. "I'm sorry, Marie. I can't stop my brain from thinking."

"It's okay. Send me a text every time you think of something else. One of us will manage it until you and Henry are home. Go in and take care of my boy and tell him that I love him."

Polly took a deep breath. "Thank you. I know you're Henry's mother, but I can't imagine doing this without you to remind me how to stay sane. I love you, Marie."

"I love you, too, sweetheart. You'll be fine."

Polly leaned against the wall and turned to the doors leading into the waiting room. At least it would be cooler in there, even if she did have to face an uncomfortable conversation. Before she went inside, though, she stopped to text Hayden that Marie was coming over with Molly for lunch. She worried that he would believe she didn't trust him with the kids. That wasn't true at all. She left him with the younger ones all the time. Polly knew that her mind was all over the place, but she couldn't stand it, so she made one more call.

"Is everything okay?' Rebecca asked.

"It's fine. Can I talk to Hayden?"

"You're giving him bad news, aren't you?"

"No, Rebecca," Polly said as measured as she could. "That's not it at all. I need to speak with him."

"Fine." Rebecca must have turned away, because Polly could only hear her in the background now. "Polly wants you, not me. It better not be bad news."

"Polly?" Hayden asked, coming on the line.

"It's not bad news. I wanted to let you know that Marie is coming over to help with lunch. She'll bring Molly."

"We've got this, you know."

"That's why I'm calling. I know you've got it, but she's worried and wants to help. I also wouldn't mind having her there if Noah and Elijah need a grandma to talk to. There's been a lot of craziness around the house this morning."

"Okay, that makes sense."

"Keep an eye on Rebecca for me, will you? Her fears are going to overwhelm her."

"Got it. Henry's okay?"

"He is. When I know anything more, I'll call you. Maybe keep your phone in your pocket so Rebecca doesn't lose her mind."

"I can do that, too. Let me know if we can help with anything else."

"You're doing exactly what I need. Thanks."

At the end of that phone call, Polly knew she couldn't put it off any longer and went back inside. The family was still sitting in the waiting room. She knew who it was by the tentative way they looked at her. How they knew for sure who she was, Polly didn't know, but she needed to at least try to communicate with them.

"Hi. I'm Polly Giller," she said, walking across the room. "Henry Sturtz is my husband." She put her hand out and the man stood up and took it. "Jeremy Conn. This is my wife, Sunny and our daughter, Amelia. I'm so sorry about what has happened. Is your husband going to be okay?"

"He is. How about your daughter?"

Sunny Conn burst into tears. "I don't know. They won't let us back there with her. A nurse came out once to tell us that they're trying to stabilize her, but it's been a long time. When will they tell us if she's going to be okay?"

Her husband put his arm on the back of her chair and shook his head. "We're trying to be patient. I don't like to make a ruckus, but I can't do this much longer."

A woman in a white coat came out into the waiting room and walked over to where Polly was sitting with the Conn's. There was no one else in the room and she sat down beside Sunny Conn. "Mr. and Mrs. Conn, we're sending your daughter to Des Moines via life flight."

The words were barely out of the woman's mouth when Sunny Conn wailed and began to sob. Jeremy Conn patted his wife's knee and stood up. "What's happening?"

"We've got her stabilized for the flight, but she requires much more than we can offer here."

"Can I go with her?" Sunny asked.

"No, ma'am. We're loading her right now. I'd recommend that you head for Mercy in Des Moines. Their team will begin caring for her immediately upon arrival. We're all focused on taking care of your daughter."

"We'll call your parents," Jeremy Conn said to his wife. "They'll head right over to the hospital and be there when she arrives. Your mom can keep an eye on Amelia when we get there."

Polly stepped back and out of the way. She didn't want to be part of this. It was traumatic, to be sure, but she didn't know these people and couldn't allow herself to be drawn into their crisis. She was grateful that Henry was okay.

She looked around for an escape and cringed when Sunny Conn began a new bout of wailing. Her husband gathered their things and took his wife's arm, then put his hand down for their daughter to grab and led them out of the hospital.

When the doors closed on his wife's wails, Polly felt her entire body relax. She wasn't prepared to deal with someone else's grief and pain.

Polly sat back down and picked up a magazine. As she flipped through the pages, she realized that she wasn't reading a word and didn't even know what magazine it was. She put it back on the table and took out her phone — no messages. It wouldn't be too long before Lydia heard the news and offered to help.

Closing her eyes, Polly leaned back in the seat and rested her head on the wall. This had been the strangest morning. What a crazy way to start a week. Last night when she went to bed, the biggest thing she had in front of her was the opening party Sycamore House was hosting for their new Beryl Watson gallery. Beryl had brought a huge number of paintings to be hung in the upstairs rooms — enough that Jeff realized it would be a perfect gallery setting. Lydia and Jeff had been working like fiends to finish the work in Polly's old apartment. She'd been in there a couple of times and loved what they were doing. The walls had been repainted, casual seating areas had been set up, and Beryl's paintings were not only hung on walls throughout the apartment, but smaller pieces were scattered throughout the bookshelves, along with an entire library of books that Jeff, Stephanie, Lydia, and Kristen had scavenged throughout the region. There couldn't be anymore stray books in the county.

Beryl's agent was thrilled that pieces the artist had kept in Bellingwood were finally seeing the light of day. He invited buyers and fans from all over the country to attend the Sunday afternoon reception. Sylvie and Rachel had been planning the menu for the last couple of weeks, practicing appetizers and desserts. Nothing like this had ever happened in town and everyone was working to make it a success. Polly felt a little left out, but she didn't know what she could do. She didn't cook and she wasn't needed to paint walls or hang Beryl's artwork. Even Rebecca was involved with the planning. She would act as a hostess along with at least two other students of Beryl's — girls that Polly had met many times over the years. Deena Elliott and Meryl Gustason were returning to Bellingwood to be part of Beryl's day.

"Mrs. Sturtz?"

Polly opened her eyes. The nurse — Audrey was her name — was standing in front of her. "Yes. Is he okay?"

Audrey nodded. "He's still a little sleepy from the drugs we gave him while we set his arm. His face is stitched up and he's going to be fine. He should stay here a while longer, but then you can take him home."

"Thank God," Polly said. "Can I sit with him?"

"Absolutely. He's asking for you. Come with me."

Polly stood and followed the nurse. Her heart jumped into her throat when she saw the bright red stitches that went from the base of Henry's jaw up his cheek. "That's going to leave a mark," she said.

His eyes fluttered open. "Scarface," he murmured.

Audrey chuckled. "It shouldn't be that bad. The doc is pretty good with a needle."

"It will just make you look tough," Polly said. "How are you feeling?"

"Like a million bucks. You should try these drugs. They're fun."

"He's almost back," Audrey said. "It won't take too long and he'll be more normal. Enjoy this while you can, though. If you want to take video of him, I won't tell."

CHAPTER FOUR

"Everyone is waiting to see you, but if it's too much, we could get a room at the hotel for tonight," Polly said as she approached their driveway. "No kids. No pets. No fuss."

"I want my chair and my bed," he said. "If that means I put up with kids and dogs, I'll live with it."

"You remember I told you that your mom and dad are bringing dinner over, right?"

"They are?" Henry thought for a minute. "Yeah. You did say that. She knows I'm fine, though, right?"

"She does. I talked to her while you were in and out of it. And I've talked to Rebecca and Hayden, too. I'm hoping they've calmed the boys sufficiently so you can get inside without being rushed."

"It's okay, Polly," he replied. "I hurt, but it's not a long-term hurt, so no big deal."

"You don't want me to run interference for you? Because I can let 'em at ya." Polly smiled at him as she turned the truck off.

Henry whimpered. "That's not what I meant. You're my tight end. I'm counting on you to block for me."

Polly slowly turned to look at him and chuckled. "Your tight end? That's what you came up with?"

"It's the best I've got." He waggled his eyes at her and then winced. "There will be no tight end stuff going on for a while. Can we agree on that?"

"I think so," she said with a laugh. "We should go in. I see little faces at the windows." Polly waved at the kids in the foyer window, got out of the truck and went around to the passenger side. Henry had gotten the truck door open and was trying to balance himself with one arm. Two strong nurses had helped him into the truck, but Polly wasn't sure how he would get out without falling to the ground.

He finally swung around and slid to the ground, then leaned into her as he caught himself and regained his balance. "Yeah, that hurt."

She walked behind him as he limped toward the side door. She hadn't noticed that before. "Why are you limping?"

"Because everything in my body aches," he said. "I was hit by a car today. Did you forget that?"

"It's going to hurt worse tomorrow."

Henry stopped at the base of the side steps and turned to her. "I thought you loved me."

"Never promised to lie to you," she said, moving past him to go up the steps.

The back door opened and Rebecca stood there with Noah and Elijah right beside her. Rebecca stared long and hard at Henry as he plodded up the steps, gripping the handrail tight enough that his knuckles were white. No one said anything as he made his way inside. The boys stepped back and let him go past them, their mouths open as wide as their eyes.

Noah reached up and took Polly's hand. She looked down at him and smiled, giving his hand a squeeze. "He's going to be okay. He just needs time to heal."

Heath and Hayden were sitting at the kitchen table and Hayden jumped up. "Good to see you home, Henry."

"Good to be here." Henry looked at the back steps, then at the kitchen table and then down the hall. "I call the recliner in the family room. Anyone want to fight me for it?"

Elijah ran ahead and stopped at the family room door. "You can have any chair you want," he said. "Are you going to sleep a lot? Does it hurt? Are you always going to have a scar?"

"Let him get settled in the chair," Polly said. "Once he's sitting down, you can ask him all sorts of questions. If he falls asleep while he's talking to you, give him a little while and he'll wake back up. He's got some strong painkillers in him right now."

Noah let go of her hand and ran to catch up to Henry, staying a step or so behind him.

Rebecca caught her arm. "He looks terrible. You can see the pain in his eyes."

"Everything hurts," Polly said, "but he's going to be fine. Do you believe me?"

Rebecca nodded.

"Where is everyone else?" Polly asked.

"Andrew and Kayla are upstairs with the dogs. We didn't think Henry wanted to have Han all over him."

"Let them know they can come downstairs. The dogs might as well get used to this. Henry can control Han, and Obiwan is pretty good with sick people."

Rebecca moved to the intercom and Polly stopped her. "Go upstairs and talk to them. They probably feel like they're intruding. Make sure they know it's okay. Both of them are part of the family."

"Thanks." Rebecca ran for the back stairs.

Polly sat beside Heath at the kitchen table. "Henry and I talked. He's going to rely on you for a couple of weeks. You'll need to haul him around and be his gopher. You know all the guys and all the work sites. Are you good with that?"

Heath's eyes lit up. "That would be great."

"That means you're stuck with finishing the rooms here," Polly said to Hayden. "I'm sorry about that."

"Hey, I've got it. Heath can help me with the heavy stuff when he gets home at night. No problem."

"Can you do one more thing for me?" she asked.

"Sure."

"There are a couple of prescriptions up at the pharmacy. Nate should have them ready any time. Would you mind running after them?"

Hayden shrugged. "No problem. Do you need anything else?"

"That's it. I just don't want to leave Henry alone with the kids and animals right now." She reached out and clutched at his arm. "Wait. Could you stop by Sweet Beans for me?"

He laughed. "I can't believe you didn't get a chance to sneak up there today."

"Worst day ever," Polly said. She sat back. "It has been a weird one so far. I hope this is all it has for me."

"Marie said she and Bill would be back around six with dinner."

Polly nodded. "Was it okay with her here earlier?"

"Yeah." Hayden smiled. "Noah and Elijah like cuddling with her. She sits down and they both want to be in her lap. Molly gets a little jealous, but Rebecca and Kayla took her upstairs to play."

"What time did Chris Dexter come get her kids?"

"It wasn't long after you left. She wanted me to tell you that the baby is fine."

"Whew." Polly sighed out a deep breath. "At least that one is okay." She put her hand on the edge of the table, bracing herself to stand up again. This day had taken a lot out of her. "I'm going to check on Henry. I'm sure the little boys are pestering him with a million questions."

"One coffee coming up," Hayden said. "Heath, wanna ride with me?"

His younger brother looked at him, a little confused, then nodded.

Polly walked down the hallway to the family room, glancing into the dining room as she passed it. Maybe tomorrow she'd have time to work on those curtains. When she stopped in the doorway to the family room, she smiled. The little boys were sitting on an ottoman in front of Henry, their eyes filled with rapt attention as they talked to him. The two dogs had found him and Han was lying on the floor beside Noah while Obiwan sat beside Henry's recliner. He turned to look at Polly, wagged his tail, got up and wandered over to her. She rubbed his head and walked around him.

"How are you doing?" she asked Henry.

"We need to have a talk," he said, a hint of scolding in his voice.

"What did I do?" Polly laughed. "I haven't been gone that long."

"The boys have been regaling me with tales of your morning adventure. Why didn't you tell me?"

"Ohhh," she said. "I completely forgot about it."

"You forgot about finding someone behind our house? How is that possible?"

Polly sat on the arm of the sofa, pursed her lips and shook her head. "I don't know. Maybe it was because I was worried about my husband who'd just been in a car wreck."

The doorbell rang and Polly jumped.

"I don't want to see anybody," Henry said. "Please?"

She chuckled. "No problem. I'll handle it."

Heath and Hayden were gone when she passed through the kitchen to the side door. Beryl opened the door as Polly crossed into the porch.

"We won't stay long," Beryl said. "I promise. But you can't expect us to stay away on a day like today."

Andy and Lydia were right behind her, both carrying grocery tote bags.

"What are you doing?" Polly asked with a smile. "I'm not broken. Henry is."

"And you have a big family that needs to be fed. You should be hovering over your husband, not sweating and slaving in a hot kitchen."

Polly laughed out loud and backed up to let them women in. It was really the easiest thing to do.

Andy handed her a bag. "The proper response is thank you."

"You're right," Polly said, giving her friend a hug. "Thank you. Telling you it wasn't necessary is ridiculous, isn't it?"

"Yes dear, it is," Lydia said, hefting the two bags she carried onto the island in the center of the kitchen. "I talked to Marie and she says that she and Bill are taking care of tonight's dinner, so this is for tomorrow."

"And the day after that," Andy said. "How is Henry?"

Polly sat down on a stool, her heart full. She found that it was hard to talk. She'd watched these women swoop in and care for people around town. They'd done so much for her over the years, but it hadn't been since the first day she met them that she'd been the recipient of such a huge outpouring.

"Is he okay?" Andy asked, concern on her face. She'd put her bags beside Lydia's and reached out to touch Polly's arm. "You look like you're going to cry."

"He's okay," Polly choked out. "I'm just overwhelmed by this. I didn't expect it at all."

The doorbell rang again and Polly stood up. "Did you bring someone else with you?"

Andy shook her head as Polly headed for the door again. She smiled at Chris Dexter, who was standing there with her oldest son, Jeremy.

Polly pulled the door open. "Hi there. I was glad to hear that your baby is okay."

"I'm a worrywart," Chris said. "Even though I've had three kids, I'd forgotten how the littlest bug can turn into a mommy's biggest fear. I'm here because Hayden told me what had happened to Henry. I saw your friends come in, so figured I'd scoot over while they were here and you weren't occupied with Henry. I won't stay long. We wanted to give you this."

Jeremy held up a huge watermelon.

"Come in, both of you," Polly said. "And thank you so much."

"No," Chris said. "I don't want to bother you."

"Nonsense. Come on in. If you don't know them, you should meet them. Jeremy, could you put that on top of the washing machine there?"

"I'll come in for a second, but Jeremy, would you go home and keep an eye on your brothers and sister?"

"Aww, Mom."

She scowled down at him. "Go home. I expect to see everyone healthy and happy when I get there. I won't be long." She held the door open while he trudged back out and down the steps. "He's a good boy most of the time. I don't think he was fully prepared to have another baby in the house. None of us were."

Polly laughed and took her hand, then led her into the kitchen, where Beryl, Lydia, and Andy had filled the counter tops with containers.

"Ladies, do you know Chris Dexter?" Polly asked. "She lives across the street and brought us a watermelon."

"It's nothing," Chris said. "We picked a few up in Boone at the farmer's market. My kids love fresh watermelon in the summertime."

"Can we spike it with vodka and have a party?" Beryl asked.

Chris started laughing. "I've never done that. It would be fun."

"We're going to have an adult block party right out front," Beryl declared. "It's time."

Lydia moved past Beryl and put her hand out. "It's nice to meet you, Chris. I'm Lydia Merritt. The crazy woman is Beryl Watson and this is Andy Specek."

"You live down past the cemetery, right?" Chris asked Andy. "I've seen you out walking with your husband."

Andy nodded and shook Chris's hand. "Yes. Didn't you have a baby a couple of months ago?"

"Yeah. That makes four. I've told Calvin that if he doesn't ..." Chris stopped, shook her head and giggled. "I'm sorry. I don't know you. I should be going."

"What?" Beryl asked. "Get himself snipped? That's what I'm saying. Snip, snip and it's done. Am I right, ladies?"

Chris laughed out loud. "He has one more month to make the appointment, then I'm making it for him. He was going to take care of this after Aiden was born and didn't. He promised." She hugged herself. "I wouldn't trade Lucas for all the world, but I'm done with babies. I'm ready for my kids to grow up."

"You'll miss this age," Lydia said quietly. She smiled. "Then you get to do it all over again with grandbabies. That's the best." She shrugged. "I'll be honest. As cute and wonderful as they are at this age, I don't miss sleepless nights and sick kids and …"

Beryl interrupted her. "And they're pretty awesome at every age, right?"

"Right," Lydia said. "I wasn't trying to be contrary. Moms have enough trouble. They don't need old ladies telling them to enjoy stuff when they're in the middle of craziness. Do you have family around, Chris?"

Chris shook her head. "Calvin is from a little town down by Keokuk and I grew up in Bettendorf, so no one is close, but I have pretty good neighbors." She smiled at Polly and turned to the back door. "I should get going. Don't want to leave the kids alone too long. They're apt to get into something. It was nice to meet you."

Polly walked with her to the back door. "Thank you for the watermelon. The kids will love it."

"If you need anything else, let us know. I know you have lots of people around to help, but we're right there."

"Thank you." Polly startled Chris by pulling her into a quick hug.

The woman smiled again and left.

"That was nice," Lydia said, when Polly got back into the kitchen.

"I like her and I'm getting to know Mona Bright better all the time."

"How about that gal at the end of the street?" Andy asked.

"Carla Wesley? Yeah. She isn't making eye contact."

Lydia patted Polly's hand. "Probably feels guilty for her husband being so horrible to you."

Polly nodded. "I know that I'm going to have to be the one to break through, but there's always so much going on and I never see her. I'm not looking forward to having to knock on her door, but I'll do it if I have to."

Andrew, Kayla, and Rebecca came down the back steps.

"We heard lots of doorbells," Rebecca said. She smiled and walked over to hug Beryl. "Are you getting excited?"

Of all Polly's friends, Beryl was the least physically affectionate. She had a special spot in her heart for Rebecca and kept her arm around the girl's shoulder. "I shouldn't be, but I am. It's like a dream come true. However, I don't expect much from the people in town. They don't think I'm much of an artist, but it will be great to have my things on display. And just think, it's all because your Polly came into town and rescued a silly old schoolhouse."

"You'd have found a way to exhibit your work in town," Polly said.

Beryl shook her head. "No. I'm afraid I would never have considered it. When I first started years ago, I tried to sell my work to people in Bellingwood and they thought I was nothing. Even when I started selling to collectors around the country, the locals didn't care. They did a piece on me in the Des Moines Register ten years ago and nobody said a word." She smiled at Lydia. "Except for my friends. I only had a couple of those back then and now see what you've done to me. I'm meeting new people every day. It's making it harder and harder for me to be a recluse."

"That's because we love you," Lydia said. "Now we should stow this food and get out of Polly's hair." She held up a container. "Andy did her thing and labeled it all. We have breakfast sandwiches for you."

"I helped," Beryl said.

Polly looked at her.

"I did. I can assemble things. We had a little food party at Lydia's house this morning. She even made enough for this old lady to have homemade meals this week."

"Thank you," Polly said.

Lydia handed the container to Andrew. "I have two of those. Would you put them in the freezer?"

He took it from her and turned to obey.

"I sliced a ham and a roast beef," Lydia said, pushing two more containers to Andrew. She took two bags of bread from Sweet Beans out of a bag. "Sylvie sliced these for you. Andy made potato salad and baked beans."

Andy pointed at four containers in front of her. "I didn't use large bowls. Thought you'd be better able to store them this way. Do you have room in this refrigerator?"

"I don't know," Polly said.

Andrew opened the door. "It will be tight."

"Maybe the fridge on the back porch, then," Andy said.

Kayla picked up two of the containers and headed out of the room, followed by Rebecca with the other two.

"I made up hamburgers," Beryl said, cackling. Then she glared at Polly. "I did. I mixed the burgers up with Worcestershire sauce and a little seasoning, then made them into patties. They'll freeze. Can we put the buns and potato chips in the pantry?"

"Wow," Polly said. She reached out and took the bags of hamburger buns from Beryl. "You all are too good to me."

Lydia pushed another container toward her. "I know how much your little boys like macaroni and cheese, so here's some of that, too."

"How do you do it?" Polly asked.

"Lots of hands make easy work," Lydia replied. She handed the bowl of macaroni and cheese to Andrew who made room for it in the refrigerator.

Rebecca and Kayla took the bags of buns and the sacks of potato chips into the pantry. In no time, the counters were empty.

The back door opened and Polly heard the clattering of her dog's feet across the floor.

"That has to be Hayden and Heath," she said.

Sure enough, the two boys came into the kitchen with Henry's prescriptions, and carrying drink carriers from Sweet Beans.

"What did you do?" Polly asked.

Hayden looked at Beryl, Lydia and Andy and then back at the drink carriers. "I'm sorry. We didn't know you were here."

"Hush," Lydia said. "How would you? And we were just

leaving. We'll bother Polly later in the week, but right now our task is done. You take care of them, okay?"

Lydia gave Polly a hug and headed for the back door. Polly followed her out. "You aren't leaving just like that, are you?"

"You bet we are," Beryl said. "There's nothing worse than well-meaning people in your space when you're trying to sort out how to handle a newly wounded husband."

Andy gave Polly a hug. "If you need anything, let me know. We'll come right over. By the way, Len wants to have a chat with you about finding bodies in our back yard."

"Yeah. About that," Lydia said. "What were you thinking?"

"I have no idea." Polly shook her head.

Beryl pushed the other two women out of the door and winked at Polly. "Gotta keep them in line. We love you, sweetie."

When Polly got back into the kitchen, she saw that Henry, Noah, and Elijah had joined everyone else there.

"How are you feeling?" she asked Henry.

"I'm sore and grouchy, but it sounded like a lot of excitement out here."

"There has been. I'll tell you about it later. What did you bring, Hayden?"

"For you, coffee," he said, handing her a cup. He put a cup in Henry's hand. "I didn't know about coffee for you, so you have your choice of coffee or a smoothie."

"Coffee would be awesome," Henry said and gave Hayden a wan smile. "I hadn't gotten much of a start on mine this morning." He limped over to a chair at the dining room table and sat down, letting out a whoof as he settled. "This damned arm is going to annoy me for the next six weeks. Heath, can I borrow yours?"

Heath grabbed up his cup and sat down across from Henry. "Polly said something about me helping. I'll do anything I can."

Henry nodded and closed his eyes, then opened them again. "We'll talk. I'm going to need you."

Hayden handed out cups to the kids. "Camille knew what you liked, so your cups are marked. Smoothies for everyone."

Polly stepped back and leaned against the counter as she watched her family. The kids all thanked Hayden and then found a spot to sit at the table, chattering. Hayden gave her a look and she smiled through tears. She gave her head a quick shake to warn him off and he grinned back at her, then joined the others at the table.

"You going to sit with us, Polly?" Rebecca asked, patting the seat next to her.

"Yeah. I'm coming." She loved this family.

CHAPTER FIVE

"Very likely, your Uncle Dick is having the time of his life," Bill said, pushing his plate back. "Once you let him loose on that property, he decided that it was time to bring it all down."

Polly frowned. "How much is coming down?"

"All of the scrub brush, that's for sure. He's cleared out everything around the buildings so you can get to them. It isn't quite so scary looking now."

"He's leaving the big trees with the overhanging branches, right?"

"Dick doesn't have the equipment to bring those down, but he says the trees which are dead on the inside need to come out. A nasty storm could bring them down on the house."

"He's been mowing that lawn and hauling rock into the driveway," Marie said. She picked up her husband's plate and set it on top of her own, then stood. "It's going to be an attractive yard again."

Polly couldn't believe she hadn't been out there this summer. She'd put it out of her head. Once they signed the paperwork to purchase it, she knew they weren't going to do much with the house for a while, so it wasn't important. Henry hadn't said anything about Dick working on the lot, but she wasn't surprised.

"When are you planning to have that barn finished at the old place?" Bill asked.

"I was going to work on it next week," Henry said. "We're close, just have some inside work to finish."

Noah and Elijah were squirming on either side of Rebecca and Polly smiled. "Would you two like to be excused?"

Elijah jumped up. "Can we watch TV?"

Polly shook her head. "Not tonight. You can play video games, play with the racetracks, or go upstairs and play in your room."

"Come on, Noah. Let's race cars," Elijah said. He grabbed his brother's hand and dragged Noah out of his chair.

"Tell Marie and Bill thank you for dinner," Polly said.

Elijah dropped Noah's hand and rushed over to Marie, "Thank you, Grandma. You're the best grandma ever."

She beamed and pulled him close, then kissed his forehead. When she released him, he stepped up to stand in front of Bill. "Thank you," Elijah said.

"You know you can call me grandpa if you want," Bill said, bending forward to get closer to the boy. He opened his arms and Elijah walked into the embrace.

Polly glanced at Henry and he smiled back at her.

Noah was never one to initiate affection. Fortunately, Marie was sensitive to that and put her hand out. "Come give me a hug, Noah," she said.

He gave her a sweet smile and put his arms around her neck. She held on to him and whispered into his ear. When she released him, he stepped back and walked over to Bill. "She says that you like to race cars too. Do you want to play with us?"

Bill laughed. "She did, did she? She knows me better than anybody else. I'd love to race cars with you." He took Noah's hand and let the little boy lead him out of the kitchen. Before they got to the door, he turned back to the table. "Hayden and Heath, and you too, Rebecca and Kayla. If you want to race with us, you're welcome to."

"We'll help you clean up," Hayden said to Polly and Marie.

"Not if you want to play with the boys," Marie said. "Go on. We can take care of this."

He nodded at his brother, who followed him into the foyer.

"Not you, Rebecca?" Henry asked.

"That's for the boys," she said. "I'd rather be here."

Polly knew that was only an excuse. Rebecca was much more afraid that she might miss out on something interesting.

"We'll clean up," Stephanie said. She turned to her sister. "Wanna help?"

Kayla was always ready to help clean. Polly didn't know why that was, but she was willing to let it happen.

"Mom," Henry said. "I'm worn out and hurt like crazy. Would you be disappointed if I went upstairs to my bed?"

Marie's eyes grew big. "Go on, honey. I'm thankful we got to see for ourselves that you're okay." She smiled at Polly. "Not that I didn't trust you. You can go with him. I'll help the girls. We'll whip this kitchen back into shape in no time."

"Are you sure?" Polly asked.

"He needs you more than we do. Come back when he's settled." Marie took Polly's arm. "And if you don't come back before we leave, we'll understand. You've had a wild day today. It wouldn't surprise me if you fell asleep before we finish. We're family. You don't have to treat us like guests."

Polly hugged her. "Thank you."

Marie waited until Henry got his feet under him and took his right hand in hers, pulling it to her cheek. "I love you, son and I'm thankful that you weren't hurt any worse than this."

"Me too, Mom." He bent and kissed her cheek. "Thank you for dinner tonight. Tell Dad I'll talk to him tomorrow."

"I will, but nobody expects you to be right back at work. Take a few days to heal up, okay? For your mother?"

He laughed and then moaned. "Stop making me laugh. I'll do what I can."

She backed away and let him move past her to the back stairway.

Polly's heart broke as she watched him take each agonizingly slow step. With only one arm, he braced himself against the banister as he went up. By the time they got to the top, he was panting.

"I'm getting old, Polly. That was harder than it should be."

"Yeah. You're ancient."

"I just want to lie down and not have to talk to anyone."

"Good thing that's what we've got planned for you for the rest of the evening."

They arrived in the bedroom and Henry sat down hard on the bed. "I love my friends and family, but I'm tired of them right now," he said.

"You're just tired. Here, let me." Polly knelt in front of him and slid his slippers off his feet. She didn't understand why he hated going barefoot. She assumed it was a family thing. Now that the floors in the house were finished, she relished the feel of the cool floors in the summer and the warm kitchen floor in the winter. If she could always go without shoes, she would.

Henry tried to undo his jeans, but his right hand fumbled with the button until he looked at her in frustration. "This is going to suck. How am I supposed to go to the bathroom when you aren't around?"

"I have no idea. You'll figure it out when you aren't so exhausted. It's not that big of a deal." She unbuttoned the button. He'd been taking care of himself all afternoon, but she wasn't going to point that out right now. He was right on the edge of falling apart. Hopefully he'd sleep tonight. Polly helped him stand back up and he walked out of his jeans and over to the bathroom. "Can you handle that by yourself?"

He stopped at the doorway. "I want to say something lewd, but I don't have the energy to even think about it."

~~~

Fifteen minutes later, after twisting and turning, rearranging and propping up, Henry was sound asleep. Polly looked around the room, trying to decide what to do next. It was only eight fifteen and she certainly wasn't ready to go to bed.

She kissed Henry's cheek and whispered, "I'm going back downstairs. I'll check on you later. I love you."

"I love you," he murmured and shifted his arm on the pillow, which elicited a small groan.

Polly waited several heartbeats to see if he'd wake up, but his breathing slowed and the muscles in his face relaxed. She walked toward the doorway and turned to look back at him again. "I'm so thankful you're okay," she said quietly. Pulling the door closed she walked to the central doors and opened those to gales of laughter. Hayden saw her on the landing and waved for her to come down.

"Wait," Elijah said. He ran up the steps and handed her a car. "You try it."

"From here?" She pointed at a track that had been anchored to a balustrade.

"Yeah. It's the fastest car we have. You should watch it fly." He waved his hands for her to start and Polly held the car over the top of the track.

"Ready?" she asked.

"Set. Go," he yelled.

She dropped the car onto the track and Elijah raced down the steps beside the track, laughing and yelling all the way. The foyer might be great for big parties, but she wanted it to always be a grand playroom for these kids. Nothing would be impossible in this room. As she looked out over the space, she saw castles made from cardboard boxes, forts of blankets and tables, tunnels and secret hideaways.

He stood at the bottom of the steps, waiting for her. "Did you see it go? That was amazing!"

"How's my boy?" Bill asked.

"He hurts, but at least he's home. That scared me today," Polly responded. "How would I ever do this without him? He's everything in my life." She felt tears threaten as Bill reached out to put an arm around her shoulders.

"You can't think that way. It just escalates. Nobody needs to do that to themselves. He's fine. He's here."

"You're right. I shouldn't let fear make up stories for me. Where did Heath and Noah go?"

Bill looked around the room. "Where's your brother, 'Jah?"

"I don't know." Elijah ran to grab Hayden's hand. "Let's do the double track. I get this car. You can have any other car you want. Race me?"

"I'm checking the kitchen." Polly went through the doors into the kitchen and laughed when she saw that it was clean. "Wow, that was fast. What am I hearing?"

Rebecca pursed her lips together in a mysterious smile. "You'll see. Marie made …"

Marie tossed a dish towel at Rebecca, interrupting her. "Hush, you. It's supposed to be a surprise."

"You're going to love it," Kayla said.

"You got the kitchen cleaned up in a hurry. That's a pretty nice surprise."

"This is even better. We thought you'd be upstairs longer."

Marie crossed the room and took Polly's arm. "Did he fall asleep okay?"

"Yeah. Those painkillers did their job and the poor guy was exhausted. We propped him up so he was fairly comfortable." Polly huffed a laugh. "I'm not looking forward to changing the bandage on his face, though. I thought I was going to pass out when the nurse showed me what I had to do."

"You know there's someone who would come do that for you," Rebecca said. "I miss Evelyn. You should invite her over."

"I'm not going to invite her over and then ask her to work for me," Polly said. "I should be able to do this."

"I'd do it," Marie said. "I don't know that Henry would be a good patient for his mother, but I'm not squeamish. However, if you hired Evelyn, you could invite her to have coffee and spend time with Rebecca. I suspect both of them would enjoy that."

"Yeah," Rebecca said. "I could show her my room and the paintings I've been working on. Would you, please?"

Polly laughed. "It sounds like I'd be abusing you if I didn't. That's a great idea. I'll talk to Henry about it tomorrow morning."

"Don't ask him. Just make the call," Marie said. "He'll try to talk you out of it. He's not very good at accepting help from people. Did you see how difficult it was for him to go upstairs tonight? And it's just us. He never had a problem walking out on me when he was a boy and living at home. Now he's polite?"

"Got it." Polly glanced back at the foyer. "Did you see Heath and Noah come through here?"

All four shook their heads.

"I wonder where they got to." Polly wandered back down the hallway and glanced into the family room thinking that maybe the boys were playing a video game, but the room was empty. She continued on down the hallway. The doors to the rooms that Stephanie and Kayla were using were closed. She couldn't imagine having to live in someone else's home.

It was a wonder that Kayla and Rebecca were still good friends. The only reason it worked was that Kayla was so easygoing. When Rebecca turned into a horrid, sulky child, Kayla found someplace else to be. She was wonderful with Noah and Elijah, and taught them how to play board games and card games. The kids had summer passes to the swimming pool and were there several afternoons each week.

She stopped outside the living room door when she heard voices in the room Hayden and Heath were using. Polly strained to hear what was going on, not wanting to interrupt by walking in. That was soon dashed when Elijah burst through from the foyer, yelling for his brother. He pulled up short beside her.

"Polly, did you find them?"

She nodded.

"Noah, what are you doing?" Elijah yelled. He grabbed Polly's hand and dragged her into the room.

"Nothing," Noah said. He pushed a stack of things over on top of whatever he was working on at Heath's desk.

"Then come here. Grandpa and Hayden set up a triple track. I need you to run one of the cars."

Noah looked at Heath and then at Polly. "I'm busy."

"Doing what?" Elijah demanded. "You said it was nothing."

"Fine," Noah said. He stood up and stomped toward his brother. "I'm coming. Let's go race your stupid cars."

Elijah looked at him in shock. "I thought you liked playing with the cars."

"I do," Noah said, "but not when I'm busy doing something else."

"You just said it was nothing."

Heath and Polly looked at each other in shock. The two boys rarely argued. They had spent so much of their lives protecting each other from the world around them, that it felt like it was part of their DNA. She wasn't sure whether to cheer that they were finally claiming a little bit of independence or worry that this might someday grow into something bigger.

"It's okay," Elijah finally said. He turned around and walked dejectedly toward the door. "I'll do it by myself." He sloughed his feet across the floor, sighing loudly with each step. The closer he got to the doorway, the slower he walked.

Just as he lifted his foot to cross the threshold, Noah ran up to him. "I'm coming. Really, I want to. I'll tell you later. Okay?"

That was all it took. Elijah brightened up and grabbed his brother's hand. "You're going to love what Grandpa did. You gotta see this."

"That was interesting," Polly said to Heath.

"I figured you'd stop them."

She shrugged. "Sometimes brothers have to be brothers. They were testing each other. I'm glad they figured it out together. What's going on?"

Heath uncovered what Noah had been working on and beckoned her over. "He's writing and illustrating a poem for Henry. He didn't want to tell Rebecca because he was worried she might think he was trying to be an artist — that he was copying her. And he didn't want to tell Andrew because he didn't want him to think that he was trying to be a writer and copying him. I tried to tell Noah that they would be proud of him, but he wasn't ready for that, so he asked me for help." Heath laughed. "Because I'm so artistic and clever with words."

Polly picked up the piece of paper Noah had been working on and read out loud, "Henry, you're my dad. Today you made me sad. I love you very much and wish you'd get better with a touch." She grinned at Heath. "Are you helping him with the rhymes?"

"He was actually working out rhyming words on his own. I only helped him get from A to B," Heath said. "He's got a ways to go, but it's pretty cute." He shook his head. "Of all the people in this house, I can't believe he asked me to help with this."

"He trusts you. That's wonderful."

"It feels kinda weird, you know, to have someone that little trust me like this." Heath covered the paper back up. "I want to do what you're doing when I grow up."

"What's that?"

"Take lots of kids in and make them feel safe. I hope my wife feels the same way."

Polly raised her eyebrows. "Your wife? Do you have someone in mind?"

"No!" he shouted and then giggled, a sound she didn't often hear from Heath. "I mean, no. I hope I'll meet someone in college."

"You know that you'll have to do more than go to class and come back to Bellingwood if you want to meet people, right?"

He sighed. "I'm not in any hurry. When it happens, it happens."

"You keep thinking that," Polly said. "Don't rush it. You're quite a catch, you know. When you find the girl who recognizes that, I'll be a very happy mom."

"Does it sound weird to you to have Noah and Elijah call Bill their grandpa?"

"No. Marie and Bill encourage it."

"You're not upset that I didn't want to be adopted and have your last name, are you?"

Polly frowned. "Upset? Not at all. We didn't need adoption

papers to claim you as our own." She smiled at him. "It's more important that you and Hayden are brothers. The two of you will always be ours. We'll never be upset at anything like that."

"I just wondered what Henry thought."

"Why?"

"If I go into business with him. I won't be a Sturtz, and it's a family business."

"You're family, Heath. The name doesn't matter. Trust me. That's the last thing Henry would consider to be a problem."

The door from the foyer burst open again and Elijah came racing toward them. "Come on, you guys. Grandma says it's time."

"Time for what?" Polly asked.

"She wouldn't tell me. She just said to come get you and bring you to the front porch."

Polly grinned at Heath. "We'd better go."

Bill and Hayden were standing at the front door, waiting for them. They opened the double doors and Polly walked out into the warm night air. There was a slight breeze, though the humidity hung close to her skin.

"It's ice cream!" Elijah said. "I've never had homemade ice cream."

"That's the sound I heard." Polly walked over to the card table.

Rebecca and Kayla stood behind it with a scoop and a stack of bowls.

Rebecca smiled. "We should hurry. It's hot out here and the ice cream will melt."

"Ice cream soup is good, too," Polly said. "And you brought toppings. You girls are awesome."

Obiwan and Han chased each other in the front yard as everyone found a place to sit on the porch. They'd installed an invisible fence in the front yard after Henry, Hayden and Heath finished the back-yard fencing. The dogs hadn't pushed too hard to get out; they had plenty of room to run and generally liked to be around their people. It was nice to finally allow them to be free when everyone was outside. The yard was finally theirs.

"I wish Henry was here," Noah said. "He likes ice cream."

"Yes he does," Polly replied. She was sitting beside him on the edge of the porch. "We'll do this again. I can't believe I hadn't thought about it before." She turned to look back at Marie. "We don't have an ice cream maker, do we?"

"You do now," Bill said. "Every house with kids needs an ice cream machine. Now back in my day, we had to crank it by hand. That was the best ice cream."

"You never cranked that stinking machine," Marie said, scolding him. "I cranked it, Lonnie cranked it, Henry cranked it. You bustled around checking the ice and salt mixture. As soon as I could buy an electric machine, I did. And if you want to hand crank your own ice cream, I'm sure I can find that old thing in the basement."

Elijah stood in front of Bill, ice cream on his cheeks and dripping from his spoon. "I'd crank it for you."

Bill wiped the boy's cheeks with a napkin. "I know you would. You're a good boy." He turned Elijah around and lifted him onto his lap. "I have a pretty good family. Even if my dear wife doesn't let me get away with anything."

CHAPTER SIX

Expecting something terrible, Polly woke up, shaken and startled. She'd heard something. Lying silent and motionless, she waited, hoping to hear it again.

"Polly," Henry whispered. "Are you awake?"

Sitting straight up, she turned to him. "Yes. What's going on? Are you okay?"

"I can't move."

"What do you mean you can't move? Really can't move?"

"It hurts. Everything hurts."

"Let me get a painkiller. Your muscles need to relax. I promise — you're okay. Remember, the doctor said you were going to stiffen up. You're okay." She was already moving toward the bathroom. She flipped the bathroom light on and drew a glass of water. When she got back into the bedroom, she checked the clock and saw that it was two-forty-eight. He'd been asleep for quite a long time.

"I should have gotten you up a couple of hours ago and made you take a pill," Polly said. "I'm so sorry." She opened the pill bottle and took one out. She started to put the pill in his hand and realized that he hurt too much to move his arm. "Open your mouth. We'll just get this right in there."

Henry swallowed the pill and nodded so that Polly took the glass away from his lips.

"Do you want to try to sit up?" she asked.

"Yeah. I'd better. Ignore my moaning and groaning, okay?"

"I'll do my best. I'm so sorry you hurt."

He let out a long moan as he tried to sit up on his own and dropped back to the pillow. "This sucks."

"I'm not going to laugh, because I know you hurt, but I'm sure it does. Here, let me do the hard work. You help when you can. Are you ready?"

"Like I said. Ignore the moaning. Keep going unless I say stop."

Polly took a deep breath and put her arm under his good side. Between the two of them, they got him turned and sitting upright at the edge of the bed.

"That's a good start, right?" he asked, panting from the exertion.

"Are you in a hurry to get to the bathroom?"

He looked at her and blinked his eyes. "I wasn't until you said something. I am now, though. Damn it, I hoped I could wait until the painkiller kicked in."

"I've got you," she said. She bent and placed herself under his right arm. "Let's go," she said. "I know it hurts and I know you feel off balance with your arm messed up."

It didn't take long and he was soon standing and walking. He dropped his right arm to his side and walked off without her. "I've got this," he said. "I refuse to be an invalid."

Polly stopped in the middle of the room and watched him limp across to the bathroom door. It was more like a weird waddle as he lumbered from side to side, hunching when the pain would seize him. He went into the bathroom and she waited.

"Polly?" he called.

"Do you need me?"

"Help me. I can't bend."

She went into the bathroom.

"Don't you dare say a word. Just take my pants down for me, please."

"This is called true love," she said with a laugh.

"This is called true embarrassment."

"When you're ninety-eight years old, I promise to be just as patient." She patted his bottom. "And I'll still love this butt."

"You're not helping."

"Sorry. You know what the worst part of this is?"

"There's something worse than this?"

"Yeah. I can't tell anybody about it. This is a great story and I can't tell a soul."

"Please leave."

"Why? I'm sorry. I didn't mean to make you laugh."

"Just go. I'll let you know when I need you."

"Oh. I see." Polly walked back out into the bedroom. It did stink that she couldn't tell anyone. Hopefully Henry would see the humor in it someday and they'd at least be able to laugh about it. She was pretty sure that wasn't going to happen tonight.

He showed up in the doorway of the bathroom, his shorts around his ankles. "Are you done laughing at me yet?"

Polly dipped her head, trying to fight back laughter. "I feel so bad that you hurt, so I'm trying not to laugh. I really am."

"Put me back together, please."

She got him straightened back up. "Do you want to go back to the bed?"

"It scares me."

"Because you had so much trouble getting out? I promise to set my alarm this time and make sure you get a painkiller before it's too late."

"How about my chair. Do you mind?"

"Henry, I only want you to be comfortable. You choose where you want to rest."

"Let's try the chair, then."

She helped him again and brought a pillow over for his arm, then sat down on his side of the bed. "Will you be able to sleep?"

He nodded. "How about you? I'm sorry I woke you up."

"Nonsense. This is that sickness and health thing we both signed up for. I wouldn't have it any other way." Polly dropped to the bed, burying her face in his pillow, taking in his scent. "We had homemade ice cream tonight. Noah was concerned that you were missing it."

"That sounds nice."

"Heath was worried about you being upset because he didn't want to be adopted and take your name. Thought you might not be happy if he came into the business and wasn't a Sturtz."

"You set him straight, right? He's still my boy."

"That's what I told him."

"Good. Polly?"

"Yes, Henry."

"I love you."

"I know." She smiled as she closed her eyes.

~~~

Polly's eyes flew open at the buzzing of her alarm. She looked to Henry and saw that he was still asleep. She hated to wake him, but after the incident last night, she'd rather be safe than sorry. Sitting up, she rubbed her eyes and gave her head a quick shake, then headed for the bathroom. When she returned with a glass full of water, Henry gave her a weak smile.

"I'm sorry about last night."

"Why? Because you were in pain? Bad Henry. Bad, bad Henry." She handed him a pain killer and after he put it in his mouth, handed over the glass.

He took a long drink and set it down on the table beside him.

"Were you able to sleep in this chair?" she asked.

"It wasn't bad. I'd like to get back in bed, though. I'm not going anywhere today. He lifted his right hand to his left cheek and touched the bandages. "This hurts like hell."

Polly sat back down on the edge of the bed. "Would you mind terribly if I asked Evelyn Morrow to come over and check your wound? I don't want to be responsible for that." Just saying it out loud made her stomach turn.

"I can handle it myself. What about Mom?"

"Marie's the one who recommended Evelyn. And Rebecca misses her. They lost touch when Rebecca went back to school. Do you mind? She can come in every day and make sure you're all fixed up and I won't have to get sick at the sight of your face."

"I knew you loved me."

"Please?"

"I don't like it."

Polly took a breath. "You don't like it because you have to depend on someone else? Or you really don't like it and will be upset if I push any harder?"

He thought about it for a minute and nodded. "The first one. She can come, but only for a day or two. I'll be fine once my body figures out how to manage the pain."

"You're my big, strong Henry and nothing hurts you."

"That's right," he said. "Now can you help me get up and moving into the bathroom again? All I need is a little push."

"I'm afraid a push would be the end of you. What do you think about breakfast? You didn't eat much last night."

He wobbled across the bedroom floor. "I know, and it was my favorite. Mom makes the best meatloaf in the world."

"There are leftovers. I'll save you a serving. Lydia, Beryl and Andy dropped off a ton of food yesterday. We have sandwiches for a week." She leaned against the wall outside the bathroom door. It was weird. They shared that bathroom every day, but suddenly it felt important to give him a sense of privacy. Then she heard him fumbling at the sink. "What are you doing in there?"

"My mouth is foul. I want to brush my teeth, but I can't get the cap off the damned toothpaste."

"Polly, I need help," she said.

"Polly, I need help," he echoed.

She went in and smiled at him in the mirror.

Henry held the toothpaste tube up to her and she unscrewed the cap.

Before handing it back, she asked, "Will you let me at least squeeze some on your toothbrush?"

"You don't know how I like it."

"You have got to be kidding me."

He looked away. "Kinda. Not really."

"I had no idea. How about I hold your toothbrush and you squeeze what you want on there."

"It's okay," he said with a sigh. "You go ahead. I can suffer the indignity of using an incorrectly prepared toothbrush." He lifted his hand to his hair and attempted to pat it down. "I'm going to need a shower. When can I have a shower?"

She chuckled. "Let's give it a day. I suppose we could put a plastic bag over your face to protect the stitches and another one over your arm."

"You're so helpful," he said with a mouthful of toothbrush and paste. He spit into the sink. "I'm not waiting very long. That's all there is to it."

"You keep talking while you're hopped up on painkillers, Mighty Man," Polly said. She left the bathroom and jumped when he swatted her behind.

"I still have my right hand. You'd best be careful."

"Yes sir. Let's get you situated so I can let the dogs out."

He looked around in surprise. "Where are they?"

"Sleeping with Noah and Elijah. You didn't need that last night."

"Do I have to stay upstairs all day today?"

"Not unless you want to. Try to get more sleep." Polly looked around the room, frustrated at the fact that his phone was gone. "She's not going to like it."

"Who? What?"

"I'm bringing Rebecca's phone to you. She doesn't need it and I want you to be able to reach me in a hurry. Your dad is going to look for your phone today. If we have to replace it, we'll do it right away."

"My tablet was in the truck, too. I'm going to need that."

She scowled at him. "Not today."

"Yes today. I can't be out of touch. I'll suffer with staying home, but I need to know what's going on."

"We'll put Heath on it. You sleep for another couple of hours and then we'll regroup. Heath can go out and be your voice today after you tell him what you want him to do. They did fine without you yesterday and they'll be fine without you today."

"Clearly you know nothing about my crews," Henry retorted.

"I know that you trust them." Polly put the pillow back under his arm and waited while he shifted around to get comfortable. "You going to live for me so I can get the day started?"

"I don't have a choice," he muttered.

She quickly changed into shorts and a t-shirt, then went out into the hallway and closed the door behind her. Polly opened the door into Noah and Elijah's room. The boys were sound asleep, but the dogs were ready to go. Both ran out, wagging their tails. They headed for her bedroom, but when they saw Polly walk down the hall to the back steps, the dogs trotted along beside her. As Polly walked past the coffee pot, she switched it on, thankful that there were plenty of adults in the house to make sure it was ready to go every morning.

Polly wasn't used to this hour of the day. Henry took the dogs out first thing, giving her time to slowly wake up. Since the kids had no daily schedule, she was usually in no hurry to get moving. It was going to stink when school started up again, but as long as she had a month or two to sleep in, she was taking it.

Rebecca, Kayla, and Andrew had marching band practice beginning soon. Polly wasn't looking forward to crawling out of bed at awful hours to drive them down to Boone for it, but Stephanie had offered to be the early morning driver this summer since she couldn't pick them up when they were finished with practice. The thought of letting someone else take that responsibility on made Polly feel a twinge of guilt, but not enough to refuse the offer. Sylvie was already at work that early in the morning and couldn't do any of it. She was the one who felt guilty. Stephanie and Polly told her to get over it and send them a muffin every once in a while.

Polly dreaded the beginning of school. This year was going to be horrendous. Rebecca was already talking about the activities she could get involved in. Andrew and Kayla would participate too, but their lives would diverge as each of the kids found their own interests. She felt like she was stuck in a strange conundrum — wishing that Rebecca would quickly turn sixteen so she could drive — and praying that the time between now and then would go slowly so they could enjoy every moment.

She followed the dogs into the back yard. Today was going to be sultry. Though the temperature was still in the upper sixties, the humidity was already high. Obiwan and Han ran and ran, chasing each other around the yard as if they were perfectly comfortable. Silly dogs. She'd purchased a couple of small swimming pools when the temperatures began to rise. Han wasn't at all sure what to do with them at first — he wasn't a big fan of baths. Obiwan jumped right in and splashed everyone in the vicinity. Noah and Elijah loved playing with the dogs in the water, refilling the pools from the hose and spraying the dogs, who barked and jumped with joy. Today would be another good day for water outside.

Polly wandered to the back fence. She could see over into the cemetery, but the bushes separating her fence from the main property obscured her view of where Tab and the sheriff's department had been working yesterday. Charlie Heller would be in there today, repairing the damage they'd done. She glanced down at Andy's house and her heart sank. She'd invited Reuben and Judy Greene to come to dinner tonight. As interesting as they were, Henry didn't need to be subjected to that. And … that was another thing she had yet to talk to him about. With all that had happened yesterday, she had completely forgotten about that conversation. She should have asked Bill and Marie about Judy Greene. They would remember her.

"Are you ready for breakfast?" Polly asked the dogs.

Han tore across the yard, then veered to the side door. Obiwan, a little more circumspect, trotted to Polly and walked with her as she crossed the lawn. When they got inside, she put food down and checked their water, then looked at the coffee pot and heaved a sigh. She hadn't been outside nearly long enough. Grabbing Rebecca's phone from the charger, she ran back upstairs and tiptoed into her bedroom.

"I'm awake," Henry said.

"You okay?"

"Yeah. I'm just wide awake. I'm done sleeping."

"You don't want to try any longer or what?"

"I'm done. I'm hungry and I don't want to sleep anymore. Don't make me."

"Honey, you can do whatever you want. Where do you want to land today?"

He moaned as he pulled himself upright and dropped his legs off the edge of the bed. "I don't know. I want to be in my truck going to work."

"Oh goodie. You're going to be such fun today."

"Maybe." He set his jaw. "This isn't fair."

Polly opened his dresser and dug around until she found a pair of loose shorts. She found a t-shirt in another drawer.

"You're not going to yell at me?"

"About life not being fair? You know better. Today it sucks, but you're alive and I love you. That's enough. You change your clothes and I'll get a brush to try to do something with that hair. If you're going to be downstairs amongst the rest of humanity, you might as well look like you belong."

"I hate my hair."

She laughed out loud. "That's my line."

"I usually wash the day out of it. Yesterday was a rough day and it's all sticky and gross."

"We'll figure something out."

"You'll wash my hair and rub my scalp?"

"Good heavens, you're pathetic," she said, tossing his clothes beside him. She hitched in a breath as they left her hands, certain that they'd either hit him in the face or land on the floor three feet from him, but they ended up on the bed beside him and she turned for the bathroom.

"Knew you could do it," he called after her.

Polly needed a shower this morning, too, but she could do that whenever she found time. Instead, she dug around in a drawer, found a hair tie, and pulled her hair back in a ponytail. That would do for now. Grabbing Henry's hairbrush, she headed back for the bedroom and watched as he struggled to change his shirt.

"Are you going to stand there watching me or will you deign to help me with this?"

"First pathetic and now a brat. It's going to be a long day." Polly dropped the brush on the bed, then helped him wiggle out of the shirt he'd been wearing. "Have you seen this?" she asked, pointing at his torso.

He looked down and grimaced at the bruises that had blossomed. "I suck."

"I'll be nicer to you, you poor thing."

"That's what it takes? Big bruises?"

"It'll do." She pulled the fresh t-shirt up over his arm, then slid his head through the hole.

He moaned while wriggling his right arm through the last hole. "I will stop hurting, right?"

"Of course you will," she said. "Imagine how bad it would be if you didn't have that happy pill working for you right now. Have you decided where you want to land?"

"I'll be fine in the family room in the recliner."

"Do you want to be somewhere else?"

He stuck his lower lip out. "Everybody is always in the kitchen, but I can't sit in those chairs all day. It's going to be lonely in the family room by myself."

"When Hayden and Heath get up, they can move the recliner into the kitchen for you. How about that?"

"That's too much. I'm being pathetic."

"Okay. You can stay in the family room. No problem." Polly walked toward the door and paused, waiting to see if he was going to follow her. She turned to see him slide his feet into his slippers.

"You're mean to me."

"Yeah. I'm sorry. I feel terrible."

"No you don't."

"I do a little. I feel awful that you hurt and I'm thankful that you're home."

"But?"

"But nothing. Just those things. Do you want to go down the back steps into the kitchen or the big steps into the foyer?"

"Is the foyer safe or will I battle racetrack?"

Polly stopped to think. "Go down the south steps and you can hold onto the banister with your right arm. It should be clear."

By the time they reached the bottom step, Henry was panting again.

"It's hard work to do anything when you hurt," he said.

"Kitchen or family room?"

"Kitchen first. I'm hungry and want coffee."

She held the door for him and smiled at Stephanie, who was pouring a cup of coffee. "Good morning."

"I knew you were up since the dogs were running around. How are you, Henry?"

"I'm an old man, but I'll live."

"I was thinking about running up to Sweet Beans for some breakfast muffins. Does that sound good?" Stephanie asked.

Polly chuckled. "You could certainly do that or you could open the freezer and take out a container of breakfast sandwiches. Lydia, Andy, and Beryl made a bunch up for us. You'll find ham, sausage, or bacon in there, all nicely labeled." She walked with Henry as he headed for the dining room table. Once he collapsed in a chair, she rubbed his back. "Which one would you like?"

"Ham," he said.

Stephanie held up the container. "I've got it. The instructions are right inside."

"Hey."

Everyone turned to the foyer door in surprise.

"Heath, you're up early," Polly said.

He blinked and stretched his shoulders. "I thought I'd better get moving. Hayden's in the shower. As soon as you're ready to tell me what I need to do today, I'll head out."

Henry nodded. "Thanks. I don't think I can ride with you today. Maybe tomorrow."

Polly let a cough loose.

"If I'm feeling better, I'm going to work," Henry said. "You can't stop me."

"Bet me," she muttered, walking over to the coffee pot. "Do you want that recliner in here or not?"

"I'll be fine in the other room."

"I'll get my laptop for you until you find your tablet."

Heath sat down across from Henry. "Who's working out at the horse barn at Eliseo's place?"

Polly shook her head and put a mug of coffee in front of Henry, who picked it up and sipped it. He smiled at her and leaned in to talk to Heath. These next few days weren't going to be easy for any of them.

CHAPTER SEVEN

"Right in here," Polly said to Evelyn Morrow as she walked into the family room. When he didn't respond, she realized Henry hadn't heard her. "Henry?"

He sat up fast and groaned. "I wasn't sleeping."

She chuckled. "It's okay. You can relax today. Evelyn is here."

"Is it ten o'clock already?" Henry pushed the recliner forward and stood, then turned. "I'm sorry. Hello, Evelyn. How are you?"

"Better than you," she said. "You look like you went ten rounds with a car."

"I feel like it too." He glanced at Polly, who nodded.

"I'll be right back," she said and headed out of the room. Henry hated taking any kind of pills. If he was reminding her that it was time for his pain medication, he was still hurting. She ran up the main steps to their bedroom and grabbed the medication, then walked back to Rebecca's room and knocked.

"Come in," Rebecca called out.

Polly opened the door and grinned. Rebecca had Noah and Elijah posed on chairs in the middle of her bedroom while she sketched. "I wondered why it was so quiet up here."

"Elijah wanted to help Hayden paint, but he agreed to sit for me instead," Rebecca said. "What's up?"

"Where's Kayla?"

Rebecca pointed toward the back of the house. "She's painting. Hayden told her he would teach her how to do it the right way so that she'd know when they got in their own place. She's never painted before. Mom and I always used to paint my room whenever the landlord would let us. It was the first thing we did even before we unpacked our stuff."

"Mrs. Morrow is here."

"Is it time already?" Rebecca leaned backward to look at the clock beside her bed. "Wow. You boys have been sitting still for a long time. That's cool."

If anybody could get away with asking them to sit still, it would be Rebecca. The boys adored her with everything they had.

"Why don't you give her a few more minutes with Henry and then come downstairs. I have cookies and treats ready in the kitchen. If Henry is doing okay, maybe I'll take Noah and Elijah uptown so you can spend time with her."

Rebecca gave her a look of surprise. "Really?"

Polly nodded. "She'd love to see your room and what you've painted. I don't believe she's had a tour of the house yet either."

"Thank you."

"You two boys put your shoes on before coming downstairs. We're going to run errands this morning."

Elijah grabbed Polly's hand. "Are we going to Sweet Beans?"

It wasn't a silly question. If Polly left the house, Sweet Beans was generally her first stop. "We'll see," she said with a smile. "Maybe fifteen minutes. Okay?"

"Okay boys. Can you sit there for fifteen more minutes?"

Polly turned and left as Noah said quietly. "We've been good for an hour. Fifteen minutes won't kill us."

"It might," Elijah said. She heard him give Rebecca a raspberry as she pulled the door shut.

She walked back down the hall and stuck her head in the first door, which would be Heath's room. Finding no one, she walked past the bathroom to Hayden's room. The door was only slightly opened and she tapped on it. "Are you in here?"

"Just a second," Hayden said. There was some shuffling around and soon he opened the door. "Sorry. I was painting that wall."

"Did I hear you have a helper?" Polly asked.

"I'm back here, Polly," Kayla said, sticking her head out of the closet. "I was afraid of making a mistake, so Hayden let me start in here. I'm almost done. He says I'm doing a nice job. This is fun."

Polly laughed. Painting a room was quite satisfying, but she'd never call it fun. "I'm glad you like it. You know this is a paying gig, right?"

Kayla came all the way out. "Really?" She was actually much cleaner than Polly expected. There was paint on her forearm. Polly recognized the smear as a newbie's first realization that the paint on the wall was still wet. There were splatters on an old t-shirt of Rebecca's she was wearing and on her shorts, but there were no big globs of paint in her hair.

Hayden nodded. "I didn't even think about that. Look at you, Kayla. Having fun and making money. That's the way it's supposed to work."

"Hayden still has to teach me how to do the taping, but painting is easy," Kayla said. "I love the way it covers up the wall and makes it look new."

"That's the best thing about a good paint job," Polly said. "I'm taking off for a while with Noah and Elijah to run errands. Mrs. Morrow is here to check on Henry and then she's going to spend time with Rebecca. I'll try to be back by lunch, but if I'm not, will you make sure Henry gets fed, too?"

Hayden smiled. "I'll make sure. When does Andrew come over?"

"He's usually here about eleven thirty," Kayla said. "We should make him help us paint, too."

Polly shook her head. "Good luck with that. I'll see you later." She went back down the steps and into the hallway. There was no one in the family room, so she hoped she knew where they'd gone and headed for the kitchen. Sure enough, she heard Henry and Evelyn's voices coming from the bathroom under the back stairway.

"There you are," Henry said, coming out first. "I thought we'd lost you."

"Just checking on the kids." Polly went over to a cupboard and took a glass down, filled it and set it on the island along with his pill bottle. It took everything in her to not open the bottle and take one out for him, but once Henry was up and moving around, the last thing he would want from her was to be treated like a child.

Evelyn smiled as she came around the corner. "This is such a nice space for your family. I can't wait to see the rest of the house."

"It's not all put together yet," Polly said. "Rebecca is looking forward to showing you around. I told her to give us a few minutes. She has Noah and Elijah sitting still while she sketches them. It's incredible."

"I'm looking forward to spending time with her," Evelyn said. "I want to hear how she's doing. It's hard to believe she is going to high school this fall. Where does the time go?"

Henry made his way over to the coffee pot and poured another cup. "I should get back to work. There are a few things I need to deal with. Thank you, Evelyn. Be sure to tell Polly that I'm fine."

Polly wrinkled her nose at him. "I'll be in to deal with you in a minute."

He slowly walked down the hall, his limp less pronounced than it had been earlier.

"Is he really fine?" Polly asked.

"He was beat up pretty badly," Evelyn responded. "I made him show me the bruises on his torso. It's going to take him longer than he thinks to heal. The surgeon who stitched his face up did a very nice job. There will only be a slight scar. I'd like to look at it again over the next few days."

"I'd love that. As long as I don't have to wipe up blood and gore, I'll be very happy," Polly said.

Thundering down the back steps announced the arrival of Rebecca, Noah, and Elijah. The two boys ran into the kitchen and pulled to a stop in front of Evelyn.

"Boys, this is Mrs. Morrow. She's a nurse. Evelyn, this is Noah and Elijah." Polly put her hands on their shoulders as she introduced them.

"It's nice to meet you, boys," Evelyn said. She put her hand out and first Elijah, then Noah, shook it.

Rebecca had held back and after Evelyn greeted the two boys, she turned to Rebecca. "It's good to see you again, dear." Opening her arms, she only had to wait a second for Rebecca to step in for a hug.

Polly bent down. "You two boys go sit at the table. You can each have one cookie. I need to talk to Henry and then we'll leave. Are you ready?"

They nodded and she pointed at the table, then headed for the family room.

"Are you doing okay?" she asked, as she went in.

"It stings. She poked and prodded, but I'll be fine."

"Would you be okay with me leaving? I'll take Noah and Elijah. Hayden and Kayla are painting upstairs. If I'm not back by lunch, Hayden said he had it covered. There's sandwich makings in there from Lydia."

"That was a lot of words," Henry said. "I keep telling you that I'm fine. I don't want you to treat me like an invalid."

Polly kissed his head. "Which is why I'm leaving the house with the boys. You have Rebecca's phone here, so if you need anything, call."

"You wanna check with Dad to see if they found anything in the wreckage? I'd like to get my tablet back."

"I thought I'd stop over there," Polly replied. "Anything else you need me to do while I'm out? I'll have two healthy little boys with me. They can carry stuff."

He gave her a weak smile. "Thanks for taking them with you. I don't know how much of their energy I could manage today."

"I got this. How's Heath doing out there?"

"Good," Henry responded. "I'm glad he knows everybody. They talk to him like he's part of the team, so at least there's that."

"Let me know if you need anything while I'm out and about. I'll be back later. There might be a quick trip to the library for the boys, so it will be after one o'clock."

"No worries. I promise not to die in the chair here."

Polly leaned over and he turned so that he could kiss her lips.

She headed back to the kitchen and found Evelyn in an animated conversation with Rebecca and the two boys. She listened for a moment and realized they were discussing the body she'd found yesterday morning. Was that only yesterday morning? She needed to remember to call the hotel and try to reach the Greenes. She couldn't ask Henry to sit through another meal with guests tonight.

"Are you ready to go, boys?" she asked.

Elijah and Noah popped out of their seats and ran to the doorway leading onto the back porch.

"Boys, say good-bye to Mrs. Morrow," Polly said.

They waved. "Good-bye, Mrs. Morrow."

"It was nice to meet you, boys. I hope to see you again," Evelyn said. She smiled at Polly and nodded, then turned back to Rebecca.

"All right," Polly said as they got outside. "Back seats. First stop is the coffee shop."

"Can we get smoothies?" Elijah asked.

"Little ones. We have a lot of things to do today. There might even be lunch in it for you." She waited for them to buckle in, then backed out and headed for Sweet Beans. It felt good to be out and about. There was a parking spot right in front of the coffee shop and Polly pulled in. The boys were out of the truck and standing in front of the door before she had her belt off — or so it seemed. Noah held the front door open for her.

"Thank you, sweetie." Polly reached down and he took her hand. Elijah trotted to her other side and took that hand and they proceeded to the front counter.

"Good morning," Camille said.

Polly loved watching Noah encounter Camille. He was head-over-heels in love with the young woman. Every time he saw her, his eyes glazed over and he smiled like a silly goose.

"Good morning," Polly said, nudging Noah's arm.

"Good morning," he echoed.

"How's Henry?"

"He's good," Polly said. "Good enough that I was okay with leaving. I need iced coffee for me and a couple of small smoothies."

"What flavors?" Camille asked, leaning on the counter. "Strawberry for Noah. Right?"

He nodded.

"Strawberry for you too, Elijah?"

"Can I have strawberry banana?" Elijah asked.

Camille looked at Polly.

"May I," Polly said quietly.

"May I have strawberry banana?" Elijah asked with an ornery grin.

"Of course," Camille replied.

"Look at the mess you made." A strident voice came from behind them and Polly turned to see who was speaking. "I swear. You are the clumsiest thing I've ever seen. I should have known better than to bring you out to a public place. You're an embarrassment." The woman speaking was someone Polly had seen around town a few times. She was about Polly's age and sitting with her husband and a girl who had to be their daughter. The husband was a bit older, maybe in his early forties; the hair on top of his head was thin and straggly. He was hunched in on himself and though it was obvious he tried to separate the woman from her daughter, it wasn't enough. He was attempting to clean up the girl's spill from the table and from her shirt, but succeeded in only making it worse.

Camille reached under the counter for a cloth and ran it under the sink to wet it.

"I've got this," Polly said. "You make the drinks. You two boys stay right here, okay?"

Noah and Elijah nodded, their mouths open wide. She'd deal with that later.

"Hi. I'm Polly Giller," she said, approaching the table. "Let me help you. I have a clean wet cloth. This is no problem."

The little girl looked up at her, fear in her eyes. Polly locked onto her with her gaze. "You're fine. Nothing a little water won't clean up." She gently wiped the girl's face and brushed the cloth across the shirt, cleaning up the worst of the mess from the glass of milk that had spilled. "What's your name?"

"Ariel."

"Look at this, Ariel. You didn't get any on your shorts at all. When I spill, I usually get it all over everything." Polly wiped the chair and then cleaned off the table in front of the girl, gathering the soaked napkins as she went. "All cleaned up. No problem. I hope you have a great rest of the day."

Without looking at the parents, Polly spun and headed back for the counter, certain that she could feel the mother's anger burning a hole in her backside. She pushed the cloth to the back of the counter as they waited for Camille to finish.

"You don't get mad when we spill," Noah said quietly.

"Mistakes happen," Polly said. "Do you know that little girl?"

Elijah tugged at her shirt. "She's in my grade. Ariel Sutter. She gets in trouble a lot."

"Here you go, boys." Camille put a cup down in front of Noah and then one in front of Elijah. "I'll be right back with your coffee."

Polly took four dollar bills out of her wallet and handed two to each boy. They knew the routine and put the money into the tip jar on the counter. It had been hard to explain to them that because Polly owned part of Sweet Beans she didn't pay for her drinks there, but she always made sure to put a tip in because that went to the servers. She wanted them to learn to be generous.

When Camille returned with Polly's coffee, she said, "Tell Miss Camille thank you."

"Thank you, Miss Camille," the boys echoed.

"You're welcome."

"Thanks so much, Camille. We're off on an adventure today. I'll see you later."

"We're always here."

Polly herded her two back out to the truck and got in, shuddering at how hot it had gotten. She turned the air conditioning on and took a deep breath before inhaling her first drink of coffee. There was never enough of this in her day. She closed her eyes as she enjoyed the taste and then opened them to look in the rear-view mirror at Noah sitting behind her. Polly nearly burst out laughing when she saw him close his eyes and smile as he tasted his drink. They were so darned cute.

"Tell me more about Ariel Sutter," Polly said. "Was she in your classroom?" It had only been a couple of months, but she couldn't remember which kids were where any longer.

"No," Elijah said, sitting up straight. "She's in the other class, but she's always in the time-out room. Kids don't like her very much. She's kinda mean. She always acts like she knows everything, but she doesn't. And sometimes she hits people. I heard that she takes things off the teacher's desk, too."

"Have you ever talked to her?"

"No!" he said, his eyes big. "She's not very nice."

"Does she have any friends?"

He shook his head. "I don't think so. Nobody likes her. It's her own fault. If she was nice to them, they'd like her." He shrugged his shoulders. "I don't like her either."

"Maybe she needs someone to be nice to her first," Polly said. "That someone could be you."

Elijah frowned. "Do I have to? She's not even in my room."

"We won't worry about that today. How about a run over to Bill and Marie's house? I want to see if he retrieved anything from Henry's truck."

"Yay!" Elijah yelled, thoughts of Ariel Sutter long gone. He took a long drink through the straw in his smoothie and sat back in his seat.

"Seat belts on," Polly said as she pulled hers across her lap. She tucked her coffee into the cup holder, waited for the boys to buckle in, then backed out and drove toward the west end of town. It frustrated her to watch parents subject their children to public humiliation. She knew it shouldn't — there wasn't anything she could do about it — but that child was going to grow up to be as angry as her mother and it was *because* of her mother. The woman had no idea what damage she was causing and would take no responsibility for her daughter's poor behavior at school. It would be everyone else's fault. "Let it go," she quietly said to herself.

"I need to speak with Bill in the shop," Polly said when she pulled into the driveway. "You can come with me, but you can't take your smoothies and you can't run around in there. Stay close, okay?"

"They'll melt out here," Noah said.

"How much do you have left?"

He held it up. It was nearly empty.

"You can either drink it down right now or let it melt. You know you don't mind drinking the juice." Polly glanced at her iced coffee. If she'd been by herself, she'd take it with her, but that wasn't an option, not after she'd just set down a rule for the boys. Being a mom stunk sometimes.

The boys sucked their glasses dry and put the empties on the console beside her.

"Take your empty cups with you," Polly said, taking one last good drink of her ice-cold coffee. "There's a trash can inside. Ready?"

"Ready!" Elijah yelled. In a flash, he was out of the truck. He loved racing her to the front door of wherever they were going. That boy had more energy than she could contain. She loved him to pieces, but he wore her out every single day.

CHAPTER EIGHT

Polly got the boys back in the truck right around lunchtime. Marie had hinted at an invitation, but Polly knew they'd be there all day if she stayed. Bill had contacted the company that towed Henry's truck and it was in transit to a garage in Boone. The thing was totaled. There was no getting around that, but Polly wanted to empty it of anything Henry might need, so after promising the boys hamburgers for lunch, she headed south. It was just as well. If Henry's phone or tablet were destroyed, they needed to replace those as soon as possible. The phone she could purchase in town; she wasn't sure about the tablet.

"If Molly calls Grandma — grandma, does that mean she's related to us?" Elijah asked.

Polly turned and glanced at him, but he was running his fingers along the window as he watched the landscape go by. She wasn't quite sure how to answer that question. "I guess so."

"I thought Henry's sister was Lonnie," Noah said.

"Yes, that's true, but Marie loves Molly and her mother."

"As much as she loves Henry and Lonnie?" That came from Noah again.

"Do you think I love you more than Hayden?" Polly asked.

The two boys didn't respond, and when she looked in the rearview mirror, she could see them process on her words.

"I don't know," Elijah said.

"He's not related to me and I didn't even adopt him, but I love him the same as I love you."

Elijah smiled at her. "You like to love all of us."

"Yes I do," Polly said with a chuckle. "Love isn't one of those things that you give only to those people who are related to you. You can love more than one or two people at a time." She stopped at the stop sign, looked around to ensure no cars were coming from any direction, pressed her foot hard on the brake, and turned to the boys. "The thing is, when you choose to love more than one or two people, you can hardly help yourself, you start loving more and more people. The more people you love, the more love you have to give. Does that make sense?"

Elijah was the first to speak. "So if I only loved Noah because he's my brother then that means I wouldn't love you or Rebecca or Henry or Heath or Hayden or Grandma or Grandpa."

"But?" Polly led him to finish the thought.

"But because I love all you guys, I am making more love to love even more people?"

"That's right," Polly said with a smile. "Maybe think of it that for every person you love, you create enough to love two more people. How about that?"

He used his fingers to count. "That's eight people." His little mind worked the problem, but Noah spoke up.

"You can love sixteen more people. That makes twenty-four," Noah said. "That's a lot of people. I don't even know that many."

"Yes you do," Polly said. "Start thinking about all of the people you know. What about Miss Camille?"

Noah gave her a shy smile and looked away.

"What about Stephanie and Kayla?"

"And Andrew," Noah said.

"And Jason and Mrs. Donovan," Elijah echoed. "Then there's Eliseo and oh yeah …"

Noah interrupted. "Sam and Gabby, Ana and Matty."

Polly drove south into Boone. "You keep thinking. I'll bet you can come up with sixteen names. And then, Noah, if you love twenty-four people and take that times two, how many is that?"

His eyes grew big as she watched him process the number in the mirror.

"That's forty-eight more."

"And take that times two again," she said.

He closed his eyes and in a second, looked up. "That's ninety-six. Almost a hundred people." He turned wide eyes to Elijah. "We could love a hundred people!"

"Two hundred," Elijah said.

"Four hundred," Noah responded.

"Eight hundred."

"Sixteen hundred."

"How many people live in Bellingwood?" Elijah asked Polly.

"Around nineteen hundred."

"Can we love them all?"

"That would be wonderful."

"How are we going to meet that many?"

Polly smiled. "I'll bet you can come up with a wonderful plan."

Elijah reached over and grabbed his brother's arm. "We could give people cookies."

"Who's going to bake all those cookies?" Polly asked.

"We'll help you," Elijah said. "Won't we, Noah?"

Noah just nodded. The poor boy wasn't nearly as gregarious as his brother. He had a lifetime ahead of being dragged by Elijah into situations that made him uncomfortable.

"You know who meets a lot of people ... ushers at church. They talk to everyone. Can we do that, Polly?" Elijah asked.

"When you're a little older. You know that you don't have to meet everybody this year, right? Maybe you start with a few and let it grow little by little."

Noah shot her a look of relief.

She drove into Boone and their attention was caught by the sight of a man in his mid-seventies riding down the sidewalk in a motorized scooter, dressed in his Harley leathers, his gray hair pulled back in a ponytail under a black, gray, and red do-rag. They waved and he ignored them, obviously focused on his destination. When she lived in Boston, Polly got used to seeing people live out their uniqueness in dress and hair styles. Returning to the Midwest, she saw less and less of that, but every once in a while, she'd see someone who couldn't contain themselves to normal white-bread behavior.

Bill Sturtz had given her the address of the body shop that Henry's company used and she drove through town until she found it. Her heart sank when she saw the damage to the front end of his truck. There was no fixing this one. Henry had realized that, but Polly hoped maybe it wasn't as bad as he remembered. The front and driver's side of the truck were obliterated, the hood crumpled, the bumper barely hanging on, and the glass in both the door and the windshield shattered. Bill said that from the pictures he'd received, the engine had taken a good hit. At some point, repair wasn't worth it.

She didn't know this garage. Henry did his business here, but most of her regular maintenance work was done at Sully's in Bellingwood. Pulling up beside Henry's truck, she turned to the boys. "You two can get out of the truck, but I don't want you getting into anything, okay?"

"I'll stay here," Noah said.

Polly knew the boys could take care of themselves in a hot vehicle, but she hated the idea of it. "Open your doors, then. I'll be right back." She headed for the front door of the garage and went inside.

"How can I help you?" the man behind the counter asked. The name tag on his shirt identified him as Chris.

"I'm Polly Giller — Henry Sturtz's wife. I need to get into his truck if I can."

"I hope he's okay. That truck took a bad hit. We're going to get it in to do an estimate on repairs. It won't be pretty. Everybody thinks the girl totaled it for him." Chris came around the counter with Henry's keys in hand. "You need these, too. We'll keep the truck key. Do you want me to help you unload everything from the bed into your truck? We can empty it right now, if you want. The bed didn't take the hit, so it should all be good."

"Let me ask Henry what he wants me to do," she said and stepped away from him. Wandering over to her own truck, she dialed Rebecca's phone.

"Hello?" Henry said.

"Hey. I'm in Boone looking at your truck. They're asking if I want to empty everything into my truck. Do I?"

"No," he replied. "That's nice, but I'd rather Heath picked it up. I'm going to be riding with him until I replace the truck, so he'll need it."

"Okay, great. I'll empty things out of the cab, okay?"

"Is it as bad as I remember?"

"Yeah, it is, and it made me realize how thankful I am that you're okay. You are okay, right?"

"Doing good. Hayden made sandwiches for lunch."

"Is Evelyn still there?"

"No, she took off."

"Did Andrew show up?"

"Just before lunch. I don't know where they are right now."

Polly didn't want to worry him, but she had a bad feeling. Her next call was going to be to Hayden. "Okay. You're really doing fine?"

"I am. Heath and I are talking on the phone. There are a few things that he can't handle, but we're working through them. I'll let him know to stop by the garage and get the rest of my things."

"I love you, Henry."

"I love you, too."

She hung up and turned back to Chris. "Our son, Heath, is going to pick up things from the truck this afternoon. He'll be driving Henry around."

"I know Heath," Chris said. "He graduated with my boy. You just want to get into the cab?" He opened the passenger door. "Maybe I should get in here for you. There's a bunch of glass. Don't want you to hurt yourself. What are you looking for?"

"All his papers, his phone and there should be a tablet." He brushed glass shards from the passenger seat and sat on it, leaning over into the driver's seat.

Polly opened the back door and climbed in. A few bits of glass had blown back, but she was able to put her hands on Henry's brief case and a cardboard box filled with papers — everything from file folders to blueprints. She collected it all and carried it to the bed of her truck, then unlatched the tail gate. She groaned. There would have been no room back here for everything of Henry's. She carried athletic equipment for the boys and it took up a great deal more room than she thought it should.

"I don't see his phone," Chris said. "This is the tablet, right?"

Polly took it from him, relieved to see no damage. It sounded like this was the most important thing to Henry. "Did you look under the seat and in the console?"

"I got everything out of the console and the glove compartment." Chris got back in the truck and she watched him gingerly pull the seats away from the console, careful not to stick his fingers down where they might get sliced by glass. He finally twisted himself around to reach Henry's seat and pulled out a ball cap. His body tensed up as he stopped moving. "I can feel it, but it's wedged in there."

"Can I get to it from the back?"

"No, it's where the seat was bent. I think ... I ... can ... Got it!" he said and sat forward on the seat. "This is bad." He handed it to her.

The phone was twisted and bent, the front glass shattered.

"That's okay," Polly said. "We can replace the phone and hopefully they can pull his contacts and data off here. Thank you so much. I didn't know what to expect today."

"Glad we can help. Tell Henry I'm happy that he's doing good and to give me a call when he can. I'll see Heath later?"

"We'll let him know," Polly said. "Thank you again."

Chris went back inside while Polly took pictures of the inside and the outside of the truck. Noah and Elijah got out and joined her.

"That was a bad accident," Noah said. "Henry could have died."

"It was bad, but he didn't and we don't have to worry about it now, do we?" she replied. "Are you two ready for burgers?"

"Yes!" Elijah said, peering into the front seat. "I'm glad Henry's alive."

"So am I. Hurry back to your seats. We still have a lot to do today. Do you want to eat in the truck or inside?"

"Inside!" Elijah yelled. The boy was always excited about everything. It made her smile.

"Inside it is. Buckle in."

Polly drove to McDonald's and pulled into a parking space. The boys raced to the front door and Noah held it open for her to walk through. Once they were through the line and seated at a table, Polly finally took a breath. Then she remembered the next call she needed to make.

"You two sit here and eat," she said. "I need to make a phone call. I'll be right over there." She pointed to the entryway, knowing that she could see them. She dialed the phone while she walked.

"Hey Polly," Hayden said. "What's up?"

"Do me a favor."

"Sure. Anything."

"Is Kayla still painting with you?"

"Yeah. Doing a good job, too."

"Where are Andrew and Rebecca?"

He took in a breath. "Just a sec."

"Leaving the room?"

"Yeah."

"They're in her bedroom, aren't they?"

He laughed. "I never thought about it. There's usually so many people around here, they never get to be alone."

"I know," she said, laughing out loud. "I don't care if you tell them that I called. If you want me to be the big meanie, I'm fine with that, but I don't want them alone in that room."

"Hang on."

Polly heard him laughing softly as he walked down the hallway. He rapped on a door and then without waiting, opened it.

"Uhh, Rebecca? Andrew? What's going on in here?" Hayden asked.

"Nothing," came Rebecca's voice.

Andrew, whose voice was beginning to crack as it changed registers, said, "I'm sorry. We'll come out."

"Yeah," Hayden said. "You will. You'll never believe who's on the phone with me."

"Nooooo," Rebecca wailed.

Polly could barely contain her laughter. It wasn't like she didn't know this was coming. Those two had waited until they had the perfect moment and grabbed it. She was kind of proud of them for being so clever, but at the same time, there was no way she was allowing this to happen. "Let me talk to her."

"Yeah," Hayden said. "She wants to talk to you."

"Don't hate me," Rebecca said to Polly. "I'm sorry. I'll never do it again."

"Never do what?" Polly asked.

"You aren't going to make me say it out loud, are you?"

"No. Not right now I won't, but you and I are going to talk about this behavior when I get home. What were you thinking?"

"I don't know."

"I want you downstairs in the family room right now. Tell me you two are still fully dressed."

"Polly!" Rebecca was aghast. "What do you mean by that?"

"You know exactly what I mean, but at least that was a good response. You can let Andrew know that I'm calling his mother."

"You can't."

"Bet me, little girl. You two just screwed up in a big way. I want you out of that room right now. You'll sit in the family room and be very quiet so that Henry can either work or sleep. If he tells you that you can watch a movie, that's fine, but you get to make no choices at all this afternoon. Do you hear me?"

"Oh, come on. Nothing happened."

"The proper response is 'Yes, Polly.' Anything else will extend the punishment that I'm going to deliver when I get home. Now, do you understand?"

"Yes, Polly." Rebecca sounded properly abashed. "I'm sorry."

"Hand the phone to Hayden as you walk out of the room."

She heard the phone slam into Hayden's hand and soon he was back. "Yes?"

"Are they out of the room?"

"Getting there."

"Close the door. They're heading to the family room with Henry. He can keep an eye on them, even if he doesn't know why. I'm sorry to turn you into the bad guy, but thanks."

"No worries." He chuckled and paused. "They're on the landing now. That was kind of entertaining."

"How bad was it when you walked in?"

"They were lying on her bed, kissing. Andrew didn't have his hands in inappropriate places, so at least there's that."

"I'm going to kill her." Polly looked up to see a woman talking to Elijah and Noah. "I've got to go. More fires to put out." She ended the call and walked back into the restaurant and over to the table. "Hi there," she said to the woman.

"Hello. I'm Jennifer Carlson. My Julia is in Noah's class at school. I thought I recognized him. Julia is at the hospital with her dad and I'm picking up lunch."

"Is she okay?"

The woman shrugged. "Maybe a broken arm. They're checking it at the emergency room. We don't have a lot of time, so since both of us didn't need to be there, I'm doing this."

Jennifer Carlson was an attractive woman, dressed in a lightweight blue business suit.

"I'm sorry to hear that," Polly said.

"She's always getting into something," the woman responded. "I'd best be on my way. I was surprised to see the boys by themselves."

"They weren't," Polly replied. "I was taking a phone call and could see them. Thank you for stopping to check."

"Can't leave the little ones alone too long. Anything can happen." Jennifer spun and walked away, then out of the restaurant.

Polly gave her head a quick shake and sat down. "You two are nearly finished."

"Noah and I wondered if we could go to Dairy Queen and get an ice cream cone."

Dairy Queen was right across the street. The Carlson woman had planted a hint of guilt in Polly's heart about leaving her boys alone, especially since they'd finished eating without her.

"Yes. We can get small cones." She glanced up at the menu board. "Would you rather get them here?"

Noah looked up with his big brown eyes. "I like twist cones."

"I know you do," Polly said with a smile. She picked up her sandwich and cold, wilty fries. "Clean up your mess and we'll get ice cream cones for you."

The boys deposited their trash in the bin and Noah held the swinging bin-door while Polly tossed her fries in. She'd work through the sandwich, and lament the passing of the fries.

The humidity seemed to be on a continuous rise and Polly shuddered as she opened the truck again. She left her door open as she turned the truck on and blew cool air through it.

"Ice cream is going to melt if we don't eat it fast," Elijah said as he put his seat belt on.

"Maybe we shouldn't get any."

"I'll eat it fast." That came from Noah.

Polly turned around to back out of the space. "I was kidding. We'll crank the air conditioning and it will be like it's winter in here."

The boys each got their ice cream cones and she drove off, heading to the phone store. She pulled into a parking space and turned around. "You have time to finish your cones while I eat my sandwich."

"Mrs. Carlson never comes to the school. Julia's dad is always the one who does stuff with her. Julia says her mom is too busy. She's a lawyer or something," Noah said.

"Hmm, that's why I've never met her," Polly said, turning in her seat. "Has Julia been in your class all year?"

He shook his head. "No, she joined after I did. Mrs. Wallers says we are getting a lot of new people in town. That's why there are so many new kids in school."

Polly nodded. "You're going to have big classes next year."

Elijah crunched the last bite of his cone. "Twenty-one," he said with a mouth full of cone and ice cream.

"Swallow before you speak," Polly said. "You're going to have a pretty big class. You know what that means, don't you?"

He obeyed and swallowed, then said, "What?"

"You're going to have to be extra good and extra helpful for Mrs. Wallers since there are so many kids in the room."

"I can do that."

"And you too with Mrs. Hastings," she said to Noah.

He nodded as he took a bite from the cone.

"You're both pretty good helpers. I don't worry very much about you. I'm proud of you."

The two boys beamed at her.

"It might take time while they fix up a new phone for Henry. Do you think you can be patient?"

"I'll try," Elijah said solemnly.

"Me too." Noah popped the last bite of the cone in his mouth, crunching it in his teeth. His eyes watered from the cold ice cream mixed in with the cone and then he relaxed. "I'm ready."

"Let's go, then." Polly got out of the truck and pointed Noah to get out on his brother's side, then walked around to join them on the sidewalk. She was glad to be at this point of the day, but wasn't looking forward to the conversation she was set to have with Rebecca. This mom-thing was hard, and as she held her boys' hands while walking into the store, she knew it was only the beginning.

CHAPTER NINE

"Use your quiet voices when you get inside," Polly said, handing the box with Henry's new phone to Noah. "Would you take this in and give it to your dad?" She handed the tablet to Elijah. "Can you carefully carry that in to him?"

"Are you going somewhere?" Elijah asked. He looked at the tablet in his hands, then gave it back to her. "I'll be careful, but maybe I should get out of the truck first and come get it from you."

"Sure," Polly replied. "I need to make a phone call before I come in. Henry will be glad to see those two things. Tell him we transferred everything to the new phone, okay?"

Elijah jumped out of the truck, ran around to her and took the tablet from her again. "I'll go slow now."

Noah was already at the back door, excited to deliver Henry's new phone. She watched them go inside and then dialed Sylvie's cell. It took a few rings, but Sylvie finally answered.

"What's up? Did something else happen?"

"We're all fine," Polly said, "but you and I need to have a conversation about Andrew and Rebecca."

"Oh no. Just a minute while I walk outside. Am I about to be furious?"

"If you'd like to be. I believe it was all Rebecca's idea. Andrew is pretty careful of running afoul of the two of us, but Rebecca will lead him down the dark path every chance she gets."

Doors slammed and Sylvie spoke again. "Okay, how bad was it?"

"I took Noah and Elijah to do some errands with me, knowing that would give Henry a little peace. Hayden and Kayla were painting the bedrooms and ..."

"Our two brats were alone in Rebecca's bedroom," Sylvie said, finishing the sentence. "You know we should be thankful it took this long, right?"

"I know that. It's so weird being an adult sometimes. I'm kinda glad they actually rebelled a little, but at the same time I can't have this going on."

"Did you catch them?" Sylvie asked. "No wait. You said you were doing errands. Who caught them?"

"I sent Hayden in. The reason I didn't call earlier was because I had Noah and Elijah in the truck with me, but now I'm home and I get to go inside and deal with this." Polly paused. "I suppose I could make them wait — not say anything at all and let Andrew come home and deal with you. That would make them sweat a little."

"That's a good idea. I like it. Oh, Polly, what are we going to do with them?"

"I don't know. I'll be honest. It scares me to come down too hard because I know Rebecca — she'll get even sneakier. The last thing I want to do is tell them they can't date or can't see each other. I'd never separate them from each other — they are best friends. Damn it, Sylvie, I don't want to be a mom."

Sylvie laughed. "I'm right there with you. I'm all for separating them for the rest of the summer. I can find a million things that Andrew needs to do around the house. There are a couple of rooms that need to be repainted. The back fence needs to be painted and he can power wash and paint the front porch. There's enough work to keep him busy until school starts. What do you want to do?"

"I like this," Polly said. "There have to be consequences. He and I have talked a lot about how he lets Rebecca talk him into doing things he shouldn't be doing. He knows better."

"But hormones," Sylvie said. "I hate boys and their hormones."

"I'm not a big fan of girls either. The list of things that need to be fixed and done around this place is big enough that I could set Rebecca to tasks starting today and she wouldn't be finished for years. They should be able to see each other during the week or it will be awful for them."

"What about video calls for a half hour every evening after supper and then what about Friday night dates with friends or he could come over on Saturday afternoons. Good heavens, Polly. We didn't see our friends every single day after school and on weekends. It's better for them to spend time apart anyway."

Polly was nodding in agreement. "You're right. You do know this is going to get harder and harder as they get more independent, right?" She shuddered at the thought of either of those kids having their driver's license. She would never know where they were.

"Jason was ... well, he *is* so much easier. He and Mel only see each other every once in a while for a date. He's so wrapped up in the horses that I never worry about what he's doing. Eliseo would tell me in a minute if Jason wasn't there or was messing around. I never thought I'd have to face this with Andrew."

"It's because he's with Rebecca," Polly said with a laugh. "I love her, but that girl is an independent thinker. I keep telling myself that she's going to be successful in life because of her attitude, as long as I don't pulverize her before she gets out of the house."

"Why don't you tell Andrew to go home right now," Sylvie said. "I can call him and do it if you want me to. He and I will discuss the rest of this after work tonight."

"I'm so sorry. I should have been paying better attention. I hate that this has happened."

"Stop it. We both knew it was coming. You've kept them busy with friends and little kids and everything else for a long time. They knew that if they chose to be foolish there would be consequences. It's all part of growing up." Sylvie chuckled. "I know I'm supposed to be furious, but this is hilarious. I'm glad that I'm going through it with you. I'd hate to have some girl's mother screaming at me because she caught Andrew with her daughter. I suppose I should ask. How far along did things get before Hayden arrived?"

"He said that Andrew's hands weren't in inappropriate places. They were just lying on Rebecca's bed kissing."

Sylvie gasped. "That made it real to me. Lying on her bed? I want to be sick. *Now* I'm furious. I will kill that little boy. It's a good thing we made the plan before I knew that. He would never see her again in his entire life. I'd put a collar on him and stick that invisible fence up around the house." She took a breath. "Never mind you talking to him. Go inside, get his phone and hand it to him. He'll be out of there faster than you can even imagine."

"Got it."

"I'm sorry. I didn't mean to sound like I was giving you an order."

"You've sounded worse," Polly said, laughing. "I still remember running scared of you when Eliseo was hurt. Give me a few minutes to get there and then you can call him. I'll talk to you tomorrow. By then I'm going to need coffee and a muffin. I love you, you know."

"I love you too," Sylvie said, breathing loudly. "And I love my boy, but I'm ready to kill him."

"Later, sweetie." Polly ended the call and went inside. When she got there, Andrew and Rebecca were sitting at the dining room table across from each other. The two looked up at her, fear written on both of their faces. Polly pulled Andrew's phone out of the charging box and walked over to him. "This is going to ring. It will be your mom."

"I'm so sorry," he said. "We're both sorry."

"Sorry doesn't cut it today." She turned to Rebecca. "We'll get to you later."

"What's going to happen?" Rebecca asked.

"Consequences."

Andrew's phone rang and Polly spun and headed down the hall to the family room. Just seeing Rebecca made her seethe because she knew the girl didn't want to take responsibility for what she'd done. Every single time something happened with her, Rebecca cried and whined trying to deflect trouble away. She always came around, but getting her there was painful.

"I got it to him with no trouble," Elijah said, jumping up from where he was sitting and running to Polly. He gave her a quick hug. "That was fun today."

"I'm glad and thank you." She hugged him and then went on into the room. "How are you feeling?"

Henry gave her a small shrug with his good shoulder. "I'm okay. Thank you for picking up the new phone. I feel normal again."

"Your truck is toast. Chris doesn't think it's going to live through this."

"He's a good guy. If he says it's done, then it's done."

"I have more of your things from the cab out in the truck. I'll get them to you later, if that's okay."

"That's fine. I don't need any of that right now." Henry held up the tablet. "This. This is my lifeline. Thank you for finding it."

Polly put her hand on Noah's shoulder. "Why don't you two boys go upstairs and ask Hayden if the dogs have been outside? Maybe you can play out there while they run around for a while."

Noah nodded and moved around her for the doorway. Elijah gave her another hug as he passed her. "I had so much fun."

"Me too," Polly said. "Thanks for taking care of the dogs." She waited until she heard them go up the stairs and sat down so she could look at Henry. "We have a problem."

"I wondered. Andrew and Rebecca showed up looking like beaten puppies. They didn't say anything and I was afraid to ask. Should I ask?"

"It hit me that they were alone since I had the boys, and Kayla was painting with Hayden, so I called Hayden and he walked in on them."

In that split second, Henry's face turned red and his eyes lit up. "In on them?"

"Hayden said that all they were doing was kissing, but her door was closed and they were on the bed. He said Andrew's hands weren't in inappropriate places. Those were his words."

"Do they understand that I will kill him?" Henry asked.

"I don't know that. I talked to Sylvie. He won't be here any longer this summer." Polly lowered her voice, in case anyone was listening from the hallway. "We'll work out a plan for them to talk and maybe go on dates with friends or us and then come over on Saturday afternoons for a while. They're best friends, Henry. I can't separate them completely and I worry that if we make this too awful, Rebecca will get even more rebellious and try harder to get away with things, and I won't know that she's being sneaky."

"I will kill him."

Polly chuckled. "That's not helpful."

"They will never see each other again, then."

"Still not helpful. The thing is, I want to confront Rebecca with you in the room. I don't want to do it without you."

Henry put his hand out and she took it. "You know I'll turn into a wimp with her, right?"

"Yes I do. That's why I'll deal with the punishment, but she needs to know how angry you are." Polly thought for a moment. "No, better yet, she needs to know how disappointed *we* are. That's a better way to handle it."

"Yeah. It always did me in," he replied. "Mom used that one quite effectively on me. It worked every time."

"I'd like to get this out of the way. Do you want to do it in here? We can shut the door."

"I have a few minutes. Heath is going to call at three thirty."

Polly nodded. "I suspect Andrew is scurrying his way home right now. Sylvie called and ordered him out of our house. Let me find Rebecca and we can get through this."

"I don't want to. You know that, right?"

She leaned over and whispered. "I hate being a parent some days."

"I know!" he said. "Why can't they figure it out on their own and make it easy on us?"

She kissed his cheek and left the room and went toward the kitchen. When she walked past the dining room, she saw Noah and Elijah running through the yard with Obiwan and Han. Exhausting them was a great idea this afternoon.

Rebecca was sitting by herself at the kitchen table, her eyes red and her cheeks tear-stained. "Did you tell Henry?"

"You know that I don't hold things back from him."

"You do if you did something wrong and don't want him to know."

Polly stepped back. "That's how you want to start this?"

"We weren't doing anything. I don't know why there's so much fuss."

Every one of Polly's muscles went rigid. She closed her eyes, took a long breath and clenched her hands together. Without looking at Rebecca when she opened her eyes, she spun. "You'd be very smart to keep your mouth shut and follow me right now. Do. You. Understand. Me?" Each word was punctuated by a long pause as Polly started back down the hallway. She went in to the family room and took a seat across from Henry on a stool in front of the television screen. Rebecca hadn't followed her.

"Where is she?" Henry asked.

"Give it a minute. She's doing her thing."

"This isn't going to be easy, is it?"

"Nope." Polly set her jaw.

They waited an uncomfortably long few minutes. At the point Polly put her hands on her knees to stand up, Rebecca came into the room.

"I'm sorry," she said.

Henry pointed to the sofa. "Sit."

Rebecca sat. She pulled her hair forward to cover the side of her face and then drew her legs up, bending her knees and wrapping her arms around them. She rested her face in the crook made by her knees, essentially hiding from Polly and Henry.

Polly nodded at him. She was so angry, she could barely speak.

"Do you have any idea why we might be upset with you, Rebecca?" Henry asked.

The girl's shoulders rose and lowered in a shrug.

Henry looked at Polly and raised his eyebrows.

She took a deep breath. "Sit up straight, Rebecca. Right now. You will look at us and you will speak. No more shrugs, no more ridiculous behavior while you play for pity. You are the one who screwed up and you will face it. Sit up."

Rebecca unwound her arms and legs and sat up straight. She had a hard time looking at Polly, but at least she was trying.

"Now answer Henry's question."

"Yes," Rebecca said softly.

Henry looked at Polly helplessly, so she went on. "I don't want to lecture you about why we're disappointed in you, Rebecca. You're a smart girl. You know what our expectations are and you deliberately chose to disobey."

"We didn't ..." Rebecca started and then stopped.

"Tell me one more time that you weren't doing anything," Polly said, fire flashing from her eyes. "One more time."

"We weren't."

Henry sat forward, his face grim and determined. "I don't know what your definition of anything is, but lying on your bed in the middle of an afternoon with a boy is something. It's a big damned deal and it breaks my heart that you don't understand that. You should never be alone in your room with any boy. Not ever. You knew exactly what you were doing. Don't try to make this into nothing. You defied us and I was right here in the house. Do you understand what integrity is? Integrity is doing the right thing even when it's easier to do the wrong thing. You chose to do the wrong thing today. You didn't have to make that choice, but you did."

Rebecca looked up at him in shock, then tears burst from her eyes. "I'm sorry," she sobbed.

"Here are the consequences of what you did today, Rebecca," Polly said. "You and Andrew don't get to spend time together any longer this summer unless there are people around. He won't be coming over here during the week. If things work out, he can come over on Saturday afternoons and we will discuss what happens after school starts. *You* did this. The two of you made choices that are now going to be painful for you."

"He's my best friend," she said through the tears.

"Yes he is and I'm sorry that you messed this up. I've spoken with Sylvie, and while Andrew is spending his summer at home, he'll be working on the house. Guess what that means?"

"I don't know," Rebecca said. "I'm cleaning bathrooms?"

"Oh, you're cleaning so much more than bathrooms. You'll be cleaning the living room after Heath and Hayden move out. You will keep your room clean. One of us will check it every night and you won't be doing much if it's not clean and neat. There are four bathrooms that you have access to. Each one will be cleaned this week by you. You will make sure that the laundry is washed, dried and sorted into each person's baskets. I don't expect you to fold anything but yours, but that will be folded and put back where it belongs. That's a start. There will be more."

"More?" Rebecca squeaked.

Henry looked at her. "You have a problem with any of this? All she's asking you to do is keep your room clean, do laundry and clean bathrooms this week. Do you not understand that Polly does that all the time? She cooks meals, does laundry, washes bathrooms and takes care of your needs during the day. You should be doing some of this as a matter of course, anyway. In fact, from here on out, you are in charge of doing your laundry along with Noah and Elijah's. You will also wash towels and bedsheets as they arrive in the laundry room. You will fold those and put them away. There's no question. You should have been helping with these things all along. It's time you grow up and act like a responsible young lady. That starts today."

Polly blinked and did her best to hide a grin. The kids were pretty good about helping around the house and Henry did all he could in the little time he spent at home. Having Hayden, Stephanie and Kayla around kept things running pretty smoothly, so she didn't have much to complain about, but if Henry wanted to get Rebecca doing more, she was all in.

Rebecca nodded. "Okay. I'm sorry. Can I go now?"

"You can. If I were you, I'd get started," Henry said. "Don't save it all until the end of the week. It's Tuesday. Pick a bathroom and do it this afternoon. Do another one tomorrow and another the day after that. Gather up laundry when you can and keep pecking away at it. And for God's sake, keep that room of yours clean. I'm tired of walking into that pigsty. If it weren't for Kayla, you couldn't even walk in there. I don't want her to take any more responsibility for it. This is on you and I expect it to be done well."

Rebecca stood up and headed for the door. Polly caught up to her. "I know this is tough, but we do love you."

"Even right now?"

"Even right now. We will always love you. We're not here only the good days, we're here for the rough days, too." Polly gave her a quick hug and let her go, then went back in and sat down and looked at her husband. "You were a little heated up there."

"Did I go too far?" he asked. "She started making me mad and I knew I couldn't react to her, but I want her to understand that she has a responsibility to this family."

"You were fine. She always figures it out." Polly leaned back on the sofa and closed her eyes. "I'm exhausted. I don't want to do another …" She bolted upright. "Damn it."

"What?" he asked.

"I invited strangers to dinner tonight and forgot all about it."

"You what?" He looked at her in shock.

"I met these people in the cemetery yesterday. They're really cool. She used to live here. Let's see. Who's her sister? You know them. Sandy Morrison. They've been living in California and are thinking about moving back to Bellingwood."

"And you invited them to dinner?"

"Yeah. It was before I found a body and then you were in a wreck and Rebecca was necking with Andrew." Polly dropped her head into her hands. "It is going to be one of those weeks. I didn't even get their phone number. Why would I need it? I live a perfectly sane life. What am I going to do?"

"You're going to wrangle a dinner," Henry said.

"Your parents were here last night and you don't feel good and Rebecca's in a mood and I haven't told anyone that this is happening, so Stephanie isn't prepared for people in the house. I could scream."

"Polly." Henry leaned forward as if he were going to stand up, then sat back.

"What?"

"Calm down. Are they staying at the hotel?"

"Yes."

"Call Grey. See if they're in their room. Call Sandy. Maybe she can reach them. Either that or suck it up and make dinner."

She looked at him and grinned. "You're on a roll."

"That could well be true. This will be okay. If you want to have them come over tonight, that's fine. They won't stay very late. Call Stephanie and tell her that we're having guests so she can be prepared. Tell Hayden and Kayla so they can be cleaned up from painting. Everyone will help you make dinner."

"Beryl brought a bunch of hamburgers. We could put them on the grill."

Henry nodded.

"Surely Hayden and Heath can grill hamburgers without you."

"You're right. They can."

"I have salads and beans from the girls, too. There's plenty to make a nice meal. Are you sure you're okay with this?"

He put his hand up to his hair. "Can you help me do something with this?"

"Of course. Let me start with the phone calls to everyone so that I know people are on board. Henry Sturtz, you are the best man in the world. How did I get so lucky?"

"Just remember that the next time I screw up. Now, tell me what made you like these people so much you invited them to dinner?"

Polly thought back to her encounter on the path in the cemetery. She could hardly believe that was only yesterday morning. So much had happened. "I don't know. They seem so interesting — like people I want to know better. I couldn't believe it myself when I heard the invitation come out of my mouth, but it felt right."

"Then here we go," he said. "Adding more friends to the family."

"I love you."

"I know."

CHAPTER TEN

"Take the dogs to my room," Polly said to Rebecca. "We'll let them out later if things are quiet." As Rebecca headed for the back steps, Polly added, "And make sure the cats have plenty to keep them occupied upstairs. We don't need them on the table tonight."

Rebecca had stayed close to Polly all afternoon, offering to help any way she could. Once Kayla and Hayden finished the first coat in both rooms, they showered and landed in the kitchen ready to assist. Polly put Hayden on grilling duty, while Kayla helped Rebecca clean the downstairs bathroom and straighten the back porch. Poor Rebecca kept glancing at her phone across the room.

Polly finally took it out of the charging station and stuck it in a drawer. "You can check with Andrew after supper. He'll live without you — I promise." Rebecca had merely shrugged and walked back out to finish folding the laundry coming out of the dryer.

Stephanie had offered to bring dessert when Polly called her, so at least that wasn't a concern. Noah and Elijah had been learning how to set the table and Polly put them to the task.

Once things were running smoothly, Polly and Henry went back upstairs. He desperately wanted his hair washed and she'd been processing all afternoon how to make that happen. She remembered once, when she was very young, that she'd gotten something bad in her hair. She couldn't remember what it was, but what she did remember was that her mother had brought out the ironing board and set it up to be even with the kitchen counter. Her mother had lifted her up and placed her on it so Polly's head was in the sink. Using the sprayer, she had gently held Polly's head while warm water washed away the mess. The memory brought tears to Polly's eyes. Those gentle moments were some of the few memories Polly had of her childhood.

She was certain the ironing board wouldn't hold Henry. Even if it could, he'd have none of that.

She helped him remove his t-shirt, Polly cringing as he flinched. "Maybe your crazy Hawaiian shirt tonight," she said. "We can button it up the front."

He chuckled as he held his side. "Don't be crazy. I have other button shirts."

"Those are all dress shirts. It's casual tonight."

"I'll find my own clothes," he said. "Now, how are we going to do this?"

Polly grinned. "I just figured it out. I need a pitcher. I'll be right back." She left him in the middle of their bedroom and ran to the pantry in the kitchen downstairs.

"What's up?" Rebecca asked as Polly ran through.

"Need a pitcher to wash Henry's hair. I'll be back in a while." She was back upstairs in a flash. When she arrived in their bathroom, she pulled up short. "What are you doing?"

Henry glanced at her while holding a wet washcloth over the sink. "I needed a bath. At least I can do this much on my own. I'm feeling better already, but I can't wait to take a real shower." He rubbed the cloth across his chin. "Are you prepared for me to have a beard?"

"You'd be sexy in a beard," Polly said. She sidled up to him. "Very sexy."

"That's mean, woman. Just mean."

"Want me to wash your back?" She used her best sultry voice.

"Still mean, but yes. That would be awesome. When I'm back to normal, you are going to be required to wash my back in the shower. Payment for this mean behavior, you know."

Polly washed his back. "Got it. How are you feeling right now?"

"Okay. I'm not looking forward to bending over so you can wash my hair. My side hurts."

"I'll go fast." The sink wasn't deep enough to fill the pitchers, so Polly filled them from the tub. Within five minutes, she had his hair washed and rinsed. When she grabbed for a towel, Henry turned, flipped down the lid on the toilet and sat.

"I hurt. This is exhausting."

"You did great." Polly kissed his cheek. "Now let me dry this for you and we'll be done."

"I feel terrible for not helping get ready for tonight."

Polly stepped back and scowled down at him. "I feel terrible for having guests here when you're recuperating from an accident and besides, you helped a lot when we were talking to Rebecca. I owe you bigtime for that."

He smiled at her and pointed at his comb on the sink. "Yeah. I guess you do. How's she doing?"

"The perfect angel. We have about a week of good behavior out of this one."

"Were we ever this bad?" Henry lifted his right arm to comb his hair and dropped it. "Man, everything hurts."

"Let me help," Polly said. She combed his hair into a mohawk on the top of his head and stepped back. "How's that?"

He looked in the mirror and then stood up. "It will go perfectly with my Hawaiian shirt, don't you think?" He headed for the bedroom and sat down on the edge of the bed. "I need more energy so I don't have to move from chair to chair."

"You don't have to come downstairs tonight," Polly said quietly. "You can stay up here and rest. No one will bother you and everyone will understand."

His eyes lit up and then he shook his head. "No. I won't do that to you."

"Yeah, Henry. You will." Polly combed his hair into place. "You can meet these people later when you feel better. When Heath comes home, I'll send him up so you two can de-brief his day. I'll have someone bring up your tablet and phone and we'll make sure you get dinner. Please, you don't have to do this."

"I don't have to dress up?"

She shook her head. "No. You can wear comfortable shorts and pull your robe on."

"You're too good to me. I feel all clean and normal, and now I get the night off. Life is heaven."

By the time she left the bedroom, Henry was safely ensconced in his favorite chair. The television was turned to a baseball game, Han was lying on the floor beside him, and Obiwan was on the bed.

Heath was sitting at the kitchen table talking to Hayden, Noah, and Elijah when she got back downstairs.

"How was your day?" Polly asked.

"It was awesome," Heath replied with a big grin.

"You might have a couple more days like this."

He nodded. "That's cool. Henry talked me through some things. He has everything up in his head. It's amazing. I hope I know everything he does someday."

"You will." Polly sat down beside him. "His phone and tablet are in the family room and he's going to spend the evening upstairs. Would you take those up to him? If you guys need to go over the day, take your time. We'll let you know when guests are here."

Heath jumped up. "Thanks." He headed down the hallway and was gone.

Rebecca and Kayla came in from the back porch each carrying two baskets of folded laundry. "We finished everything that was in there," Rebecca said. "I'll take these upstairs and put things away where they belong. Should I gather everybody's dirty laundry?"

"Maybe tomorrow," Polly replied. "The machines don't need to run tonight. By the way, the bathroom looks fantastic. Thank you."

Rebecca gave her a small smile and the two girls went up the back steps. Yeah. This next week was going to be fabulous. Cleaning and organizing would happen all over the place.

The back door flew open and Stephanie gave a little yelp. "I'm stuck," she cried out.

Polly and Hayden jumped up and rushed to the back porch to find Stephanie, with her arms filled, trying to unhook her belt from the handle on the screen door.

"I knew I cut it too close."

"Here, let me," Hayden said, taking a box from Sweet Beans from her hands.

Polly took her purse and two paper grocery bags and Stephanie backed up to free herself.

"Sorry about that. You won't believe what happened to me this afternoon," Stephanie said.

"What?"

"We're moving this weekend. We have a place again."

"The apartments are finished?" Polly was confused. The last time she looked, things were still a jumbled mess there. It hadn't been that long since she'd gone past.

Stephanie took one of the paper bags and set it on the counter, then took her purse as Polly put the other bag beside it. "No. We're moving into the upstairs of a house. You know the Worths up on Tyler and Walnut Streets?"

Polly shook her head.

"It's the pretty light green house with the dark green shutters. They have those white wrought iron chairs in the front yard around a pond?"

"Sure," Polly said. "That's a big house."

"I know and the upstairs is an apartment. They built it for their son to live in and it's been empty for a couple of years. She was in last week to talk to Jeff and me about her husband's Christmas party and I don't even know how it came up. Jeff told her that I was looking for a place to rent because I'd lived in those apartments that burned. I'll pay less than I did before. We have our own entrance and there's space in the garage that I can use, too. She said we could move in this weekend if we want. And I want to! I went up to see it this afternoon and it's wonderful. The living room furniture is nice so I don't have to buy that right now and she has pretty curtains up, so I don't have to worry about any of those. I signed a contract and we're moving!" Stephanie looked around. "Where's Kayla? I can't wait to tell her." She pointed at one of the bags. "I brought ice cream from the General Store."

"I'll make sure it goes in the freezer," Polly said. "Kayla and Rebecca are upstairs."

Before she could say anything else, Stephanie crossed into the foyer.

"That's going to empty out the main floor," Hayden said.

Polly took the ice cream out of the bag and bit her lip. "And make life rough for Rebecca. She lost Andrew and now she's losing Kayla."

He opened the box from Sweet Beans. "She still has us, and anyway, band starts in a week. She'll see them every day."

"Two weeks," Polly said, "but yeah. I know this is only short-term. It's still going to be hard on her."

"We'll make it better," Elijah said, somehow showing up beside Polly when she shut the freezer door. "We'll keep Rebecca busy."

Polly rubbed the top of his head and smiled. "I'm sure you will."

~~~

"Can we help?" Elijah and Noah had been helping Rebecca and Kayla as they cleared the dinner table after supper was finished. Now, they were standing beside Polly, who had taken containers of ice cream from the freezer.

Polly pushed the platter of cupcakes toward Rebecca. "Would you take those? And Kayla, would you get down bowls?" She opened the silverware drawer and counted out spoons, then handed them to Elijah, making sure the handles were in his hand. "Don't touch the spoon part and take these over to the table. Thank you."

Noah looked at her expectantly.

"I have vanilla, chocolate, and …" she looked at the label. "Peach ice cream. Noah's going to come ask what you'd like." She turned to him. "Can you get a count of what everyone wants? This won't be easy. If they want one of each, you'll have to remember."

"I can do it," he said, a grin breaking across his face.

Polly kept an ear to the table and started filling bowls with vanilla, according to the orders. He returned after a few minutes and rattled off three orders for her. She smiled at the realization that he'd taken their guests' orders first. She let him take those three orders back to the table and he returned with three more, serving Rebecca, then Heath and Hayden. Kayla took her bowl and Elijah ran over to get his, but Polly allowed Noah to return with his own and hers as she stowed the nearly empty containers back in the freezer.

"What about Henry?" Noah asked, coming back over.

"We'll take ice cream up to him later. You go on and get settled at the table."

"This is very good," Judy Greene said. "It's from the General Store downtown?"

Stephanie nodded. "They have the best ice cream and there's a new flavor every day. They don't have peach very often and it's my favorite. I couldn't believe it when I walked in. It's like today was the perfect day."

"It must be fun working at the Sycamore House," Judy said. "Do you meet a lot of interesting people?"

"Most of the time. Many of them are brides and their mothers. That can get stressful, but Jeff is pretty good with them."

"Bellingwood has changed so much since the last time I was here," Judy responded. "It's nice to see that the town is growing and looking forward rather than backward. Not what I expected at all."

"Do you believe you'll move here?" Polly asked.

Reuben and Judy looked at each other with knowing smiles. "We've talked a lot about that the last few days as we've driven around the area. Judy would like to move back to Iowa and I believe the town is nearly ready for us."

Hayden chuckled. "What does that mean?"

"We're not your regular run-of-the-mill folk," he said. "When we were here for Judy's mother's funeral, I got a lot of strange looks."

"Because your hair is long?" Elijah asked.

Rebecca looked at Polly, horrified. Polly shrugged. There was something perfectly wonderful about his innocence. She wasn't going to stifle it.

"That's exactly right," Reuben replied. "We aren't comfortable in stiff and formal clothing either. We're pretty laid-back. I wore my best khakis and sandals to that funeral and those brought more than a few judgmental glances."

"Everyone should get to be who they want to be," Rebecca announced. "If you try to be what everyone else thinks you should be, you run out of time to go after your dreams."

"That's pretty smart," Judy said. "What are your dreams?"

"I'm young," Rebecca said, "so I'm still trying to figure them out, but if I waste too much time trying to decide what other people want me to do, I won't have time to choose for myself. What do you want to do?"

Judy sat back, grinning at the question. "I'm still trying to figure it out, too." Then she nodded. "To answer your question, I'd like to have a little greenhouse where I can do what I've always loved doing. Whether winter or summer, I want to be able to sink my hands down deep into dirt and grow beautiful flowers and plants. You have a beautiful garden over there at your Sycamore House."

"I had nothing to do with it," Polly said. "There are people in town who are much better at gardening than I am."

"Tell them what your dream is, Reuben," Judy said.

He frowned. "My dream?"

"He's a metal worker. A welder and a blacksmith," Judy said. "He designs beautiful metal sculptures. If he could spend his days in a shop, he'd be happy."

"That's not a dream. I'm already doing that," Reuben said. "Wherever we move, there will need to be enough space for us to have a smithy."

"When we were in Hannibal, Stephanie took me to see a glass blower," Kayla said shyly. "They used fire, too. I'd like to learn how to do that someday."

Reuben turned to her. "Then you should. I'm certain there are artists in the area who would be interested in teaching you their craft." He smiled. "I'd like to be in a location where I can teach others to forge metal, too. There is no end to what a person can create."

"Would you teach me?" Elijah asked.

"Son, if you want to learn how to be a blacksmith, I'll be glad to teach you. That is, if your mother will allow it."

"Maybe when he gets a few more inches on him," Polly said. "I believe it would be great fun, though."

"What about you, Hayden?" Rebecca asked, turning to the young man sitting beside her.

He chuckled. "You all are talking about these wonderfully creative things and my favorite place to be is in a laboratory. I can't believe how much I've missed it this summer."

Polly nodded and smiled. "You'll be the one to figure out how to cure MS or Parkinson's or another dread disease."

"That would be nice," he said. "Not that I was the one to do it, but that they'd be cured."

Rebecca looked across the table. "What's your dream, Heath?"

He'd been quiet through most of the evening, watching and listening. That was usually his go-to unless someone spoke directly to him. He looked tired tonight, too. Henry mentioned that he'd had Heath all over the area. It made Polly wonder how much she understood about what Henry did all day long. He was always engaged with the family in the evenings and he had to be tired.

"I just want to work," Heath said. "It sounds weird."

"No more weird than me wanting to be in a research lab," Hayden said.

"You want to work with wood, too," Polly said quietly. "Henry and I need to move faster on clearing a space for you to do that."

"What kind of woodworking?" Reuben asked. "I've been thinking about adding wood to some of my pieces, but I'm not interested in learning how to turn things on a lathe."

"There's a guy at Henry's shop who is good," Heath said.

Reuben smiled. "I don't know him. I know you. If we move here, I'd like to talk to you about how we can work together."

Heath nodded.

"How long will you be in Bellingwood before you head home?" Polly asked.

"A couple of weeks," Judy said. She peered at Noah, who was sitting beside Polly. "We haven't heard much from you. What do you dream about doing?"

His brown eyes turned up to Polly. "I don't know."

"You've never thought about what you want to be when you grow up?"

"Maybe fly a plane." He pulled Polly's arm and she bent to hear him as he whispered, "Maybe be a policeman."

"You'd be a great policeman." She looked at Judy. "He knows a lot of law enforcement officers. His teacher's husband is the police chief here in town."

"Ken Wallers?" Judy asked. When Polly nodded, she continued, "He's younger than me, but I knew his family. They were good people. We need good policemen, Noah. That's a pretty wonderful dream."

He looked at the floor, but Polly could tell he was smiling.

Reuben pushed his chair back. "We should head back to the hotel. I'm sorry we didn't meet your husband this evening, but I hope he heals soon."

"That sounded like a horrible crash," Judy said, pushing back as well. "If I'd put two and two together, we wouldn't have come."

"I'm glad to have had a chance to get to know you," Polly said. "How long do you think it will be before you return to Bellingwood if you do?"

Judy stood. "We need to put our house on the market and pack things up. We'd like to be back by late November. There will be short trips back and forth as we look for a place to live. I understand there aren't many homes on the market here in town, so we might move into an apartment, if necessary."

Polly walked with them to the back door. "I know my invitation to dinner was kinda out there, but it has been good to get to know the two of you. I look forward to you moving here. The town keeps changing and I believe you will have fun. Did you know Beryl Watson when you lived here, Judy?"

Judy put her hand on the door handle. "Beryl Carter?"

"Yeah. That's her maiden name."

Judy smiled. "She was two or three years younger than me. Kind of a wild girl. Had her own mind about things. If she'd been a little older, we would have been friends. One of her brothers was in my class. A real stick-in-the-mud, that one. I heard she's an artist?"

"Yeah. A really good artist. She's having a show at Sycamore House. If you're still in town, you should come to it."

"We're in no hurry to leave. We can stay, can't we, Reuben?"

"I'd like to meet her. Thank you for your hospitality. You have a wonderful family," Reuben replied.

"Yes you do." Judy reached out and pulled Polly into a quick hug. "You have your own mind about things, too. I can tell you're living out your dream in this crazy town. Don't let anyone ever stop you from doing what you do."

Polly smiled as Judy released her. "It's a great life. I never imagined it would happen, but now I can't imagine anything else. Thank you for coming."

CHAPTER ELEVEN

Heaving a sigh, Polly turned over. Morning was here and she needed to get out of bed. Last night had been another bad night for Henry. He couldn't get comfortable and since she worried about him, every time he moved or changed position, she came awake. Then she waited for him to drop back to sleep, holding absolutely still so he wouldn't think he was bothering her. The dogs had left about three. Even as much as the little boys tossed and turned, Han and Obiwan were safer in there.

She looked around the room for Henry and when she didn't see him anywhere, listened for sounds of him in the bathroom. Nothing.

"Henry?" she asked quietly. When there was no response, Polly jumped out of bed, slid into her slippers, threw her robe on and headed for the bathroom. He wasn't in there, so she walked out into the hallway. Everyone else was still asleep — not even the dogs were moving. She headed to the back stairs and went down to the kitchen, hoping to find Henry. She breathed easier when she saw the coffee brewing. He was up and around. She did a quick check of the family room and didn't find him there either, then looked out the window to the back yard and smiled. Henry was sitting at the table in the gazebo while the dogs chased each other through the yard. Polly ran back to the kitchen, poured two cups of coffee and headed outside.

"Henry," she said. "I thought I'd lost you."

He looked up from his phone. "I wanted to let you sleep. I know you were up all night with me."

Polly climbed up the steps into the gazebo and put a cup down in front of him. "I thought I was hiding it so well."

"Yeah. No. I'm sorry. I can sleep in the chair in the family room tonight."

"Yeah. No," she echoed. "If you're sleeping there, I'm sleeping on the couch. Remember how that works?"

"I feel so useless. There is so much work to be done and I pant just getting up to go to the bathroom. I'm exhausted all the time and everything hurts."

She reached out to touch his right hand. "It hasn't even been forty-eight hours. You have to give yourself a break."

"I'm letting you all down, too. Hayden and Heath are supposed to move upstairs this weekend. Now Stephanie is moving into her new place and I can't be there to help. Damn it." He slapped his hand down on the table. "I'm useless."

Polly laughed. "You are a terrible patient. What would you say to me if I'd been in an accident?"

"Let us take care of things for you." The corner of his mouth turned up. "I wouldn't put up with any of your crap."

"That's a good boy." Polly stroked his forearm. "Are you coming inside for breakfast?"

"After a while. Nobody's in a hurry this morning, are they?"

Polly took a breath and settled back into her seat. "No, we can take it slow today. There's nothing going on. I want to run over to Sycamore House. Beryl and Lydia will be upstairs working and I'd like to check in with them. We haven't talked since they dropped all that food off on Monday. Kristen sent me a text last night that there were bills I needed to approve, and I'd like to see how that new girl is working out with Rachel."

"Sometimes I wish we'd been able to keep living on site for you," Henry said. "You miss a lot because you live here."

She nodded. "Yeah. I do, but it's okay. Life can't always stay the same. We couldn't live there and have this big family. I'd rather do it this way."

He grinned at her. "You know I keep wondering when you'll bring the next person in to live with us."

"What do you mean by that?"

"I mean that Hayden is within a year or two of leaving for good. He is going to want to live on his own soon. Heath will be gone most of the time when school starts and with Rebecca in Boone for school activities, it's going to be pretty lonely around the house."

"You're going to be the lonely one. I have a bad feeling that until Rebecca gets her driver's license, I'll be on the road a lot." Polly gave a shudder. "Rebecca with her license. I am not ready for that."

"She does pretty well when she's driving with you, right?"

"Uh huh, but that's not what I'm talking about. She'll be a great little driver. It's the independence thing that worries me. Just about the time I think she's taking responsibility for her life, everything falls apart and I want to lock her up until she turns twenty-five. I was so mad at her yesterday."

"So was I," he said. "I felt kind of bad for unloading on her, but I will not have that girl acting like an entitled brat with you. She's old enough to take responsibility for more than herself."

"You're right." Polly smiled at him. "I get so caught up in the busy-ness of managing everyone and forget that I'm supposed to be helping them become independent. Where is that danged training manual for being a parent?"

Henry stood and tried not to flinch as he moved. "I'm getting better. I really am. The dogs are lying down at the edge of the lawn. I think they're trying to tell us how hungry they are." He reached out and Polly took his hand as they walked back across the yard. "You're a pretty wonderful parent. I'm proud of what you've taken on."

"Couldn't do it without you." Polly kicked a stick, then bent over to pick it up. "You'll like Reuben Greene. I hope they do move back."

"You haven't said too much about last night."

She went up the steps and held the door. Obiwan and Han dashed inside and then Henry held on to the railing as he made his way up. "It was a nice evening. They didn't say much. The kids were busy talking and they worried that because you'd been hurt, I would rather have been hovering over you."

"They don't know you yet." Henry put his mug and phone on the counter and headed for the pantry.

"I can feed the dogs," Polly said. "Go to the family room or the dining room table and sit. I'll take care of it."

"Okay, thanks."

She waited until he was in the hallway before opening the pantry door. "He's so macho sometimes," she whispered to Obiwan as she filled their bowls. "But I don't know what I'd do without him."

Stephanie walked into the kitchen as Polly was pouring another cup of coffee. "Good morning."

"Hi there. Want me to pour you a cup?"

"No. I'm going up to Sweet Beans."

"Is Skylar working?" Polly taunted.

Stephanie giggled. "Yeah. I want to ask him to help move us this weekend. I talked to Hayden and Heath last night. They said they'd help if you don't have something for them to do. Can we use Heath's truck?"

"Of course you can. Rebecca and I will help, too."

"I can't wait to show Sky the new place." Stephanie held up a key. "Mrs. Worth said I can go over any time. Maybe I'll take Kayla over at lunch. Polly, you won't believe how cute it is. There are two bedrooms, a big living room and a cute kitchen. There's only one bathroom, but Kayla and I can share that. There's room for my table in the kitchen and she says I can hang anything on the walls as long as I'm careful. She also said we could paint the bedrooms. It's going to be so awesome."

Polly hugged her. "I'm excited for you. I suspect you're ready to have some peace and quiet again."

"This has been better than I thought it would be," Stephanie said. "I was so upset when I found out we were homeless and had to rely on you again, but it's been good being here. I worried about Rebecca and Kayla being with each other too much and fighting, but they did pretty good." She looked around the kitchen. "I'm going to miss this room, though. It's like everything happens in here."

"I know it sounds phony," Polly said, "but I want you and Kayla to feel like you can stop by any time. We can always set extra places at the table."

"Thanks." Stephanie waggled her keys again. "I can't wait to move."

"Good. Now go tell Skylar all about it. If I can find time, I'll be up to pester him."

~~~

Polly was hemming another panel for the curtains to be hung in Heath's room when Rebecca, Noah, and Elijah all came into the dining room.

"Can we go for a bike ride?" Elijah asked.

"Sure," Polly said. "Where are you going?"

"Just around."

She looked at Rebecca. "Where are you going?"

"Really. Just around. I thought maybe we could go down to the elementary school and ride in the parking lot. Maybe even swing on the swings. It's boring around here."

"I could find things for you to do," Polly said.

"I already cleaned the bathroom upstairs."

"It's clean," Elijah said effusively. "She did a good job. It sparkles."

Rebecca smiled down at him. "And I washed their clothes and my clothes. Those are in the dryer. I'll fold them and put them away when we get back."

"What about Kayla?"

"She's painting with Hayden again. They're nearly done with the second coat and he said they'll have the first coat in the other room done this afternoon. She's boring, too."

"Sure, then. Go ride your bicycles. I'd rather you didn't go downtown."

"No problem. I'll grab my phone so you know where we are."

Polly smiled. There it was. "No. You'd be upset if you dropped it while you were riding. Leave it in the kitchen."

"What if something happens and we need to reach you?"

"You'll be barely three blocks away from home. A good scream and I'll know. Leave the phone here."

"But it's *my* phone. Why can't I take it when I leave?" Rebecca whined.

"Boys, go get your bicycles out of the garage. Don't leave the yard without Rebecca, though. Okay?"

Noah gave Rebecca a quick glance, trying to decide whether he should help her out, but with another look at Polly, he grabbed his younger brother's arm and the two of them ran for the back door.

Polly swallowed. "Do we really have to have this conversation now? I can't begin to tell you how disappointed I am in your behavior these last two days. If I need to have a sit-down with you, Andrew, and Sylvie, I will do it. What I won't do is tolerate you sneaking around and lying to me."

"I'm not sneaking or lying," Rebecca said defiantly.

"So you didn't want your phone to call Andrew while you were out?"

"No." Rebecca glared at Polly, daring her to challenge her assertion.

"Well then, I'm sorry."

"So I can take the phone?"

"No. I didn't say that. I apologize for believing that you were trying to sneak something past me. Go on and take the boys up to the elementary school. I'll take out cookies and we can make lemonade when you get back."

Rebecca started out and got well into the kitchen before she turned around and ran back to stand beside Polly. "I'm sorry. I *was* going to call Andrew. You were right. Why do I keep doing things that make you mad?" Tears ran down her face.

Polly turned in her seat and reached for Rebecca's hand. When Rebecca took it, Polly pulled her in so she could hold her tight. "Because you are bright and independent. Those are excellent qualities in any person, but you need to figure out how to work within my rules. You have so much life ahead of you. These short moments that you are facing today will soon be forgotten, but learning how to be a strong-willed young woman who is trustworthy will last you for a lifetime."

"I *am* sorry."

"I know." Polly kissed Rebecca's cheek. "I love you. Now go take the boys for a ride. It will be good for you."

Rebecca left and Polly smiled as she lined up the fabric on her machine. That child was going to be the death of her.

~~~

"Polly, Polly!"

She'd finally finished the curtains for the two upstairs rooms and was standing at the ironing board waiting for the iron to finish heating up.

"Still in here," she said.

Elijah came dashing in. "Guess where we went."

"The elementary school."

"No. After that."

"I have no idea. Tell me."

"Rebecca took us around the neighborhood and we went to the old people's house."

Polly creased her brow. "The old people's house? Which old people?" There were so many in this neighborhood, it could be anyone. "Mr. And Mrs. Lynch?"

He shook his head. "No. Where those old people live. Down there." He pointed to the south.

"The nursing home. Very nice."

"There were people sitting outside and we stopped to talk to them. Then they took us inside for cookies and milk. They were really nice. Can I go tomorrow? Benny said he was going to teach me how to play chess. I've never played chess before. He said I'd be a good chess player. Can I go? Noah wants to go too. And it's right down there. Can we?"

Noah and Rebecca had joined them in the dining room.

"I suppose," Polly said. "You weren't bothering people, were you?" She looked at Rebecca for affirmation.

"I don't know why I was scared to go," Rebecca said. "The nurses and staff were cool. They said the boys could come over any time they wanted. Best time is in the afternoons, they said."

"They paint and play games and do all kinds of fun things. And there's a piano. I played some of my songs for them," Elijah said. "They clapped when I was done!"

Polly laughed out loud. He was doing fine with his piano lessons, but things were still pretty elementary. "It's wonderful that you want to go back."

"I'm going to tell Henry." Before she could stop him, Elijah was out of the room, heading to the family room.

"How did you like it, Noah?" she asked.

"There was a lot of people in wheelchairs. I remember that Miz Evie was in a wheelchair and then she had to go away. Gramma said she went to an old folk's home. Is that what that is?"

"Yes, I suppose."

"Why aren't those people living with their families? Miz Evie had to go because her daughter went to jail and there wasn't anyone else around to take care of her."

"Sometimes people need more help than their families can give them," Polly said. "They need medicine and help getting in and out of bed or they can't cook for themselves anymore. They live where there are nurses and people to help."

"When you get old, you can live with me forever," he said. "I'll give you your medicine and cook for you. Maybe that's what I want to do. Maybe I'll be a nurse so I can take care of people when they're old."

Polly pulled him close and held on to him. "I love you, Noah. You have the biggest heart. If you want to be a nurse, then you will be a fantastic nurse. Do you want to go back tomorrow, too?"

She let him loose and he nodded solemnly. "Maybe they'll let me help do things."

"I suspect the best thing you could do is make friends."

"There weren't any other kids around."

"Then you can go be a kid. Go find your brother. Tell Henry what you did."

He left the room and Polly turned to Rebecca. "Are you sure this is okay?"

Rebecca handed her a business card. "That's the activities director. She told me to give this to you and you could call her. She says she knows you."

Looking at the card, Polly tried to remember how she might know Brianna Hoffman. "I have no idea."

"She said she worked at Pizzazz."

"Bri?" Polly said. "I love her. I should go over and see her."

Rebecca laughed. "She said you weren't welcome."

"What do you mean?"

"She said that if you came in the front door, people would worry who you were there for."

"Oh, come on."

"You never know. They're kinda old." Rebecca was still laughing as she left the room.

"Wait, Rebecca?" Polly called.

"Yeah."

"You have a half hour with your phone. I want to see you back downstairs with it on time, though. I'm setting my timer."

"Thank you!" Rebecca ran off and Polly heard her head up the steps.

She set the timer on her phone, then dialed the number on the card in her hand.

"Bellingwood Care Center, this is Bri."

"Hello, Bri. This is Polly Giller. I didn't realize you were working there."

"Just started this summer. It was kind of my dream job. I didn't know if I'd be able to get the job here, but they've been without for a few months, so here I am. I met your sons and daughter today. They're good kids."

"Thank you. I'm sorry that they barged in on you, but Rebecca tells me you're fine with them visiting."

"The residents loved them. Elijah has so much energy and he isn't scared of anyone. Nothing phased him. He walked right up to everyone and started talking to them. There were plenty of smiles on faces by the time they headed home. A couple of people asked if I would find out who they belonged to and invite them back again."

"The boys will be back tomorrow, then. Can I send anything with them?"

"No. We've got it. Do the boys have any food allergies?"

Polly laughed. "Not at all. They can eat anything. Elijah is a bottomless pit, so don't worry about spoiling their dinner. For now, let them enjoy themselves."

"Thank you. I'm hoping to work with teachers at the elementary school this year. Too many of my people don't get to see their grandchildren and they miss children's laughter and energy. We have so much to offer."

"For now, let them lavish it on my boys," Polly said. "They'll lap it up and come back for more. If Noah is a bit more hesitant than his brother, it's okay. He's loving and kind, but not as effusive. He'll be the one that latches on to one or two and sticks close to them."

"Then I know just who to introduce him to," Bri responded. "Mrs. Walker needs a friend. Does he read well?"

"He loves to read and he's getting better at reading out loud all the time."

"Mrs. Walker has difficulty staying focused when she reads and she often falls asleep when she's listening to an audio book, but having Noah read to her might be good for both of them."

"They're yours to manage," Polly said. "I look forward to seeing what comes of it."

"Me too. It's good to talk to you again. Are you ladies still going up to Pizzazz every Sunday night?"

"We are. You should join us, but as a customer."

"Really?"

"Yes. We'd love to have you. The more the merrier."

"Maybe I will, then. I like all of you. Everyone else is still part of the group?"

Polly thought back to when she'd last seen Bri. "We may have added one or two more. You're welcome any time."

"Thanks. Tell the boys I'll see them tomorrow afternoon."

Polly put the phone down and smiled. Her boys were going to make their way in this town without her help. They'd already found more people to love. She could hardly help herself when a few tears spurted from her eyes.

CHAPTER TWELVE

Every night this week had been rough and Polly was exhausted. She and Henry had spent yet another restless night while he tried to make himself comfortable. He'd decided that he wasn't going to take any more of the pain medication unless absolutely necessary. She tried to talk him into taking a pill so he could relax enough to sleep, but he insisted that he could handle it, so he handled it. And Polly only got a few hours of sleep.

Kayla was having a blast painting with Hayden. Polly was certain there was a hint of a crush there, but she recognized that Kayla also liked to see projects get completed and painting walls would do exactly that for her. Rebecca was doing her best to maintain a sense of equilibrium without having Kayla and Andrew around. She wanted to paint something for Kayla and Stephanie's new apartment, so she was working in her bedroom.

Polly sent Noah and Elijah outside with the dogs again. They missed having Kayla and Andrew around, too. Polly almost felt bad that she'd excommunicated Andrew, but she shrugged it off. This wouldn't kill any of them and it simply couldn't be healthy for those two to spend so much time together.

She'd finished the curtains this morning and had them ironed and ready to hang as soon as the paint dried in the bedrooms upstairs. She looked at the table filled with piles of everything from fabric to papers that needed to be scanned and managed, junk mail that needed to be recycled, and paper the boys used to draw and write on when they wanted to be near her. She looked up as Rebecca walked in.

"What's up?" Polly asked, unplugging the iron.

"I was wondering."

Polly grinned. "Wondering what?"

"Kayla and Hayden are almost done painting the bedrooms and Hayden says he doesn't need her to paint the bathroom. Can we go to the swimming pool this afternoon?"

Polly glanced out at the two boys running around in the back yard. They'd had a month of swimming lessons in June and were actually pretty good in the water. They loved going to the pool. She started to slowly nod.

"Before you say yes, I wanted to ask if we could invite Andrew, too. I know that he isn't supposed to be here, but can we spend time together at the pool?"

"No problem," Polly said. "Let me call Sylvie and ask if she has plans for him this afternoon." She looked at Rebecca to make sure that this plan hadn't already been set into motion and Rebecca was alerting her to it at the last minute. There was no sign of deceit in the girl's eyes, something that was generally quickly apparent.

"Thank you."

"We've all been stuck in the house for a couple of days. What if we go downtown for lunch?"

Rebecca's eyes lit up. "Really?"

"Yeah. You guys like Sylvie's sandwiches at Sweet Beans, right?"

"Yes!"

"I'll call her to make sure. We can pick Andrew up and then you can go to the pool from there."

Rebecca rushed in and grabbed Polly into a hug. "Thank you."

"You're welcome. How long until Kayla will be ready?"

"I'll check." Rebecca ran out and up the steps, yelling for her friend.

Polly opened her phone and called Sylvie.

"Hello. Are you giving in?" Sylvie asked.

"You dirty rat. Yes. No. Maybe."

"What does that mean?"

"Rebecca asked if she could invite Andrew to go swimming with everyone this afternoon. If you say yes, I'll pick him up and we'll eat lunch at Sweet Beans before they walk to the pool. What do you think?"

"Thank God," Sylvie said. "I've never seen such a morose little boy. He's pathetic. He mopes around the house like the end of the world has come. I'm not sure how I'm going to put up with two more weeks of this."

"It's only been a day."

"A day from hell, let me tell you. I had to send him to his room last night. He was depressing me. I have to buy some paint so he can start doing something constructive with his time. I thought I'd do that after work tonight. Maybe I'll ask Jason to take him. I don't know."

"Do you want me to call him? Or Rebecca?"

"If you don't care, Rebecca can call him. How's she doing with these new rules?"

"There's a lot of activity around here, so she's better than Andrew, but with Stephanie and Kayla moving out this weekend, I'm afraid next week is going to be awful."

"They're such stupid kids," Sylvie said. "Not that I was any better at that age."

Polly chuckled. "When I think of how bad kids can be, I realize we're both pretty lucky."

"You're right. See you later?"

"Yeah. Tell Camille to be prepared. I need my coffee."

"Got it," Sylvie said with a laugh. "Bye."

Polly went into the family room and sat down in front of Henry.

He grinned at her. "What's up?"

"Want a nooner?"

"That's mean. Parts of me say 'hell, yes' and other parts of me shrivel up at the thought of the pain involved."

"Are you keeping busy?"

He set the tablet down on the table beside him. "Actually, this has been good. I've caught up on a lot of paperwork. Quotes and contracts are done. I haven't been this close to finished in months."

She smiled. "How are you feeling?"

"I'm okay. Tomorrow I'll ride with Heath until I can't take it and then he can drop me off at the shop."

"Are you sure?"

"I expected you to tell me that I wasn't allowed to leave the house."

"No," Polly said, shaking her head. "I figured that I had two good days of keeping you home. At least you aren't driving yourself."

"Doc said I couldn't, so I won't. At least until I replace the truck. I heard from Chris. They're totaling the thing. Heath and I will run down and make sure everything is cleared out of it."

"Do you have a problem with Andrew going swimming with Rebecca and the boys this afternoon?"

He furrowed his brows, looking at her quizzically. "Why would I?"

"I just wanted to check."

"They can do things together, just not alone and not here. He's not trying to wheedle his way back into the house, is he?"

"No," she said with a laugh. "This was Rebecca's idea and she was very upfront with me about what she was thinking. I talked to Sylvie and she's okay with it, too. Do you want to have lunch with all of us at Sweet Beans?"

"Do I have to?"

"No." Polly chucked. "Not at all. Do you care if we're all out of here? Except for Hayden. He's painting the bathroom. It sounds like he might be ready to move things upstairs tomorrow."

"Wow. With him and Heath upstairs and Stephanie and Kayla in their own apartment, that empties us out."

She gave him a knowing smile. "I can hardly wait. The living room is in good enough shape that we can move in. I need to paint the walls in Kayla's room and then I'm moving the desk in. We *will* have an office here. Then it will be time to start thinking about bookshelves in the library."

Henry lifted his broken arm. "I can't make shelves right now."

"Put your silly arm back down. I know that. I was actually thinking that I might dig through the garage. Once I decide which pieces to move into the house, I'll work on refinishing those. Then we'll move Dad's shop equipment in so Heath has a workshop. If the two of you work out there, he can be part of building those shelves too."

"You have us all working nonstop, don't you?"

She gave him a toothy grin. "That's my job." Polly sat forward and put her hands on his knees. "We need to talk to Rebecca about the sweet studio the boys built for her. I'm afraid she's never going to use it as intended. Before you get heat and air conditioning out there, she'll be in college. She's perfectly happy working in that beautiful bedroom."

"I'm glad you bought her a tarp for the floor."

"What do you think, though? She feels guilty for not using it the way it was intended."

"We'll figure something out." His phone rang and Henry looked at the screen. "I need to take this."

"Do you want me to make something for you for lunch?"

He rolled his eyes. "I can take care of myself. Go do your thing and don't worry."

Polly kissed Henry's forehead as he answered the call and she left the family room. She wandered past Kayla and Stephanie's closed doors, then down the hall toward the living room where Heath and Hayden were living. Having these rooms open again was going to be wonderful. She looked forward to spreading out.

~~~

Polly and Sylvie watched as the kids left the coffee shop for the pool.

"Those two are happier," Sylvie said.

"They've been friends for so long, it's hard to not be able to talk to each other all the time."

"They'll learn."

Polly laughed. "You're such a good mom. You inspire me, you know."

"Look who's here."

Polly turned to see Tab walking toward them. She was dressed in her uniform, so Polly assumed she was on duty.

"You find a body in your back yard and then you go incognito," Tab said, putting her hand on Polly's shoulder.

"Not my fault."

"It never is. I have news for you, though. I'll be right back. Let me order my coffee."

Polly opened her mouth to say something, then closed it when Tab walked away without finishing the story.

"That wasn't very nice of her," Sylvie said with a laugh.

"I probably deserve it, but no kidding."

"I was going to go back to work. Now I have to stay here and wait for Tab's news."

"How's Marta doing?"

Sylvie's latest employee, Marta, loved working in the bakery at Sweet Beans. It was obvious in the way she interacted with people every day. She'd told Polly it had almost been like she was given a second chance at life.

"I love her. Sometimes I feel bad that she works so hard, but she insists that she's having the time of her life. Marta has taken Elise under her wing, too."

"Elise? Our Elise? Timid, professorial Elise?"

Sylvie smiled. "Yeah. That Elise. Marta convinced her to participate in the next production at the Boone Community Theater."

Polly sat back, her eyes wide. "Elise is performing on stage?"

"Oh no," Sylvie said. "She's going to help Marta with props and building sets."

"I don't even know what to say about that. Isn't this the theater that Nate performs with sometimes?"

"Yeah. He isn't participating this fall because of so many new kids at their house. Joss said he could, but he'd rather be with his family while they're getting used to each other."

"How do you know all of this and I don't?"

"Because you've been gone for a couple of days. Life keeps going on around here."

"This happened in two and a half days?" Polly let out a breath. "That's not fair."

"I'm sure there's more." Sylvie smiled up at Tab. "You'd best sit and tell Polly what's going on. I've been trying to keep her entertained with the news of the day, but she won't last much longer."

Tab blew out a laugh. "It's still preliminary, but do you remember that body you found last May?"

"Yeah."

"We're pretty sure that one and the body you found Monday are related."

"As in the cases are related, or the people are related?" Polly asked.

"Both. We're waiting for complete results, but everything points to them being brothers."

Polly peered across the table at Tab. "That's weird, right? Do you know how long each of them had been dead?"

"The guy you found in May had been dead for several weeks." Tab slowly nodded her head. "This latest one died a couple of weeks before you found him."

Polly groaned. "And then he was delivered to the field behind my house on Monday. That's crazy."

"The first man's DNA isn't on record anywhere and the bodies were decayed so badly we couldn't get fingerprints." Tab shuddered. "Critters had gotten to both men. We aren't giving up, but we don't know for sure where to look next."

Sylvie stood. "I need to go back to work. It looks like you have a job ahead of you, Polly. Time to kick in and solve these murders."

"I'll take Andrew home after they're finished at the pool," Polly said as Sylvie walked away.

The woman turned. "Thanks. Maybe he'll be a happier boy tonight."

"What's up with that?" Tab asked. "Something wrong with Andrew?"

"He got caught making out with Rebecca in her bedroom."

Tab's mouth opened into an O. "That was probably a very bad scene."

"Yeah," Polly drawled out. "He doesn't get to spend afternoons at our house for the rest of the summer and they can only talk on the phone for a half hour after supper. They are trying to figure out how to live with those restrictions. I don't have a problem with them spending time together, but I should have known better than to let them have very little structure this summer. They're growing up. I still see both of them as fifth and sixth graders, but they'll be in high school this fall. Andrew's voice is dropping and Rebecca is filling out and, oh Tab, I'm not ready for this."

"I don't know if any mom ever is." She looked up and grinned. "The whole world knows you're out and about today, Polly."

"There you are," Joss said, rushing up to Polly. "I saw your truck out front and hoped I would find you here."

"Sit," Polly said. "What's going on?"

"Nate's father had a heart attack and we have to head back to Indiana. He's on his way to Des Moines and is flying out this afternoon. The kids and I are leaving tomorrow morning."

"What can I do?"

"I don't want to travel with Jasmine. Can you help me?"

Polly nodded. "Sure. Do you want her to come to our house or do you want me to check on her at your place?"

Joss wilted. "I hate to leave her alone since she's used to having tons of kids around. Is it too much to ask you to take her to your house? I can bring her over tonight." She stopped and put her head down, taking deep breaths.

"You have too much to do tonight," Polly said. "Why don't I come get her after supper."

"That would be wonderful." Joss let out a sigh of relief. "The kids don't know about this trip yet and Lillian is going to be heartbroken at leaving Jazz, even for a few days. Some days, that dog is the only person Lillian speaks to."

"I can't imagine taking a trip like this with five children," Tab said quietly.

Joss looked at her sideways. "Neither can I. Andy just showed up at the library. I'm so glad she's back from her vacation. She'll take care of things while I'm gone. Hopefully we'll be back this weekend. I have to go to the grocery store and I should run to Boone and ..." Joss stood back up. "I need to keep moving. I have a few hours to myself and better use them." She put her hand on Polly's arm. "Can you come after eight thirty or so? The kids will be in bed and it will be easier to get Jazz out of the house. Is that asking too much?"

"Not at all," Polly said. She put her hand over Joss's. "If you need me to do anything else, call or text me. I can go be a librarian, too, if necessary."

Joss nodded. "I guess you did do that once upon a lifetime."

"A long time ago," Polly said. "Can I do any shopping for you right now?"

"No," Joss said with a quick shake of her head. "I don't know what I need."

"I get it. I'll see you later."

Joss left and Polly looked at Tab. "Five little kids in a car for eight hours? Is she nuts?"

"I couldn't do it." Tab stared off toward the door and then looked back. "How's Henry?"

"He's okay. Says he's riding with Heath tomorrow. I had to get out of the house today and he has to be feeling some cabin fever. Have you heard anything about the girl who hit him? No one's told us anything."

"Just rumors. She's in pretty bad shape."

"That's awful. My heart aches for them. She's a dumb, stupid kid who does what every dumb stupid kid does. I'm terrified that one of my kids will make a mistake and it will cost them everything. No matter how hard I try, they're still just kids." Polly rubbed her forehead. "When I think of the idiotic things I did at that age, I can't believe how lucky I was. And I was a good kid. I knew what Dad's expectations were, but sometimes I had to try life on my own."

"Testing the waters," Tab said. "I'm never having kids."

"What does JJ say?"

Tab laughed out loud. "We are so far from even thinking about that. I can't tell you for sure that we'll still be dating at Christmas."

"Is something wrong?"

"No," Tab said. "We aren't engaged or anything. We're just dating."

"You've been dating for a few months now. It's not serious?"

Tab took a long drink from her coffee. When she put the cup back down on the table, she still didn't say anything.

"What's going on?" Polly asked.

"Nothing's going on," Tab said. "This is all my problem. You know I don't want to settle down. I want my own life. I like living by myself. I'm not ready to be part of a couple that has to be together all the time."

"That's not a bad thing. Have you and JJ talked about that?"

"He understands that I want to be my own person and he's cool with it. There's no pressure from him. It's the pressure from everybody else that drives me out of my mind. Why does everyone want me to suddenly be married? Why can't I enjoy being Tab Hudson without everyone trying to make me into something else?"

"I get it," Polly said. "When Henry and I were trying to figure out what our lives were going to be, it was hell fending off the pressure from my friends to get married and start a family. They couldn't bear the fact that I might be happy alone." She put up her hand. "Don't get me wrong, I'm thrilled to be married to him and we have an amazing life. I wouldn't want it any other way, but it had to be on our time, not everybody else's. Sometimes it feels like the whole world can only be happy for you if you are doing things the way they did or making decisions the same way they did. No one gets to be an individual any longer. Your most important decisions are community property."

Tab slapped her hand on the table. "Exactly. When I'm ready to settle down, then it's my decision and if I'm never ready, that's my decision, too."

"So I should never ask again?" Polly asked with a smirk.

"I kind of came unglued, didn't I."

"No. You reminded me of something I'd forgotten."

"What's that?"

"How important it is to let people live their lives the way they decide, not the way that makes me comfortable."

"You're getting all crazy now."

"Don't let people push you. When I was dealing with it, there were times I wondered if it would be easier to push Henry away. At least then I wouldn't have to worry about disappointing everyone who thought I'd be so much happier if I were married and having children."

"That's exactly how I feel," Tab said. "I like JJ, but if I'm going to be pushed into marriage, it would be easier to be by myself again."

"Don't let us do that to you. You have plenty of time."

"Sal is so happy," Tab said. "She and Mark didn't waste any time. They were always together."

"First date," Polly said. "I introduced them and it was all over. My friends each made different decisions about being in relationships at different times in their lives. Beryl is one of the happiest people I know and a lot of that is because she made the choice to be single and enjoy it. I'm sure she could have been married if that was what she wanted, but she didn't want to do that again."

"And she shouldn't."

"Andy didn't like being alone after her husband died. It took her a while to come to grips with it, but she and Len are happy together. Sylvie and Eliseo are having fun together, but I don't think either of them are in a hurry to be married. They like their lives just as things are. She's happy because she earned independence all on her own. That house is hers. No one helped her get it. Eliseo is in a home surrounded by his sister and her kids. He adores those kids and right now it would kill him to leave them. I know people think they'd be happier if they got married, but the thing is, they're perfectly happy right now."

"And then there's the sheriff and Lydia."

Polly smiled. "Then there's Aaron and Lydia. Those two are rock solid."

Tab pointed at the front door. "No, there they are."

"Are you kidding me?" Polly turned and waved.

CHAPTER THIRTEEN

"Now what are you two doing here today?" Lydia asked with a grin. "This looks like it could be trouble."

"I should get back to work." Tab stood up. "It's good to see you, Mrs. Merritt. Sheriff." She took her coffee cup and headed for the front door.

"Something I said?" Aaron asked.

Polly grinned and pointed to the chairs. "It's terrible that you don't allow your deputies coffee breaks. Why aren't you at work today?"

Aaron held a chair for his wife and she sat down beside Polly. "I'll get our coffees. Do you need a refill, Polly?"

She looked at her nearly empty mug and held it up. "Yes, please."

As he walked away, Lydia took Polly's hand. "How are things at your house? Since you're out and about, does that mean Henry is better?"

"Yeah. We haven't had a lot of sleep. He has a hard time getting comfortable, but that's only temporary. What are you two doing?"

Lydia leaned in. "He said he missed me, so he took the day off. We went over to Dayton to see Marilyn and the kiddos this morning. It was wonderful. We're driving up to see Sandy and Trinity this weekend."

"How will Bellingwood ever live without you?" Polly asked.

"They'll get by," Aaron said, putting Polly's mug in front of her. "How's Henry?"

"He's better. He told me that he's riding with Heath tomorrow. If I have cabin fever, his has to be worse. He's usually out and about every day. He's going to be very frustrated carrying around a bum arm, I can tell you that. We talked about projects that we want to work on at the house and it bothers him that he won't be able to help. This weekend, Stephanie and Kayla are moving into a new place and the boys are moving upstairs into their own rooms. All of that lifting and carrying and Henry can't do any of it. I might have to drug him into senselessness."

"I'd be glad to come help."

Lydia looked at her husband in surprise. "We aren't going to Edina?"

He chuckled. "Oops. I won't be in town. Sorry."

"We'll be fine," Polly said. "Tab just told me that the two men I found were related."

Aaron nodded. "It's strange, that's for sure. Both were pretty violent deaths, too. Someone was very angry."

Polly was a little surprised he was talking so openly to her and wondered if maybe she'd finally crossed the point where he trusted her. "Do you have an idea what was used to kill them?"

"Honestly, we aren't sure yet. Both men had trauma to the back of their head." He touched Lydia's head, just above the neck. "After they hit the ground, a multiple-pointed tool was used over and over. The killer was enraged — taking the time to turn the bodies over and continue tearing them apart."

"Wow. In Bellingwood?" Polly asked. "I don't know anyone who would do that, do you?"

Aaron gave her a wan smile. "There are plenty of sick people living in and around town. Who knows? I was surprised to find a link between the two men, but once we saw the similar puncture wounds in their bodies, we dug deeper."

"I want Bellingwood to be a quiet utopia," Polly said.

"Then you wouldn't have anything interesting to do," he said with a chuckle.

Lydia leaned in and whispered, "Speaking of interesting."

Polly turned and saw Reuben and Judy Greene coming into the coffee shop. Lydia was right. The couple stood out.

He was dressed in cut-off denim shorts, a tie-dye button down shirt and brown sandals. His hair was loose and hanging down his back. Judy wore bright purple and yellow baggy pants that looked like pajamas. She had on a white sleeveless t-shirt and her long gray hair was tied loosely in the back.

Standing up, Polly put out her hand to greet them. Judy took it and smiled warmly.

"Reuben and Judy Greene, I'd like to introduce you to Lydia and Aaron Merritt," Polly said.

Aaron stood and shook their hands. "Are you folks new in town?"

"We're thinking about moving in," Reuben said. "We're staying at the hotel right now and looking around the area to see if this is where we want to spend our twilight years."

His wife swatted his arm. "Twilight years, my hiney. I'm not having a twilight, thank you very much." She smiled at Lydia. "Do not go gentle into that good night, old age should burn and rave at close of day; rage, rage against the dying of the light."

"Dylan Thomas," Lydia said. "I don't know that I fully understood that poem until I passed the age of fifty."

"When you pass sixty, it becomes even more meaningful," Reuben said.

Judy nodded. "I intend to rage for a very long time."

Aaron pulled out a chair from a nearby table and then held it for Judy. "Join us."

She looked at her husband and he shrugged. "We'd love to," she said. "I've enjoyed getting to know people in town. What were you discussing when we came in?" She looked at her husband. "Herbal tea and maybe a raspberry biscotti." Turning back to the table, she asked, "Would anyone like something sweet to eat? We've been walking all over town and I feel the need for some quick energy."

Polly shook her head and Lydia said, "I'm fine, but thank you."

Aaron sat back down and Reuben headed for the counter.

"We were talking about murder," Polly said.

Judy's eyes grew wide. "Murder! That sounds exciting. Do you get many of those around here?"

Lydia put her head down and her hand over her mouth. Polly soon realized she was laughing and having difficulty controlling it.

"What did I say?" Judy asked.

"Judy, I introduced Aaron, but he's also the sheriff in these h'yar parts," Polly said.

"You would encounter more murder than most people."

Aaron lifted his eyes over his glasses at Polly. "Tell her the rest."

Polly sighed. "I might be the person who finds dead bodies."

"I don't know how to respond to that," Judy said, peering at Polly with a quizzical look.

"Since she moved into town," Aaron said, "if there's a murder, Polly is right there on scene. She is usually the person who comes across the body and calls me to investigate. We have an interesting relationship."

"It's not my fault," Polly said. "I didn't ask for this."

"She's very good at it," Lydia said. "If she invites you to ride along to an out of the way location, or take a walk in a dark forest, run the other way."

"That's quite some talent. I'm surprised we haven't heard about it yet."

"People in Bellingwood are pretty protective of Polly," Aaron said. "It's surprising."

Polly frowned at him. "Surprising? Why?"

"Because you're a relative newcomer and you've introduced many new ideas into the community. You make people nervous."

"They only get nervous if she shows up when they're sick or hurt," Lydia said with a giggle. She covered her mouth again. "I'm sorry. That wasn't nice."

Polly grinned. "I spoke to the new activities director at the nursing home today and while she's very happy to have my boys come over to visit, I don't think I'm welcome."

Lydia laughed out loud. "Oh dear, that's awesome. Noah and Elijah are going over to the nursing home?"

"They went yesterday and had a blast. The kids are swimming right now. When we get home, they'll want to run right over again."

"They're such cute boys," Judy said.

"You met them?" Lydia asked.

"Judy and Reuben came over for dinner the other night. I met them Monday morning in the cemetery just before I found that last body."

Judy sat back. "You found a body Monday morning after we left?"

"Yeah." Polly rolled her eyes. "I'm helpless against my talent."

"In the cemetery?"

"What was in the cemetery?" Reuben sat down beside his wife and put her tea and a plate with biscotti in front of her.

"A dead body."

He gave them an incredulous look. "That doesn't sound surprising."

"A newly dead body. Polly finds dead bodies."

"I seem to have missed a large part of this conversation." He waved his hands. "Go on, though. Don't explain. Continue. If I have trouble keeping up, Judy can enlighten me later."

"What were you two doing in the cemetery?" Lydia asked. "Do you have family here?"

Judy nodded. "My sister is Sandy Morrison."

"You're Judy Grady?" Lydia asked. She turned to Aaron and then waved him away. "You weren't around then, so you wouldn't know. Where did you go when you left Bellingwood? We never heard from you again." She paused to think. "I did see you at your mother's funeral ten years ago, but you were in and out so quickly no one got a chance to talk to you. And you want to finally move back to town? What does Sandy think about that? She's never said anything about you and Tim being gone, but then I don't see her all that often, just at church and around town sometimes. She and Bob are pretty busy with their farm."

Judy had tried to speak several times during Lydia's monologue and finally gave up. She waited a beat and opened her mouth, but Lydia had only gotten started.

She reached across the table and took Judy's hand. "It is so good to see you. I was pretty young when you left, but that was a big deal. You were the smartest person in town. Everyone thought you could do anything you wanted in life and then you took off and never came back. A couple of years later, your brother left too. Did you meet your husband in college? Do you two have children?"

Aaron gently put his arm around his wife's back.

"I'm sorry," she said. "I should let you talk, but you've been a mystery all these years. I can't believe I'm sitting here with you. You were kind of a hero to me."

"I was?"

"It was the sixties," Lydia said. "I wasn't even in junior high yet. Somebody said you went to San Francisco and I was seeing news reports of all the hippies out there." She bit her lips together.

"I participated in a few sit-ins," Judy said with a smile. "You know — make love, not war. I could never understand why people were so angry at the soldiers who came home, though. I refused to participate in any of that. How could folks not understand that those boys were drafted and not responsible for the choices our government made? I protested the government's decisions, that's for sure." She chuckled. "I've never stopped making my voice known when the government makes poor decisions for our country, but that's neither here nor there. And yes, we're looking at moving to Iowa if we can find a good place to live."

"From where?" Lydia asked. "Still San Francisco?"

"Across the bay — Oakland," Reuben said. "Judy taught at Stanford."

"What do you do?" Aaron asked.

"I'm retired and starting my next life," he replied. "Welding and blacksmithing have always been a hobby. Now I'm ready to take it to another level."

"Knives? Guns? What do you make?"

"Beautiful outdoor art," Judy said. "Using reclaimed steel and iron."

"Do you help him?" Lydia asked.

Judy shook her head. "No. I love my plants. I would love to put up a greenhouse. I've been a plant biologist my entire life and I don't want to give it up."

"Your mother had beautiful gardens," Lydia said.

"So did my grandmother. I lived in their gardens as a child. It was a natural progression."

Polly's mouth had dropped open and Aaron looked at her across the table. "What's going on in your head, Polly?"

"I had a thought, but I don't know what to do with it, so I'll keep it to myself for a while."

"What kind of a thought?" Lydia asked, then a smile curled across her lips. "It might be a great thought."

"What?" Aaron asked. "That's not fair."

"I can't say anything right now," Polly said, glaring at him. "It was just a thought that ran through my head. No big deal."

Aaron flinched and Polly realized his wife had pinched his thigh. Fortunately, he was well-trained and his automatic response was to shut the conversation down.

"Women make me nuts," he said to Reuben. "Do you have a forge?"

"I'll build one when I settle somewhere. I built the one at our home in Oakland, but it isn't worth it to pull the whole thing apart and move it across the country. I learned a great deal though and my next one will be even better."

Aaron and Lydia looked up when the bell on the front door rang out. Polly decided she was never sitting with her back to the door again. This was killing her. Within moments, though, she realized that her boys had come into the coffee shop wearing only their damp swim trunks.

"What are you two doing here?" she asked, craning her neck to see where Kayla, Rebecca, and Andrew were.

"We're done swimming," Elijah announced. "I want to go to the nursing home."

Noah didn't say anything, but stood quietly beside Polly. She reached out and put her arm around his waist, pulling him close. "Were *you* done swimming?"

He nodded.

"Were you done swimming because Elijah said so or because you wanted to be done?"

"I wanted to be done. I'm not going back there."

"Why not?"

He shrugged.

"Where is Rebecca?"

Elijah pointed outside. "They're at the truck putting more clothes on." He shivered. "It's cold in here."

"We should get more clothes on you, too," Polly said. She stood up. "I should get these boys home. It was good to see you two again." She shook Reuben and Judy's hands and turned to Lydia. "Have a great rest of the day off and if I don't see you before Friday, have a good weekend in Minneapolis."

Polly was confident Aaron and Lydia would enjoy chatting with Judy and Reuben. It was funny to think of Lydia holding anyone out as an idol. Polly had such respect for Lydia. She was an amazing woman, filled with confidence, generosity, kindness and love. It never occurred to her that Lydia would have childhood heroes. The things you learned about your friends.

She opened the front door and held it as the boys went out into the warm sun. "Why did you leave the pool so early?" she asked.

"Somebody said something bad," Elijah said.

Her heart sank.

Rebecca slumped when she saw Polly. "I hoped we could be out longer. We have to go home now, don't we?"

Polly glanced back at the coffee shop. "I don't want to have to shuttle you around any longer today. If I'm taking Andrew home, I'm doing it now."

"I can walk," he said.

"If that's what you want to do, you can spend one more hour here. You will stay at the coffee shop." She took out a ten-dollar bill and handed it to Rebecca. "When an hour is up, I want you to come straight home. You don't get to walk Andrew to his house. He goes one way and you go another. That means that in an hour and fifteen minutes, the two of you girls need to be walking in the door. Deal?"

Rebecca took the money and smiled at Polly. "Thank you. This is nice. I promise we'll be home on time. Kayla has to start packing this afternoon and I'm going to help her. We want to get most of her things packed before Stephanie gets home from work."

"Perfect. We'll see you later." Polly waited for Noah and Elijah to get into the back seat. She pulled her seatbelt on and then unbuckled it and turned around. "Okay. Who said what to you?"

"We've heard it before," Elijah said quietly. "It's easier to ignore it."

"Tell me what they said."

"She called me a nigger and said I should go back to Africa because nobody wanted me here." Noah looked at Polly, his eyes glistening with tears. "I've never been to Africa."

They'd had similar conversations before. People were so ignorant in their bigotry. All she wanted for her boys was that they would be able to succeed in life. They were both bright and ready to take on any challenge they faced. The challenges that were impossible for them to handle were those handed out by people who were willing to speak their hatred and fears out loud.

"Maybe one day you'll get a chance to go visit Africa," Polly said. "There are many wonderful people who live there. We've talked about this. People are afraid of anything that is different from them. Who said this to you?"

"Ariel," Elijah said. "She's mean."

"I know that, sweetie," Polly said. "Is this the same Ariel I saw at the coffee shop?"

He nodded.

Polly continued. "They're unhappy people and when that much unhappiness builds up, it spills out and they make everybody around them unhappy too."

"That's stupid," he said.

"You're right. It is." She hitched herself up on her knees and put her hands over the seat, reaching out to the boys. Polly waited until they'd each taken her hand. "I know that it's hard to remember this when people say nasty things to you, but Henry and I love you very much and we're proud of you all the time. When people are mean to you and you turn around and treat them with respect, that's important. It's hard to do, but it's the right thing."

She gave their hands a squeeze. This was never going to get easier. After all these years, bigotry was still as ugly and nasty as it always had been. She wanted to wrap her beautiful boys up in her arms and never let them back out into the world. "What say we go home and after you change clothes, you can run over and visit your new friends at the nursing home."

Elijah took his hand back and bounced in his seat. "Can I take some of my cars to show them?"

"I suspect they'd love that." She dropped Noah's hand after another quick squeeze and turned back in her seat. Pulling her seatbelt back on, she started the truck and looked around before backing out of the space. Elijah would always bounce back. Polly was more worried about Noah. He took these things in and held on to them. He was more protective of his brother than Elijah realized and she knew he felt impotent at not being able to stop that horrible girl from saying hurtful things. Polly wondered if Ariel even realized the depth of pain she caused, or if she was just looking to get a rise from the boys.

She pulled into their driveway. "Don't forget to take your things inside. Run upstairs and change your clothes and don't leave the house until you find me, okay?"

They scrambled to pick up their clothes and towels and then ran to the house, slamming the truck doors as they left. Polly took a deep breath. What she wanted to do was go charging to the Sutter's home and raise a stink, but she knew better than to believe that would do any good. All she could do right now was provide a safe environment at home for Noah and Elijah. She smiled as she thought about how the boys' day would progress. They were excited to go to the nursing home and spend time with people who were glad to see them. That would be a good balm for this heartache today.

CHAPTER FOURTEEN

Rebecca gave a little whimper as Polly drove away from their house to go pick up the Mikkels' dog. "I can't believe Kayla and Stephanie are moving out tomorrow. It feels like they've always lived with us."

Polly nodded. "You two will have fun decorating her new bedroom."

"If you're okay with it, Stephanie wants to take us thrift store shopping in Ames sometime next week. What do you think?"

"That sounds great." Polly waited for cars to pass before she turned south on the road that passed in front of Sycamore House. It was strange to see the place dark with nothing on but security lights. She didn't like driving by here at night. As much as she loved her new home and knew it was important to have the extra space for her big family, she missed the apartment. So many memories had been made in there. She thought back to those nights when Doug and Billy brought their friends in to play video games. They'd finally found a place in town with plenty of electricity, plenty of internet capacity and better yet, room to spread out and have fun. They'd grown up so much since then and now Billy was married. She shook her head. Billy was married. Wow. And Doug was dating Anita. She'd hoped something would work out between those two and apparently it had, though they were loath to admit how much time they spent together.

"What are you thinking about?" Rebecca asked.

"How much I miss living at Sycamore House."

"Me too. Things have really changed, haven't they?"

"They really have."

When she went past the barn, Polly looked in, knowing she wouldn't see anything. Everyone was tucked in for the night. She drove on past and turned onto the road leading to Joss's house.

"Thanks for letting me come with you," Rebecca said.

"You were being a sad sack, moping around like your world was coming to an end. I thought you might need a break."

"I can't believe I screwed everything up. First, Andrew got kicked out and now Kayla is leaving. I'll be all alone again."

"All alone. Yeah, that describes life at the Bell House."

"You know what I mean."

"I know what you think you mean, but this is only a small blip. Before you know it, your life will be so busy you can't breathe. Hold on. It will be here soon enough."

"I can't wait."

Polly pulled into the driveway and turned the truck off. "Don't rush your life, sweetie. Slow down and enjoy the journey. I know that doesn't mean much to you today, but one of these days you'll wish you hadn't wasted so much time waiting for tomorrow." She opened the truck door and got out. Rebecca met her at the sidewalk and they walked up to Joss's front porch.

"What are you waiting for?" Rebecca asked, her hand heading for the doorbell.

Polly pushed it down. "I don't want to wake the kids if she finally got them all to sleep." She opened the screen door as Joss pulled the inside door open. "I was going to knock."

"Thanks," Joss said, holding Lillian in her arms. "This one won't go to sleep."

Lillian recognized them and reached out for Rebecca, who took her from Joss. Rebecca and Kayla had spent quite a bit of time here this summer helping Joss with the five children. Joss was hoping to find a more permanent nanny once kids rolled into the area for college.

"Why aren't you going to sleep, Lillian?" Rebecca asked.

"I'm not tired." Lillian crossed her arms over her chest.

"Let's go to your room and I'll read two of your favorite books to you. Do you think that might make you tired?"

The little girl shook her head in a defiant no, but Rebecca headed for the stairway.

"She's so good with them," Joss said. "So much like you. Won't take any crap from the kids, but lets them think they're in charge."

"Ain't nobody in charge but me at my house," Polly said. She bent down to pat Jazz's head. The dog wagged her tail and ran upstairs to join Rebecca and Lillian.

Joss pointed at a small tote bag beside the front door. "That's her toys, food and her leash. Come on in. Do you mind if I work while we talk?"

"I didn't expect to stay long enough to bother you," Polly said. "Tell me what to do and I'll help."

"The kids need at least five outfits and maybe one or two more for accidents. We can do laundry at the house once we're there, but I want to be safe." Joss gestured to stacks of clothes around the living room. "That's Sophie, Lillian, Cooper, Owen, and Lucas. I think I have everything they'll need. I just have to pack it up."

"In this suitcase?" Polly asked.

"Do you think it will all fit?"

Polly lifted her shoulder. "All I can do is try. Do you need me to keep it in any order?"

"The boys' clothes in back and the girls' in front. I'm going to the porch for their shoes."

"More than they're wearing on their feet?" Polly called as Joss left the room.

"In case there's a funeral. That's what we're worried about. It sounded serious when Nate's mother called."

"Oh no." Polly set the opened suitcase down on a chair and began placing neatly stacked piles of clothes inside. She did quick calculations and counted as she worked through, making sure that each child had plenty of outfits, underwear and socks. She could not imagine packing for a trip with five children. Joss was some kind of saint. At least these clothes were itty bitty and fit into the case. The woman was so organized, each stack of clothing had exactly what the child needed.

"I'm finished," Polly called out. "What next?"

Joss stuck her head into the living room. "There's a case next to the entertainment center. Could you fill it with movies? They like everything on the top shelf. I don't care which ones go with us, just make sure it is packed full. Lillian likes Doc McStuffins. Make sure there are a couple of those in the case."

Polly grinned and sat down on the floor. DVDs were neatly ordered alphabetically on the shelf, but the cases wouldn't fit into the tote, so she took the time to open each and pop out the disc and place it into a slot.

"What next?" she called.

Joss came out with a pile of blankets and pillows and dropped them onto the sofa. "Would you mind packing up coloring books and things?" She held out two brightly colored bags. "Everything is in a cabinet on the south wall of the playroom. Right in the middle. There are three small containers of crayons and a stack of coloring books and two folders filled with plain white paper. If you see anything else there that they could draw on or color or write on, go ahead and pack it. I'll have each of them pick two toys out before we leave tomorrow. It won't be enough, but there are more at Grandma's house. They'll be fine." She rolled her eyes. "If nothing else ... oh!" she said. "Their music CDs. Just a second." She ran up to the second floor, leaving Polly standing at the top of the basement stairs. In a flash, she was back with another disc case. "On the west wall, on the first shelf above the counter is a stack of CDs. Fill this up. Don't worry about being organized. We listen to everything, so whatever you put in will be fine."

Polly smiled at her.

"You think I'm insane."

"I think you're a hero. I don't know anyone else who could put a trip like this together and maintain their hold on sanity."

Joss took a breath. "I feel like I should stop and talk to you and ask questions about Henry and tell you about Nate and find out about the body you discovered on Monday, but I can barely breathe. I'm so worried about not getting enough sleep tonight and getting up in time to start this trip and I'm worried about Nate's dad and how Nate is feeling and I hope that we don't have to have a discussion about death with the children and I am so thankful you are taking Jazz, but I'm still worried about how much she'll miss the kids and how much they'll miss her."

Polly put her hand out. "Breathe. You can do this. Keep telling me what you need me to do and I'll keep doing it. We'll try to get you to bed on time."

Joss turned to go back up the steps, then stopped. "I'm so sorry. You have a husband at home who needs you. You shouldn't be here helping me. That's not what you signed up for." Tears filled her eyes. "I'm so glad you're here." She pointed back up the stairs. "And Rebecca? She's singing to Lillian right now. I don't know what I would have done. My baby girl got caught up in my stress and couldn't settle. Then you two showed up like angels and I feel like I might be able to make it."

"We're good. You keep going and I'll take care of these things." Polly held up the totes. "We're on it."

Polly found everything exactly where Joss had said it would be and was adding CDs to the case when she heard footsteps coming down to her.

"How are you doing?" she asked Joss.

"The trip's off."

Polly turned. "What? Is everything okay?"

"Yeah. It wasn't a heart attack after all. He's coming home from the hospital tomorrow and Nate will be flying back to Iowa on Saturday."

"What happened?"

"Apparently, he had been moving boxes in their garage yesterday and didn't realize how badly he'd strained his back. When he woke up this morning, he couldn't breathe and the first thing they thought of was a heart attack. Nate's mother called the kids right away, putting everyone into a panic. She didn't bother to call back to tell any of them that she'd made a mistake." Joss took a deep breath. "She's going to milk this one for a while. I love her, but I know she's happy to have Nate there without me or the kids so she can dote on him." Joss sank into a rocking chair and pointed at a second chair. "I'm not going to kill her. Instead I choose to be glad that Nate called me before I was on the road."

Polly started opening CD cases again. "I might want to kill her."

"Stop doing that. I'll put things away tomorrow," Joss said.

"I just got started. I can at least manage this for you tonight."

Rebecca came into the room. "Lillian is finally asleep. Did I hear you talking to Nate and saying you aren't leaving tomorrow?"

"Nope. We're staying here. His father is fine."

"That's wonderful," Rebecca said.

"Thank you for spending time with Lillian. She adores you."

"All of your kids are awesome. Since I thought I heard you say you weren't going anywhere, I figured it was okay to leave Jazz in there with Lillian. Is that right?"

"That's perfect," Joss said. "Both of them will be happy." She stood. "I should let you two go home."

Polly handed her the empty totes and the case, then pulled her into a hug. "I'm glad it worked out this way and no other."

"Me too. Nate was so worried. His mother might treat him like a little god-king, but his father is normal and Nate would be lost without him."

They walked back upstairs.

"Are you still going to take tomorrow off?" Polly asked. "You should. Andy would understand."

"I have to," Joss replied, walking with them to the front door. "I don't have anyone here to watch them. I'll rearrange things again for Saturday, but we'll be here all day tomorrow." She grimaced. "I didn't buy food for the weekend. I can worry about that later."

"If Polly says it's okay, I can come over for a while," Rebecca said. "I'm not sure about Kayla. She has to move tomorrow night, but I'd be glad to."

They walked out onto the front porch.

"It would be fine," Polly said to Rebecca, then to Joss, "Give me a call. We'll work it out."

"You've been my sanity tonight," Joss said.

Polly looked across the way. She could barely see the security lights at Sycamore House from here. She opened her mouth to respond and they heard the scream of a horse.

"What in the hell?" Polly asked. "Is that one of my horses?"

"It sounds like it."

"Get in the truck," Polly commanded as she ran to the driver's side.

Rebecca was in and buckling her belt as Polly slammed the truck into reverse and tore out of Joss's driveway. She hit the gravel road and sped toward the highway, her tires squealing when they hit the pavement. Both she and Rebecca were breathing hard when Polly turned into the barn's parking spaces.

Polly turned the truck off, jumped out and ran for the gate, horrified to find it open. Rebecca was right behind her as they bolted through.

"Shut that gate," Polly yelled, running ahead to the barn.

Eliseo had installed locks last year and she fumbled to unlock the main door. She got inside and flipped on the lights and instantly felt weak when the stalls were empty. She hit the buttons that would flood the pasture with light and ran through Demi's stall, sinking to her knees when she saw the four horses at the far end of the pasture. Startled by the sudden lights, Nan threw her head back and whinnied. The donkeys were nowhere to be found yet, but she hadn't covered much ground.

In the bright lights, she saw that the horses were obviously scared. They paced along the fence line and not a one of them paid attention when Polly called their names. She wasn't sure what to do — whether to walk out to bring them back or let them return on their own. Then she saw that the gate in front of the bridge leading to the pasture on the other side of the creek was also open.

"Damn it," she swore and started across. "Tom. Huck. Where are you?"

The donkeys still hadn't responded and she began to worry. Why would someone mess with her animals?

The walk took long enough for her to gather her wits and she dialed Eliseo's phone.

"Hey, Polly. What's up?"

"The horses are out. The gates are all open and I can't find the donkeys."

"The what?"

"I'm going to shut the gate to the bridge, but I'm afraid that Tom and Huck might have crossed it. The horses are pretty freaked out and I'm scared to approach them."

"We'll be right there. Call Demi. He'll respond to you immediately if any of them will."

"I have," she said. "He's not coming."

She heard noise in the background and he returned. "I'm bringing Elva. The kids will be fine here. She's going up to talk to Samuel."

"I'll cross the bridge and look for Tom and Huck."

"Okay."

He ended the call and she couldn't believe how relieved she was to have just heard his voice, knowing that he'd be here as fast as humanly possible.

"Polly?"

She spun to see Rebecca coming across the pasture. "Go back. I can't find Tom and Huck."

"I brought this." Rebecca held something up and ran toward Polly. As she got closer, Polly realized it was a bag of carrot chips, the donkeys' favorite treats.

"Thank you. Go back to the barn and keep an eye out. Eliseo will be here in a few minutes. See if Hansel and Gretel are there."

Rebecca turned back and Polly went on. She heard a groan and turned again.

"No worries," Rebecca said. "I need a new pair of shoes. Can't believe I didn't see that."

Polly chuckled in spite of her fear. As she got closer to where the horses were still moving skittishly back and forth, she spoke to them in low and quiet tones. "We're here, guys. Eliseo will be here in a few minutes. I don't know what upset you, but we've got it now. Have you seen your buddies?" She pulled two pieces of carrot out of the bag and held them up. "First one to come over and give me some love gets a treat. What? No takers? Come on. I know that you like this stuff."

She stopped in front of the gate and looked across the bridge, hoping to see the donkeys coming her way. They usually showed right up whenever they heard voices. Those two were gluttons for human interaction and could barely contain themselves at the thoughts of a few treats.

"Tom! Huck! Where did you go? Come home." She pulled the gate shut and walked across the bridge. It was darker over here, the sycamore trees along the creek blocking much of the light from the pasture, so she turned her phone's flashlight on to help her walk in the rutted paths the animals had created.

"Tom? Huck? Are you here?" Polly looked to the north. Eliseo's sweet corn field was between this pasture and the highway and the street light didn't reach too far, but she was certain she saw at least one dark form moving among the stalks. "Seriously, boys. I need you to come home. I don't care what anyone else promised you, I have carrots and lots of hugs. Come here."

The sound of hooves on the ground made her smile as the two donkeys rushed toward her. Polly bent at the knees and filled her hands with carrot treats, moving them one by one into her fingers so she could feed the boys who made her smile.

Huck nudged her arm and she rubbed his forehead. "What were you two doing out here? Was someone trying to take you away from us? You're not supposed to trust strangers. You know better than that." She hugged Tom's neck and gave each of them another treat, then walked toward the bridge with the two donkeys flanking her. She stopped and put a hand on both of their backs, then dropped her head. The donkeys stopped beside her and turned their heads, hoping for something more. "You two are important to us. I don't know what I would have done if you'd been taken." She hugged each of them again and led them across the bridge. When she opened the gate, she saw Eliseo and Elva in the pasture, talking to the four horses.

Eliseo turned at the sound of the gate and nodded at Polly. "You found the boys."

"They were following a bad person, I'm afraid. I saw someone cut through the corn field."

His sister, Elva, had her hand on Nat's shoulder and slowly walked with him back to the barn, talking quietly enough that Polly couldn't understand her words.

"They're really lathered up," Eliseo said. "Were they back here when you arrived?"

"Yes. They looked skittish, but they were here."

"Then they'd been running quite a bit before that. What made you show up?"

"I was at Joss's house and heard a horse scream. We'd been in the basement and I could have missed something before that. All I know is that as soon as I heard it, I tore over and found the front gate and this gate open. The stall doors were all open, too."

Elva had returned to the pasture and approached Daisy, who backed away, still agitated. Elva stopped and spoke softly to the horse, then took another slow step.

Eliseo had his hands on Nan and Demi, but stopped to watch his sister. He turned to look at Polly and smiled. In a few moments, Elva was standing beside Daisy, who dipped her head and nudged Elva's shoulder. The two of them headed to the barn and Eliseo talked to Demi and Nan as they followed him.

"She's pretty amazing," Polly said, doing her best to stay upright with Tom and Huck crowding around her. Tom stumbled on a rut and Polly put her hand on his neck to calm him.

"I'm glad she's finding herself again," he replied. "She's been traveling around the region lately looking at horses. She says there are a couple that she'd like to bring into the stables. One that would be great for anyone to ride and she found a stallion whose owner is terrified of him. She wants him."

"Then she should have him."

He smiled and nodded. "I agree."

They went in through Demi's stall again. Elva had Daisy and Nat in their stalls.

Rebecca was sitting on a bench, stroking Gretel. "I think I found where someone broke in," she said. "There's a couple of boards hanging off the door in the donkey's stall."

Eliseo frowned. "They broke in? That was a lot of work."

"There was a flat bar and a hammer lying on the ground. They pried off a hinge. I didn't want to touch it in case you call the cops."

He looked at Polly.

"Yeah," she said. "We should call them. This was deliberate."

"We need to brush these horses down again," Elva said, stepping into the alley. "You can't leave them like this tonight."

"I can do that," Eliseo said. "You go on home. I'm spending the night. I don't want to leave them alone after this."

"Can I help?" Rebecca asked. "I'd like to. Daisy usually lets me." She looked at Elva. "Will she let me tonight?"

Elva smiled. "She's much better now. Let's find what we need." The two walked into the tack room and Polly could hear Elva explaining to Rebecca the tone of voice she should use while talking to Daisy.

"I'm calling the police," Polly said. "I'll be back to work with Demi."

Eliseo nodded absentmindedly and followed after his sister and Rebecca.

CHAPTER FIFTEEN

"You all did good work," Eliseo said, standing beside Nan while he stroked her shoulder.

They'd gotten the horses settled back into their stalls and the four of them gathered in the alley. Elva sat down on a bench and brushed sweaty hair from her face. Rebecca sat beside her and looked down at herself, covered in sweat and horsehair.

"I'm a mess," she said with a laugh. "A hot, sweaty mess."

"You have water in the fridge, right, Eliseo?" Polly asked.

"I'll get it," he replied.

"No, you sit. I'll get it. Everyone?" At their nods, Polly headed for the feed room. She glanced into the stall that the donkeys shared. "Eliseo! Elva!" she shouted as she rushed in.

Both Tom and Huck were lying on their sides, completely out.

Rebecca came in with Elva and Eliseo.

Polly knelt beside Tom's head, praying he was still breathing. What had happened? She heard deep, long breaths coming from him and took out her phone. "I'm calling Mark. What happened?"

"I don't know," Eliseo said. He rubbed down Huck's back, Elva following his lead while working on Tom. They were both trying to discover what had taken the donkeys down when Mark answered.

"Polly?"

"Mark. I'm at the barn. Something happened. The horses are fine, but the donkeys aren't responding. I didn't think anything of it, they followed me in and they're just lying there in their stall."

"What are you talking about? What happened?"

"Too much to explain. Can you come over?"

"I'll be right there. Have you called Eliseo?"

"He and Elva are here. I should have called you sooner, but they said the horses were okay, so I didn't think we needed you. Mark, I need you!" The shock of what had happened finally caught up to Polly and a sob caught in her throat."

"I'll be there. Hold on."

She bent over and grabbed her knees, her phone falling into the hay on the floor of the stall.

Rebecca bent over to pick it up and rubbed Polly's back. "They'll be okay," she said quietly. "They have to be okay."

"They've been tranqed," Eliseo said, holding up a small dart.

Elva frowned. "Where did you find that?"

"This was beside his tail."

"Nothing on this one. I've been all over him." She nodded as she scooted back up to Tom's head, shifting it so she could nestle it in her lap. Elva stroked his neck. "If it's only a tranq, you'll be back to normal soon. Who wanted to mess with you?"

Eliseo began pulling hay away from the fallen donkeys. "We should find that dart before someone steps on it. We're cleaning out the stall tonight, you wanna help?"

Polly nodded and went out to get the wheelbarrow. It had been a long time since she'd done this work.

"We're going to clear it slowly," Eliseo said. "I'm hoping it fell off in here and not out in the pasture."

"What if it did?" she asked.

"Depends. The horses' hooves could have crushed it and buried everything into the ground, or ..." He shook his head. "I don't want to think about it. We'll find it."

Polly began sweeping the hay out of the corners, shifting it around while keeping an eagle eye out for anything that might glitter in the light. Eliseo did the same while sweeping hay away from the donkeys.

"I found it," Rebecca said, coming in from the main alley. "I saw Tom rub his butt on the door and thought maybe he was trying to get rid of it." She held out the offending dart like it was a snake that might turn on her.

"Thank you," Eliseo said. He took the dart from Rebecca and motioned for Polly to stop. "Might as well leave the hay. We gave the stalls a thorough clean-down today, so this is still fresh. Who tried to steal your donkeys?"

"I have no idea," Polly said. "There are plenty of donkeys available in this state. Nobody needs to take mine. She knelt beside Huck. "And besides, I love my boys."

They all turned at the sound of the front door opening.

"Polly?"

"That's Mark," she said and stepped out of the stall. "Back here, Mark. Eliseo says they've been tranquilized." She gave a sad chuckle. "The movies make it look like tranquilizing happens in a couple of seconds. These guys were walking around for a long time."

"Depending on the dose, it would have taken fifteen minutes to a half hour for them to have gone down completely." Mark knelt beside Huck first and opened his case.

"Polly?" A new voice came from the front door.

She blew out a breath. "That has to be Bert. I'll be back. Take care of my boys." Polly stepped back out into the alley and found Bert Bradford looking into Demi's stall.

Everyone in town knew that Demi was the calmest and most easy-going of the four Percherons. While the others were friendly enough, it was Demi that always attracted a crowd.

"I'm sorry it took me so long to get here. I was in the middle of a domestic. Dispatch said it wasn't an emergency, but I just saw Doc Ogden come in. What's going on?"

"Somebody tried to steal my donkeys."

He frowned. "Why?"

"That's what I wondered," Polly said with a laugh. "Of all things. I haven't had time to check out where Rebecca said they broke in, but I'm sure Eliseo will want to fix that before we leave tonight, so I'm glad you're here. We haven't touched anything."

"Show me."

She took him past where Mark was checking on Tom and Huck, out the back door, then around to the stall door where Rebecca had seen the tools lying on the ground.

"They pried that lock right off and broke the door by the handle," Bert said. "Shouldn't be too hard to patch closed for the night. Why are your donkeys on the ground? What happened to them?"

"Eliseo found tranquilizer darts in them. Hopefully that's all it is. When I called Mark, I wasn't sure. I just screamed for him to show up." Polly smiled at Bert. "I wasn't that insane when I called dispatch for you. I promise."

"I could understand it, though," Bert said. He took two plastic bags from his back pocket, shook them out, then placed the hammer in one and pry bar into the other. "I'll want those tranquilizer darts, too," he said.

"Sure."

"Tell me what happened here tonight."

They walked back outside and Polly pointed toward Joss's house. "Rebecca and I were leaving the Mikkels' house and I heard a horse scream. I'm glad you weren't around, because I tore over here and ignored every single traffic law on the books.

"You probably shouldn't tell me that," he said with a smile. "What did you find?"

"The gates were open, the horses were freaked out, and when I got into the other pasture, I saw someone cut through the cornfield going toward the road. The donkeys came to me right away. When we crossed into the main pasture, Eliseo and Elva were here. They brought the horses inside and brushed them down. They were really worked up by whatever happened. When we were finished, I found the donkeys there and called Mark."

He held the door open for her as they walked back inside.

Mark came out and gave Polly a smile. "They're fine. Just getting a very nice nap. They will start waking up in a half hour or so. You'll want everyone to be out of that room by then; the boys will be confused and a bit annoyed. I'll stop by tomorrow and make sure they're back to normal, but there's no need to worry tonight." He held out a plastic bag with the two darts inside. "I assume you want these."

"Yeah, do you know where they could have been purchased?" Bert asked.

"Any vet supply."

"Do you carry them?"

Mark shook his head. "No." He chuckled. "I'd end up shooting myself in the butt, I'm afraid."

Bert nodded and continued to write in his notebook. "Have you heard of anyone looking for donkeys?"

"No." Mark shook his head. "It makes no sense to steal Tom and Huck. I know of at least three donkeys in the county for sale. There might be more, but those are the three that I'm aware of."

"If I have more questions, can I call you tomorrow?"

"You bet," Mark said and put out his hand. "Good to see you."

Bert shook it and walked with Mark to the front door, essentially leaving Polly standing alone.

"No big deal," she muttered. "They're my donkeys and my horses. By all means, walk off and don't bother with me any longer. I don't feel slighted at all."

"Polly?" Bert turned and spoke.

"Yeah?"

"I'll let you know if we find anything."

"Thanks."

He and Mark left together and she turned back to the donkeys' stall. Elva had stood and was talking animatedly to Eliseo in the corner beside the broken door.

"What's going on?" Polly whispered to Rebecca.

"They're arguing about him sleeping here tonight. She says that his life doesn't have to revolve around this place."

"Hey, guys," Polly said. When Elva and Eliseo turned to her, she continued. "I'll stay here tonight."

"That's ridiculous," Eliseo said. "Henry needs you and there is no reason for me to be at the house. I need to repair this door. You both know I've slept here before."

"You have a perfectly good bed," Elva protested.

"I might have a better idea," Polly said. "What if I call Jason and ask if he'd want to spend the night here with one of his friends. They'd think it was a great adventure."

"I still need to repair the door."

"Elva, if you want to go home and be with your kids, I'll bring Eliseo out as soon as Jason arrives. How does that sound?" Polly asked. "Maybe you could take Rebecca home for me?"

Rebecca frowned at Polly. "I'm staying with you."

"Are you sure? It's Kayla's last night there."

"It's not our last night of being friends. She'll understand. I'm staying."

Elva walked toward Polly. "I'm sorry," she said quietly. She took Polly's arm, leading her out into the main alley. "He's been having trouble sleeping. I can't tell if it's physical or emotional pain."

"You do know that he finds peace here at the barn," Polly replied. "I've found him sleeping here in Demi's stall when things have gotten bad for him."

Elva deflated. "I never know the right thing to do for him. I'll go on home. Tell him to text me if he's staying, okay?" She stalked toward the main door and walked out, not stopping to speak with or touch any of the horses.

Polly hated stepping between those two. Their tenuous relationship had gotten better this last year, but Elva hadn't been part of her brother's life for years and was unsure how or when he wanted her around.

"What do you want me to do, Eliseo?" Polly asked when she went back into the stall.

He shrugged and knelt beside Tom to scratch the donkey's head. It was one of his go-to calming mechanisms. If an animal was nearby when Eliseo was stressed, his first response was to reach out to it. Polly had seen this in him over and over. She watched him take a few deep breaths.

"I need to fix that door." He waited for Rebecca to follow Polly out and then closed the stall behind them.

"If you want to stay here by yourself tonight, all you have to do is send Elva a text. I won't call Jason. This is up to you."

"Give me a few minutes," he said. Instead of walking into the feed room, Eliseo went down the alley to Nan's stall. He opened the door and slipped in. Polly dropped onto a bench and Rebecca sat down beside her.

"What's wrong?" Rebecca asked in a low voice.

"He's stressed. Nan brings him back to center."

Rebecca nodded. "Kind of like you and Henry."

Polly put her arm around Rebecca's shoulder and pulled her close. "Yeah. Kinda like that."

"Do you think he feels that way about Sylvie, too?"

"I don't know," Polly said. "People are different. We all have expectations of him. He's so driven because he does his best to meet everyone's expectations. These horses are pretty straightforward. Feed them and take care of them and they'll offer you indomitable strength as a response."

"That's a big word."

"They're big horses."

"Do you feel that way about Demi?"

Polly nodded. "There have been times I've relied on his indomitable strength."

"Sometimes I cry into Wonder's back," Rebecca said.

"I get that. I've done the same to Obiwan."

"Really?"

"That's why we love our pets so much. They don't judge us when we fall apart. They don't expect us to come up with reasons or have a conversation about why we're falling apart. All they want is to be close. And if that closeness helps, then they're satisfied."

"It really is that simple, isn't it?"

"Yeah." Polly stood up. "Let's get a bottle of water. I wouldn't be surprised to find some of Sylvie's goodies in the fridge."

"I'd love a brownie." Rebecca ran ahead of Polly. "It's weird to think about best friends and boyfriends and moms and dads and then add pets, too. Everybody has a different role in your life, even cats and dogs. I never thought about not having to explain anything to Wonder. She lets me cry it out. Do you think Henry ever does that with Han?"

Polly opened the refrigerator and handed Rebecca a bottle, then took one for herself. She lifted the lid of a plastic container and grinned. "I knew there would be something here. It's not just a chocolate brownie, looks like cheesecake, too."

"Those are my favorite!" Rebecca took two and held her hand out so Polly could pluck one away. "So, what do you think about Henry? And what about Hayden and Heath? They don't have a pet that they can cry on when they're upset."

"I don't know," Polly said. She sat down on a sawhorse. There were a couple of comfortable chairs in here. One was filled with catalogs and Rebecca took the other.

"Do you think they ever cry?"

"I don't know that, either. I know they have. It's not something we talk about a lot."

"Kayla asked me if you guys were going to sue that girl who crashed into Henry."

"No," Polly said.

"Why not? She shouldn't have been texting and driving. The whole thing was her fault."

"What if you had been the driver?"

"I wouldn't have been texting and driving."

Polly looked at her. "Really?"

"It's illegal."

"I'll ask again. Really? Everybody makes bad decisions and to get all judgmental about someone else's bad decisions makes you look dumb, because yours are out there for people to see, too. And sometimes kids do stupid things because they think no one will catch them. Am I right?"

Rebecca looked at the ground. "You aren't going to forget that any time soon."

"Nope, but the truth is, people make bad decisions every day and kids are the worst. They haven't experienced enough yet to have the wisdom to avoid mistakes. We aren't about to rub salt in the wounds she's created for herself. Her family's insurance will handle it, but if we have to handle part, we will. It's not worth destroying her life or the lives of her parents for this. They have enough of a difficult road ahead of them with her recuperation. Why would we make that worse?"

"Lots of other people would."

"Then that's their decision. It just isn't ours. By the time you get to my age, you'll realize that people gave you a great deal of grace as you were growing up. The least you can do is return it in kind when it's the right time."

Polly's phone rang. She bit her lip when she saw that it was Henry. "And here I am about to ask for more grace. I totally forgot to call Henry."

"You've been kinda busy."

"Yeah. I was only going to pick up a dog. We should have been home a couple of hours ago." She swiped open the call and said, "I'm so sorry."

"Are you okay? Tell me you didn't find a dead body out at the Mikkels' place."

"No, and Joss isn't driving to Indiana tomorrow. Nate called and his dad is fine. It was a pulled muscle. His mom kinda went out of control. I should have called you. I was helping Joss pack for the trip before he called."

"Okay. Are you leaving any time soon?"

"Do you need something?"

"No, but Elijah and Noah wanted to say goodnight. Hayden and Heath have been hauling things up to their rooms while Kayla and Stephanie have been filling boxes up and taking them to the foyer. I finally escaped up to our bedroom and shut the door. Too much chaos around here."

"Rebecca and I are at the barn," Polly said.

"Why? Did something happen?" He chuckled. "Did you need to use the bathroom?"

"Someone tried to steal the donkeys. Everything's fine, but I had to call Bert Bradford and Mark Ogden. They're gone now and we're waiting to see if I need to take Eliseo home."

"You aren't going to tell me the story right now?"

"If you'll let me get away with it, I'd prefer telling you face to face. I am sorry about not calling. It's been one thing after another."

"What about Noah and Elijah?"

"Tell them to get ready for bed and go into their room and read until I get home. I don't care how late they're up tonight, but they should start settling down. Are you okay with that?"

"You bet. Come home and tell me stories."

"I've got 'em," she replied. "Thank you. I love you. Are you heading out with Heath tomorrow?"

"I can't be trapped inside one more day. Evelyn said I can go." The last sounded like a pleading child.

"Then if she said so, it's okay. Will you be able to sleep tonight?"

"I feel better. Let's hope so. Send me a text if you're driving out to Eliseo's, okay?"

"I'll try. I love you."

"I love you too."

"You don't get into much trouble with him, do you?" Rebecca asked when Polly put the phone down.

"As long as I'm honest, he understands."

"That's a big thing with you two."

"Honesty?"

"Yeah. It's what always gets me into trouble."

"When you lie, I get angrier than when you screw up. It's so disrespectful to me. It's as if you think I'm ignorant."

"I know you aren't. I can't help it. I do try, though."

"You keep trying and I'll keep expecting the truth. We'll get there. And besides, I love you." Polly smiled and looked at the door as she heard Eliseo approach. "How are things?"

"I called Elva. I don't want to ask the boys to come out at this hour. I'll be fine here by myself."

Polly stood and reached her hand out to Rebecca. "That's fine, then. I appreciate this a lot. I wouldn't be able to leave them alone tonight."

He nodded, but wouldn't look her in the eye. "I'll talk to the boys about camping here this weekend. If we give them a little notice, they can make a party of it." He backed out of the door as she and Rebecca approached.

Stopping in front of him, Polly touched his arm. "I can't thank you enough for being here tonight. And Elva, too. It means the world to me that you two showed up to calm the horses down." She walked over to look inside the donkeys' stall. "And these boys too." Huck lifted his head and looked around, surprised at where he was. He struggled to get his feet under him. "They're waking up."

"I should fix that door right away," Eliseo said. "Don't worry about us. We'll be fine."

"I know you will be. Thanks for everything. Come on, Rebecca."

Rebecca took Polly's hand as they walked to the other end of the barn, past the four horses. Polly turned around and smiled. She still couldn't believe this was part of her world. Even in the mess of this evening, she was thankful for these animals and the people who cared for them.

CHAPTER SIXTEEN

"I told you to watch out! You're going to drop it!"

Polly tried not to laugh as Heath and Hayden carried a dresser up the stairs into Stephanie's apartment. Heath was always going to be the younger brother and Hayden would always tell him what to do.

"I got this," Heath said. "You watch out for your end. You're going to jam that foot into her wall."

She knew exactly how lucky she was to have two healthy young men who were willing to help. Her dad had helped her move into her last apartment in Boston. The two of them had carried everything she owned across town in a rented truck and piece by heavy piece taken it in and put it all in place. Sal would have been useless and she hadn't known Drea's brothers long enough to ask them to help.

Polly smiled to herself. She had a wonderful family here in Bellingwood, but sometimes she missed Drea and her family. She couldn't believe how lucky she was that Sal had moved to Iowa.

When Polly cleared the top step, Stephanie read the top of the box and pointed her to the other side of the living room.

"I don't know where to put half this stuff yet," Stephanie said. "This place is going to be a wreck for a long time."

"Whatever," Polly said. "You'll have it all put together by the time you go back to work on Monday if I know you."

Skylar and Jason came up the steps with another dresser.

"That goes into Kayla's room," Stephanie said. "Along the west wall. Put it anywhere and we'll adjust."

Polly waited for Kayla and Rebecca to go past with more boxes and went back down the steps.

"How are you two doing in there?" she asked Noah and Elijah.

The two boys were sitting in the bed of her truck waiting for small boxes to be uncovered. They were under orders to stay close to the truck until they could help, so Hayden had lifted them into the bed so they could watch it all happen.

"I'm bored," Elijah said. "Can't I carry anything?"

"I'll bet you could take this up." Polly lifted up a fabric grocery tote bag, jammed with toiletries. A second bag filled with cosmetics and hair items was beside it and she handed that to Noah. "Stay upstairs and don't get in anyone's way. Got it?"

The boys wriggled around the chairs and tables still in Polly's truck. They jumped down from the tailgate, each taking a bag and running up the steps.

"Beds next," Hayden said.

Heath moaned. "I hate mattresses."

Henry and Heath had gotten home early this afternoon. Fortunately, Henry's crews usually shut down by four o'clock on Fridays, because today, he was absolutely exhausted. He had walked in the side door, kissed Polly, then went upstairs to fall into bed. Hayden had other plans for his brother. The two boys had hauled their own beds and dressers upstairs at the Bell House. Hayden was intent on spending the night in their new rooms. He'd gotten most everything else carried up during the day and was ready to be finished on the first floor.

After they vacated the living room, Polly had walked in. It was always surprising how dirty a room could get even when you worked to keep it clean. Scrubbing this room down would be a good project for Rebecca next week. Polly could hardly wait to put her to work.

"These are the last two," Hayden said. "Then we're done. Think how well you'll sleep tonight. You'll be exhausted and in your own room, without me snoring to keep you awake."

Andrew came back down the steps and grabbed two of the straight-backed chairs from the bed of Polly's truck.

They had plenty of help, and soon everything would at least be in Stephanie's apartment.

When Stephanie had talked to the Worths about moving in this evening, the older couple decided that dinner and a movie would be a perfect way for them to spend the evening. What a great way to handle this. They wouldn't have to listen to the noise of people going up and down the stairway, banging furniture back and forth, and none of this group would worry about disturbing them.

By the time the last box was stacked against a wall and Stephanie had made a final check of the vehicles to ensure nothing else needed to be moved, everyone had dropped into a chair or sat on the floor, waiting for the air conditioning to catch back up.

Stephanie, red-faced and with sweat dripping from her forehead, stepped into the kitchen doorway. "I didn't think you'd want pizza tonight."

They all looked at her, confused.

"Isn't that what you're always supposed to offer? Pizza when people help you move?" she asked. "Anyway, Jeff and Rachel should be here any time." Stephanie looked at her watch. "They're bringing ice cream and toppings. Grab another pop out of the fridge if you want. Kayla and I can't tell you how much we appreciate your help. This went a lot faster than I thought."

"While we're sitting around, we could help you make sure your furniture is where you want it," Hayden said.

Heath must have made a noise because his brother glared at him.

Hayden stood up and put his hand out for Heath to grab. "Let's put those beds together first." He hauled Heath up from the floor and they headed into the Kayla's room.

"Do you want help unpacking your kitchen?" Polly asked, standing up from where she was sitting. "I can do that."

Stephanie shook her head and smiled. "I'd rather take my time and figure out where I want everything, if you don't mind, but thank you."

"I get that. This is the fun stuff. Do you like the living room?"

"The couch is nicer than the one I had at the other apartment. I can't believe Mrs. Worth is letting us use all of this."

"If I were you, I'd have a hard time ever leaving this apartment," Polly said. "It's cute. Is there *anything* I can help you do?"

Stephanie looked around at the boxes. "I have no idea where things are. We were in such a hurry to move out of that apartment that we jammed things in boxes. I tried to label them."

"You haven't looked in them for a couple of months either," Polly said. "Are you okay for dishes until you're unpacked?"

"We have plastic cutlery and paper plates. I can't wait to cook our first meal in the kitchen. I'm going to have to learn how to use a convection oven, but Rachel says it's no big deal and if I need help, she'll teach me."

They turned at the sound of footsteps on the stairs.

"No one will be able to surprise you," Polly said.

"That's good." Stephanie was already at the door and opened it to Jeff and Kristen. "Welcome to our new home. Come in. I thought Rachel was coming?"

Jeff smiled. "She said she'd come over next week. Billy was taking her to a show in Ames. It came up at the last minute and Anita got tickets for all of them."

"Cool. We only just finished unloading, so nothing is put away yet. They're putting beds together in the bedrooms. What do you think?"

The relationship between Stephanie and Jeff was something quite special. She trusted him with her life and looked at him as a brother and protector. When she first began working at Sycamore House, she'd had a bit of crush on him, but that had worn off and left them with a great friendship. What she had with Skylar was growing into a nice relationship, too. Polly was a little surprised at how easily Stephanie trusted these two men after what her father had put her through. Both Skylar and Jeff were good men and understood how much Stephanie needed them to be honorable. They might make mistakes, but they wouldn't fail her.

"Where do you want us to put this bed?" a voice yelled from one of the bedrooms.

"Jeff, could you put the ice cream stuff out on the kitchen counter?" Stephanie asked. "I'll be right back."

Kristen followed him out to the kitchen and then came back into the living room and sat down beside Noah on the sofa. "Did you carry a lot of boxes up?"

"No. Just a few things. They said I'm too small."

She slumped her shoulders and sighed. "That's too bad. I'll bet you wanted to help."

Elijah jumped up from where he'd been peeking into a box and sat beside his brother. "I wanted to help, too."

"You are probably good helpers."

"We helped Hayden carry things up to his new room today. Then he let us put his clothes away. I can't reach the top drawers yet, but he brought a chair over so I could. Noah made sure all of the clothes were folded up neat and I put them in the drawers. Hayden said we did a good job."

Polly smiled. Those two wanted to be involved in everything, even if it required them to work.

"I'm sure you did a good job," Kristen said.

Jason and Skylar came out into the living room, looked around and then turned back.

"We beat you," Jason yelled.

"Just by a minute," Heath yelled back.

The four boys came into the living room.

"Beds are set up and where they want them," Hayden said. He turned to Jason. "We pushed the dresser into place for Kayla and made sure her desk was where she wanted it. Check that out."

Skylar started laughing. "Okay, so you're faster than us, but you had all of that extra help."

"I'm not sure those three constitute extra help," Stephanie said, coming out, followed by Kayla, Rebecca, and Andrew. "Let's have ice cream."

Polly pointed at the basket of clean sheets. "Let me make up your beds while you eat ice cream. That way you can work until you're ready to crash and have a nice fresh bed to drop into."

"I can do that," Stephanie protested.

Looking around at all of the young faces who were anticipating ice cream, Polly suddenly felt old. When had that happened? Everyone else in this room other than Jeff was under the age of thirty. She loved that her kids were growing up with this group of people, but the realization hit her like a ton of bricks. "No. You eat ice cream and then we'll get out of your hair so you and Kayla can start falling in love with your new home. I can do this for you."

She picked up the basket and headed for Kayla's room. She'd helped Stephanie with laundry all summer and knew which sheets belonged to Kayla. She lifted them out and sighed as she stretched the mattress pad across the mattress.

Rebecca walked in. "Can I help?"

"Go eat ice cream. This won't take me long at all."

"Okay, but Kayla wondered if I could spend the night so we can stay up and put her things away."

Polly shook her head. "Not tonight. Let Kayla and Stephanie have their first night together in their new place. You can come over tomorrow."

"But Kayla asked."

"I said 'not tonight,'" Polly repeated.

Rebecca spun on her heels and left the room. It was never going to be easy.

~~~

The ride home was quiet. Jason was heading to the barn after picking up his friend, Scar, so Polly had taken Andrew to his house. Before she'd gone a block, Noah and Elijah were nodding off. Rebecca hadn't said much else to her the rest of the evening and Polly was tired enough that she didn't care. She was fully aware that for the first time in a long time, Rebecca's house was emptier than she was used to.

"Boys?" Polly said after she turned the truck off.

"Huh?" Elijah asked. He woke up and looked around. "We're home?"

"Yeah. Go on in and head upstairs. You should both take a shower before crawling into bed."

"I'm not ready to go to sleep," he said. "Can we stay up for a while."

"Go take your showers and we'll talk about it when you're finished," Polly said.

Rebecca got out of the truck and headed inside.

"That was fun tonight," Elijah said.

"Yes it was." Polly waited for them to exit the truck, made sure the doors were closed, and followed them inside.

Hayden and Heath were already back. She assumed they were upstairs in their rooms since the lights were out on the main floor. Rebecca had gone to her room where she'd stay for the rest of the night. Polly checked the charger to make sure her phone was where it was supposed to be. It did look a little lonely there by itself. It was going to take some adjustment, but they'd be back to normal soon.

She walked up the back steps and down the hall. Heath was sitting on his bed, looking around the room.

"What do you think?" she asked.

"This is so cool. Thank you. I like the curtains, too. You're pretty awesome."

"I'm glad you're here. Thanks for all your work tonight. And thanks for taking care of Henry today. I didn't say that earlier. Did you two have a good day?"

"It was good having him around again. He makes decisions fast. The guys are glad he's back."

She smiled at him. She was weary. This had been a long and crazy week. The door to the bathroom between Hayden and Heath's room was closed and the shower was running, so she assumed Hayden was in there. Polly walked on down toward Noah and Elijah's room and rapped on the door.

"It's me. Polly. You two getting ready for the shower?"

"I'm going first," Elijah said.

"Okay. I'll be in our room if you need me." She headed back to her bedroom and pushed the door all the way open.

Henry was sitting in his recliner watching television. He turned it off when she walked in.

"I'm beat."

"Did you get everything in?"

Polly nodded. "Beds are set up and made. The rest is Stephanie's to deal with. I'm a sweaty mess. Give me a few minutes to get clean and I'll be back. Rebecca's annoyed because I wouldn't let her stay with Kayla, Noah and Elijah are supposed to be taking a shower and Hayden's finishing his. It was hot and humid hauling that stuff. I'm getting too old for that."

"Nah. You're just a baby."

"Uh huh. I can barely stand myself right now. Let me take care of this."

He nodded and turned the television back on.

Polly didn't take long in the shower and felt a million times better when she stepped out. She put on a pair of shorts and a t-shirt, then grabbed her robe and went back into the bedroom. Henry turned the television off again.

"What are you watching?"

"Silly stuff. It will be there later."

"More of *your* silly stuff?"

He laughed. "Yeah. You know I love to watch how things are made."

"I know you do." Polly flopped on the bed and waited for the dogs to readjust so they could be close to her. "Did you get something to eat after your nap?"

"Yeah. I'm good. The dogs have been out and fed. The cats are all fed. You can relax now."

"I'm old, Henry."

"What does that mean?"

"I stood in that apartment tonight with all of those young people and realized that I don't fit in. Jeff is barely thirty, so he's at least kind of close to my age, but the rest of them are kids. Heck — half of them were *my* kids. It was the strangest sensation."

"You aren't old."

"I feel old. All I want to do right now is curl up here and not wake up until Monday. Jason is picking up Scar and they're spending the night in the barn with the horses. Stephanie and Kayla will be up all night unpacking and rearranging. Heck, Skylar will stay until she kicks him out. Rachel and Billy didn't come over because they were going to a club in Ames with Doug and Anita. They're going out late tonight. What is that about? I'm old. That's all I've got."

A light tap on the door and Hayden said, "Guys?"

"Come on in," Henry said after Polly nodded.

"I got a call from friends in Ames. After Heath's out of the shower, we're going over to a party. We won't get back until late. That cool?"

Polly gave Henry a sideways glance. "See. Even ours are going out late tonight." She grinned at Hayden. "That's cool. Just remember to send me a text when you're home."

"Thanks. See you in the morning."

"Don't hurry to get up tomorrow. We'll do breakfast late."

"Okay. Got it." He left and closed the door.

"Poor Rebecca has to be miserable," she said to Henry. "She won't be happy when she finds out they went to a party."

"She'll get over it." Henry yawned. "Didn't she and Kayla spend time with the Mikkels kids today?"

"Yeah. About an hour so Joss could get some things done."

"She's had plenty going on. How were the donkeys? I assume you stopped by to see them while the girls were babysitting."

"They were back to normal. Eliseo saddled them up and let Noah and Elijah ride around the pasture. I have to tell you, that is just about the cutest thing in the world." She shook her head. "Though I still can't imagine why anyone would want to steal Tom and Huck."

"Because they're so well trained. They'd be great on a farm. Everybody around Bellingwood knows those two have been trained to pull carts and let kids on their backs. If you want a donkey, you want one of Eliseo's."

"So bring him a donkey and let him train it. Why go to all that work to steal my boys?"

"Do you think they'll try again?"

"They went to so much work to get them, I really do. I hope we figure it out. It's one thing for Jason and Scar to camp out in the barn over the weekend, but they can't keep doing that."

"Hire a bodyguard for the overnight hours."

Polly laughed out loud. "That's funny."

"I'm serious."

"Eliseo would never let me get away with that. He'd sleep there himself."

"Ask him."

She rolled her eyes. "Enough about my stuff. Heath said you had a good day. How was it really?"

"It was exhausting."

"Yeah. You never take naps when you come home from work."

"It was good to feel like I was kinda normal. Dad's looking for another truck for me." Henry chuckled. "Because I'm still a kid and can't find my own truck."

"He just wants to be part of getting you back to normal."

"I know. He's got a couple of leads. Heath and I will check them out next week." He held up his broken arm. "Don't worry. As soon as I'm allowed to drive, I want to have a truck in place so I can get back to normal. Heath will start school in a few weeks and I won't be able to rely on him."

"You can rely on me, you know."

"I love you, Polly Giller, but I would make you crazy before the end of one of my work days."

"That's your way of telling me that I'd make *you* crazy?"

"Something like that."

Another light tap on their door preceded Elijah's voice. "Can I come in?"

"Come on in, honey," Polly said.

"We're all clean, but Hayden and Heath left. Can we watch TV with you?"

"No. No TV tonight. Why don't you go choose a good book that you both want to hear and I'll come in and read to you. Then you can go to sleep and tomorrow will be another big day."

"Noah said you wouldn't let us. Never hurts to try." Elijah turned and went out into the hallway, then stuck his head back in. "How long?"

"I'll be there in a few minutes." She smiled at Henry. "I want them to stay sweet and innocent forever. Can you please wave your magic wand?"

"Maybe when the cast comes off. Right now the wand feels a little iffy. It might cast the wrong spell."

Polly sat up and patted the bed beside her. Obiwan crawled over. "Shall we go put the boys to sleep? You can sleep with them tonight if you want."

He slithered his body off the bed to stand on the floor and waited for her. Han jumped off the end of the bed and beat them both to the door.

"You can come too, you silly oaf," Polly said.

CHAPTER SEVENTEEN

Not wanting to leave her without knowing that someone was here, Polly waited until Rebecca's knock was answered by Kayla. The girls waved at her and she backed out of the driveway, grateful to have Rebecca out of the house for a few hours. Kayla had called early this morning, asking Rebecca to come over and help her unpack and plan her room.

Noah and Elijah were chattering in the back seat. After a quick trip to Sweet Beans for coffee, they were heading to the barn. She wanted to make sure that last night had gone well with Jason and Scar there alone. Polly considered stopping by to say hello to Beryl since she was just down the street from the Worths, but didn't want to bother her. The woman was head down, trying to finish things for the exhibition at Sycamore House next week. Instead, when Polly left the Worth's driveway, she headed east toward Spruce Street to look around. It was so interesting to her that much of the town backed up onto farm fields.

"Hey, that's Ariel," Noah said, pointing out the window.

She had certainly been hearing a lot about this little girl after meeting her in the coffee shop. Ariel Sutter was standing in the driveway of a small home. The house sat on a huge plot of land with several sheds and small barns. Pieces of equipment, a small tractor and other implements were parked in front of the largest building. The land right up to the back of the house and buildings was either freshly tilled or had things growing. Polly had no hope of identifying any of it. She'd heard about a small organic farm in town and wondered if this was it. Apparently, the family sold to quite a few restaurants who wanted to offer locally sourced produce — everything from blueberries and strawberries to tomatoes, cucumbers, sweet peas and beans.

Ariel looked up and started to wave, then turned and ran into the large building.

"Huh," Polly said. "I never would have paid attention to this if you hadn't recognized her." She'd been past it several times, but it blended in with the landscape of the community.

The Sutters didn't participate in any of the local community projects with their produce. Eliseo was thrilled to be able to offer the surplus from his gardens, as were many others in town. After meeting the couple one time, it wasn't surprising. They weren't friendly, and evidently had no desire to make friends with the people who were their neighbors.

She drove on around and came back down Walnut Street. Glancing at Beryl's house, Polly was surprised to see the woman standing on her porch, until Polly realized she was looking through the mail that had just been delivered. Polly pulled into the driveway. "We're not staying," she said to the boys. "I'm only saying hello."

Beryl came over to the truck and Polly opened her door.

"What are you sweet things doing here?" Beryl asked. "Do you want to come in?"

"No, we won't stay. I know you're busy. I dropped Rebecca off down the street."

"The Worths are good people. Stephanie landed in a good place there. You know they built that apartment out for their son. He had a whole mess of issues and couldn't live on his own, but they did their best to give him a sense of independence."

"How long has he been gone?"

"It's been at least ten years now — he was pretty young when he died. They've rented it off and on since then. He was their only child. They'll like having Stephanie and Kayla there. Nora is a good soul. Orville took his son's death kinda hard and he's pretty gruff. Felt like life didn't give him a fair shake."

"I hope this works out for everyone. Stephanie is excited."

"A new home is always exciting," Beryl said with a smile. "What are you doing today?"

"Coffee and then over to the barn to see the horses and donkeys."

"Heard there was a little excitement the other night. Sylvie told us that Eliseo spent the night there."

Polly nodded. "I'm worried."

"We rode the donkeys yesterday," Elijah said, poking his head over the front seat.

Beryl looked in and smiled back at Noah. "You two were so quiet I didn't know you were here."

"I was just being polite," Elijah said with a big grin on his face. "Polly's teaching me."

"She's a good teacher."

"So … the Sutters …" Polly pointed back the way she'd come.

Beryl rolled her eyes. "Yeah. Friendly folk."

"What do they do back there? Is that the farm I hear about?"

"They've got a nice-sized production going. Lots of different types of things. They provide seasonal produce from April to after October. Don't know how they do it all with just the two of them. They hire temporary workers to harvest the bigger crops, but then those people always move on. She won't hire anyone permanent — doesn't want to be responsible for them, I guess. The rest of us try to ignore that they're back there. They stay quiet for the most part. Sometimes we have to deal with flatbeds coming through to haul produce away, but it's no big deal."

"I've seen those go through town," Polly said. "There are so many things that happen around me and it never occurs to me that I should ask questions. Are you ready for your exhibit?"

Beryl pursed her lips. "I am. We're moving my entire front room over there this afternoon."

"What?"

"That painting of the tree I have? Jeff thinks that if he relocates it to Sycamore House, he should take the chairs and tables, along with my vases and flower arrangements." Beryl gave a small laugh. "I don't think he's going to give any of it back either. Now I have to come up with a brand-new decorating theme for that room. Maybe I'll put a hot tub in there and open the curtains when I …" She looked into the truck and tossed a wicked smile at Polly. "I believe I enjoy entertaining my neighbors. Even with my sixty-three-year-old hot self."

"You go, girl," Polly said. "Just don't ask me to join you."

"Actually, I might re-paint the walls to look like an English garden with hollyhocks and wisteria and other pretty flowers. It would make a lovely tea room, don't you think?"

"You have the most creative ideas. Let me know if I can help you."

"I believe that I will spend time with our local antique dealer and see what he might come up with for me," Beryl said. She smiled. "Instead of complaining about your Mr. Jeff taking away my furniture, maybe I should tell him how wonderful he is because I get an opportunity to do something new and creative. Yes. That's it. I haven't painted roses and phlox in quite some time. A pale yellow-green background would be a good place to begin." Beryl turned and slowly wandered back to her house, talking to herself the entire time.

Polly sat in the driveway with her truck's door open until Beryl went inside and shut the front door.

"Put your seatbelt back on," she said to Elijah.

"Did she know that she didn't say goodbye?" he asked.

"No," Polly replied with a laugh. "She was thinking about something else completely."

She headed south on Walnut, marveling that there were still plenty of surprises for her in Bellingwood. She had lived here for nearly five years now and still didn't feel as if she knew everyone who lived in town. About the time she felt as if she had a handle on things, something like Sutter's Farm leapt out at her and she realized how much there was yet to learn.

"Polly?" Noah was sitting forward in his seat.

"What?"

"I asked you if we could go see Grandma Marie."

"Sure, honey. Is there something you want to do over there?"

"No. I just miss her."

Polly put her hand over her heart. What a little sweetie. She pulled into the Lutheran Church parking lot and took out her phone. "Let me see what she's doing today."

"I didn't mean we had to go now."

"It's okay. I'll ask her."

Polly waited as the phone rang.

"Hello Polly," Marie said. "How are things today?"

"Everything is fine."

Marie chuckled. "You know, I worry a little when you call me. I know I shouldn't, but I do. What's up?"

"I was wondering when you might have time to play with two little boys."

"Noah and Elijah?"

"Yeah." Polly didn't want to land the guilt of Noah missing her on Marie. She'd tell her after they'd set up a time. That would make Marie feel wonderful.

"I was just thinking about them. Bill and I picked up tomatoes and corn this morning and I'm setting up to do some canning. We talked about heading out tomorrow to pick raspberries for jelly. Would they like to spend the weekend with us? We'd love to have them."

"Let me ask," Polly replied with a smile. She turned in her seat. "Grandma wants to know if you two would like to spend the weekend with her. She's going to work in the kitchen today canning tomatoes and then tomorrow she's going to pick raspberries to make jelly. Are you interested?"

Elijah bounced — like he always did when he got excited. "I'm interested. Does that sound like fun, Noah?"

Noah's eyes lit up with joy. "All weekend?"

"Whenever you're ready to come home tomorrow, you can come home. What do you think?"

"Can we go now?" he asked.

"Instead of going to the barn?"

Both boys grew solemn and looked at each other. As if in unspoken agreement, they smiled back at Polly.

"Can we see the horses on Monday instead?" Noah asked.

"Absolutely." She put the phone back to her ear. "I have them in the truck right now. We can either go home and pack their things or I would be glad to bring them over and drop clothes off later."

"Bring the boys now," Marie said. "Bill found Henry's old wagon in the shop last week. He's been cleaning it up for them."

"We'll be right there. Thank you." Polly ended the call. She drove through the parking lot and out the other side, heading for the Sturtz's. "Thank you for asking, Noah," she said. "I don't always remember how much you like going over there."

"I love it," he said. "When you bring my clothes, will you bring the book on my bed?"

"Grandma doesn't have any good books?"

He stopped and thought for a minute. "She has great books. Never mind. You don't have to bring any clothes for me if you don't want to. I can sleep in my t-shirt."

"Me too," Elijah said.

"I'll bring clean clothes to you. Grandma has you take a shower at night, doesn't she?"

"Yeah."

"And you don't want to put dirty clothes back on your clean bodies."

"Okay," Elijah said with a big sigh. "If you insist."

She laughed until she snorted. "I do. Maybe I'll bring extras and we can leave them at Grandma's house."

"There's an empty dresser in the room where we sleep. Maybe she'd let us put clothes in there."

"I'll bet she would."

Polly drove in and parked beside the house. The boys jumped out of the truck and ran to the door where Marie was waiting for them. She waved at Polly and hugged each boy as they passed her when going inside. Rather than waiting for Polly to get out, Marie followed them in, so Polly backed up and drove away. Two down. She fully expected Rebecca to call her asking to spend the night with Kayla. That would leave Hayden and Heath, who were planning to be gone again tonight. Hayden's friends were beginning to return to Ames in preparation for the school year. Though the first day of classes was still a few weeks away, there were plenty of things going on to draw students back early. Hayden enjoyed showing his brother around campus and introducing him to his friends. Once Heath got involved in his own classes, he'd meet friends closer to his age, but he was getting more and more comfortable about where things were on campus due to his brother's attention.

Polly had to drive around the block and ended up parking along the side of Sweet Beans. Parking spaces were filled downtown today. She liked seeing that. There were still several empty spaces, but there was more life down here than ever before and it was exciting. She walked through the patio area and inside, glad to find people scattered at tables around the large room.

Skylar was behind the counter, talking to two high school aged girls who were obviously flirting with him. He caught Polly's eye and smiled. She shook her head. The girls went back and forth between him and the bakery displays, finally settling on something. There was much too much giggling as they took their plates and drinks and settled into a booth.

"Hi Polly," he said. "Your usual?"

"Just a cold brew today. You have fans."

"What do you mean?"

"You're kidding me, right?"

Skylar gave her a small frown. "No. What?"

"They were flirting with you."

"Aww, they were just being nice. They're sweet girls."

"I'll bet. How late were you at Stephanie's last night?"

He blushed and turned to pour her coffee.

"I didn't mean anything," Polly said. "I only wondered how late everyone worked to help them get unpacked." Then she grinned. "Did you spend the night?"

"I slept on the couch."

She laughed out loud. "Seriously, Sky. It's none of my business. I wasn't trying to put you on the spot. This whole conversation happened because I simply wondered how they were doing getting settled in."

"We worked until about one o'clock. Kayla fell asleep around eleven thirty, then Stephanie and I finished unpacking the kitchen. I'm going back after work. Did you take Rebecca over? I know Kayla wanted her help."

"Yeah. She's there now. I suspect they'll try to talk us into letting her spend the night."

"Kayla said it was weird to not be around her."

"It will take some getting used to. We've enjoyed having them stay with us this summer." Polly took the cup from him and dropped a dollar in the tip jar. "It was nice getting to know you better, too. You're okay."

"I'm going to miss hanging out with those little boys. They're sweeties."

Polly sent a quick glance to the girls who were still giggling and looking at Skylar. "So are they. I'll leave you to your adoring fans."

"Stop it," he said. "I had no idea."

"That makes it all that much more fun." She headed out the side door and went back to her truck. With no kids at home, she might actually get things done. Either that or she was going to take a nap. Henry had finally slept through most of the night last night which meant that she did as well, but it still wasn't enough. Just the thought of it made her yawn. She took a long drink of her coffee when she got in the truck. She headed home, wondering what Henry had done with himself today. When she'd been out of commission with a broken collarbone, she'd nearly lost her mind. Henry was even more active than she was so Polly couldn't imagine the frustration he had to be feeling — especially now that he didn't hurt quite as much. Evelyn had checked on him one last time earlier this morning and removed the large bandage on his face for good, declaring it to be healing nicely. The stitches would come out early this week and Henry told Polly that Heath would take him in for that — she didn't need to worry. It was a little creepy to see him with a bright red scar and stitches, but she kept reminding herself that he was alive and healthy.

Heath and Hayden were painting something in the grass beside the garage when she pulled into the driveway. Grabbing up her coffee, she jumped out and walked over to them. "What are you doing?"

"We're waiting on the first coat to dry," Hayden said. "Henry showed us this old table in the garage and said it was a piece of crap and not worth refinishing, but it's solid and he thought it might be good for your sewing machine."

"This is for me?"

Heath nodded. "We're putting primer on it and then you can tell us what color you want it. I'll run up to the hardware store and get it. If we can finish tonight, we'll move it in for you tomorrow."

Hayden nodded toward the garage. "There's an old buffet in there that you could use to store your fabric and stuff. There's another old dresser up in the attic if you want to use that, too."

"I want to use the buffet in the dining room. It goes with the set," Polly said.

He shook his head. "No, not that one. There's another one in the back. It's scarred on top. Like someone put a machine on it or something. We could haul it to the shop and sand that."

"I have a sander," Polly said. "If the top is badly scarred, we should paint it. I'm thinking bright, wild colors."

Heath looked at her, his eyes big. "Bright and wild?"

"Yeah. Paint the table blue. Maybe paint the dresser a wild yellow with teal and pink accents and paint the buffet a bright red."

"You're kidding me, right?" he asked.

She shrugged. "Kinda. Not really. I'd like to do bold and wild colors. If I can't have a natural wood finish, then I'm certainly not painting things brown or grey or black. Maybe I'll let Rebecca loose on these things. She can go crazy with spray paint and then do complementary canvases for the walls." Polly nodded. "I love that idea. I'll give her a call and see what she thinks. Thank you for bringing this out and if you want to retrieve that buffet, you might as well prime it. Let's just say you're prepping the canvas for the artist."

Pulling out her phone, she went inside and dialed Rebecca's number.

"Hello? Polly? Is everything okay?"

"Yeah. I had a thought. Do you want to do wild spray painting on furniture for my sewing room?"

"Okay … what do you mean?"

"Your brothers are preparing furniture to be painted, but I don't want boring. I want you to go crazy. Are you up for it?"

"That would be fun."

"Fantastic. How are things there?"

"This is such a cute apartment. I can't wait to get my own place someday. Not now, not for a long time, but someday."

"You'll have fun, but I'm not ready for you to move out on your own yet."

"Can I spend tonight with Kayla? Stephanie already said it would be okay. She's out right now getting groceries. Sky is coming over and she's making a fancy dinner."

"Yeah, sure. Have fun and I'll see you tomorrow."

"Thank you!" Rebecca shouted. "Kayla, she said I can stay!"

Polly heard Kayla's shout in the background. "Noah and Elijah are staying at Marie and Bill's tonight, so the house is going to be empty. I'll be glad to have you all home tomorrow night."

"Thank you again. And I can't wait to paint those things for you. You're the best."

"I love you too."

CHAPTER EIGHTEEN

Running up the back steps, Polly headed for the bedroom, only to discover no one there. "Henry?" she called out. When there was no response, she wandered back down the hallway to peek into the bedroom that was about to become an all-purpose sewing and craft room. The buffet would work perfectly at the end of the room under the windows. While the table would work for now, she wanted something bigger for the many projects that she and the kids worked on. And one small dresser wouldn't hold much. Maybe Henry would build cabinets and shelves in this room down the road. She could be patient. Working out of tubs and boxes was fine. This house needed his attention in other places.

Every time they came up from the kitchen, they passed through the unused wing of this second floor. Polly hadn't stepped foot into the rooms there in months, always in a hurry to get somewhere else. The rooms had ugly, dingy walls. A couple of them had been re-wallpapered, but it was peeling away and looked horrible. She had no interest in trying to restore any of that. Unless something came up, those bedrooms and the bathroom on that end could wait until next summer. Hopefully

Hayden would be around again to help with the demolition and reconstruction. She didn't hold out much hope that Heath would be free. Once he began feeling more confident about what he was learning, he would drop into Henry's business with ease. It was a catch-22. She loved having him here working on the house, but if he and Henry shared more responsibility, that would make it easier for Henry to be around. Maybe they could even take a family vacation.

Marie had pushed and encouraged them to go away with the kids this summer. Polly had ended up taking five kids to the Grotto of the Redemption in West Bend on a Saturday. Henry hadn't been able to take the time. Noah and Elijah were awestruck. They went from one display to the next and could barely contain their excitement. The three older kids — Kayla, Andrew, and Rebecca — took it more in stride, but eventually, the little boys' excitement rubbed off on all of them. Then, one by one, each of the kids was overwhelmed by the story that was told in marble and stone. It had been a wonderful day, but it hadn't been a family vacation.

Polly went down the back steps and into the kitchen. "Henry? Where are you?"

There was still no response.

She wandered down the hallway and peeked into the family room to see if he'd fallen asleep. He wasn't there. Kayla's bedroom was empty and so was the room where Stephanie had stayed. They needed to do a lot of work to clean those rooms again and finish them for use. Polly could hardly wait.

"Henry?"

"In here," he said.

"Where is here?"

"The living room."

She walked through the library, into the bathroom and then into the living room. "There you are. I've been looking all over."

"Sorry. I heard you call from the kitchen, but I was on the phone." He held it out, then put it in his pocket.

"What are you doing?"

"Just looking around. Things are empty down here again."

"Isn't it great?"

He smiled at her. "I guess so. After all that's been going on this summer, things are so quiet. Where are Noah and Elijah?"

"Your mom wanted them to spend the weekend and Rebecca is spending the night with Kayla." She grinned. "Hayden and Heath are going out again. Believe it or not, it's just us tonight."

Henry reached his hand out to her and she took it. "I've missed just us. I know that I've been way out of it this week. You and I connected better when I was working every day. I'm sorry."

"Don't be sorry," she said, leaning against his good arm. "You've been healing." She huffed a laugh. "I'm not very good at being a caregiver. I never know whether you need me to help you or leave you alone and I tend to just leave you alone."

"That was fine. I can't bear it when people hover. You were there when I needed you."

Polly looked up at his head. "Your hair is clean." Then she sniffed. "You're *all* clean. What did you do?"

"I took a shower."

"You aren't messing with me, are you?"

"I jerry-rigged a big plastic bag for my cast and once Evelyn said my face wouldn't be a problem, I showered. It was awesome. I feel like a human being again."

"You waited until I was gone, didn't you?"

He chuckled. "Maybe."

"Since you're all fresh and clean, do you want to go out tonight?"

"Yes, please," he said. "I'm tired of this house. Where shall we go?"

"We could go to Davey's." Polly shrugged. "I suppose we could go up to the Alehouse."

Henry shook his head. "I don't want to put up with that noise tonight. Davey's would be great."

"There's a group playing music out at Secret Woods. After dinner, we could sit on their patio and drink wine."

"A real date night."

"Yeah." Polly wrapped her arm around his waist. "What do you think?"

"I could be up for that. Should we invite friends?"

She hadn't wanted to even ask. It was enough that he wanted to leave the house, but inviting friends was always a welcome choice. "Who? Nate's coming back into town today. They won't want to go."

"Sylvie and Eliseo? Or are they working a wedding reception?"

"Probably." Polly could hardly breathe. He'd never considered them as friends to go out to dinner with before. This was kind of cool. "Mark and Sal?"

"Yeah," he said. "Sure. Do you want to give her a call? She'll need a babysitter, right?"

"Right." Polly laughed. "I'm glad we have the night free. And I'm glad I have built-in babysitters with Rebecca, Hayden and Heath. I would hate having to figure that out every time I wanted go somewhere. I'll call her. What are you doing in here?"

"Just trying to get a feel for the space. I was in the office and the library. I want Heath to help me build the bookshelves and cabinets for the library. It will be good practice for him. He likes the idea of transforming the door to the bathroom into a bookcase. I'm going to show him next week how to measure for it. Do you know who he wants to impress with that?"

Polly shook her head.

"Andrew. He can hardly wait for Andrew to see it, so we're not telling anyone — not Rebecca, not the little boys, no one."

"That sounds great," Polly said with a smile. "I'm excited about that room. I'd love to get a dark walnut table. Not a large one, but something the kids can use as a study table. We'll put a couple of those green banker's lamps on it. Then I want to find two wing chairs and a little round end table for that rounded corner. You won't build bookcases there, will you?"

Henry heaved a big sigh. "I can build bookcases on a curve."

"I didn't even dare hope. You can't bend wood, though."

"I can curve a thin sheet of plywood for the back, but I'll cut the shelves out of larger pieces."

Polly smacked her forehead with the base of her hand. "I didn't even think of that. Then, cool. I get bookshelves in the curve."

"It's never going to be easy with you, is it?" He hugged her close. "Go call Sal. This is the first day I've felt like a normal human being and I want to wander these rooms a little longer."

Polly reached up to kiss his cheek and went back into the hallway, then into the foyer. She headed up the steps to the second floor while waiting for Sal to answer her phone.

"Hello there," Sal said. "What's up?"

"Do you have plans tonight? Henry and I were thinking of going to Davey's for dinner and then to Secret Woods for wine and music."

"He's doing better? That's great."

"Yeah. He was out at the job sites yesterday with Heath, but he's still got cabin fever. What do you think?"

Sal hesitated. "I can't believe I'm about to say this, but I need to check with Mark and see if I can find a babysitter. When did I turn into this person?" She laughed. "My first reaction was to say yes, then I had to get responsible about my family. Can I call you back?"

"We're going anyway. If you can only do one or the other, that's fine, too."

"I want to do both," Sal said with a whine. "Going out on a date with Mark and no Alexander would be fantastic. I love my little boy, but today has been a very long day. Rebecca isn't available, is she?"

"No," Polly said. "She's spending the night with Kayla in the new apartment."

"That's right. Sky was talking about how excited those girls were. There go two of my possibilities."

"What about Andrew? He's probably available."

"Do you think he would?"

Polly laughed. "He'd love it. I'll have to tell you what happened this week. He's been banned from our house until school starts back up."

"Who caught them?" Sal asked, cackling with mirth.

"It was Hayden. I sent him down to her room. They wanted to crawl in a hole. How did you know?"

"It's the only thing he could possibly do that would bring down that much hell on the two of them. Rebecca's been cleaning again?"

"Yeah, and she's barely begun. Hayden and Heath moved out of the living room and with Stephanie and Kayla gone, that opens up the library and office. We need to clean everything before I put furniture in those rooms."

"You'd think she would learn."

"Nah," Polly said. "They have to test the limits. If she didn't, I'd be worried. It would be a different worry, but I don't want her to be a simpering goody-two-shoes. The girl is feisty and I refuse to beat that out of her. However, she needs to learn how to play the game and be responsible to the rules set down. Henry was furious when I told him what happened."

"You told him?"

"I tell him everything. He has a lot of trouble with their relationship. I understand. I have trouble with it, too, but those kids have been best friends since before I knew her. We can limit their exposure to each other, but I could never separate them completely. I keep telling Henry that the more we clamp down on their relationship, the more that rebellious Rebecca will want it. As long as I keep it casual and don't turn it into a big deal, she'll have nothing to rebel at. Andrew is hilarious, though. He loves her, but doesn't want to screw anything up, so he's the one who holds back. He's very careful with us — even when Rebecca isn't."

"You're lucky. That could be all kinds of a mess otherwise."

"Oh, I know."

"How did Sylvie handle it?"

"Andrew is painting and cleaning and doing yard work and extra jobs around the house. She was livid. Jason was so caught up in those horses that he didn't have time for girls until this last year, so this is a learning experience for her, too."

"If you think she'll let him watch Alexander, that would be great."

"Call her. She'll be glad that he has something to do tonight." Polly almost hung up, then said, "Sal?"

"Yeah."

"When you talk to Sylvie, tell her that she and Eliseo are welcome to come out to the winery after they're done at Sycamore House."

"That would be fun. Mark loves to talk horses with Eliseo, especially now that they're building those stables." Sal paused. "Will that be weird for Henry?"

"Not at all. He's involved in building that barn, too."

"I'll call you back."

~~~

"I suppose we could walk home," Henry whispered to Polly as she poured another glass of wine.

"This is only my second. I'm fine."

"That's what this place should offer," Sal said. "Shuttle services to our houses if we relax too much. And this? This is relaxing. A beautiful evening and wine under the stars. Thanks for inviting us." She ran her hand up Mark's arm and caressed his cheek. "We need to go out more often."

He took her hand and kissed it, then smiled at his inebriated wife. She'd had a couple of glasses of wine with dinner and was well on her way to being quite relaxed.

The group that had been playing was taking a break, so Polly stood and stretched. "I'm going to walk around. Anyone want to walk with me?" She looked directly at her husband.

"We'll be back in a few minutes," Henry said with a laugh. "Apparently, we're taking a walk." He hooked his good arm through Polly's. "What are we doing?"

She turned the corner of the building and pulled him in for a kiss. "This. I've missed this, too."

Holding her as close as he could with his arm strapped across his front, Henry returned the kiss. When they stopped, he smiled at her. "I love what alcohol does to you."

"I won't get too crazy on you tonight. I know you're still wounded, but I wanted to taste your lips — more than a hello and goodbye kiss. I like them when they're flavored with just a little bit of wine."

He kissed her again and Polly melted against him. They held on to each other for a moment, enjoying the quiet of the evening.

"We should go back," she said. "They're going to know."

"We've been married a few years. We're allowed."

She laughed and took his hand as they walked back onto the patio.

A woman looked up at Polly and gave her a little wave. Polly wasn't sure who it was, but smiled in acknowledgment. When they got back to their table, she nudged Henry. "Do you know who that is? She acted like she recognized me."

"That's the Carlsons," he said. "Roger's his name and she's a lawyer. I built their new house two years ago. They've got a little girl."

"Julia," Polly said, nodding as she realized who it was. "I met the woman in McDonald's last week. Her daughter was at the hospital — a broken arm or something. She said Julia was in Noah's class. Maybe it was Elijah's. I don't know. Okay. That makes sense now. She freaked me out when she walked up to Noah and Elijah and started talking to them. I was on the phone and away from them and she was suddenly there. It was kind of weird."

"She's a trial lawyer. Tough woman, from what I hear. When I built the house, she had the plans all laid out. Her husband didn't have a say in anything."

"That woman over there?" Sal asked, nodding to the Carlson's table.

"Yeah. Do you guys know them?"

Mark gritted his teeth. "I had to put their dog to sleep last year. She made me go to the house to do it."

"That's too bad."

"The dog had been hurt. She said it was hit by a car. I'm not sure about that, but I wasn't in a position to question it."

"What do you mean?" Polly asked.

"The injuries didn't feel right to me." He shook his head in disgust. "And they made their little girl watch while the dog died. The dad tried to let her leave the room, but Mrs. Carlson insisted, saying that she needed to be exposed to death anyway. Yeah. That was a weird day."

Polly shuddered. "Now I'm totally creeped out." She pushed the wine glass toward Henry. "At least I got a good kiss before this all got up in my mind."

"Look who's here," Sal said, pointing at the door to the main building.

It hit Polly that she was sitting with her back to the door again. She needed to stop doing that. She turned and saw Eliseo and Sylvie coming toward them. "Hello there!" she called and stood up.

There were extra chairs stacked beside the building and she walked over to grab a couple of them.

Eliseo saw what she was doing and picked two off a stack instead. "I have this."

Polly took Sylvie's arm. "You look wonderful tonight. I've never seen this," she said as she fingered a thin woven wrap Sylvie had over her shoulders.

"Elva gave it to me. It's pretty, isn't it?"

"It's lovely. I'm glad you're here. We were talking about weird things and I need to think about something normal."

"What weird things?"

"People. Those weird things."

"You should have seen the reception tonight. It was a doozy."

Eliseo held a chair for Sylvie and then sat beside her.

"What was doozical?" Sal asked, giggling.

Sylvie laughed. "You sound like you've had a fun evening so far."

"They were starting to harsh my buzz, but now that you're here, you can get us back on track." She turned to Mark. "We need another bottle. Can you round one up? I'll make it worth your while."

He stood and kissed her forehead. "I'm on it. Anything to keep my gal Sal happy. Does anyone want anything special?"

They shook their heads and he left.

"Now dish," Sal said. "I need a funny story."

"It was going to be so romantic," Sylvie said. "Toward the end of the evening, a groomsman decided to propose to one of the bridesmaids. He'd spoken to the groom who thought it was a great idea, but no one thought to talk to the bride's mother and she threw a fit. He started to go down on one knee and the woman walked in between the couple, grabbed the microphone from the DJ and let everyone know that this wasn't happening at a party she was paying for. The bride cried, the bridesmaid cried, the bride's father looked like he wanted to crawl under a table and that was pretty much the end of the party. I've seen some crazy mothers over the years, but this was new. Usually they lose their minds right up until the reception is in full swing, then they calm down and relax. Not this woman. It surprised all of us."

"She wasn't ready to have her daughter leave," Sal said.

"Who knows."

Sylvie looked up when Mark came back to the table. "Eliseo says that Elva's found a couple of horses she wants to purchase. Have you looked at them yet?"

"Not yet," he said. "She'll know better than anyone what she's looking for, though." Mark patted Eliseo's shoulder. "As soon as things get going out there, I'm looking forward to bringing out a couple of my own. That sister of yours is pretty impressive. Once people find out about her, she'll be in high demand as a trainer. I asked her the other day about going with me out to Stafford's place. They have a couple of horses that need a firm hand. They bought them for their kids, but the kids don't know what they're doing. Good kids. Good horses. They just need guidance."

Eliseo nodded. "Thank you. She told me that you said something, but thought maybe you were just being nice."

"Well, yeah," Mark said, "but also sincere." He leaned to Henry. "We might have to put that second barn up sooner than we thought."

"Hello there. JJ said you were here. Can I join you?"

Polly looked up to see Tab standing beside her.

"What are you doing here?"

Mark jumped up to get another chair.

"I finished my shift and came up for the last set. I didn't expect to see you all here tonight." She smiled in thanks at Mark who held her seat for her.

"We're decompressing," Polly said. "This is Henry's first night out. I thought wine was a good idea."

"You look pretty good for a man who was attacked by a car," Tab said to him.

JJ dropped another chair beside Tab and put a full wine glass in front of her on the table. "This is turning into quite the party. Do you have everything you need? Can I bring you anything else?"

They all shook their heads.

Sal held her glass out and Mark poured more wine into it. "I'm relaxing," she announced and scooted her chair so she could lean on her husband. "We need to do this more often."

"How was Andrew with Alexander when you left?" Sylvie asked.

"They were having a great time. He was on the floor playing games and Alexander was laughing and crawling all over him. Thank you for saying yes."

"It's good for him." Sylvie chuckled. "He has more time on his hands right now, so whenever you'd like a babysitter, be sure to call."

Sal waggled her eyebrows at Mark. "You heard that. Andrew has plenty of time on his hands. We should use it."

"Anything you say, baby." He pointed to where the musicians were picking up their instruments again. "They're back. Drink and be quiet."

"Yessirree," Sal responded. She winked at Polly and held out her glass in a toast. "To a wonderful evening."

CHAPTER NINETEEN

"Every time I turn around, I see these people. I didn't even know they existed before this last week," Polly complained. She nodded toward Jennifer Carlson and her husband, who were having a heated discussion at a table near the front door of Pizzazz.

Camille smiled and turned to check it out. "That's because you recognize them now. I doubt that they suddenly decided to show up where you are on purpose. He comes into the coffee shop every once in a while — not usually with his wife, though. They have a little girl. She is sweet and polite, but the poor child jumps at everything. She seems absolutely terrified of the world."

The loud sound of a harsh slap turned everyone's attention to the couple as Jennifer Carlson pulled her hand back ready to hit her husband's face again. He caught it, said something under his breath, then nodded in apology to the other guests. Her response was to yank her hand away and stalk out. Her husband quickly drew cash out of his wallet, set it on the table, and followed her.

"I would have noticed that behavior if I'd ever seen it before," Polly said. "What a bitch. How does she think that behaving like that in public is appropriate?"

"No manners," Sylvie said.

"She's a lawyer, right?" Polly asked.

"Sometimes a good education doesn't mean you've learned a thing about life."

Sal came in the front door of Pizzazz and turned to look back out at the street. She gave her head a quick shake and strode across the restaurant to their table in the back. Polly would never cease to be amazed at how tall and gorgeous her friend was. Even in casual shorts, flip flops, and a t-shirt, Sal commanded the attention of every person in the room, whether they were male or female. And she didn't even notice.

"What in the world was that about?" she asked, sitting down beside Camille. "I nearly got clipped pulling into a parking space. Was that the same woman you and Mark were talking about last night?" she asked Polly.

Polly nodded. "She was mad at something her husband said or did or … whatever. She has to be hard to live with. Can you imagine never knowing if you were going to set someone off by saying the wrong thing?" Polly dropped her head and took Sylvie's hand. "I'm sorry. I didn't think."

Sylvie creased her forehead. "What? Anthony? That was years ago now. It's like that's a life someone else lived. I'm not the same person that I was when he and I were married."

"That makes sense," Polly said. "Do your boys ever hear from him? Isn't he living in Fort Dodge? You never talk about him."

"Nothing," Sylvie said. "I worried for about six months after he came into town that he was going to try to insinuate himself back into our lives. I called my lawyer and had everything ready to go just in case, but he vanished." She grinned at Polly. "You haven't found his body yet, so I'm assuming he's still alive."

"Stop it. He was so insistent that he be part of their lives. It surprises me that he's not around."

Sylvie shook her head and shrugged a shoulder. "I'm not about to start asking questions. I worry that if I ask anyone about him, he'll interpret my curiosity as interest and be right back here making life difficult."

"And the boys never ask about him?"

"They did a couple of times. Mostly Jason. We had to have a few conversations about how they didn't need to be defined by him and whether he was in their lives. I talked to them about how I knew that he loved them, but he had never learned how to express love the same way that the people who are around them all the time do."

"Alexander loves your son," Sal said. She winced. "I'm sorry. I know you were talking about something else, but he had so much fun last night with Andrew. Today, he would point at a toy and say Andrew's name. I'm certain he wanted to tell me how Andrew played with him and that toy. It was pretty cute. Thank you for letting him come over."

"He liked the cash," Sylvie said with a grin. "He also had a good time. It will be good for him to have more outlets this year. It seems that Polly and I will be working harder to keep our kids separate so we can keep them from landing themselves in trouble."

Camille looked at Polly with curiosity.

"Yeah, they got caught making out." Polly shook her head. "It's my fault for not realizing how much I was expecting of them. You can't be that age and be together all the time and not want to experiment a little."

"I'm glad it was only a little and not a lot," Sylvie said. "Where's Elise tonight?"

"This is her weekend to be in Chicago with her family. She wasn't looking forward to the trip, but they love her and it will be great. I told her to keep telling herself that. She's coming back into town on Tuesday."

Sal leaned in. "I was kinda hoping you would tell us she was out on a date."

Sylvie waved and everyone looked up to see Joss rushing back to the table.

"I'm sorry I'm late. Have you ordered without me?"

"We're just getting it all together," Sylvie said. "Weren't you going to be in Indiana? I heard Nate's dad had a heart attack."

Joss rolled her eyes as she sat down on Polly's other side. "No heart attack. Crazy wife. She was the problem. Nate came home yesterday which meant I didn't have to travel with five kids. He and I got them into bed this evening and I took off. He's on duty now." She cackled an evil laugh. "That'll serve him right for having a couple of nights' sleep without children." Then she grew sober. "He had to put up with his mother and I'm not sure that was any easier. The poor woman worries all the time about every little thing. And it isn't something that anyone can talk her out of. Once a crazy idea shows up in her head, she worries about it for the rest of her life. Nobody can convince her that her husband didn't have a heart attack. She was furious with Nate for leaving yesterday because she was certain that as soon as his plane lifted off, his father was going to die, clutching his heart. I swear that she's gotten worse every single year as she grows older."

"Has she been tested for dementia?" Sal asked. "It's a real thing."

Joss sighed. "I don't know how they'll get that done. Nate says she's always been like that, but it's getting worse. I know Nate feels guilty about not being there to help, but at the same time he's so thankful he isn't there to listen to it all the time. I try to be supportive when he wants to talk about it. Whatever he needs to do, we'll make it happen."

"You can't move back to Indiana," Polly said.

"No we can't," Joss declared. "That's not even a consideration. We're happy here. Nate's happy here. This is where our family is going to grow up. Period."

"You tell 'em," Sal said. She looked up as the waitress arrived. "Is this all of us tonight?"

No one had heard that others weren't coming, but these Sunday evening gatherings were casual and they weren't about to take roll.

The front door opened and Tab Hudson rushed in. "I'm here, I'm here," she said as she dropped into a seat beside Camille.

"Were you over at the winery?" Sal asked, waggling her eyebrows. "Playing with the owner a little?"

Tab laughed. "Whatever. Have you ordered? I want an iced tea." She looked back at the group around the table. "Sandy can't be here tonight. She completely forgot about a dinner they had to be at — one of Benji's clients."

"How's Will doing?" Joss asked.

"Good," Tab said with a nod. Then she smiled. "I interrupted Traci. She's being awfully patient with us."

"It's okay," the young waitress said. "You're fine."

The group finished with their orders — nothing any different from what they usually had — and Traci left.

"I saw Bri this week," Polly said. She giggled. "See, now I'm interrupting. Finish talking about Will. I'm sorry."

"I don't have much to tell you," Tab said. "I only talked to Sandy for a few minutes today. She says he's doing okay. The doctors aren't telling her much. They're still in the middle of treatment and while they have one doctor who says he's cautiously optimistic, the others don't want to say anything yet."

"Drives me nuts," Joss said. "Sometimes the thing that gets us through to the next step is hope. Surely they understand that." She looked away and then back. "I laugh about my mother-in-law worrying about everything, and the truth be told, I sublimate all of my fears about my kids into frantically cleaning the house, keeping them occupied with healthy activities, and then I pour myself into work at the library. I'm as bad as she is."

Sal reached out and touched the top of Joss's hand. "I don't think you can have kids without worrying that they'll be okay. If Alexander ever understood the number of times I silently weep into his shoulder while he sleeps on my chest, he'd need more therapy than I'm ready to pay for. I'm so thankful for him and so glad that he's in my life, but then I make too much of it in my head and worry that something will happen and he won't be here long." She scowled at them. "It's sick. I know. I don't like to talk about it and he will never know. It's just private idiotic stuff in my head." She wiped a tear from her eye. "Damn it. Look what I did." After pulling her phone out, she swiped through it and showed them a picture of Alexander sleeping on Mark while Mark slept on the sofa. "Then I have to look at pictures of these two guys to remind myself that everything is okay and I should stop my insanity."

"Does it work?" Joss asked, taking out her own phone.

"No, but I keep telling myself it does."

"They are sweet when they're asleep," Joss said. She showed them a picture of the five kids and Jazz, the dog, sound asleep on pillows under what looked like a blanket fort. "We did this Friday night since Nate was gone. I crashed on the couch while they all slept better than they usually do. Maybe I should put bunk beds into one of the rooms and let everyone sleep together."

"How are Cooper and Sophie enjoying their new siblings?" Tab asked. She took the phone from Joss and looked more closely at the picture. "They're so sweet. Cooper is tucked right up against Owen, isn't he?"

"He adores those boys," Joss said. "So does Sophie. She and Lillian are having a little trouble figuring out who's the boss. There's going to be competition there. If Lillian is sitting on my lap, Sophie wants to be there, too. They do the same thing to Nate. We keep pouring out as much love as we can for now."

"I don't know how you do it all," Polly said. "That many little ones would put me over the edge."

"It's exhausting," Joss acknowledged. "We're still looking for a part-time nanny. If you hear of anyone who might want the job, let me know."

Traci returned with their drinks and cheese bread, moving around the table as she set things down. "Pizza will be out in a few minutes. Do you need anything else?"

Polly caught her eye and smiled while shaking her head. "Thanks."

"So, you said you saw Bri," Sylvie said. "What's she doing?"

"She's the new activities director at the nursing home."

Sal laughed. "What were you doing at the nursing home? Looking for more customers?"

"Stop it." Polly huffed out a breath. "Bri told me I wasn't welcome — for exactly that reason. Apparently, Noah and Elijah are welcome any time. They love all of the attention those folks give them. I'm going to have trouble keeping them away. They play games and Noah has found their library. When I called over to make sure they weren't in anyone's way, I talked to Bri. Had no idea it was her."

"That's so cool," Tab said. "More kids should be encouraged to visit the nursing home."

"Bri said something about working with the elementary school to bring activities over there. If it works out, that would be great."

"But you can never go with them," Sal said.

Polly nodded. "There's that. It's a little intimidating to be shut out of a place because they're afraid you'll find dead people."

"Surely she was kidding," Tab said.

"I doubt it," Polly replied. Then she cackled a wicked laugh. "So how serious is this relationship with you and JJ?"

Tab looked up in surprise. "What just happened here?"

"Looks like she changed the subject," Camille said. "That was smooth."

"You're one to talk. I'm pretty sure that JJ and I saw you having dinner with a young man last week."

Every single person turned on Camille.

"What?" she asked. "I can't eat out?"

"Not with a man and think you're going to get away with not telling us," Sal said. "Why haven't I heard about this?"

Sylvie leaned forward. "Why haven't I heard about this. I work with you every day. What's up?"

"I'm sure that I told you Elise was going to introduce me to a professor she knew."

Pursing her lips, Sylvie looked skeptically at Camille. "That was months ago. We never heard anything more and assumed that nothing came of it."

"It's no big deal," Camille protested. "Trevor and I have dinner every two or three weeks."

"Trevor?" Sal sat forward with a grin. "At least we have a name now."

"What does he teach?" Polly asked.

Camille chuckled. "Guess."

"Math?"

"On the first guess," Camille said. "Elise doesn't get out much beyond her own realm. Lucky for her that department is big and she's expanding her acquaintance-base in a hurry."

"She found you a winner first time out?"

"He's a nice guy. Neither of us are looking for a deep and undying relationship. It's just dinner whenever we both have time." She turned on Tab. "And why didn't you come over and introduce yourself to him? Were you spying so you could tattle or were you and JJ doing something that you didn't want me to see?"

"It looked as if you were deep in conversation and I didn't want to interrupt." Tab grinned at the rest of them. "And maybe I wanted to bring it up when you least expected it."

Their pizza arrived and Traci passed pieces around. They had tried to tell her that they could take care of it many times, but she insisted, saying it was her job.

"Do you know anyone who'd want to nanny for five little kids?" Joss asked when Traci put a piece of pizza on her plate.

"Your five?" Traci asked.

Joss nodded.

"Is it full-time? Live-in? Or what?"

"It doesn't have to be full-time. We hadn't considered a live-in," Joss replied. She reached down into her purse, took out a small container, and drew off a few business cards. "If you know anyone, have them give me a call. Everything is negotiable right now."

"I'll think about it. Would you be interested in talking to *me*?"

Joss nodded again. "Sure. Call me tomorrow and we'll set up a time to talk. Aren't you going to school?"

"Not this year. I can't afford it right now, so I'm working and trying to save money. I was thinking of taking online classes to try to get ahead, but those are expensive."

"Give me a call and we'll talk."

Traci finished handing out pizza and walked away, looking at the business card.

"That was smooth," Polly said. She picked up a piece of pizza and bit into it, then pulled the piece back out of her mouth. "Every damned time. Why do I forget how hot this stuff is?" She blew on the pizza and then took another bite, holding her mouth as wide open as possible as she chewed.

"You're such a dork," Sal said, daintily cutting her pizza with a fork before putting a piece in her mouth.

"Takes one to know one," Polly taunted.

"Dork."

"Girls," Sylvie scolded. "Grow up. Were you two this bad when you lived together?"

"Worse," Sal said. "Her manners were atrocious. I was embarrassed all the time."

"What?" Polly asked. "My manners? It was your mother who loved having me come to her fancy teas because I was so proper and sweet. They all loved me."

"Whatever." Sal turned to Tab. "I was going to ask you last night, but you were gone before the music was finished. Have you found anything more about that body Polly discovered? Why did they put it in her back yard?"

"Probably wanted to make sure it was finally found," Tab said. "All we know is that the two were brothers. We're still searching databases, but their DNA isn't on file anywhere. Missing persons hasn't turned up any links in the Midwest. It sure would have been helpful if they'd been dumped with identification. Without it, we don't have a clue why they were even in the area, much less killed. Just one little break in the case would help. When we discovered they were related, we thought that might move things along, but it didn't. It gave us more questions."

"Don't you wish you could wrap it up in an hour like they do on television?"

"Yeah, those shows span a bunch of days."

"Okay, a bunch of days," Sal said. "Polly found the other guy last May."

"She needs to up her game," Tab replied. "I'd like to close this case. When Sheriff Merritt assigned me to Polly's cases, I thought

I'd won the lottery since all of her cases are closed."

"No pressure," Polly said under her breath. "I thought I made it clear that if I had to find them, you guys had to solve them."

"That hasn't happened so far," Tab said. "You've been involved in every case right up to the end." She chuckled. "I seem to remember you driving one of the murderers right to our back door and he was tied to the front seat of his car. We still laugh about that poor guy. He didn't know what hit him when you and those crazy ladies showed up. I think he was grateful that we were there to rescue him from you."

"That was all Beryl."

"Yeah, no. It was all of you. Sheriff Merritt can't believe that his wife was involved in that. You do tend to take your friends along for entertainment."

"How about we finish our pizza," Polly said. "No more harassing poor Polly. Especially since this all started when I was asking about you and JJ."

"We're just fine." Tab took another bite of her pizza and glared at Polly, who just grinned.

CHAPTER TWENTY

"Are you kidding me? What are you doing up so early?" Henry asked Polly when she came into the kitchen. He closed the pantry door, having just fed the dogs after they'd been outside.

"Heading to the barn. Jason and Scar have been spending the last few nights there and I'm going to send them home. I can help Eliseo this morning. How are you feeling today?"

"Like it's been a week after I was in a wreck. Much better." He grimaced as he turned back to the coffee pot.

"What was that?"

"That was nothing. I'm fine. Things are still a little tender."

Polly stood up on her tip toes and kissed his cheek. "I'm not going to give you any trouble. You're a smart man and I trust you to take care of yourself. I believe that you understand how important you are to this family. If anything awful happened to you, we'd be devastated, so you'll make good decisions."

Henry laughed until he snorted, then grabbed his waist. "Woman, you're awesome. No guilt there. None at all."

"The thing is, I believe everything I said." She tipped her head up and he pulled her close.

They were still kissing when Heath walked in from the foyer, rubbing his eyes. He turned around and went back through the door.

"It's okay, Heath," Henry called. "It's safe now."

"Mornings are supposed to be G-rated around here," Heath said. "That was unexpected. What are you doing up so early, Polly?"

"Gonna haul hay and feed so Jason can go home for a few hours. Is your brother up?"

Heath nodded. "He's in the shower. It's nice being upstairs and having that bathroom to ourselves. And my own room? That's awesome. I love my brother, but now I can read or do whatever I want and not worry about him yelling at me because he's trying to sleep. I saw an old desk out there in the garage. Would you care if I fixed that up and used it?"

"The one under that far window?" Polly asked.

"Yeah. It's got really cool handles on it. They're all there, too."

She looked at Henry and he shrugged. "If you want to use that desk, it's yours. Figure out what you want for a chair and we'll make it happen."

"I want to build a set of bookshelves, too," he said.

Henry grinned. "Son, you are going to be so tired of bookshelves by the end of this year. With all the furniture you've pulled out of that garage these last few days, we're closer to getting space in there to set up equipment for you."

"Don't get too comfortable, though," Polly said. "That building is coming down so we can put up a decent garage and shop."

Henry looked at her with concern written on his face. "When?"

"Not for a year or so. Don't panic. I just don't want Heath building cabinets in there that he has to destroy later on."

"Do you want coffee here or shall we stop for breakfast?" Henry asked Heath.

The boy's eyes lit up. "Can we get breakfast?"

"If we leave right now." Henry kissed Polly's cheek and rubbed his hand down her back. "I'll talk to you later today. Be careful at the barn."

"As long as you're careful out on the work sites," she said. She stood in front of the coffee pot, staring at it as she debated in her head whether to drink what she had here or stop by Sweet Beans on the way to the barn. She didn't want to waste any more time chatting with people who might be getting their breakfast downtown, so she opened the cupboard, took down a travel mug and filled it. She'd find time to stop there later.

Buzzing Hayden's room, she said his name.

"Yeah, Polly. What are you doing up and around so early?" he asked.

"I'm going over to the barn to help Eliseo. Will you keep an eye on the hordes this morning?"

"Have the dogs been out?"

"Yeah. Just the human hordes. Do you mind?"

"No problem. Do you care if I put Noah and Elijah to work outside painting some of that furniture we discussed?"

"That sounds great. Say, Heath wants that desk under the far window. Don't paint that."

"He told me. If we can haul it out, I might clean it up for him."

"Cool. I'll see you later." She grabbed up her mug and after a few sloppy kisses from Obiwan and Han and snuggles with Luke and Leia, she headed for her truck.

The sun was up, but just barely. The sky was filled with dark clouds. Polly hadn't had time to watch the weather lately and had no idea what might be coming in today. They needed rain and she loved a good thunderstorm. Hayden might not find it quite so easy to paint furniture, but he'd figure things out. That wasn't hers to worry about.

She pulled in beside Eliseo's car. There was never going to be a time that she would be here earlier than he was, even when she tried.

Crossing through the gates to the main door, Polly looked up at the sky again. It continued to get darker. She could almost feel the rain trying to pour out of the clouds.

"Good morning," she called out when she got inside the barn. "Anybody here?"

Eliseo stepped out of the feed room. "What are you doing here this morning?"

"I figured that Jason had been here long enough. He should take time off — go home and take a shower and make himself breakfast. I'll do his job this morning."

Jason and his friend, Scar — short for Oscar — came out of the feed room. "You don't have to do that, Polly."

"You've spent two nights here and I know you've also been working here during the days," she replied. "Go home. It's not like you're going to work with the horses outside anyway. Have you seen that sky?"

Both boys shook their heads and went into the donkeys' stall to look outside.

"You're okay with this, right?" she asked Eliseo.

He nodded in agreement. "It's a good idea. They've been here plenty this weekend."

"That looks bad," Scar said as they came back into the main alley of the building. "Mom's probably a little scared. Can I call her?"

Eliseo nodded as sirens began to sound throughout town. "To the main building. Now," he said. "You need to get to the basement."

The horses began to shift in their stalls as the sound of the siren pierced the air.

Polly pushed the boys toward the main door. "Are you coming?" she asked Eliseo.

He looked at her as if she was an idiot and shook his head. "They need me. We'll be fine. Just get the boys to safety."

Storms like this never came through in the early morning. It was strange to feel the air change around them as they ran up to Sycamore House.

No one else had arrived for work yet this morning, so Polly swiped the lock open and they went inside only to find three surprised guests coming out into the main hallway.

"What's going on?" a young man asked. His wife was still in her robe, her eyes barely open.

A man in his late fifties, dressed in shorts and a t-shirt, clutched two camera bags and a tripod and looked at Polly questioningly.

"The basement is right over here," she said. "Apparently there's a bad storm coming this way. Follow me."

They crossed the main lobby to the basement stairway and Polly waited as Jason and Scar led the way down the steps. She was about to follow them when the auditorium doors crashed open and Doug came through.

"What's this about?" he asked.

Polly shook her head. "I don't know. There's a storm coming through. Might as well be safe, don't you think?"

"I guess. Dad likes to watch storms. Would it be crazy for me to look out the front door?"

"I'm not going to force you downstairs. You're an adult."

"You want to come with me, don't you?" he asked, a smirk on his face.

She leaned in and whispered. "A little, but I have guests downstairs with Scar and Jason. Shouldn't I be responsible?"

"Come on. Just for a minute. Then we'll go down. Let's see what's coming."

She walked with him to the front door and he pushed it open against the wind. Dust swirled up from the ground as leaves and small branches flew down from the trees. As they watched, rain burst forth and pelted the parking lot and sidewalk. Wind caught the rain and blew it toward them soaking Polly's front. She jumped and laughed as Doug allowed the door to slam shut.

"That's crazy," he said.

"It's moving through fast," Polly said. "We'll be back to normal in no time. Were you already up?"

"I don't have to get up for another half hour. Oh well." He headed for the basement door.

Polly shook her head. "It happened so fast, I haven't called home. Go on down. I'll be right there." She dialed Hayden's phone and waited for him to answer.

"Polly? Are you okay?"

"Yeah. Did you get everyone to the basement?"

"We're missing two of the kittens so Rebecca's freaked out. She says we need more carriers."

"She's right. Are the boys okay?"

"Yeah. They're playing with the lanterns. Luke and Leia weren't too happy about me scooping them up from their breakfast, but otherwise, we're good. Have you talked to Henry?"

"I'll call him next. He and Heath were headed somewhere for breakfast. Guessing it's Sweet Beans and they have a basement, too. They'll be fine. Thanks for being there."

"I heard a crack in the back yard. Sounded like a branch went down. I'll check when this is over."

"Thanks again." Polly hung up and dialed Henry's phone.

"I'm fine," he said when he answered. "Where are you?"

"At Sycamore House. Jason, Scar, Doug, and our guests are in the basement. I'm at the top of the stairs. Where are you?"

"Watching the storm from the front door of Sweet Beans."

"Why are you not in the basement?"

"Why aren't you?"

"That's not fair."

He laughed out loud. "It's a pretty cool sky out there. The clouds are moving fast. Nobody's seen a tornado yet, so this is the fun stuff. Everybody at home okay?"

"Rebecca is missing two of the kittens, but the rest are in the basement. We need a better way to gather animals for an emergency. She and I will think about that."

"We could put kennels below the laundry chute and she could dump them down. We'd get them the rest of the way down."

"Yeah. You tell her that. I'm not going to."

"Whoa!" he yelled. "That was close."

Polly had heard the crack of lightning too. "How close do you think?"

"I saw it hit a block or so west of here. Like where those apartments are on Pine Street. I hope everyone is okay."

"Me too. That place may never get rebuilt after the fire last May if they keep having things hit them. I'm glad that Stephanie and Kayla are living somewhere else."

"First weekend in a new place and you get a crazy storm on Monday morning. There's some excitement for you."

"I'm going to head down to the guests," Polly said. "Talk to you later?"

"You bet. I love you."

"I know," she said with a smile.

She headed down the steps and into the room where she'd once set up a bed for Eliseo. The bed was long gone, but the rug had remained. Jeff had purchased several inexpensive comfortable chairs and brought them down here for events such as this. There was more room available in the rest of the basement in case something happened when there was a large event going on upstairs, but this room was a nice place to spend time while waiting out a storm.

"How bad is it?" the photographer asked.

"Windy and rainy right now," she replied. "Lightning and lots of thunder."

"When I checked the weather app on my phone before the siren went off, it said things were cloudy," the young man said. He and his wife were sitting on a sofa that had been set up against a wall. "Those things are useless."

"I'm Polly Giller," she said. She walked over to the photographer and put her hand out.

"Davis Warren," he replied.

Polly turned to the young couple and offered her hand.

The young man stood and shook it. "I'm Matt Lipton and this is …" he paused and smiled down at his wife. "This is my wife, Cicily. We got married on Saturday. We're flying to Jamaica this afternoon."

"Congratulations," Polly said. "This will be one way to remember your wedding weekend."

"Our groomsmen and bridesmaids had the other two rooms, but they left yesterday." He smiled at his wife again. "I can't believe I can finally call you my wife." He sat back down beside her. "We've been dating since we were in junior high. I've loved her my whole life. It feels like I waited forever and here we are."

Cicily took his hand and smiled at him.

"Are you two from around here?" Polly asked.

"We grew up in Grand Junction, but we live in San Diego. One more year of college."

"I hope you have a wonderful honeymoon," Polly said. She sat in a chair next to Jason, whose knees bounced up and down. "Not happy about being stuck down here?"

"How long do we have to stay?"

"Give it a few more minutes, okay?"

"Do I really have to go home? I can work."

"You really have to go home. Take a shower. Lie down in your bed. Do the chores you're supposed to do on the weekends for your mom."

He grinned at her. "I don't have any of those this weekend."

"Why not?"

"She made Andrew do all of his chores and all of mine. She's still mad at him for messing around with Rebecca at your house. He had to totally empty out the upstairs bathroom yesterday and tape it off. Today he gets to paint it. He's going to be painting and cleaning and doing yardwork for a whole year."

Polly chuckled. "It wasn't that bad."

"Yeah, but he got caught. I'd never get caught."

"Never?" Polly asked.

He looked away from her and shook his head.

"What?" Scar asked. "What did he get caught at?"

"It's nothing." Jason gave Polly a look, begging her to stay quiet.

She smiled at him and shook her head.

Doug Randall jumped up and headed for the stairs. "My weather app says that the worst has passed. It's just raining. Let me go check."

In a few minutes, he yelled down. "Yeah. It's cool. Just rain now."

"It was nice to meet you all," Polly said. "I hope you have a safe trip to Jamaica and a wonderful honeymoon."

The Liptons smiled at her as they walked past.

"Can we help you with your equipment?" she asked Davis Warren.

"I can get it," he said, hefting a bag up on each shoulder and lifting the heavy tripod.

"Let me carry the tripod," Jason said, putting his hand out.

"Thanks."

"I can carry one of the bags," Scar offered.

"No. I've got those."

Polly followed him out of the room. "Are you staying in Bellingwood long?"

"Another week," he said. "I come through every year now. It's a nice place to stay while I travel around central Iowa. I was getting ready to head out and catch the morning light, but when I saw the clouds come in, I went back to bed. Didn't think I'd end up in your basement."

"There's always tomorrow morning, right?"

He nodded as he crested the top step, then took a few deep breaths before heading toward the addition. Jason was waiting for him there and handed off the tripod.

Polly watched the guests enter the main hallway of the addition and then looked outside. Rain was still coming down, but it wasn't quite as violent as it had been earlier. "Gonna run for the barn?" she asked.

"I'll race ya," Scar said. He bolted out of the door and Jason raced after him. They ran pell mell through the rain toward the barn, never looking around to see if she was following.

"Are you coming?" Jason yelled back when he got to the first gate.

"On my way." Polly jogged toward them, feeling only a little guilty that he'd waited for her.

They got into the barn and she wasn't surprised to see the donkeys surrounding Eliseo who was sitting on one of the benches. The two cats, Hansel and Gretel were with him as well — Gretel in his lap and Hansel perched beside him, ready to run at a moment's notice.

"Everything good down here?" she asked.

"It wasn't that big of a deal. We're waiting for the rain to clear."

"Did you talk to Elva?"

His eyes crinkled in his attempt to smile. "They only had a little rain. Everything else missed them."

"That's so weird," Scar said.

"You two boys go on home," Eliseo said, standing up. "I don't want to see you back here until this afternoon. The storm interrupted my morning plans anyway, so I won't need you until later. Got it?"

Jason looked into Nat's stall. "Are you sure?"

"I'm sure."

He reached in and rubbed Nat's forehead. "Okay then. I'll see you later, Nat." Jason spoke to each of the horses before he left with Scar by the front door. He turned back. "Do you want me to bring you some lunch, Eliseo?"

Eliseo turned to Polly and his eyes sparkled. "That would be great, Jason. Call me later."

"Okay." Jason finally left and Eliseo took a deep breath.

"Did the guests come down out of the addition?" he asked.

"Yeah. You and Jeff have made a nice place in the basement there. It's very comfortable."

He chuckled. "We've talked about putting a refrigerator and television down there so the staff can have a place to hang out. Especially on weekends when we're between receptions. So far, I have plenty that I can do, but maybe I'd like it someday."

"It's a great idea." Polly walked over to Demi's stall. "So where shall I start?"

"He's as good as any. Might as well open the doors and let them go outside. A little rain won't hurt anyone."

Polly walked in and rubbed Demi as she walked past him to open the outside door.

"Uh, Eliseo?" she called out.

"What's up?"

"You have visitors." She put her hand on Demi's shoulder, hoping to stop him from leaving the stall.

Eliseo walked in and moved Demi back in before shutting the door behind them as they stood under the eaves. "Where the hell did they come from?"

Two new donkeys were standing at the large pile of hay, quietly chomping away. They had looked up when Eliseo and Polly emerged, but from the looks of them, they were hungry and desperately glad to find something to eat.

"What do we do now?" she asked.

"Call Mark, first of all," he said. "We need to find out if he knows who these two belong to. I'm not ready for them to stay here, but Elva has room."

"I'll call Mark. You'll call Elva?" she asked.

"Yeah. Tell him we need his trailer."

"We should get one of those," Polly said.

"It's an investment we'll make one of these days," he replied as he took out his phone.

Polly drew hers out and dialed Mark's cell phone.

"This is awfully early for you, Polly Giller," Mark said. "What's going on?"

"I'm at the barn this morning and rather than stealing our donkeys, someone has deposited two in our pasture." She looked across at the gate leading to the bridge. It was standing open again. "They don't look too healthy. Eliseo doesn't want to house them here. He wondered if you'd take a look at them and bring your trailer to take them up to Elva. He's talking to her right now."

"Not healthy?"

"I didn't mean that, because I have no good way of knowing, but they're definitely skinny and in need of attention."

"That barn isn't ready."

"You talk to him about that. Will you come see if these are donkeys you recognize?"

"I don't know any skinny donkeys, but I'll be right over."

CHAPTER TWENTY-ONE

"Let's go upstairs," Rebecca said to Polly. "I want you to see what we did."

Polly turned off the truck and followed her daughter to the door. They were only here to pick Kayla up for the afternoon and even though she didn't want to get caught up in anything else, she understood Rebecca and Kayla's excitement.

"Hello there," a woman said, coming out from behind the house.

"Hello, Mrs. Worth," Rebecca replied. "Have you met Polly?"

Mrs. Worth removed a pair of work gloves from her hands and reached out to Polly. "It's nice to meet you. The girls have all been working very hard to make a cozy living space upstairs. Stephanie and Kayla invited us up yesterday evening and I must say, it's quite attractive." She took Polly's arm. "They're very nice girls and we promise to keep an eye out for them. There is no need to worry."

"That's good to know, Mrs. Worth. I love them both very much," Polly said. "I'm thankful they have a beautiful place to live."

"Stephanie told me what you've done for her, letting them live with you after that terrible fire. And in the old Springer place, too. It's so good to see that corner of town come back to life. Maybe your neighbors will finally take care of their homes, now that you are showing them the way. Such a pity that they care so little about the house they live in. I don't understand. If you can't do the work yourself, find someone to do it. There are plenty of handymen in town who need work." She smiled at Polly. "I suppose even your husband could do that kind of work if he wanted. When are you planning to have an open house so the town can see what you've done inside that building? You know, everyone is curious. It was so good to see that you finally trimmed those bushes back. They looked awful. I'm always telling Orville that I can't bear to see untrimmed bushes. It's almost as bad as an unkempt lawn." She patted Polly's arm. "Orville tells me that I shouldn't worry about other people's things so much — that I have enough to concern me right here at home. Maybe he's right. People don't seem to care as much about how things look as they did when we were younger."

They were standing at the door that led up to the apartment and Rebecca looked as if she desperately wanted to bolt, but she remained in place.

"Would you girls like to come in for iced tea? I brew it out on the patio every morning when the sun shines down. We've had quite a lot of rain these last few mornings, so I've had to brew it in the afternoon on the front walk. That's incredibly low-class, though. It's like telling everyone on the street about your private business."

"We can't come in today," Polly said, carefully extricating herself from the woman's hands. "I have quite a bit of work to do at home and we're here to pick Kayla up. The girls want to show me what they've been working on since last Friday evening when Stephanie and Kayla moved in."

"They are very sweet girls," Mrs. Worth said. "We've had a couple of doozies. I don't like married couples. They make too much noise." She turned so her back was to Rebecca and leaned in. "The walls are much too thin to have to hear that. I don't know why they weren't more embarrassed. I was so thankful when they moved." She stood up straight again. "And I don't like young men. I had to ask the last young man to leave after he'd had a loud party. He should have been much more aware of the time. The contract states that there is to be no loud music after ten o'clock. Young people should be in bed by ten o'clock so they can get a good night's sleep. Don't you agree?"

Polly nodded slowly and Rebecca put her hand on the handle. She slowly twisted it and the door opened.

"You go on and enjoy your afternoon. Maybe we'll have time for tea another day," Mrs. Worth said. She held the door as Polly and Rebecca went up the steps. "It was very nice to meet you."

"Nice to meet you too, Mrs. Worth," Polly said. She goosed Rebecca in the butt, pushing her faster up the steps.

Rebecca knocked and Kayla opened the door immediately. "You're here. I saw your truck come in, but you took forever."

As soon as Polly shut the door, Rebecca laughed out loud. "We got caught by Mrs. Worth. I didn't think we'd ever get away. She invited us in for iced tea."

Kayla looked at Rebecca and then at Polly. "I like her."

"She's a busybody," Rebecca said.

"She's nice to me and Stephanie. Last night she and her husband came up to welcome us and she brought brownies and these yummy lemon cookies. They loved everything that Stephanie and I did around the apartment. Mr. Worth said he had another old set of bookshelves in the basement if I wanted them. He's going to clean them up today for me."

"She's very nice," Polly said. They hadn't done much in the living room. The furniture was just as it had been when they'd moved in, but Stephanie and Kayla had put several of their personal knick knacks out on the tops of tables.

"Come in and see my room," Kayla said. "Rebecca helped me do it all and I love it so much. You have to see!"

Rebecca grabbed Polly's hand and tugged her along. The door to Kayla's bedroom was closed and they stopped in front of it.

"Are you ready?" Kayla asked.

Polly nodded and smiled as Kayla threw the door open.

They had draped yards of sheer burgundy fabric from a point about six feet above the head of the bed to two points on either side of the bed and then allowed it to fall gracefully to the floor. On the wall within that frame, they'd hung a sketch that Rebecca had done of Kayla and Stephanie. Another swath of the fabric was tied on each post of the headboard and swooped up to the top of the sketch. Polly didn't think that would last long with a cat in the house.

The crates that had held most of Kayla's items were stacked neatly in a corner beside a desk. Above the desk was a framed corkboard. Someone had glued flowers and pictures, beads and buttons to the frame.

"I love the frame," Polly said.

"I made that," Kayla replied proudly. "I'm going to make one for Stephanie for Christmas."

"That's a wonderful idea."

A bright yellow beanbag chair sat in another corner and a short wooden bench that had been stenciled with colorful flowers sat beneath a window. The sliding closet door was pushed open enough so Polly could see the litter box in a corner.

"Where's the kitten?" she asked.

Kayla shook her head. "Around here somewhere. There are so many things for her to check out, she gets exhausted and falls asleep wherever. Usually it's in a sunbeam, though. She loves watching the squirrels and birds from the living room window. Can you believe it? This place is so awesome."

"You two have done an excellent job in here. You'll be happy for a long time in this room," Polly said.

"I'd show you Stephanie's, but we're not done yet." Kayla pointed at the bench. "Isn't that cool? We're going to stencil on Stephanie's wall and if we do a good job, she said we can do it in my room too. Mrs. Worth thought it was a pretty way to add color. She said that she might do it in her kitchen." She stood in an empty spot along one wall. "We'll put the bookcase here."

"She's barely going to have enough room to walk," Rebecca said with a laugh. "You should put the bookcase in your closet."

Kayla pushed the closet door open. "That would work. This isn't a very big room, but I like it."

"It's lovely," Polly said. "You girls have done a great job decorating."

"We're getting a new shower curtain for the bathroom," Kayla said, pushing the bathroom door open. "I wanted seashells, but Stephanie says maybe a pretty colored one. We're going to get matching rugs for the floor, too. It isn't very big, but we don't have to be in here at the same time, so it's fine." She led them to the kitchen and opened cupboards. "I couldn't believe everything fit in these cupboards, but now we can use our plates and glasses again." Kayla looked at Polly. "I don't mean that it wasn't nice at your house, but it's fun to have our things out again. We found everything. Mr. Worth took our boxes out to his garage. He says he's going to keep them so if anybody ever needs them to move, he can offer them. Of course, he asked us first. Stephanie was going to recycle them, but he saves everything."

She picked up a little cow cream pitcher. "Isn't this the cutest? I found it at a thrift store last year. Now we can have it out again." Then she pointed to a crystal butter dish. "We got that in Missouri on vacation."

Polly pulled Kayla into a hug. "I'm so glad you two girls are happy. You're going to love it here. It sounds like Mr. and Mrs. Worth are ready to totally take you under their wings."

They walked into the living room and Kayla pointed at the kitten behind the couch. "See, she's back on the window sill. I know she misses everyone at your house, but it's okay. We're going to be okay here."

"Do you want to bring her with you this afternoon?" Polly asked.

"Can I?"

"The cats will be glad to see her."

"I'll be right back. Her carrier is in my closet." Kayla took off at a run.

"Mom and I used to live in little apartments like this," Rebecca said quietly. "We never got to decorate very much. She always did my room, but nothing else."

"She would have, given enough time," Polly said. She took Rebecca's hand. "She wanted the best for you."

Rebecca smiled up at her. "That's why she asked you to take care of me, right?"

"Right."

~~~

Stephanie drove away with Kayla after picking her up at the end of the day, and Rebecca came back into the kitchen, sloughing her feet across the floor. "I can't wait for school to start. This is boring. I don't get to do anything. Summer isn't fun anymore."

"You spent the afternoon with Kayla," Polly said.

"Yeah. Cleaning and taping walls to be painted. If I never see another dirty rag, it will be too soon."

"Tomorrow is going to be too soon, then."

"Why do I have to do all this? Shouldn't we be out buying supplies for school? New clothes? All of that stuff?"

"School isn't for a few more weeks. Yes, marching band is starting next week, but there's plenty of time for that. And besides, I thought you and Kayla were going shopping with Stephanie."

"Well, yeah, but I'm bored."

Polly pursed her lips. "You probably shouldn't say that again."

"Why?"

"Because if you're really and truly bored, I have plenty of things that you can do."

"I don't want to do your things. I want to do fun things."

"How much whining about this do you have left in you?" Polly asked.

"What do you mean?"

"Are you nearly finished whining or do I need to get involved right now? That's what I mean."

"I'm finished." Rebecca sighed. "I'm just bored."

"Here. Start peeling."

"What?"

"Start peeling. You know how. I'm making mashed potatoes for dinner. You can peel."

"There are so many."

"More whining?"

"Fine." Rebecca threw herself into the chair at the island and dramatically pulled the bag of potatoes close, making loud sighs and groans and moans with every move she made.

The back door flew open and Elijah came running in, but stopped short when Hayden yelled his name.

"Take your shoes off," Hayden said.

Elijah put his hand on the door sill and kicked first one shoe off and then the other. He pushed them back toward his cubbie with one foot until he caught Polly's eye. With a small grin, he turned and picked them up before putting them where they belonged.

"You're kind of a mess," Polly said.

"Noah's worse. Hayden is hosing him off before he can come inside."

"What happened?"

Elijah shrugged. "I tipped the paint over on him."

"On purpose?" Polly held back a laugh, in case he'd done something awful.

"No. I tripped and ran into him while he was holding it. I didn't mean to." He remained in the doorway, hesitant to come the rest of the way inside.

"The whole can?"

"No, we each had one of those plastic bowls. Hayden said it was so we could hold on to it."

She grinned at him and watched his little body relax. "It sounds like you two need an early shower tonight. Run on upstairs and clean up before dinner."

Hayden came in with a soaking wet Noah. He held Noah's clothes in one hand and his shoes in the other. "We got most of the paint out. I'm going to hang these here to dry."

Noah tiptoed into the kitchen, scooted around Rebecca's back and ran for the back stairway.

"Noah, honey?" Polly called out.

He stopped and waited, not turning around.

"Elijah is in the shower, but you take one right after him, okay?"

"He can use ours," Hayden said. "I'll go up and make sure they've cleaned most of the paint off. I took a hose to the mess behind the garage. They were pretty funny."

She chuckled. "There will always be something with them. As long as they don't team up, we'll stay safe. How are you doing?"

"The table is dry now. We should be finished tomorrow. The boys have had a blast playing in the yard. They painted a little, but mostly played. Tomorrow is supposed to be hot. Maybe I'll put them in their swim trunks and they can play with the hose. If they get any paint on them, it will be easier cleaning it off their bodies than their clothes."

"Maybe we could go to the pool in the afternoon," Rebecca said.

Hayden nodded. "That's a good idea. I'll take you guys over if you want."

She lit up. "Will you go swimming with us, too?"

"Sure," he said.

After she was certain that he was out of earshot, Rebecca said, "Whenever he goes to the pool, all the cute boys come around to talk to him. He knows everybody."

"I thought you were serious about Andrew," Polly teased.

"I am! But these guys are way cute."

"Can I call Andrew and Kayla and see if they can go to the pool tomorrow?" Rebecca was already heading for the charger to get her phone.

"After dinner," Polly said. "You know the rules."

"What if they make other plans?"

"Then they've made other plans." She pointed back to the counter. "Peel."

"You're no fun."

"I know. I'm the worst."

The back door opened again and Henry came in with a big smile.

"You look happy," Polly said.

"I found a truck."

"You can't drive yet."

"I can in a couple of weeks and I'll have a truck when the time comes."

"What color is it?"

"Blue. Almost the Sycamore House color, but not quite." He kissed her cheek. "That's one pressure off my mind. We stopped out at Elva's place before coming home tonight." He turned as Heath walked in. "Saw your new donkeys."

"They aren't mine," Polly said. "We don't know who they belong to. What did Elva say about them?"

"They're settling in. And the kids have named them, so it looks like they're home for now."

"What are their names?"

Henry smiled. "Nothing quite as literary as your animals. They are now named Woody and Buzz. Matty was playing one of the Toy Story movies for the donkeys while we were there."

"You don't have the barns done yet."

"They're done enough. Elva would have brought them into the house until they were healthy if she thought she could have gotten away with it. Heath is going out this weekend to help them put up more fence. All they had was that small area behind the house. Nobody thought they'd need this to be finished so fast."

"Around here, you get animals and people before you have everything completely ready. At least Elva was willing to take them. Eliseo didn't want any more at Sycamore House."

Henry sat down beside Rebecca and picked up a peeled potato. He took a bite out of it and set the potato back down in front of her.

"What are you doing?" she asked.

"I like 'em raw."

"That's gross."

"Elva said that Eliseo felt bad about rejecting them. He was pretty shaken up by that storm coming up so fast. She also said that he was upset someone could get into the Sycamore House pasture so easily. He got new chain for that back gate."

"They cut the other, right?"

"They cut the lock. He's ordered one that can't be cut. I suspect he felt helpless."

"He doesn't like that," Polly agreed. "I still can't figure out who would be moving donkeys around like this. Jason and Scar can't spend every night at the barn and I'm tired of getting up early every morning."

"We could go sleep in the hay," Henry said, winking at Polly.

"That's even grosser," Rebecca said. "Stop it."

"What?" he asked.

"You know what."

"Little girl has been reading too many romance novels," he said.

"Have not."

"I need to get some work done before dinner. Okay if I go hang out in our room?"

Polly laughed. "That would be fine. We finished cleaning the walls and floor in the living room. We'll paint the office tomorrow. Maybe this weekend we can move furniture around again. I'd like to get the desk set up in the office so you can work in there."

He nodded. "It drives me nuts that I can't help."

"We have plenty of strong bodies around. No worries."

Rebecca held her arm up and flexed. "I'm strong."

"Yes you are," Henry said, squeezing her upper arm. "Nobody ever said you weren't."

Polly's phone rang and she was surprised to see that it was Eliseo. She picked it up and walked out onto the back porch. "Hey. What's up? Is everything okay?"

"Yeah. I wanted to tell you that you don't need to come early tomorrow morning. Jason and Scar are going home tonight. I'll stay instead."

"That's crazy," Polly said. "Why won't you let me hire someone to guard the place?"

It had been nearly a week since thieves had broken in and tried to steal the donkeys and it had been two days since the two new donkeys had been dropped off. They hadn't had any other excitement and she assumed that whatever had been going on, it was over now.

"Just through this weekend," he said. "Don't argue with me. I sleep better here than anywhere else. You know that. Elva and the kids are going to come over and bring dinner. We're all set."

"I'm not happy about this. It's not what I hired you to do."

"Yes it is, Polly. I care for these animals as if they were my own. I wouldn't have it any other way. If you didn't have a big family to take care of, you'd be the one in this barn tonight and you know it."

"I should be."

"No. I should be. I'm happy here. I didn't call you for permission, by the way. I only called so that you could sleep in tomorrow. You've been here early for the last three mornings. Take one off."

"Okay, but I'm not happy about it."

He chuckled. "I can live with that."

CHAPTER TWENTY-TWO

Driving over to Sycamore House, Polly smiled at the two sleepy boys in the back seat of her truck. They hadn't complained about her getting them up early this morning, and were looking forward to the day, but they certainly weren't used to being awake at this hour.

She'd appreciated the additional sleep yesterday morning, but at the same time, she enjoyed her mornings with the horses and donkeys again. Noah and Elijah were spending the day with Elva and her kids. If that hadn't been enough to motivate them out of bed, the fact that she and Eliseo were taking them out to the house on horseback was about more than they could handle. Polly couldn't figure out how they might possibly stop for coffee at Sweet Beans, so she filled her travel mug.

Today would be busy for everyone. Rebecca was at Sycamore House, helping with finishing touches for Beryl's art show on Sunday afternoon. Henry and Heath were already gone for the day, and Hayden had appointments in Ames with several of his professors to discuss his research project. This was how the next year was going to look and Polly was doing her best to not complain about her family spreading out.

Two years ago, she didn't have a family and now, she had a love / hate relationship with the idea that they were growing into their own lives.

When she pulled into the parking area beside the barn, she double-checked the time, surprised to see Jason's car already gone. She wasn't late, so at least there was no guilt.

"Come on, boys. Let's go."

They'd been quiet during the drive over. Elijah stretched his arms out and yawned before unbuckling his seatbelt. "People rode horses all the time before there were cars, didn't they?" he asked.

She held his door while he jumped to the ground, surprised to see Noah climb across to jump out of the same door. "They did."

"We should do that more," Noah said.

"Ride horses?"

"Yeah. Instead of cars. It's better for the planet."

"You're right, but it sure takes a lot longer to go places."

"But it's more fun," Elijah said, dancing in front of the gate. He'd finally come awake. "Grandma says we shouldn't be in such a hurry. We miss out on things."

"Grandma Marie?" Polly asked.

He nodded as she opened the gate. "She's always telling me to slow down."

Polly laughed out loud. "You are full of energy, that's for sure." The large door into the barn was open and she went in to find Nan and Demi already saddled up. "Eliseo?" she called out.

He came in from the outside through Daisy's stall. "Good morning."

"Are they ready for us to ride?"

Eliseo nodded. "Noah, you're going to ride with me this morning. You can sit in the saddle and I'll sit behind you. Polly, I want you in the saddle on Demi and Elijah will sit behind you. Boys, remember, don't swing your feet into the horses. Keep them still. We've practiced this around the pasture, right?"

The two boys nodded.

Noah and Elijah were still trying to come to grips with riding these big horses. They were getting more comfortable on the backs of Tom and Huck and while Eliseo's training with the Percherons had those horses as gentle as they could be, neither of the young boys were in control enough to manage this ride on their own. While it was only a couple of miles, Polly wanted them to enjoy the trip. She looked forward to Elva having more normal sized horses. In all her life, she'd never imagined that she would be comfortable on the back of a horse, much less have a family who rode. Rebecca wasn't quite as passionate about the horses as she had been in the beginning. There were too many other things in her life right now. At least she wasn't afraid of riding. That was enough.

Eliseo waited for Polly to climb onto Demi's back and then helped Elijah up behind her. The horses were fine with having two people on their backs, especially since the boys weighed practically nothing. Once they were settled, she turned and headed out the main door. Eliseo got Noah situated, adjusted the stirrups so he was comfortable, then led Nan out. He closed the barn door, and once they cleared the gate, he shut it and used the bar to swing himself up behind Noah. He wrapped his arms around the boy and gathered the reins into his hands. Polly never ceased to be amazed at how natural this was for him. She was so proud that he was part of her life.

She rolled her shoulders in order to force herself to relax and then patted Elijah's arms that were around her waist. "How are you doing back there?"

"Good. I can't believe we're out on the road."

"It is fun, isn't it? What do you think people will say when they see us going through downtown?"

"They'll think we're cool." Elijah was practically vibrating with excitement. He squeezed her. "You do the funnest things."

She covered his hand with hers. "I like doing fun things with you."

As they rode through the downtown area, she felt his head turning back and forth while he looked to see who might be paying attention to him. He waved to someone, startling Polly when his hand left her side, but it was soon returned. Once they passed Madison Street, Eliseo slowed and beckoned for her to catch up and ride beside him.

"How are you doing over there, Elijah?" Eliseo asked.

"I'm good. This is fun."

"One of these days you two boys will be able to ride all by yourselves. You need to come over and practice more often."

"That's on me," Polly said. "We get so busy."

"Maybe we should set up a regular schedule."

Polly chuckled. "My life is going to be scheduled to death this next year. I can see it now."

"That was funny," Elijah said.

"What? Schedules?"

"No. I felt it when you laughed."

She laughed again. The heat of the day had yet to take hold, the sky was clear, and Bellingwood was just waking up. A man standing on his front porch waved as they rode by, and further down the street, they rode up on a young woman who was out for a run. She slowed and turned as she heard the horses' hooves on the pavement, then stepped up onto the grass as they went past. The boys both waved at her and she waved back with a smile.

"Do you know her?" Elijah asked Polly.

"I don't."

"Cheryl Tindale," Eliseo said.

Polly looked over at him, surprised. "*You* know her?"

"She owns the flower shop. Her husband works at the farm store in Boone."

Polly blinked and nodded. "Okay, I didn't expect that."

"What?" he asked, his eyes twinkling with mirth. "You don't think I'm meeting people?"

"Whoops," she replied with a laugh. "Of course you are."

They went past Ford Street, the last real street in town and he picked up the pace. Polly nudged Demi to keep pace with Nan.

"I know Don because of how much I buy from them. He's brought a few things up when I got too busy. They live out west of town and have horses there, too. Cheryl used to ride competitively."

"She doesn't now?"

"They bought the flower shop a few years ago and she hasn't had time. He thinks that maybe someday she'll get back to it."

"Do you know Cheryl very well, too?"

He shrugged. "I've bought a few things from her."

"For Sylvie?" Polly taunted.

Elijah laughed behind her. "She's his girlfriend. He buys flowers for her. That's what boys do, isn't it, Eliseo?"

"You're right, bud. That's exactly what boys do. They also buy them for their sisters and if they think about it, they should buy them for their bosses, too. Flowers are always a nice gift."

"If I had money, I'd buy you flowers, Polly," Noah said.

"So would I," Elijah echoed.

Polly could hardly believe they were already at the corner leading to Eliseo's home. The trip hadn't taken long at all. He turned Nan onto the gravel road and Polly followed him down the road and then into the main driveway. Before Eliseo was able to dismount, the front door flew open and four kids were on the porch waving at them. The plan was to drop Noah and Elijah off and turn right around. He didn't want to leave the barn without a human there for too long. The rest of the staff wouldn't be at work for another hour. Polly shook her head at the realization that she was well into her day at seven o'clock in the morning.

Eliseo was on the ground and lifting Noah off Nan before Polly realized what was happening and then Elijah released her and allowed Eliseo to help him down from Demi.

"If you make me get down," Polly said to him, "I'll need a stool to climb back up here."

He nodded. "It's up to you. Do you want to see Woody and Buzz? They seem to be happy in their new digs."

"Sure."

She swung her leg over Demi's back and let Eliseo help her down. He led the two horses toward the back of the house where Elva had already put out buckets filled with water for them.

He tied them to a fence and walked up to the back door. "Do you need more coffee? You can come on in."

"I really don't," she said, knowing full well that once she got back to town and was on her own, the first place she was going was Sweet Beans. She followed him inside and up the few steps into the kitchen. This was a very cozy space. The window over the kitchen sink looked out on where the stables were being built and two small bouquets of flowers adorned the sill. Elva had a big cookie jar on the end of the counter just as you walked in, and the table, which only had room for four people, had another small vase of cut flowers sitting in its center.

Elva walked in from the dining room. "The kids have been watching for you. They're excited about Noah and Elijah being here today. Are you sure they'll be fine for the whole day? We're going to be working outside."

"They're good workers," Polly said. "They are both looking forward to whatever you have for them to do."

"You know," Elva said, looking around to make sure that there were no kids to hear her. "If they'd like to spend the night, my kids would love that. We're still burning quite a lot of brush out back and we could have a bonfire. All you'd have to do is drop clothes and stuff with Eliseo today. He could bring it back with him."

Polly nodded. It was one thing for her to sign the boys up to spend a night at Marie and Bill's house, but she wasn't sure how they'd feel about this. It had taken a few months for Elijah to finally sleep soundly every night. Even though it had been chaotic, she knew that in those early months, he'd felt safe because Heath and Hayden were only a few steps away. When they finally moved upstairs, the transition had been made easier because of the presence of Obiwan and Han, as well as the fact that Polly and Henry were right next door. She couldn't believe that it had been just a year ago when those two boys first arrived in her life and needed the comfort of the sofa backs, as well as warm dogs to make them feel safe. They'd come so far, but she wasn't going to expect them to have come this far.

"I know, you need to talk to them, right?" Elva asked.

"I do. I'm not sure how they'll feel about being in a stranger's house. They've been through so much."

Elva smiled. "I understand. Maybe they'd like to stay for the bonfire and then Eliseo or I could bring them home around ten thirty. Is that too late?"

"They might fall sound asleep on the way home, but that could work, too. There's every possibility you will be very tired of them before that time arrives, though," Polly said.

"I don't think so. We have a full day. My kids usually wear out about three o'clock and everything stops for an hour or so before we start thinking about dinner. We all collapse in the living room." Elva shook her head. "I don't even let them turn the television on. No sound, just lots of pillows and quiet talking. I usually need a nap, but they can read."

"Wow," Polly said. "That's awesome."

"We've been working pretty hard this summer. Everything is changing for my kids. It used to be they watched television all the time, but Eliseo doesn't like it, so I've been weaning us off." She shrugged. "I miss some of my shows, but the kids are doing better without it, so I won't complain. They have a few movies that they like to watch." She grinned. "Toy Story is one of them. Even Eliseo likes that one. You should come meet Woody and Buzz again. They're going to be sweet boys, but they've been through some stuff. I wish I knew where they came from."

"Me too," Polly said. She saw the kids run past the back window. "What are they doing now?"

"Who knows. I suppose I should get out there and start organizing the troops. Are you and Eliseo staying?"

Polly looked around. "Where did he go? I saw him come inside."

Elva pointed out the window. "He moves so quietly sometimes. He's checking on the donkeys."

"I want to talk to Noah and Elijah before I leave."

"If they need to come home for any reason, we'll make it happen," Elva said. "I understand this is a big deal for them. I'm so used to my pack of crazies that I figure they can incorporate anyone into the fun."

"You've settled in nicely," Polly said with a smile. "I'm happy for you."

"Me too. I didn't expect to find my home with my brother, but it's good." She gestured to the back door.

Polly went down the steps and put her hand on the door. "I haven't seen one of these in years," she said, pointing to a cloth bag hanging on a peg on the wall.

"My clothespin bag?"

Polly turned. "You hang laundry?"

"Yeah. Here I am, out here in the country — a whole new girl. I love the smell of sheets after they've been on the line. Sammy is tall enough to help me and the girls are figuring it out."

They went out into the yard and Noah ran up to Polly. "We should have brought our bikes."

"That would have looked funny on Nan's back," Polly said. "Go get your brother, I want to talk to you two."

He looked at her wide-eyed. "Did we do something?"

"Not at all. Just want to work out the schedule."

"Elijah!" he yelled, running to the pack of kids. "Come here. Polly wants to talk to you."

Elijah stopped in his tracks. Polly saw the wheels in his head spinning as he tried to figure out what he'd done. Slowly turning, he walked toward her.

"You're not in trouble," she said. "Come here. I just want to say a couple of things."

"We'll be good," he said. "I promise."

"I know that. I trust you. But ..." Polly waited for the two of them to gather to her and she knelt down. "Elva asked if you wanted to spend the night here. They're going to make a bonfire after supper."

Since neither boy reacted with joy or glee, Polly was pretty certain where this conversation was going to go.

"It's all up to you," she said. "If you want to stay for the bonfire and then come home to sleep in your own beds, that's perfectly fine. We'll come get you. If you want to come home before the bonfire, all you have to do is tell Elva to call me. I'll come get you. It's completely your decision. And if you want to change your mind later today, that's okay, too."

Elijah looked at Noah and then back to Polly.

"He's afraid that Sam will be upset if we don't stay tonight, but we want to come home," Noah said.

"Nobody is going to be upset," Polly assured them. "If you don't want to do it tonight, maybe another time will work out better. Maybe we'll invite Sam to spend the night with you first."

Elijah smiled and nodded. "That would be fun."

"Do you want to stay for the bonfire?" she asked.

He jumped up. "Can we help make it?"

"You'll be helping with a lot of projects today. Are you ready for that?"

"Yes!" he shouted.

She stood and hugged both boys, then watched as they ran to catch up with their friends.

"What do you think?" Elva asked.

"I think they'll come home tonight."

Elva nodded. "Eliseo can bring them whenever they're ready."

"Or call me. We can come get them." Polly watched Eliseo walk into the makeshift pen. The donkeys were hesitant at first, but came over to him for scratches and affection.

"It's going to take time," Elva said. "You saw that with your horses, didn't you? Eliseo wasn't always there."

"No, but I was glad when he showed up. It took a lot of work to make sure they had the right food and care. You two are lucky that you know what to do."

"I never thought I'd get a chance to use what I learned growing up, but I'm looking forward to getting started." Elva walked with Polly over to Demi. "Thanks for bringing the boys out. Sometimes I worry that my kids are too far away from friends, and I don't know that many people in town yet."

"It will take time, but pretty soon you'll be overrun with people out here and you'll want everyone to go away."

Eliseo arrived, carrying a step stool. Elva laughed. "I forgot that you'd need this. Demi is so tall."

"It's embarrassing," Polly said. "I'm not quite as smooth as your brother."

She and Eliseo were soon back on the road, heading toward Bellingwood.

"Your sister is happy," Polly said.

"That makes me happy. I never thought we'd be together again. It's funny how things work out."

They rode in silence, enjoying the peace of the morning as they re-entered town.

Polly pointed to the east. "Do you know anything about the Sutters' Farm?"

"Yeah," he said, nodding. "I've met them. Bought plants from them for the garden this year. He's a bit odd and she's kind of rough around the edges. It's not easy doing business with her, but she's the one in charge. She does all of the business interactions." He paused. "She does most of the work, too. From what I've seen, he works on some of the equipment, but he's not much help in the gardens."

"How does she do it all?"

"Transient workers come through during the different harvest seasons. I know a bunch of them come into town in the fall. They work at the winery, harvesting grapes, and some are up here clearing out the gardens for next spring. They do pretty well, but I'm sure it isn't easy." Eliseo turned the horses east on Taylor Street — it was only two blocks back to Spruce Street where the farm was located. "Have you met them?"

"I saw them at Sweet Beans one day when I was there with the kids. They have a daughter in Elijah's class. He says she's mean. I kind of introduced myself to them. They weren't friendly."

Eliseo nodded. "Sounds about right." He gestured out at the fields to the east once they turned onto Spruce. "All of this is theirs. That field will be filled with pumpkins in a month or so. They sell to a bunch of grocery stores around here. Their greens are a big seller — kale, arugula, lettuces and the like."

The peace of the morning was shattered at the sound of a screeching yell, followed by cursing and more yelling.

"Sounds like she's up and at 'em," Eliseo said. "Wonder who she's yelling at this early?"

"I'm so glad I don't live across the street. I'd hate waking up to that."

"I've talked to some of her workers downtown at the bar. They don't last very long, that's for sure. Sometimes it's only a week. They get their pay and get out. I'm surprised she can keep bringing in new ones. You'd think they would talk to each other. There are a couple of people who seem to come back time after time. The money isn't bad and if you need the work, you'll put up with about anything to feed your family."

She watched him as they rode and wondered exactly how much he had put up with in his lifetime. It couldn't have ever been easy, especially when he had to face all of that while worrying about how people perceived him because of his burns.

"I'm glad you're here, Eliseo."

He looked at her in surprise. "Me too. What's that about?"

"I'm just glad you found us." Polly leaned forward and patted Demi's neck. "I couldn't have done what you do with these horses. I've said it before and I'll say it again. You gave me the freedom to love them and not worry that I was making terrible mistakes. Your sister is here and you two are building a life. I'm glad that it's all worked out this way."

They turned on Tyler and headed west again.

"That's where Stephanie and Kayla are living," Polly said, pointing to the Worth's house.

"Doesn't Mrs. Watson live down there?"

"Yeah. Bellingwood isn't that big. Everybody lives by somebody."

"Now you're being profound. You need more coffee."

"Yeah. And you're going to walk me right past my favorite place. It's not fair."

"Maybe we should stop in and give everyone a thrill."

CHAPTER TWENTY-THREE

As they approached the main cross street, Eliseo beckoned to Polly and turned into the alley behind the coffee shop.

"What are you doing?" she asked.

"Getting coffee for you. The dock is high enough back here that you should be able to step right off Demi and go inside. You'll never find an easier place in town to get back on him when you return."

"You should come in, too. There are posts back here you can use to tie them up.

He shook his head. "I'll wait outside."

"Can I get you something to drink?"

"No, thank you. I have coffee back at the barn."

"Come on," Polly said. "A croissant, a muffin? Anything?"

He looked at the watch on his wrist. "I'll bet Sylvie still has breakfast muffins. One of those would be nice."

She turned Demi around and sidled up to the concrete dock. Eliseo was right. After handing the reins to him, she stepped right off onto it. "I'll be right back. I promise."

"We aren't in any hurry," he said. "Take your time."

Polly wasn't about to abuse the privilege and ran to the back door of the coffee shop and went in. When she tapped on the kitchen door, both Sylvie and Marta looked up in surprise.

"What are you doing here?" Sylvie asked. "I can usually see what's going on out front."

"I came in the back door. Eliseo is out there with Demi and Nan. We took the boys up to Elva's place this morning."

Sylvie smiled as she brushed flour from the front of her apron. "He told me you were doing that. Did they have a nice ride?"

"We did. He let me stop to get coffee and said he'd like one of your breakfast muffins. Out front?"

Marta waved at Polly. "I'm pulling a fresh batch out now. When you come back with your coffee, I'll have them packed up."

"Thank you." Polly ran down the hallway to the main room and shook her head at how busy the place was. She couldn't get over how Bellingwood had embraced this little shop. She stepped into line behind two others and waited.

Skylar looked up and caught her eye. "Your regular today?"

"Just iced cold brew — black," she said. "Go ahead and finish with them."

He nodded to where Camille was mixing something into a tall glass. "She's got it. Anything to eat this morning?"

"Not now. Just coffee."

"I didn't see you come in the front door."

Polly smiled. "The horses are waiting for me out back."

"You rode up on the horses? That's cool. Can I come see?"

"Sure."

"Do you care, Camille?" he asked, filling a glass with ice.

"Don't be long," she replied.

Polly slipped two dollars into the tip jar and took the iced coffee from Skylar, then met him in the hallway.

"How are Stephanie and Kayla doing?" she asked, knowing full well that he was over there all the time.

"Good. That old Mr. Worth is quite the character. He and I put shelf strips on the wall in Stephanie's closet last night. He's going out to buy the wood for shelves today and I bet he has them painted and ready to install by the time I get over there tonight. Stephanie has to be at Sycamore House, but he said that he'd let me in since I'm there all the time anyway. Kayla will be with Rebecca, right?"

"I hadn't heard anything. Is she at Sycamore House today helping to set up for Beryl's show?"

"Oh yeah," Sky said. "That's what's going on. I'm sure she is. They're going to have a busy weekend. There are two weddings tomorrow again — one reception in the early afternoon and then one in the evening. And that's after the rehearsal dinner that's happening tonight."

The kitchen was empty and when Polly opened the back door, she smiled at Marta and Sylvie standing beside Demi.

"He's a beautiful horse," Marta said, running her hand down his neck. I've always wanted to see them up close, but didn't think I should bother anyone. This is a special treat."

"Any time you'd like to ride, I'd be glad to take you out," Eliseo said. "Maybe you could convince Sylvie that she'd like to go for a ride, too."

"You've never ridden?" Marta asked her boss.

Sylvie blushed. "There hasn't been time yet. Someday I will." She glanced at Eliseo. "I will. I promise."

"You all heard that," he said. "Howdy, Sky. You should come down and ride sometime, too."

Skylar tentatively reached out to touch Demi. "I've never been on a horse. You sure he won't throw me off?"

"I never say never," Eliseo said, winking at Polly. "These horses are as gentle as any you'll ever meet."

Polly handed her coffee back to Skylar. "Hold this, will you?" She climbed back onto Demi's back, got herself settled and took the reins that Eliseo held out to her, before taking the coffee back. "Are you ready?" she asked Eliseo.

He held up a bag that held more than one breakfast muffin. "I am, now. Thank you, Marta." He gave a small wave and they rode back down the alley to Elm Street and headed south, waiting at the new stop sign for two cars to pass.

"That was nice. Thank you, Eliseo."

He shrugged. "It was an easy stop."

They continued until they got to the highway and waited for cars to pass before crossing.

Polly pointed toward the road south of the barn. "What is that? Is that our donkeys?"

"Damn it," Eliseo said. Suddenly, he and Nan were racing down the road.

She signaled Demi and he took off. It had been a long while since she and Demi had run like this and even though she was nervous and worried, the sensation of being on the horse's back while he ran full out was glorious. The muscles in the body under her were incredibly powerful. She took a moment to revel in it.

"Stop!" Eliseo yelled. He got close enough that he used the same technique he used with his dogs and clicked his teeth together, then yelled. "Huck! Tom!"

The two donkeys ground to a halt, surprising the man who had their leads in his hand.

Polly raced on around them, then slowed Demi, turned, and trotted back only to find herself face to face with Roger Carlson and his gun.

"What in the hell are you doing? Don't you point that gun at me."

"Get out of my way," he growled. "I'm taking these two with me whether you like it or not."

"I don't like it at all. Are you going to shoot both of us *and* our horses? You don't want to do this."

"I don't care. This is the way it has to be." His hand shook as he held the gun up.

Eliseo had come up beside him. Polly barely saw it happen, but he used one of the reins as a whip and knocked the gun out of Carlson's hands, sending it to the ground.

Roger Carlson promptly brought both hands close to him, groaning in pain.

Polly brought Demi closer to the man, crowding him toward the ditch and away from the gun, while Eliseo jumped down.

He kicked the gun away, then grabbed Carlson's shoulder. "Kneel," Eliseo spat out. "On your knees."

"I'm not kneeling," the man said defiantly.

"Like hell." Eliseo pushed at the back of Carlson's knees, bending them and shoved the man downward.

Roger Carlson kneeled.

"What are you doing with our donkeys?" Polly asked. "Was it you who brought those two starving animals to our pasture?"

Carlson refused to look up, much less speak.

"Fine," she said. It took a moment for her to balance her coffee so she could dig out her phone. Fortunately, Demi had a wide back.

"Bellingwood Police Department," a familiar voice said.

"Mindy, it's Polly Giller. I need Ken or Bert south of the barn on Elm Street."

"What did you find now?"

"A horse thief. He tried to take the donkeys again — this time in full daylight." Polly nudged Demi closer to Roger Carlson, eliciting a look from Eliseo. His eyes were twinkling again, so she wasn't worried she'd gone too far.

"Do you know who it is?"

"Roger Carlson."

There was a long silence on the other end of the phone.

"What's wrong?" Polly asked.

"Not mine to tell you. I'll send Ken right over. Bert's off right now. Don't be too hard on the man. He does his best. That's all I can say."

"He had a gun," Polly said.

"Damn it. You're safe?"

"Yes. I'm with Eliseo. He was just like a Wild West deputy, chasing down villains and bringing 'em to their knees."

Mindy chuckled at that. "I've sent a message to Ken. He should be there soon. Can you hold him?"

"He ain't a-gonna like it, Miss Mindy," Polly said in her best cowboy accent. "We wrangled this here rustler and don't aim to let him get away."

"It's never boring with you. I can't wait to hear what Ken has to say."

"Thank'ee ma'am." Polly grinned as she tucked her phone between her legs. "Chief's on his way, Eliseo. That was a nice trick with the rein. I have to ask, how did you know his finger wouldn't hit the trigger and shoot me?"

Eliseo glanced back at the gun. "When people own guns and don't know how to use them, they do stupid things like leave the safety on." He shook his head. "And besides, this one doesn't even have a magazine in it. There could have been a bullet in the chamber, but it seemed doubtful."

That brought Roger Carlson's head up. He looked at the gun as if it were completely alien, then slumped his shoulders.

"It's not even your gun, is it?" Polly asked. "Have you ever touched it before today?"

Carlson started to open his mouth, but instead looked back at the ground.

The sound of a siren got their attention. Roger Carlson tried to stand up. He braced his hands on the pavement and pushed away from Eliseo toward the ditch, but Eliseo caught the collar of his shirt and pushed him so that he ended up lying face down on the ground.

"Stay put," Eliseo said.

Polly shook her head. It was easy to underestimate the man who worked for her. The burns on his face might make a person think he was weak — that he was less of a man because of his scars. In reality, years of working to return to health, as well as the last few years of working daily with the horses and donkeys, made him strong as well as quick. He wore shirts that covered the burns and scars on his arms and down his torso, but they also covered the powerful muscles he'd built up. She wouldn't want to be the person who tangled with Eliseo Aquila.

The Chief of Police — Ken Wallers — drove up to them, his siren turned off when he passed Sycamore House. He parked behind the two donkeys, who had been wandering back and forth until Eliseo took their leads in his hands.

"Well, howdy folks," Ken said. "Looks like you caught yourself a donkey rustler. What do you have to say for yourself?" He bent down, and pulling Roger's arms behind him, whipped a zip-tie closed on them. "Roger Carlson, I'm surprised. Why would you be out here stealing donkeys?"

"Not stealing. Just borrowing."

Patting down the man, he pulled another gun out of his jacket pocket. "What's this?"

Roger Carlson looked down. "For the tranquilizers."

Polly backed away and Ken helped Carlson stand. Eliseo took the time to walk back to the donkeys. He rubbed his hand across their backs and then swore out loud as he pulled another dart from Huck's shoulder. He checked Tom and found a second. "Chief, I need to get these boys home right now. They're going to go down again and I want them to be in their stall."

Ken nodded. "I've got this one. Why did you do it, Roger? What did these donkeys ever do to you?"

"Polly," Eliseo said, "could you bring Nan home with you?"

"Uhhh, sure," she replied. "Will she be okay with that?"

He nodded. "She'll be fine. If I asked, she'd probably follow me, but I don't want to watch her. I need to hurry." He clicked his teeth and started trotting with the donkeys back to the pasture's entrance north of the barn.

"Tell the lady," Ken said. "Why are you stealing her donkeys? We both want to know."

"I want a lawyer."

Ken rolled his eyes. "You have to be kidding me. This isn't a murder investigation. It's barely even a crime. Tell me what you've done."

"I don't know, Ken. If those mistreated, starving donkeys belong to him, Mark Ogden might have something to say about there being a crime," Polly said.

"You aren't like this, Roger. You're smarter than this and I know your mother didn't raise you this way."

Roger Carlson looked at Polly and then at Ken. "I'm so sorry. Julia wanted a horse, but her mother said they were too big. We found two donkeys cheap and brought them home." His entire body seemed to sag in on itself. "I couldn't. I just couldn't."

"Couldn't what?" Polly asked. "Couldn't feed them when they needed to be fed? Couldn't hire someone to take care of their hooves? Couldn't call a vet when they needed help? Couldn't keep yourself from hitting them and hurting them?"

"Couldn't stop her," he practically whispered.

"Couldn't stop who?" Ken asked. "Who did this."

"Jennifer." The word was spoken so quietly, Polly wasn't sure if she'd heard him correctly.

"Your wife? What does she have to do with it?"

"It's hard to explain," he said. "She'll kill me. I might as well admit to it and be done. Put me in jail, but if you do, please get Julia out of that house. I'm the only thing standing between her and her mother."

Polly took a breath, then made a quick decision. She put her phone back in her pocket, took one last drink of the coffee, knowing it was about to spill all over everything and swung her leg over so she could jump to the ground. When she stood up straight again, she couldn't believe the coffee was still in her hand. Taking Demi's lead, she approached Nan and took her lead. Approaching Roger and Ken, Polly waited a breath. "Your wife is an abuser."

He nodded.

"Does she hurt your daughter, too?"

His body went rigid.

"Say something," Ken said quietly.

"Not if I'm there. I never leave them alone."

"Mark Ogden said that he had to come to your house to put a dog to sleep — that it had been hit by a car. Was that the truth?" Polly asked.

Roger Carlson shook his head. "She beat the animal practically to death because it had chewed a pair of shoes. When she tried to shoot it, I stopped her and she made me call the doctor. She was going to make Julia watch it die one way or the other. I thought that would be less cruel." He grimaced. "It was bad that night."

"So why the donkeys?" Polly asked.

"I was only going to borrow yours — they're so well trained. That night you almost caught me, I had the other two in the trailer and hoped that you would rescue them if you found them in your pasture. I needed Julia to have one last good experience with the donkeys before I told everyone that I had to put them down."

"Surely your wife would have seen that Tom and Huck were healthier than those two you brought over," Polly said.

"She's in the middle of a trial right now. She won't be home until Saturday night and then only for a day. She sleeps in the office when it gets like this. It's the only time Julia and I get any peace. She's a different little girl when her mother is gone. We both are different." He pointed toward the gravel road that went east. "The trailer is around that corner."

Ken looked at Roger. "Is your daughter home alone right now?"

"Yes. I was only going to be gone a short time."

"And your wife is at her office."

"Until tomorrow."

Ken finally picked the gun up from the ground. He pulled the slide back and frowned. "Roger, there aren't any bullets in this."

"That's what the other guy said. I didn't know."

"You've never used it?"

"It belongs to Jennifer. She keeps it in our closet. I brought it with me to scare you if you caught me." He gave an apologetic glance at Polly.

"What do you want to do, Polly?" Ken asked. "I can take him in if you want to press charges."

"I can't," she replied. "Mr. Carlson, how can you stay in that house?"

"How can I go? I have no money. We can't go anywhere that she won't find us. She'll never let me have custody of Julia and if I'm not there to deflect her, I'm absolutely certain that someday she will kill our daughter. When Jennifer loses control, there is no stopping her." He shuddered. "The reason the donkeys were in such bad shape is that she wouldn't let me buy feed and she wouldn't let me give them to someone else because Julia wanted a horse. And if Julia wanted a horse, then Julia was going to get a donkey. And if the donkey died, then it was Julia's fault. And mine too, because I can't make food out of nothing."

"Do you and Julia get enough to eat?" Polly asked quietly.

"It's better when she's in school," he replied.

Polly turned to Ken. "We have to help."

"What can we do?" he asked. He slit the zip tie and removed it from Carlson's wrists.

"Surely there are safe havens around here."

Ken shook his head. "The ones around here don't have the capacity to take men in because so many women there have been badly traumatized by their husbands."

"That's not fair."

"She'll fight me in court for Julia," Roger said. "She knows lawyers and judges all over the state. There's no way that I can win that battle and I won't leave my daughter with her. If we run, she'll hunt us down and then she'll throw me in jail for kidnapping Julia. It's useless. I've tried and tried to come up with ways to escape, but she's got too much power. If you let me go, I'll tell Julia that the donkeys died. Her mother will be furious with me for upsetting our daughter, but I can live through it. I've lived through everything else. There isn't any hope." He put his hand out. "Can I have the gun?"

"No," Ken said. "I won't do that. Does your wife have another gun in the house?"

Roger nodded. "Yes. Maybe she won't notice that this one is missing. I'll have to come up with a reason that it isn't there anymore." He put his hand out to Polly and she shook it. "I'm sorry that I involved your donkeys. I didn't know what else to do. They're so well trained I thought Julia might be able to ride once before I returned them. My mistake. I won't make it again."

"I'll follow you home," Ken said. "If Polly isn't pressing charges, you're free to go, but son, you've got to get some help. I can put you in touch with folks that know how to help with situations like this."

"Not like this," Roger said. "You don't know Jennifer."

"You aren't the first person in this type of the situation and you won't be the last," Ken said. "You aren't alone. Let us help you."

"There's no help." Roger shook his head and walked past Demi as he headed for his truck. "I *am* sorry, Ms. Giller," he called back.

Eliseo was walking back down the road toward her and she waved at him. This had taken much longer than she'd expected.

"If I can do anything," she said to Ken. "If they need money or a place to stay, please let me know."

He patted her shoulder. "Thanks. I don't know what we can do for him until he's ready to face this, but I'll keep that in mind."

"It's hard to believe these things happen here in Bellingwood."

"More often than anyone realizes. I'm going to follow him home and check on his daughter. Thanks for working with me on this."

"When you *asked* what I wanted to do, I realized that you didn't want this to escalate further. I'm fine with that. His donkeys are safe at Elva's place and my donkeys are home. Do you think he will leave them alone now?"

"Yes I do. He's been defeated and knows there is nothing more he can do. He told you that he wouldn't try again. You don't need to worry."

"Thanks for coming over so fast, Ken," Polly said as she walked with him toward his car. He stood beside the vehicle as she walked on past with the two horses to meet Eliseo.

"What was that about?" Eliseo said, taking Nan's reins into his own hands.

"Oh, Eliseo, you won't even believe it. That poor man is in more hell than we could possibly imagine."

CHAPTER TWENTY-FOUR

Nothing was better than having her family all together around the table this Saturday morning. It wouldn't last long; everyone was busy again today. Stephanie was picking Rebecca up within the hour to spend another day at Sycamore House helping Beryl and Lydia prepare for tomorrow's showing.

Rebecca had come home last night enthralled with the thought of meeting artists that would be coming in to Bellingwood this weekend. Polly didn't recognize a single name, but Beryl's excitement poured over onto her young protégé. Several of Beryl's art students from years previous were already in town; some were professors at universities across the nation, while others were working as artists. It surprised everyone to realize how long Beryl had been encouraging young people to go after their dreams. One young man had captured Rebecca's attention. He was living in Belgium, making very little money, but he painted to his heart's desire. All Rebecca had done last night was talk about the fascinating people she was meeting.

This morning, she could barely sit still at the table and refused to eat anything, asserting that she was too nervous. She had been in and out of Polly's bedroom five or six times while trying on outfits. It had to be perfect. Tomorrow was going to be even worse.

Heath and Henry were spending the day working toward building the library bookshelves. They'd come home last night and measured the room several times. When Heath brought in a roll of brown Kraft paper, Polly had followed him back into the library and watched as they created a template for the curve in the wall. It was hard to believe they were going to start on this. For now, Heath would work at the main shop. He and Hayden were also taking the time to rearrange things in the old garage so they could bring over several shop tools that had belonged to Polly's father. Even if it took him all winter, Heath looked forward to this project.

Hayden and Polly had hauled furniture from the foyer into the living room yesterday afternoon. Although she had barely begun to work on decorating that room, at least there was a place other than the kitchen table or the cramped family room for the family to hang out together ... or escape from each other. Hayden planned to work in the room upstairs today. He and Polly would haul things up from the dining room. Though it might confuse the cats for a day or two, the cat trees would also be removed from the room. One would go upstairs and the other into the office.

Noah and Elijah didn't make it to the bonfire at Elva's last night. They were exhausted from working all day and when Elva asked if they were doing okay, Noah told her that Elijah needed to go home. Their timing had been perfect, since Heath and Henry were at the shop dropping off supplies. They drove up and got the boys. Polly ordered pizza, and they picked that up on their way through. Hayden was out again last night — with friends — or so he implied to them. He wasn't saying much and his brother was also cryptic. That made Polly wonder if there was another girl in his life. He'd tell her when he was ready — or when she could no longer stand it.

Rebecca jumped at the sound of a car turning into their driveway. "That's Stephanie."

"Have a good day," Polly said.

She ran over and stood by the phone charger. "Can I take my phone?"

Polly shook her head. "You won't need it. Leave it here. There are phones all over Sycamore House you can use to reach me."

"But …" Rebecca took one look at Polly and then another at Henry and decided to say nothing more. She nodded slowly and headed out the back door.

Henry leaned over and gave Polly a kiss on her cheek. "We'd better get moving. Dad wants to ride with us while we're picking up lumber today. You have to believe he's chomping at the bit."

"Will I see you at lunch?" Polly asked.

He hesitated. "Maybe not. If we're with Dad, he'll want to go somewhere to eat. He says he never gets out of Bellingwood."

"Okay," Polly said with a laugh. "It looks like you're fully back in business now."

"Yes I am." He tapped at the scar on his face. "This makes me look rakish. Don't you think?"

"That's one word for it." She stood and kissed him. "We've got the dishes. You don't need to worry about those."

Henry laughed out loud. "Pow. Right between the eyes. You knew cleaning up wasn't even on my mind because I was thinking about what I needed to do next."

"Yep," she said. "Noah, Elijah, and I have this. If you are focused on my bookshelves, I'm not complaining in the least."

Kissing Polly on the lips, Henry wrapped his right arm around her and pulled her close. Then he whispered in her ear. "These are the moments I treasure."

"Okay, now I can't think straight."

"Good. It's time for me to leave. You ready to go, Heath?"

Heath shook his head. "Mornings are more treacherous around here when Polly gets up with you." He nudged Noah's shoulder. "Do you see all this kissy-kissy they do?"

"I like it," Noah said with a smile.

"You're not helping." Heath laughed and picked up his plate, as well as Henry's. "I've got your back, Henry." He rinsed them off in the sink and put them in the dishwasher and then ran to catch up to Henry on the back porch.

"They're gone. Shall we have a party?" Polly asked.

"A party!" Elijah yelled, startling Han who had come back in to lie in front of the table after Henry walked out without him. "What kind?"

"First, a cleaning-up-the-kitchen party," Polly said and laughed when he sagged back into his seat. "Then we're going to have a moving-things-around party."

"That's not any fun," he complained, then he brightened. "Can we do a fire outside tonight? We didn't get to have s'mores last night because I was sad."

Polly put her arms around him and squeezed him tight. "We'll talk Henry into a bonfire." She reached over him and stacked up the breakfast dishes while Hayden gathered up the casserole. There was only a small amount left in the pan. All of those years that Polly had cooked for one person and ended up putting food down the garbage disposal because she couldn't eat it fast enough were long since passed. Now, her refrigerator was almost always empty and leftovers rarely made it through the day.

She had the dishwasher open when her phone rang.

"Maybe somebody wants us to come visit them," Elijah said hopefully.

"Maybe," Polly replied. She took her phone out of the charger and was surprised to see the call was from Eliseo. "Good morning. What's up?"

"This might take you off guard, but I wondered if you and the boys might want to come over to the barn this morning."

"Sure. Why?"

"I got to thinking last night. You know about Roger Carlson and his daughter and how all she knows is how to abuse animals?"

"Yeah? What did you do, Eliseo?" Polly was grinning. She had a good idea where this was going.

"After I talked to Sylvie, I decided to call him. You said that his wife isn't around right now, so I figured it was safe."

"And?"

"And I invited him to bring Julia over this morning to see how people treat animals with respect and love, and maybe give her a ride around the pasture. He talked to me for a very long time last night, Polly. That man is in a world of hurt."

"And you're going to rescue him?" she asked.

"I'm going to try to make his life easier at least for a few minutes. If we do this early enough, he and Julia can be home before his wife returns. Like in a half hour? You said his daughter was in Elijah's class. If she sees someone her own age enjoying the donkeys and the horses, maybe it will help her acclimate to kindness a little easier."

"I love you, Eliseo Aquila. We'll be right over."

"Could you do one more thing?"

"Sure, what?"

"Sylvie has a box of breakfast muffins and other treats ready to go. Would you mind picking those up, too?"

"I have to go to the coffee shop? What a dreadful thing to ask of me," Polly said with a laugh. "The boys need to put on jeans and I need to change. We'll hurry and be right there. I'm so danged proud of you, Eliseo. You have no idea."

"Don't make too much of it. I felt guilty for assuming the worst about him. I'm going to schedule a time to take him out shooting, too. If that man has to live in a house with guns, the least he can do is figure out how to hold one properly, much less shoot it. That was embarrassing to watch."

"Like I said. I love you. Let me go and we'll be over as soon as possible." She put the phone in the charger and turned around to see Noah wiping down the kitchen table.

Elijah, however, was standing at the end of the island looking at her with anticipation. "Am I one of the boys that needs to put on jeans?"

"Yes you are," she said, rubbing his head. "We're going to the barn. Eliseo needs our help. Noah, you and your brother need to put on your jeans from yesterday. Make sure you put on socks and your boots, too. We're out of the house in five minutes."

Noah ran back to the sink and dropped the cloth into it, then chased his brother up the back steps.

"I'm sorry, Hayden. We'll be back before lunch."

He shrugged. "No problem. I can do it all by my lonesome. Don't mind me here in this big old house with no one else around. It seems almost sad and depressing, doesn't it?"

"Do you want company? Andrew is probably available. He'd love to come over and help you. From what I hear, Sylvie has him doing all sorts of terrible tasks at his own house."

"Nah." Hayden shook his head. "I'll do what I can and then I'll find something else to do. I should spend time sitting in front of my laptop preparing for classes this fall anyway."

"Do that instead," Polly said. "There isn't anything around here that can't wait until you have plenty of help."

"We'll see."

"And crank up the tunes as loud as you want. Nobody will be able to hear you."

Hayden laughed. "That's not a bad idea." He rubbed his foot across the kitchen floor. "Maybe I'll slide down the hallway with my air guitar." He struck a pose and strummed an imaginary guitar. "Just take those old records off the shelf ..."

"You are much too young to know that movie," Polly said.

"Mom loved it. Especially that scene."

She smiled. "You're a nut. Okay, the boys will be ready before me. I'd better scoot."

~~~

"I certainly didn't expect anything like this to happen, especially after what I did to you," Roger Carlson said.

They were all standing inside the training pen as Noah and Julia rode the donkeys around and around. Eliseo showed Julia how to sit in the saddle, then walked with her a few times around the pen. It didn't take long for her to want to try it by herself. Sitting on the back of Huck, she was perfectly safe. Especially with Eliseo standing mere feet from her at any given moment. Demi stood behind Polly with his head over her shoulder, watching the activities. Elijah stood beside her and every once in a while, tentatively reached out to touch Demi's leg. The big horse had stepped back the first time, but moved forward again, making himself available to the little boy.

Nan and Daisy were racing through the pasture, playing with Eliseo's dogs. Polly knew that Obiwan and Han missed coming over here, but once they'd been given freedom in their own yard, things were much better for them. There were always plenty of children around who wanted to come in and run with her big dogs.

"She's very comfortable on the donkey," Eliseo said. "Maybe one day she will graduate up to a bigger horse."

Roger shook his head. "We talked about it this morning. She knows this is the last time she'll ride one. I won't bring another animal into our life." He closed his eyes. "I've never talked about any of this before to anyone. I don't know why I'm telling you things."

Polly said nothing. Something had clicked between Eliseo and Roger. She wasn't part of it at all. He hadn't intentionally turned his back to her, but Roger was engaging with Eliseo and ignoring her. She gave a slight shrug. Not that he wasn't used to ignoring women. With what he dealt with every day, it was surprising he could speak to any woman. How would he possibly raise his daughter to be different than her mother? The girl's behavior went back and forth between shriveling into a ball and defiant anger — all in a matter of seconds.

She had so many questions for him and wondered at how he'd gotten himself into a marriage with a woman who was so abusive. Surely Jennifer Carlson had shown her true colors long before she was pregnant with Julia. But then, Sylvie had said that her ex-husband had gotten much worse after the boys were born. Oh, she had questions. Like, did he have a job or what did his family think about all that was going on?

When she looked at him, she realized how thin the man was. She had brought the box of goodies into the barn just as he and

Julia arrived. Eliseo opened the box, offered it around and promptly took one of his favorites — Sylvie's breakfast muffins — and bit into it. The box was filled with food, so Polly encouraged her ravenous boys to take something they would like. Before long, Roger and Julia had both eaten quite a few things and Eliseo had filled their glasses of milk and juice several times. How could a woman, who obviously made a great deal of money, not allow her husband to feed her child well? They could afford it, but he spoke as if he was unable to access any of their money. She was slowly destroying the two people on earth who would have loved her without question.

"Oh my God," Roger breathed. Then he shouted. "Julia, get off the donkey. Right now."

The little girl looked up in confusion.

Without missing a beat, Eliseo ran to her, stopped Huck's movement and swung her to the ground. "Go inside," Eliseo said.

Polly looked around. Then she saw a BMW turn into the parking space beside her truck, squealing its tires on the pavement. "Jennifer Carlson?" she asked Eliseo.

"I guess."

Roger Carlson had grabbed up his daughter and run into the barn.

"Put the donkeys in the pasture, please," Eliseo said to Polly, handing her the reins. "I need to help Roger get his daughter's helmet off."

"Come on over, Noah," Polly called out as she watched Jennifer Carlson get out of her car and approach the first gate.

"Roger Carlson, what in the hell are you doing here? I did not give you permission to leave the house today," she screamed. "And don't think for a minute that I don't know what you're doing. Julia killed those donkeys with her neglect and now you're trying to make it okay. Get your ass out here right now!"

"Those donkeys aren't dead," Elijah whispered to Polly. "They're at Sammy's house, right?"

She nodded and handed him the reins to Huck after Tom and Noah passed through the gate. "You two stay in the pasture. Go around to the back where the wagon is. Don't come into the barn or around front until I tell you that it's okay. Promise? Don't leave the donkeys either. Stay with them."

The little boys nodded, their eyes wide and frightened. The woman's rage scared Polly, but there was no way she would cower in the face of it. Polly watched her boys do what she had asked of them, then she went back into the pen and the front gate.

"Can I help you?" she asked calmly, suddenly thankful that there were no guests at Sycamore House yet. There were a few cars at the front entrance as family members set up for the first reception of the day, but at least this would be dealt with before the event began.

"Get out of my way, you bitch."

"No. That won't work here," Polly said. "Please calm down before you go inside."

The fury that lit the woman's eyes grew even more frightening. Her face was bright red and her nostrils flared as she tried to draw in enough breath to speak. What came out instead, was shouting, the likes of which Polly rarely experienced. "Don't you tell me to calm down! I checked his phone calls this morning and discovered that he'd been talking to that ugly spic you've got working for you. He should have asked me first, but he knows I would never allow it. I knew that you people would try to get in between us. You have no idea what I have to put up with. That lazy asshole and his prima donna daughter. I'm going to make him pay for this."

"For what? Julia is in Elijah's class. Is it not okay for her to play with her classmates on a Saturday morning?" Polly knew she was playing with fire, but if she could divert any of this woman's fury away from Roger and Julia and to herself, she'd take the risk. One woman wasn't enough to scare her.

"Them little nigger boys? Oh, hell no. He knows better than that, too. That man isn't going to see the light of day after this little excursion."

"Are you threatening his life?" Polly held out her phone and brought up Ken Wallers' number.

"He's my husband and I can do whatever I want with him. You can't stop me. Now, let me past. I will not allow him to disobey me this way. Get back!"

"No," Polly said, pasting a grim smile on her face and shaking her head. "I will not allow you to act this way on my property. My family, my animals, and my guests are my priority and you are threatening them. You need to leave."

Jennifer Carlson leaned across the gate into Polly's face, her eyes flashing and her cheeks bright red. "Get out of my way, bitch, or I will make sure that you pay as much as he does."

"Now you're threatening me?" Polly asked, standing her ground. She chuckled in spite of the situation. She'd faced much worse than this woman and the stakes were much higher today.

"You want to see a threat?" The woman reached into her purse and took out a handgun — one smaller than the gun her husband had held the day before.

"I'm right here," Roger Carlson said calmly from behind Polly. "You don't need to threaten Polly."

"Polly? Now you're calling her by her first name? I suppose you're sleeping with her. Oh hell, of course you are. Why else would she want you around, you lazy, no good, piece of shit. I've warned you over and over not to mess around with other women and now, here you are flaunting it in my face. I will kill you for this!" She took aim and pulled the trigger on the pistol.

Polly grabbed her ears and ducked to the ground, the ringing sound of the explosion from the bullet leaving the chamber and whizzing past her almost painful. Panting, she pressed the green button on her phone to call Ken, barely able to see because of the tears filling her eyes. Still holding one side of her head, Polly turned to see Roger Carlson lying on the ground.

Jennifer Carlson pushed the gate open, ramming it into Polly's body, then stalked to her husband, who lay deathly still.

Polly had no idea if he'd been hit or not and through her pain and tears couldn't see if he was breathing.

"I should have done this years ago," Jennifer Carlson said, taking aim once again. "I've had the most stressful week of my life and this is what I have to contend with from my family. I'm done with you."

Ken Wallers was saying something, but Polly had lost her phone in the melee. However, she wasn't about to let this woman kill her husband — not in front of Julia Carlson and absolutely not in front of Noah and Elijah. She stood and rushed Jennifer Carlson, tackling her to the ground. The gun went off again, but Polly couldn't tell where the shot had landed.

Jennifer Carlson was no pushover. She turned underneath Polly while they wrestled in the dirt. When she brought her hand up, she seemed surprised to find that she no longer held the gun, so she clenched her hand into a fist.

The thing was, Polly had been in a few dirty fights — with people bigger and meaner than this crazy woman. She knew she had leverage and with one quick punch, hit the woman in the face, snapping Jennifer Carlson's head to the side. As she raised her hand to bring it down again, she heard Eliseo's voice. "I've got this, Polly."

"Daddy!" Julia Carlson ran to her father and Polly sighed with relief as he sat up and with his left arm, took the girl into his lap. Blood ran down his right arm. At least she knew now where he'd been hit.

Eliseo quickly turned Jennifer Carlson back onto her stomach and tied a quick knot in the rope he had efficiently wrapped around her wrists. "I'll gag you if you open your mouth again, lady," he said.

She spat on his shoes.

"I've dealt with worse," he said as condescendingly as he could.

Sirens screamed through town. Polly stood and gave a small wave to the crowd of people who had gathered in the side door of Sycamore House, letting them know the altercation was over. Turning back to the pasture, her heart sank as both Noah and Elijah stood beside Tom and Huck at the inner gate, tears streaming down their faces.

"Go," Eliseo said.

She ran over to them and passed through the gate, falling to her knees in front of them. She opened her arms and both boys allowed her to hug them close. "I'm okay," she said.

"She was going to shoot you," Noah said through sobs.

"No, she wanted to shoot her husband. Not me."

"She had a gun."

"To scare me. But look, everything is okay."

Elijah clung to her. "No it's not. You can't die." He clutched her again and buried his face in her neck.

It was one thing for her older kids to see her head into danger, but these two boys had already seen too much of this in their short lives. "I'm so sorry," Polly said. "I didn't mean to scare you."

"Will they put her in jail?" Noah asked.

"Yes. In fact, I believe that Chief Wallers is here now, am I right?" Polly turned to look over her shoulder.

Noah nodded.

"Once he finds out what she did, he will arrest her and take her to jail."

"Because she's a bad person?"

"Because she did a bad thing. She knew it was a bad thing and chose to do it anyway." These boys worried all the time that they would be punished for mistakes they made. It was something she confronted regularly with them. "If you make a mistake and don't do something on purpose, that won't get you arrested, but she knew that shooting her husband was bad and she did it anyway."

"But she didn't kill him," Elijah said, rubbing at his eyes with the back of his hand. His other hand held tight to Tom's reins. Polly couldn't believe the donkeys were standing so still with all that was happening. The horses were at the other end of the pasture. She didn't blame them. She'd have preferred being far from this situation, too.

"No, thank goodness she didn't kill him," Polly said. "It's good that Julia still has her father. Now, I'm going to talk to Chief Wallers. Can the two of you walk with Tom and Huck around the barn to their stall door and take them inside? As soon as Eliseo can, he'll come in and take their saddles off. Okay?"

Noah nodded solemnly.

"We'll talk more about this later," Polly said. "Think about all of the questions you want to ask and then we'll discuss them."

She stood up and watched them take a few steps. Heaving a sigh, she turned and crossed through the gate again. This was going to be a long day, and when Henry found out what had happened, she was going to have more difficult questions to answer.

CHAPTER TWENTY-FIVE

"Go ahead." Roger Carlson nodded as the EMTs lifted his gurney into the ambulance. His daughter had refused to let go of his other hand, wailing when they tried to pry the two apart. His wife, Jennifer, had already been taken away. She had never stopped screaming at the man, accusing him of everything from adultery to attempting to kill her, from trying to sabotage her career to deliberate destruction of their home. When Chief Wallers asked for proof of any of her accusations, she pointed at Roger and told the police to ask him, stating that he knew everything.

"Thanks again," Roger said to Polly.

She nodded at him. Polly was certain his wife would end up pleading not guilty by reason of insanity. It was obvious that Jennifer had been calculating the reactions of the police as she spewed her ravings on them. At the very least, Roger and Julia would be safe for a while.

"Polly!"

She turned at the sound of Rebecca's voice. Her daughter was standing on the sidewalk, unwilling to cross into the pen in her good shoes, so Polly went over to her.

"Did someone really shoot at you?" Rebecca asked, worry etched in her face.

"No, she was shooting at her husband. I was just in the vicinity."

"Found it!" Bert Bradford came out of the barn holding a small plastic bag. "It had lodged on an inside wall. Glad there wasn't a horse in there."

Polly's stomach lurched and she fought to control herself.

"What's that?" Rebecca asked.

"The second bullet." Polly took a long, deep breath. "I'd forgotten about it."

"She shot twice?"

"I don't know if the second was intentional. She was being tackled to the ground." Polly turned away so Rebecca couldn't see her face.

"Who tackled her?" As soon as the words were out of Rebecca's mouth, she gasped. "You did, didn't you."

"I couldn't let her shoot her husband."

The siren spun up as the ambulance pulled away. Polly breathed a sigh of relief that the Carlsons were out of her life for now.

"Ms. Giller, we found your phone." A young man approached and handed it to her. "It's kind of a mess, but it still works."

Polly laughed. She'd completely forgotten about it once she had started the call to Ken Wallers. "Thank you." She brushed dirt away from the back and slipped it into her jeans. She couldn't worry about that right now. "I need to check on Noah and Elijah," she said to Rebecca. "You go on back up to the building. How are things going up there?"

"A bunch of us are going to Davey's for lunch. I'm having so much fun."

"I'm glad. Let me know when you'll be home this afternoon."

Rebecca nodded and as she turned, looked back toward the barn. "Tell Noah and Elijah I was here, would you?"

"Sure." Polly headed for the barn and stopped when Ken Wallers stepped in front of her.

"We haven't had time to talk yet," he said. "Do you want to tell me what happened here?"

"How much do you know already?" Polly asked, still trying to make her way into the barn. She hoped that Eliseo was with her boys — she didn't want to leave them alone much longer.

"Roger Carlson told me that you tackled his wife. Do you want to explain yourself?" Ken asked with a small grin on his face.

"I wasn't letting her shoot him. She was aiming straight at his head and the way she was ranting and raving, she meant to kill him. I couldn't let her daughter become an orphan. Not today."

"What about yourself?" Ken asked.

"What about me? She didn't see me coming. I tackled her from behind and when she fought back, I popped her in the face. Then Eliseo arrived and it was all over."

"Is that how you're going to explain it to your husband?" he asked.

Polly shuddered. "I don't want to think about that right now."

"You know he's heard about it by this point, don't you?"

She frowned. "How? You didn't tell him, did you?"

"No," he replied with a laugh. "Of course not, but this kind of news spreads pretty quickly."

Pointing to the barn, Polly edged closer. "I want to check on my boys. I don't know how much they saw."

"Of course. Take care of them. I'll have more questions for you and Eliseo later. You have a big weekend here at Sycamore House. Mrs. Watson's art show is tomorrow afternoon, isn't it? We've seen a lot of out-of-towners around."

"Rebecca's more involved in that than I am," Polly said. "I haven't even thought about what a big deal it is. I know it's big for Beryl, and it's pretty cool that all of that attention has come to Bellingwood. Can I?"

"I'm sorry. Go. I'll catch up with you later."

Polly went into the barn and headed to the back to find Noah and Elijah. She glanced into the feed room and found them sitting up on a bale of hay. The two cats were sleeping beside them as the boys held Eliseo's tablet, watching a movie.

"Hey, boys," she said.

"We're watching *Toy Story*. Is that okay?" Elijah asked.

"Of course it is. How are you doing?"

Noah shrugged. "Nothing we haven't seen before."

Eliseo walked in. "The donkeys are back outside with the horses and the dogs — none the worse for wear. I let the boys watch a movie. I hope you don't mind."

"Thank you. That's perfect." Polly blew out a breath. She wasn't sure how to begin this conversation with them. "Are you two at a point you can stop watching?"

"Just a couple more minutes," Elijah said, then heard himself. "Please?"

She smiled. "That's fine."

He looked at Eliseo. "Why isn't Jason here today? He's always here."

"His mother has him busy today." Eliseo grinned. "He's taking Andrew shopping. They have a list of things both boys need for school and then they're picking out paint for their rooms."

Polly laughed out loud. "She grabbed the brass ring with this one, didn't she?"

He nodded. "If she could have figured out how to put Andrew to work for Elva, she would have done that, too. I believe Sylvie thinks it is time for him to start pulling his weight."

"I've made it too easy for him," Polly said. "He's helpful, but with as many people as there are around my house, he never has to dig in and work very hard. Rebecca is finding herself working harder too. It's good for everybody."

They both turned at the sound of the front door crashing open.

"Eliseo!" Henry yelled. "Is Polly here?"

She stepped out as he ran up to the feed room. He stopped short, looked her up and down and then pulled her into his arms ... well, only one arm since his left arm was still in a sling.

"What's going on?" Polly asked.

Bill Sturtz and Heath came into the barn and she watched as both men sagged with relief upon seeing her.

"You're okay," Heath said.

"Why wouldn't I be?"

Henry finally let her go and stepped back while checking out every inch of her. "You aren't hurt," he stated plainly.

"I'm fine. Why did you come tearing in here like this?"

He sat down on a bench and put his head between his knees.

"What?" Polly asked.

"We heard you'd been shot," Heath said. "It's all over Twitter and Facebook and Henry got a bunch of texts from people who said that you were involved in a shooting down here at the barn."

Elijah and Noah came out of the feed room. Elijah ran over to sit beside Henry. He hooked his arm in Henry's good arm. "There was a bad lady here. She had a gun. We were scared, but Polly told us to take care of Tom and Huck, so we stayed back in case they were more scared than us."

Henry looked up at Polly with frustration and fear written all over his face. "The boys were here? What happened?"

"It's my fault, Henry," Eliseo said. "I asked Polly to bring the boys over so that Julia Carlson would feel more comfortable learning to ride a donkey. And I'm the one who invited her dad to bring her to visit. After all they'd been through this week, I was just trying to reach out." He huffed a laugh. "I won't be in quite such a hurry to do that again."

"You do it any time you want," Polly said. "It was the right thing to do. We can't take responsibility for a woman's crazy behavior."

"What happened?" Bill Sturtz asked. "It's better to get the straight story. Marie's going to want to know, too. She's home worrying."

"I'm so sorry," Polly said. "Why didn't you call me?"

Henry glowered, a look she didn't often see on him. "I did. Over and over. When you didn't answer, we left the lumberyard and Heath drove here as fast as he dared."

Bill chuckled at his son's words. "It was quite the trip. I sat in the back seat and held on. Haven't ridden in a truck doing those kinds of speeds since I was a kid. How fast were you going, Heath?"

"I'm not telling." Heath flinched when Bill patted his back. "I hoped that the police were here and not watching for me flying down the highway."

Polly took her phone out of her pocket and realized that it had been powered off. "I didn't turn it off," she said, "but it was lost in the chaos for a while and a young technician gave it to me. I'm so sorry. I had no idea. After the police and the rescue squad finally left, the only thing I could think about was Noah and Elijah. We haven't had time to talk much yet either. I'm not even sure what they saw."

"You still haven't told us exactly what happened," Henry said. He tightened his hold on Elijah. "Did someone shoot at you?"

"No," Polly said, shaking her head emphatically. "She might have aimed the gun at me to get me to move out of the way, but the person she wanted to hurt was her husband."

"She shot him," Noah said.

"Did you see that?" Polly asked.

Elijah jumped up. "You told us to stay in the back. We heard the two shots and then when we heard you yelling at her, we came around. I'm sorry. We should have stayed where you told us to stay."

Henry rubbed his hand up and down Elijah's back. "You aren't in trouble."

"Is Polly?" Noah asked.

Polly smiled. "Yeah. Is Polly?" She turned to Elijah. "I was yelling?"

His eyes grew big and he nodded his head up and down. "You yelled loud. That's when we snuck around. You smacked that lady right in the face."

All eyes turned on Polly.

"You hit her?" Henry asked.

"I might have tackled her to the ground, too. When she decided to wrestle with me, I didn't have time for that, so, yes, there might have been a punch. I needed her to stop. She'd shot her husband and was prepared to do worse."

"How much worse?" Bill asked.

Polly shot her eyes to Elijah. "Let's just say it could have been much worse and I couldn't let that happen — not when her daughter was inside the barn and my boys were nearby."

"Where were you through all of this?" Bill asked Eliseo. "I'm glad you weren't hurt."

"I was inside with Roger and Julia. He went out to try to intercede with his wife who was aggressive and threatening. I'm glad that I was with Julia — especially when the first shot rang out. I knew it had hit someone and realized that it was her father when he let out a howl."

"He let out a howl?" Polly asked. "I didn't hear any of that." Then she nodded and rubbed at her ear. "Yeah, the gun went off right beside my head. I'm still having trouble hearing clearly."

"The EMTs didn't look at you?" Henry asked.

"You know better than that," she replied. "I told them I was fine and I am. They had a crazy woman and a wounded man to deal with. At least she only shot him in the arm. I heard someone say that the bullet went right through, so he won't be hospitalized very long."

"So today you had an encounter with an insane woman who shot at her husband. Then you tackled her to the ground, wrestled with her, and ended up punching her in the face," Henry said. He pulled Elijah back so the little boy was sitting on his lap, then nestled his face into Elijah's shoulder. "Your mother is going to make my hair turn gray before its time."

"Me too," Elijah said.

Bill took out his phone. "I need to call Marie and tell her that you weren't actually shot today." He looked pityingly at Henry. "Son, I don't envy you this marriage. It is never going to be easy with her."

"Hey," Polly said. "I'm easy to get along with."

"Hello, Marie. It's me." He rolled his eyes at Polly and walked away. "Polly's fine. The crazy lady wasn't shooting at her."

"I'm sorry I messed up your day," Polly said. "If I'd realized that my phone had been turned off, I would have fixed that. There's been so much going on."

Henry released Elijah, who had gotten distracted by Tom, who walked in from his stall. "I do understand. At some deep down level, I knew you were okay, but when I read that you'd been shot and then couldn't reach you, the only thing I could think to do was rush over as fast as possible. It's good that Heath was driving instead of me. I don't know that I would have been quite as safe."

Polly smiled at him.

"What are you smiling at?" he asked, with only a small amount of belligerence in his voice.

"The fact that while you were worried about me being shot, you would have considered driving like a fool. You know how dangerous that can be. I'm hungry. What do you all think about getting lunch?"

Once again, every eye in the place was on her.

"You're hungry?" Heath asked. "I've barely started breathing again."

Elijah ran back in from the donkeys' stall. "I'm hungry."

"You're always hungry," Polly said. "Maybe it will just be you and me if nobody else wants to eat with us."

Noah put his hand up. "I do. I'm hungry, too."

She turned to Eliseo. "How about you? Do you want to go to the diner for lunch?"

He shook his head. "No. I need to help out up at the main house this afternoon. Sylvie will be bringing wedding cakes over any minute now."

"Bill, how about you? Lunch at the diner? I'm buying," Polly said as he walked back into the building.

"I could eat. Maybe Marie should join us. That way she can see for herself that you're alive." He turned and went back out to make the call.

"Henry?" she asked.

He dropped his head and then slowly shook it. "More gray hair than I ever imagined."

"It will just make you more distinguished," Polly said. She walked over to him, ruffled the hair on his head and then pulled him close. "I'm sorry I scared you and I'm sorry that I didn't

271

answer the phone. I do know how frightening it is to not be able to reach someone when you hear bad news. I'm sorry that you went through that today."

"I'd like to ask that you never get yourself into these situations, but I know there's nothing anyone can do — especially you. And I also know why you tackled that woman. You are so strong. Even though I'm terrified for you most of the time, I know that you do your best. I trust you."

Bill walked back in again. "Marie would love to meet us at the diner. You'd think it was because she loves me and wants to eat lunch with me, but the deciding factor was when I told her that Noah and Elijah would be with us. She can't wait to see them again."

"I should call Hayden," Polly said. "He's home by himself."

Heath put his hand out. "I'll call him. We already talked. He's worried too."

Henry reached out and brushed down the side of Polly's jeans. "You're kind of a mess."

"That's from rolling around in the dirt." She slapped her hands against her legs, releasing billows of dust.

"Turn around," he said.

When she did, he swatted at her bottom, making her yelp.

"Dust," he said with a laugh. "Lots and lots of dust."

CHAPTER TWENTY-SIX

Easing into traffic off the exit from Highway-30, Polly smiled at Henry. "Are you sure you want me to go with you?" she asked. "I'm dangerous, you know, and it won't be nearly as much fun as going to the lumberyard with Bill and Heath."

"I'd like to keep you in my sights today," he replied. "Polly, I haven't been that scared since ..." He sighed. "I haven't been that scared since the last time you chased down a murderer. This is just as well. Hayden needs help to finish things at the house. I can't and Heath can."

"Then I'm looking forward to it. You and I never get to do things like this together."

He looked at her. "You want to do these things with me?"

"Sometimes," she said, lifting a shoulder in a small shrug. "It's fun to hang out with you."

"Weird woman. We're only walking through a big tool store and lumberyard. If you don't mind, I want to buy a small utility trailer for home."

She looked up into her rearview mirror. "I have a hitch back there, don't I? I find it every time I help the boys get their soccer gear out of the truck."

"That's what those bruises are on your leg."

Polly laughed. "I don't even notice them anymore." She reached across the console and gently rubbed his shoulder. "I'm sorry that I couldn't reassure you this morning. It never occurred to me that you would find out what happened before I got a chance to tell you. Social media is screwing with my life."

"I'm better now. Reading that shots were fired down at Sycamore House's barn is not a pleasant thing to see when I'm more than a half hour away."

"Marie seemed glad to meet us for lunch."

"She's never had anyone like you in her life," Henry said with a smile. "Until you and I got married, the only thing she had to worry about was whether Lonnie was coming home for the holidays or if I was ever going to find someone to be happy with. Oh, and keeping Dad busy enough so he'd stay out of her hair."

"All of those things are pretty much fixed now," Polly said. "We have to keep her on her toes."

"You definitely do that." He shifted in the seat so he could face her better. "Noah and Elijah are doing okay. It scared me that they'd seen the whole thing happen."

"I didn't want them anywhere near that crazy woman. Once she started screaming, I knew things were going off the rails. I'm just sorry that her daughter had to experience this." She pursed her lips, then said, "And I'm sorry that Roger is going to have to face so much now. I was so surprised when Eliseo called me this morning. I've never known him to extend himself like that to anyone, but something made those two men connect."

"Hopefully they'll continue to do that. Roger is going to need someone in his corner. And he's going to need someone who is strong and steady. I've known him a little bit from around town, but in the last few years, he pretty much became a recluse. Now I see that it was his wife controlling him."

"She was horrible, Henry. Eliseo asked me to pick breakfast up on my way. I don't think she kept enough food in the house to feed them."

Henry frowned. "But his wife is ..." he stopped himself, "was a successful lawyer. They must have plenty of money."

"He said she wouldn't let him near any of it. She doled it out a little at a time and it was never enough. Why would she do that?"

"You and I will never understand people who act that way. It's not in our nature."

"It certainly was in hers. I hope Roger gets enough help for Julia so that little girl can move past the trauma her mother put her through."

"You're about to get involved, aren't you?"

Polly shook her head. "I don't think so. I'll let Eliseo do with it what he wants. Sylvie knows who Jessie used when she needed to find ways to manage the rape and then her mother's abandonment. The same woman helped Stephanie talk through her stuff. If he wants to get involved at that level, he can. Other than letting the boys visit if she goes to the barn or seeing them at the school, I guess I'm out. I've done enough."

"I'll say. I still don't understand how you are so strong after dealing with something like you did this morning."

"What am I supposed to do?" Polly asked. "Throw a fit and wail like a baby until you come in to rescue me?"

"That wouldn't be so bad, would it?"

She hesitated before looking at his face, then laughed when she saw the smirk he wore. "I always hated movies and television shows where the weak-willed female screams and screams upon seeing anything awful. A dead body — the girl screams. A monster — the girl screams. A bad guy — the girl screams. Always with the screaming. If screaming is useful and necessary to protect yourself, then scream to your heart's content, but otherwise, shut up and deal with what you've got in front of you. And besides, screaming hurts my throat."

"That's my practical pragmatic Polly," he said.

"Triple-P. Kind of like Triple X, but without Vin Diesel's gorgeous body."

He burst out laughing. "Oh, oh, okay," he stammered. "That's one way to look at it." He pointed toward a parking space in the immense lot she'd driven into. "Go here. We'll buy the utility trailer first. Then we can load lumber, paint, and stain onto it."

"This is going to take forever, right?"

"No, why?"

"You have to pick out all of that stuff?"

Henry laughed again. "You don't understand. We were here when those texts and emails starting coming in. I started trying to call you and when Heath was taking everything through the checkout line, I panicked since I couldn't get to you. I had to come find out if you were alive. They know me here and set it aside for me."

"That's great. Let's go, then."

He led her inside and they made their way through the store to where there were several styles of utility carts on display. As Henry walked through the area, Polly recognized the woman from the organic farm. She couldn't help but run into these people this week.

"Mrs. Sutter?"

The woman looked up, peering at Polly as if trying to place her. "Do I know you?"

"I'm Polly Giller."

"Oh yeah. Her. I do know you. My daughter Ariel is in a grade with one of your boys, right?"

"Yes. You're looking for a trailer, too?" Polly pointed at Henry. "I'm here with my husband."

"Is he as worthless as mine?" the woman asked.

Polly was a bit taken aback. "No, Henry is wonderful. Henry Sturtz? He's a contractor in town."

"Sure. I know of him. People like him. One of these days I should get him to give me a price on putting up a greenhouse. I keep saying that I'll get it done, but my worthless jack of a husband has me spending money on everything else. I may never get ahead. Like this trailer." She rattled the trailer in front of her. "I spent good money on one of these, and then last April, it was just gone. I don't know if one of those guys working in my field stole it for extra money or what. All of a sudden, both the worker and the trailer were gone. I told Manny to make sure that he locked those barn doors up at night, but he never listens to me. Had to buy a new wheelbarrow last week. Not that the old one was all that good, but it still held whatever I put into it."

Polly peered at the woman. Surely not.

"A trailer?" Polly asked. "And then a wheelbarrow?"

"Yeah. It's been a bad year for equipment. I had to replace the tires on our skid loader last week, too. Manny got into something and they were wrecked. It was like he got into a bad patch of barbed wire, but I know we've pulled most all of that out of the fields. I suppose there might be something far out in the corners, but I've been pretty careful." She gave her head a shake. "I never know what that man gets into."

Polly opened her phone and quickly flipped through the photo album until she landed on the trailer in which she'd found the body last May. "Is this your trailer?" she asked.

Mrs. Sutter snatched the phone out of Polly's hand and peered at it more closely, then touched it and expanded the photo, peering at it. "Yeah. That looks like it." She pointed at a mark in the side. "Well, hell yeah, that's my trailer. See that mark right there? That's where I hit it with a shovel when I was digging potatoes. I didn't realize I was so close."

"You hit it pretty hard."

The woman gave her a sardonic grin. "Don't know my own strength sometimes. You work out in the fields every day like I do and you'll surprise yourself. So, where is this and why do you have a picture of my trailer?"

"I saw it out in a junkyard," Polly said hesitantly. "I don't think it's there any longer."

"Why? Did someone steal it a second time?"

"Maybe. Excuse me just a minute." Polly hurried over to Henry and whispered. "Make an excuse and get me out of here. I'll tell you why later."

"I found the one I want," he said out loud without missing a beat. "We'd better hurry."

"This is Mrs. Sutter," Polly said. "Mrs. Sutter ..."

"It's Lorianne, Mr. Sturtz," the woman said, smiling sweetly at Henry and putting her hand out. The woman looked like a cat purring at her owner for a dish of milk.

He shook it and smiled back. "We should be on our way. It's nice to meet you."

The woman reached into her back pocket and pulled out a battered business card holder. She took a card out and handed it to him. "I'd like to talk to you about some work you could do for me on the farm. Give me a call next week and we'll set up a time to talk about how we can work together. Okay?"

"I'll do that," he replied. Taking Polly's arm, he turned them into an aisle and walked away. "Now why am I walking away from a cart that I want to buy?"

"Because I have to call Tab. Remember that body I found last May in a utility trailer?"

"Yeah?"

"It was her trailer."

He stopped walking. "I'm sorry, what?"

"It's hers. She identified it from a picture I had in my phone."

"Wait a minute. You carry a picture of where you find dead bodies?"

"Not really. It's just that …"

"It's just that you have pictures of where you find dead bodies. Dear lord, woman. You're creepy."

"You don't mean that."

"You're right, I don't, but seriously?"

"Anyway," she said. "I need to get outside and call Tab. I don't think Lorianne Sutter is the murderer, but her husband might be. She also said that she had to buy a new wheelbarrow. And she said that she had to buy new tires for her skid loader because it had run over barbed wire. There's a pile of barbed wire sitting at the corner behind the cemetery where I found that body in the wheelbarrow."

They hurried out of the store and to her truck where Polly climbed into the driver's seat and took out her phone. She dialed Tab's number and was frustrated when there was no answer.

"Where is she?" Polly asked.

"Call Aaron."

"He'll think I found another body."

"After the excitement of this morning, surely he couldn't believe something else might happen to you."

Polly pointed at the store. "Well, this happened."

"Call him."

Taking a breath, she placed the call and waited while shaking her head. This wasn't going to go well, she was sure of it.

"I was afraid someone new was going to find *your* dead body this morning," Aaron said when he answered his phone. "What were you thinking, Polly? You don't get near crazy women with guns. Even I know that."

"I didn't know she had a gun until it was too late," Polly responded. "I couldn't let her kill her husband."

"Yeah, yeah, yeah. Do you have any idea that you weaken my heart every time I hear about these things? Now, tell me you don't have another body for me to deal with. Tab is driving up to Sioux City. One of her brothers or sisters or someone was in a car accident."

"That makes sense, then. I tried to call her first, but she didn't answer."

"Good for her. If it isn't a body, then what is it?"

"I know who killed those men. I don't know why and I don't know who they are, but I know who did it."

"Who did it?" he asked.

"Mr. Sutter. I just talked to his wife."

"And how do you know that he killed those two men?"

"Henry and I were looking at a trailer and she was complaining about how she had to buy a new one — that her old one had gotten stolen." Polly paused for effect. "Last April. And then she said that she just bought a new wheelbarrow and put new tires on her skid loader."

"Those are good clues, but how are you sure?"

"I showed her a picture of the trailer. She said it was hers. She recognized a mark that she'd made on it with a shovel."

"You had a picture?"

"Hush. Henry and I already had that conversation. Aaron, she'll recognize the wheelbarrow and I'm guessing that as he was moving that wheelbarrow into place, he used his skid loader and didn't realize that he was driving over the pile of barbed wire right there."

"Yeah, that got in the way for my guys pulling the body out, too. I don't know what to think about this. You're pretty certain she isn't involved?"

"She'd have to be a heck of a liar to be able to look at me and talk about needing those new pieces of equipment. She told me that she had an employee leave at the same time the trailer was stolen. She assumed he took it. Blamed her husband for not locking up the barn. She does *not* like that man."

"He's not much help for her. I know that," Aaron said. "I've never thought about whether he had it in him to kill someone."

"Here's the thing," Polly said. "From what she says of him, I'd bet that if he killed those men, he didn't clean up after himself. You'll still find blood ..." she stopped talking. "I know what made those holes in the bodies. It has to be one of those big rake thingies they use to break up ground for planting."

"A garden till?" Aaron asked with a chuckle. "You're right, though. That's exactly the pattern. I don't know why I didn't think of that. I hate mine."

"What do you mean you hate yours?"

"I hate it. Lydia thinks it's good exercise for me. I hate that damned thing, but it works. With Tab out of town for the weekend, I'd best get busy on this. I'll call Stu Decker and we'll head up to the Sutters' place. Can I talk you into staying away?"

"I'll try," Polly said. "Now I have to figure out how to get Henry's trailer purchased so we don't have to come back here tomorrow."

"Don't you have an art show to attend tomorrow?"

"Oh yeah. I should go to that."

"Yes, you'd better. I know my wife needs to see your face. She was pretty shaken up by all that happened at the barn this morning, but didn't feel as if she dared come down and get in the way. When Rebecca told her that you were okay, she settled some, but not nearly enough."

"I'll try to call her later."

"No more today. You've done enough," he said.

"Like I always say, this stuff is not my fault."

"Good-bye, Polly. I'll see you tomorrow."

Polly put her phone down on the console. "I don't know what to do now."

"Take me home," Henry sighed. "I'll deal with it. When I left earlier, I told them I wasn't sure when I'd be back. They offered to deliver it. Maybe I'll just take them up on that. Boomer wouldn't mind adding one more thing to the order for me."

"I'm sorry," she said.

"It's no problem. You're my adventure."

~~~

When they pulled into the driveway, Noah and Elijah bolted out the side door.

"You're home!" Elijah said. "We've been waiting and waiting."

"For what?" Polly asked.

"For you."

She turned to Henry, worried and concerned.

"Were you worried something had happened to me?"

Noah nodded slightly, but Elijah jumped in. "No. We just wanted to see you."

"Okay. What have you been doing?"

"Hayden and Heath are moving furniture around. We're kinda in their way. Will you come play in the backyard with us? Hayden said the dogs need to go out. We could throw tennis balls for them. Please?"

Henry smiled at her. "Looks like you're playing outside for a while."

"Okay," Polly said. She'd done this a few times over the summer. Usually the boys were fine with playing by themselves with the dogs, or the neighbor kids would come over when everyone was outside; but after what had happened this morning, it made sense that Noah and Elijah wanted to spend time with her. She opened the garage door. "Go get the tennis balls."

Henry opened the side door and let the dogs out. Elijah tossed one of the balls into the back yard and Obiwan chased it, then brought it back to him. It was good exercise for everyone. The dogs ran and ran until they wore themselves out and the boys chased all over the yard. The more time they spent outside playing, the better they slept at night and the better behaved they were. She figured they had to be exhausted most evenings after a day of raucous play. She knew she was.

"Throw one of them here," Polly said. Elijah tossed it and sure enough, Polly missed it completely. No matter how hard she tried, this wasn't her strong suit. "Okay, guys. Watch my aim very carefully and see if I can finally get one to you."

The moment the ball sailed out of her hands, she knew she'd missed. It didn't even have a chance to hit the ground on the other side of the fence before Polly was walking to the gate. "I'll be right back," she called and went on through to the space between their property and the cemetery.

It took a few minutes of searching to find the yellow tennis ball. Polly picked it up and threw it, frustrated when it hit the top of the fence and fell back down a few feet ahead of her. "I need to practice throwing," she muttered.

A woof alerted her to the fact that Obiwan had joined her.

"What are you doing out here?" Polly asked. "You know you aren't supposed to leave the yard."

He ran and picked up the ball between his teeth, then let out a low growl.

"I won't take the ball from you. I promise. Whenever you want to let me have it, that will be fine."

The hair on his neck and back rose straight up and he growled again.

"What is it, Obiwan?" Polly looked around, but couldn't see anything.

He dropped the ball, barked and ran on ahead of her, snapping and barking at something at the far end of their property.

"Stop," Polly demanded.

He obeyed and stopped where he stood, his face jutted forward and his lips pulled back in anger. Polly caught up to him, watching the ground, sure she was going to see a snake or other animal, even though her dog had never reacted to anything like that when they lived at Sycamore House. He'd had plenty of small animals and wildlife along the creek to play with.

Obiwan took another step, growled, and then began barking wildly. Polly was about to put her hand on his collar to pull him back when a man jumped up from behind the bushes along the outer edge of the cemetery, not far from where she'd found the last body.

"Get back," the man said.

Polly put her hand on Obiwan's collar and tugged at him, trying to pull him away from whatever was about to happen. Then she realized who was standing there. "Mr. Sutter?" she asked. "What are you doing over here?"

His eyes darted back and forth, looking for somewhere to run. There was no way he knew she had accused him of murdering two men, so at least she had that on her side. She was going to play innocent as long as possible and hope that she wouldn't end up in another situation that stressed Henry out. It occurred to her that right now wasn't the time to worry about Henry.

"You need to get out of my way," he said.

"Is everything okay?" Polly asked, her hand still on Obiwan's collar. "Do you need my help?"

He glanced over his shoulder, back toward the field. Polly realized that further on down, Jim Bevins' beanfield butted up against the Sutter farm. She should have put that together earlier. No wonder he'd dropped the last body over here. He came around the edges of the field.

"Just get out of my way." He was obviously nervous around Obiwan and frightened to move past the dog, in case Obiwan lunged at him.

"Why don't we walk with you," Polly said. "Do you need to use my phone to call for help?"

Voices carried across the field. Aaron and his team were searching for the man. He heard them too, and started to move past her, but Obiwan lunged out and barked again. Polly knew her dog wouldn't bite anyone, but Sutter didn't.

"Call off your crazy dog," he said. "If you don't, I'll hurt you both."

Polly waited for him to pull out a gun or even a knife. When he didn't, she relaxed. "I don't think you will, Mr. Sutter. We aren't threatening you. In fact, I'm trying to help you."

"There's no help for me now."

"Why's that?"

Everything in him gave out at that question. "Because it's over. It's just over. I shouldn't have done it, but I was going to lose everything. She wanted him. I know she did. I couldn't lose her to some loser field worker. I could see it happening. Whenever he made a recommendation, she listened. She never listened to me like that. And then his brother came looking for him. I knew right away when I saw him. I thought it was a ghost coming to haunt me. She wasn't home that day. I couldn't have him asking questions. They're just migrants. Nobody knew he was here. She's going to hate me now. I'll never get her to love me again. Why did he have to show up in the first place? All smart and good-looking. He turned her head the moment he walked onto our property. When I saw him, I knew that this was the one. This was finally going to be the one that ended it for us. I couldn't let that happen. I couldn't lose my sweet Lorianne. She's everything to me. I'd do anything to keep her close. No man is going to come between us."

Somewhere in the middle of his rambling soliloquy, he'd begun sobbing. He dropped to his knees, his head in his hands. Polly wondered why these men felt the need to confess their sins to her.

Stu Decker had crossed onto her property about the time that Mr. Sutter spoke of losing his sweet Lorianne and at seeing him, Obiwan calmed and sat down beside Polly.

"Mr. Sutter, you're under arrest," Stu said.

"I did it," the man said. "I killed them both. I couldn't lose my Lorianne."

"Yes, sir," Stu said. "We're going to take you to Boone and you'll tell us everything, won't you?"

"I want to see Lorianne. She needs to understand how much I love her." He looked up at Stu. "Wouldn't you do anything to keep your wife?"

"I don't know, sir," Stu said noncommittally. He spoke into his walkie. "Bring a car to the cemetery. I've got him. He's admitted it all."

"You can cut through over here," Polly said, walking alongside the fence. She picked up the tennis ball Obiwan had dropped and flung it. This time it went over. She flinched when she heard a yelp. How could she have possibly hit Han?

"Did you?" Stu asked.

"Apparently. I have the worst aim — even when I'm throwing blind." They walked together to the gate and Polly pointed at the access she used to walk down to Andy's house. "How's your wife doing?" she asked Stu.

He chuckled. "That's a story for another day. Pregnancy doesn't suit this woman."

"Oh?"

"She loves it and we love our children, but she can be meaner than a snake when her hormones get up a full head of steam. I thought we had a safe word, but evidently, she's forgotten what it is." He laughed. "I'm making too much of it. When she's back to normal, we tease about this. To answer your question, she's actually fine. Physically everything is going well. I just wear armor."

"Does she take it out on your kids, too?"

"Not at all," he said. "Not at all. Just me. It's my fault. I accept the blame. It's easier that way. She's a wonderful wife and mother, her hormones just get the better of her some days." He turned Mr. Sutter down the lane. "Thanks again for catching our murderer for us. Don't know where we'd be without you."

Stu was still laughing when Polly went back inside the gate. Neither boy was in the back yard, though Han came running over to them. "Where is everyone?"

Henry came out the side door. "You did it again, didn't you?"

"It's not my fault?" Polly said.

"We were working upstairs, not paying attention to anything. Then Elijah came in and said you'd gone after a ball and hadn't come back yet. He was worried, so I looked out the window and saw you walking with Stu Decker and Mr. Sutter. How do you do this, Polly?"

"I have no idea. He was just there. Obiwan saw him before I did and scared him to death. When I asked a simple question, he broke down and confessed everything to me. There was nothing to be scared about, he was more frightened than I was. He's a pathetic, pitiful man who thought that one of the workers was going to steal his wife from him. She means everything to him." Polly used air quotes for emphasis.

"If I tell you that you mean the world to me, will you believe I won't murder anyone to keep you?"

"Good. Because I want you to stick around for a while."

He gave her a warm smile until Polly gestured around the place. "At least until more of this work is completed. I need sliding glass doors in the kitchen and a back porch and a new garage and ..."

Henry wrapped his good arm around her. "I'm glad I found a way to be useful."

"You're very useful and the best part is that I love you." Polly reached up and kissed his cheek. "So much."

CHAPTER TWENTY-SEVEN

Running his fingers up Polly's arm, Henry whispered in her ear, "You're the sexiest girl in the room."

She laughed. "What do you want?"

"What? It's the truth."

"You want to go home early."

He tilted his head and lifted his eyebrows. "Can I? I'll even take Noah and Elijah with me."

"The show is nearly over," Polly said. "I don't think anyone will mind if you leave now."

Henry heaved a huge sigh. "I'm about arted out. I've looked at every one of Beryl's paintings at least four times, chased down our sons three more times than that, answered questions from strangers regarding the construction of this place and not had nearly enough alcohol."

"I've made up for it," Polly said, holding up her wine glass. "I might have to walk home."

"One of these days Rebecca will be able to drive and she can escort your drunk butt home."

Polly glanced over at Rebecca, who was deep in conversation

with two of Beryl's oldest art students. Andrew stood off to the side, as uncomfortable as a young boy could possibly be while watching his girlfriend engage with handsome young men in their late twenties and early thirties. She shook her head. "I don't think I will ever ask Rebecca to drive me after I've been drinking. Not the standard I want to set for her."

"It isn't like she doesn't know you've gotten tipsy," Henry said.

"She hasn't ever watched it happen and that's not about to change today." Polly walked with Henry out to the kitchen. This place looked so different from when they'd lived here. Lydia and Jeff had transformed the rooms into beautiful gathering places. The living room was now filled with cozy seating areas, utilizing everything from overstuffed chairs to wing chairs and settees. The colors were quite eclectic, and instead of distracting the eye from the paintings that had been hung on the wall, drew out the beauty of Beryl's work. Persian rugs of different shapes and sizes were scattered throughout the room, softening the sound of people's steps on the hardwood floors. While bright lights illuminated Beryl's artwork, LED candles were placed on tables throughout the room, tempering the effect where people sat together.

Polly's favorite painting — the tree and its accompanying smaller pieces that highlighted life within that tree — had been moved from Beryl's front room to the front bedroom where Heath had once lived. They actually brought over everything from that room in Beryl's house, setting it up so that the paintings hung on the inner wall. The chairs and side tables, along with bookshelves and plants were placed far enough back that it was easy to sit and gaze at the entire piece. She wanted to sit there for several hours and uncover all that Beryl had created.

Beryl's agent, Jasper Farmington, had negotiated several nice sales for Beryl today and made contacts with galleries in Iowa that were interested in showing her work.

The agent was as smooth as they came, and Polly's first impression of him wasn't positive, but he made an effort throughout the afternoon and she was warming up to him. He had to be a good person — Beryl and he had been working together for over twenty years. She liked and trusted him, so there was no reason Polly should have a problem with the man. She'd known people like him when she lived in Boston — all sleek and pretty, but with no substance on the inside. They loved to move in social circles, but didn't have the ability to make a personal connection with others. She was glad to be proven wrong, though she doubted they'd ever be good friends.

"Can I have more of that cheese?" Elijah asked Polly, pointing to a platter that had been left on the counter. Guests had been in and out all afternoon, and during the height of the excitement, four or five young people had moved throughout the crowd serving food and drinks.

"You've had enough," Polly said. "I've been watching." She smiled down at him. That little boy could put food away faster than anyone she knew. "Henry is looking for Noah, it's time for you to go home."

He yawned, but then frowned at her. "I'm not ready to go."

"Yes you are. You can't fool me. Heath and Hayden are waiting for you — think about that. So are Obiwan and Han. When you get home, you can change into your shorts and go outside and play." Heath and Hayden had come early, stayed long enough to see everything and everyone, and then were gone. This wasn't their crowd. She could hardly blame them.

Henry came back into the kitchen with Noah. "What say we stop at the convenience store for chocolate milk before we go home."

Elijah's eyes lit up. "I'm ready right now!"

"You're horrible," Polly said with a laugh. "But smart."

"I learn. Will we see you home for supper?"

"I don't know. Don't plan on it. Is that okay?"

He kissed her cheek. "It's fine. You've had a heck of a week. You can spend a few hours with your friends. Have you had a chance to talk to Lydia?"

"Not very much. She hugged me and yelled at me about being careful and then was whisked away by Jeff. Important people she needed to meet or something."

"Does it feel strange to not be part of all the planning here?" He trailed his finger down her arm and then grasped her hand in his.

"It doesn't. It's nice to be on the outside. Beryl's a star, Lydia is in heaven, people are raving over Sylvie's food, and Andy is beside herself with joy for her friend. Stephanie and Jeff have made a slew of connections today and look at Rebecca — she's in heaven. I've had the best time watching them enjoy themselves. All I have to do is ooh and ahhh over art, decorating and food. I'm quite good at that."

Henry kissed her again, this time on the lips. "You are an amazing friend, Polly Giller. I love you and I'll see you whenever you get home. If you need a ride, just call me."

"I'll be fine. I love you too." She bent her knees, having to concentrate on keeping them together because the dress she wore was just a little snug on her legs. She'd never have chosen a dress like this, but Rebecca had insisted that it was perfect. Polly hugged Noah and then Elijah. "I love you boys, too. Have fun."

She watched them leave by the back door. It was strange to think about how different everything was now. Andrew's little nook was about to be destroyed by an elevator. Her bedroom and Henry's office would be turned into additional storage for the kitchen, especially needed now that Sycamore House catering was increasing its business. That little closet behind the stage could no longer handle everything. Rachel, Sylvie and Jeff had purchased two additional coolers and a large freezer that lined one wall of the garage. Growth was exciting and change was necessary. Polly was thrilled to see it happen.

Their old media room had been transformed by Lydia into something that looked like an old-fashioned library or study. She'd filled the bookshelves with old books. Smaller pieces of Beryl's were interspersed among the books along the shelves, along with more LED candles and framed old black and white photographs of people that no one recognized. Leather chairs and dark side tables lent an air of authenticity. Lydia had done such a terrific job with this.

"Polly?" Rebecca touched Polly's arm.

"Hey. Are you having fun?"

"It's the best. I never want this day to end."

"That's awesome. Do you think being an artist is what you want to do with your life?"

"Absolutely. And I can't wait to travel around the world with Beryl. She says we can go anywhere I want to go. I want to see it all. I want to sit on the Champs-Élysées and paint the Arc de Triomphe and I want to watch the sun rise on the Acropolis and ride on the back of a camel to see the Sphinx. Then I want to hear Big Ben chime and lie among the heather in Scotland with sheep grazing on a nearby hillside." Her eyes were sparkling as she spoke.

"I want you to do all of those things," Polly said. "That sounds amazing."

"Beryl said she'll go with me wherever I want to go. Will you let me?"

"Of course we will."

"Can I go to the Alehouse with Jeremy and Dave? Meryl and Dena are going, too. Nobody is going to drink. They said I'd be safe. Can I go?"

"What about Andrew and Kayla?"

Rebecca nodded effusively. "They're asking permission too. I just don't want this day to end. Can I go, please?"

Polly took a deep breath, then smiled. "Yes, but you can't be out too late. Remember, tomorrow morning you have marching band practice. This is the first one and you don't want to miss it. That would be bad form. I want you home by nine thirty. Deal?"

Rebecca took a moment to think before she spoke, something Polly thought was a huge improvement. "That's a deal," she finally said. "We'll still have lots of time to talk. They have so many stories. All about college and traveling. Do you know that Jeremy took a whole group of students to New York City for a month? Can you believe it? He's so cool."

"Do you need money for supper?" Polly asked.

Rebecca was about to turn away, but swung back. "I didn't even think about that."

Polly opened the small clutch she carried. There wasn't any place in this dress to stow even her small telephone wallet. "Here's enough to pay for you, Andrew, and Kayla. If you don't use it all, you can deposit it on the counter when you get home."

"Thank you," Rebecca cried out and threw her arms around Polly. "I'll be home on time." She started to walk away and then came back and hugged Polly again. "Thank you."

Oh, to be young and enthusiastic about everything that was coming.

"Excuse me," one of the wait staff said.

Polly moved away from the peninsula, a funny sensation fluttering through her. This person had no idea how many meals Polly had prepared in this kitchen or how many times Henry had kissed her while she washed dishes right there in that sink, or how many times she'd sat at her dining room table laughing with her family. She gulped back tears and gave her head a quick shake. Those were wonderful memories. She was making more in a new home, but it still felt odd to have strangers milling about in a room where she'd started her life in Bellingwood. They knew nothing of what had happened here. That was all in the past.

"Let's get fresh glasses and another bottle of wine," Lydia said from behind Polly. "Cindy, could you take care of that? We'll be out in the lounge."

"Yes, ma'am," the girl said with a smile.

"The lounge?" Polly asked as Lydia led her back into the main room.

"We don't know what to call it yet. That works as well as anything. We haven't had any time at all to talk today. I'm so glad you didn't leave with your family." She dropped into a chair and kicked her heels off, then pointed at the settee on her right. "Take off those crazy heels you're wearing. Your feet can't be happy."

"They aren't bad," Polly said, though she slipped her feet out of them. "At least they aren't as high as Sal's. Did you see her?"

"That girl is hot stuff," Lydia said. "It's a good thing Mark doesn't care if she is taller than him when she puts on those four-inch pain-makers."

"Sal is so used to wearing heels, she feels like a peasant without them," Polly said with a laugh. "She could move faster than anyone I've ever known on the streets of Boston while wearing stilettos. And she'd never trip or falter. It was impressive. If I had to wear heels for something at work, I always arrived in flats and then changed when I got there. I'd have face-planted in a puddle wearing those on the sidewalk."

"Me too."

"You've done a beautiful job here, Lydia. You should be very proud of yourself."

Lydia smiled. "Thank you. I've had the time of my life. Aaron says I should go into business so he could retire."

"Who would cook for all of us?" Polly asked.

"That's what I told him. I'm proud of him, though. He hasn't complained a whit these last few weeks while I've been so busy. He's had to eat at the diner a few more times than usual, but then we learned how to shop for groceries online and he picks them up in Boone for me. By the time I get home, he has everything put away. I certainly couldn't have done this while all the kids were still home, but there's no reason I have to sit around the house waiting to serve my lord and master."

Polly laughed out loud. "I'll bet he'd love to hear that."

Andy dropped into the settee beside Polly. "Hear what?"

"Aaron is my lord and master," Lydia said.

"That fits." Andy looked up as Cindy arrived with a bottle of wine and two glasses.

Sylvie came up beside her and saw what was happening. "We're going to need more glasses and more wine. Beryl's agent-man is about to leave. Jeff and Stephanie are heading over to the Alehouse with the rest of the young people and ..." she looked around, "... it's pretty much over. I'll be right back."

"I don't want to bend over to pour that wine," Lydia said. "I'm beat."

Polly sat forward, poured a glass and handed it to Lydia and then poured the second for Andy. "I'm supposed to slow down if I have to drive home."

"You don't have to drive home," Andy said. "There's a town full of people that will make sure we get where we're supposed to be."

The front door opened and someone said, "Are we too late?"

Polly turned and saw Judy and Reuben Greene standing there. She jumped up, leaving her shoes where they were. "Come on in. Things are winding down, but we aren't going anywhere." She pointed at the bottles of wine that now sat on the table where her friends were gathering. "We might be just getting started. Wander around and then come join us. Have you met Beryl Watson?" Polly turned to include Beryl, who was dressed in a gorgeous dress in shades of purple and mauve. It was actually one of the more sedate dresses Polly had ever seen her in, but she looked wonderful. "Beryl, this is Judy Greene and her husband, Reuben."

"Judy Grady?" Beryl asked. "I remember you." She turned. "Andy, this is Judy Grady."

Judy smiled. "It's been a long time."

"I hear you're thinking about moving back to Bellingwood. Is that true?" Beryl walked away with the couple as they wandered to take in the artwork hanging on the walls.

"Unless they are large investors, I shall be off," Jasper Farmington said to Polly. "You have a lovely facility here and it is managed by highly competent people. I'm quite impressed with the whole thing. This is a perfect venue for Mrs. Watson's artwork. I've tried to convince her for years to open a gallery in Iowa. She has refused for exactly the same number of years, but this will do nicely. Thank you for your hospitality."

"It was nice to meet you," Polly said. "I hope you've enjoyed your stay."

"Very much. I'm staying at your quaint little hotel, where many of Beryl's out of town guests have stayed this weekend. You don't expect much from small town hotels like that, but again, I'm very impressed. You seem to have brought a level of class to town."

"I didn't bring anything," Polly said. "They already had what they needed. All I did was restore a couple of buildings. The people in town did everything else, but thank you very much for your nice words." She stood at the front door. "I hope to see you in town again someday."

He nodded and smiled, then bent to pick up a briefcase he'd left by the door. "I'll bid you adieu, then. Thank you again."

She sighed as he walked away and down the stairs. It was good that Beryl liked him. Polly wouldn't be able to take many conversations with that man before reaching out to swat the hoity toity right out of him.

When she returned to her seat beside Andy, she picked up the wine glass that had been placed in front of her. "This is nice. Nothing to worry about, the day is finished, everyone is where they should be, and I'm having wine with my friends.

"Would you like me to leave a container of appetizers here?" Cindy asked, holding two plastic containers in her hand. "Otherwise I can take them downstairs and put them in a cooler."

Lydia, who was taking a drink, pointed at the table. "Right here would be perfect. Is there another box of those crackers to go with the cheese?"

"I'll bring it right out," Cindy said. "How are you doing on the wine?"

"I'm doing just fine on the wine," Lydia said. "We'll need three more glasses and maybe another bottle. How are you doing for bottles back there?"

The girl laughed. "There's plenty. When we're finished cleaning up, I'll make sure everything is ready for your party."

"Party?" Polly asked.

"Apparently, she's a mind reader," Lydia said. "And we're paying them very well." She tucked her feet up underneath her and rearranged her skirt. "I'm working on demure. How'm I doing?"

Sylvie bent a little and said, "Nothing's showing. You're fine."

"Cindy?" Lydia called out. "Maybe napkins, and there are paper plates in the cupboard. Would you mind?"

"I didn't know you had it in you," Polly said.

"What?"

"Asking someone else to do what you could easily do. I'm surprised you aren't up and running back and forth for all of this."

Lydia leaned toward Polly. "This old lady hurts so bad right now all she can do is drink wine and hope someone will care for her." She held out her nearly empty glass. "Please care for me?"

Polly re-filled it and offered the bottle to Lydia. "Do you want to tuck this in beside you?"

"That's not a bad idea, but if we're having company, it might be a bit embarrassing. Keep pouring, will you?" She reached out and grabbed Polly's forearm. "I forgot. I'm supposed to be mad at you."

Sylvie laughed. "Why are you mad at her?"

"Because yesterday she nearly got herself killed by a crazy woman and then walked up on a murderer. How am I supposed to keep you safe if you won't even try to help, Polly Giller?"

"I'm perfectly fine," Polly said. "I didn't even get a small scrape when I tackled Jennifer Carlson." She rubbed her ear. "Though that gunshot was kinda loud."

"Eliseo was pretty upset about the whole thing," Sylvie said. "He felt like it was all his fault — that if he'd never invited Roger Carlson to come to the barn, you wouldn't have had to get involved."

"That's just silly," Polly said with a scowl. "Things happen. It's not anyone's fault but the crazy lady's. We live our lives doing what we do. We can't help it if someone suddenly decides to go off the deep end. To be honest, it all worked out for the best. She's in jail, her husband and daughter can try to live good lives now, and I learned that I can still pack a punch." Polly shook out her right hand. "Okay, that's a little sore today, too."

"Eliseo called Roger Carlson again last night."

Polly looked up in surprise, then reached for the bottle to refill her own glass. She poured more into Andy's while she had the bottle in hand. "He did? That man of yours is full of surprises."

"He knows something about post-traumatic stress and he's pretty certain that Roger is going to deal with a lot of that, coming from what he's had to deal with. Eliseo talked to him about getting Julia into counseling right away. Roger isn't interested in that for himself right now and I get that, but while Julia is talking to Leslie, Roger is going to start spending time at the barn with Eliseo. He wants to learn how to take care of the horses."

"I love that man," Lydia said. "He's been through so much and the first thing he does when encountering someone else who has endured hell is to find a way to help."

Polly smiled at Lydia's tear-filled eyes. "You're a softie."

"Is this for us?" Beryl asked, gesturing at the three empty glasses.

"We're getting all soggy and drunk," Lydia said. "You might as well join us. This is what Bellingwood has come to since you've been gone, Judy."

"It actually looks pretty nice," Judy said. She sat down on a second settee and patted the seat beside her for her husband.

Beryl took the chair between Sylvie and Lydia. "You look like you have a big head start on me. Are you going to have to call the sheriff for a ride home?"

"If I must," Lydia said. "He'll take you home, too." She waved her hand around the group. "He'll take all of you home." Then she giggled. "Except for you, Judy. That would be a long trip to California. When are you going back?"

"We're flying out tomorrow, but we'll be back," Judy said.

"Have you found anything that looks interesting here?" Polly asked. "You know, a place to live?"

Judy shook her head. "Nothing yet, but I'm not giving up. We'd like to be back here by early December. Before the snow flies, you know. I remember what Iowa winters can be like. We'll leave town for the Christmas holiday, but I'd like to be settled in somewhere so we can both get started with our new lives in the new year."

"Are you wanting to buy a home?" Polly asked.

Judy shrugged. "If we sell our place in Oakland, we'll have to put the money somewhere, so buying a home seems like the right thing to do. Why do you ask?"

Polly could tell she'd had too much wine. She needed to put a clamp on her mouth, but all of a sudden, words spilled out. "Have you ever thought about running a bed and breakfast?"

Judy took her husband's hand and smiled up at him. "We've dreamed about doing that our entire lives, but I wouldn't know how to even begin."

"Polly can set you up," Lydia said. Her eyes grew big and she clamped one hand over her mouth.

"What do you mean?" Judy asked.

Polly took a deep breath. "I'm going to be in so much trouble for saying anything."

Beryl laughed at her. "With who, Henry? You know that if it's the right thing to do, he's not arrogant enough to be upset that you didn't ask his permission. He trusts you. You have great instincts about people. In fact, we all trust you with that. Go ahead. Ask them."

Andy nudged her. "She's right, you know."

"Really?" Polly asked. She turned to Beryl. "Really?"

"I knew it as soon as I met them," Lydia said.

Polly smiled. "So did I. That's so funny."

"We're quite curious now," Judy Grady said. "What did you know?"

"My husband, Henry, found a property north of town that feels like it would be a perfect place for a bed and breakfast and we bought it. The price was so ridiculously cheap, we couldn't let it go. It's a huge mess right now, but he and his dad walked through the big old house that's there, and though there are a few floors that need to be replaced, the house is in pretty good shape. Okay, it needs to be pretty much gutted on the inside, but it's a great place. There's an old broken-down greenhouse on the lot and a bunch of outbuildings that need to be taken down, but the location is so pretty."

"A greenhouse?" Judy asked.

"It needs a lot of repair work." Polly smiled at Reuben. "And once those outbuildings are down, there would be plenty of room to build something for you to have a forge."

Reuben put his arm around his wife. "You know, we could buy one of the storefronts downtown rather than a house this way. Put a little gallery in there for my work." He looked at the painting Beryl had on the wall. "We could even put your pieces in there. Make a real art gallery. Surely there are other artists in town who aren't getting any attention."

Beryl nodded. "Actually, there are people who create in many different mediums around here. Glasswork, jewelry, fabric arts, wood creations. You might have a hit on your hands."

"There's that great building at the other end of the block from the coffee shop," Polly said. "I know it's available."

"I still don't know anything about running a bed and breakfast."

"See that's where my staff comes in," Polly said. "You'd only have to take care of the guests. The business end would be run out of Sycamore House."

"If I didn't have to do the bookkeeping and scheduling, I'd have plenty of time to play in the dirt," Judy said. "What do you think?"

"It's something to consider," Reuben replied. He chuckled. "I certainly didn't expect to have this type of conversation today. We were a bit distressed that we would have to leave tomorrow without a plan."

"It's not a full-fledged plan yet," Polly said, "but it's something to think about."

"We're coming back over Labor Day," Judy said. "By then we should have our ducks in a row and can make more solid decisions. Does that sound good?"

Polly nodded. "That sounds terrific."

"Are we done with business now?" Beryl asked. "Because I'm ready to take off my shoes, get a little drunk and dance on the tables. This has been an incredible day. Did you see that my brothers even showed up? And they acted like they were proud of me." She kicked her shoes off and jumped up onto the table in the center of the group. "I want to raise a toast. To my friends who support me no matter what."

"Hear, hear," they all said and lifted their glasses.

After Beryl took a long drink, she lifted her glass again. "And to this crazy little town I live in. I never thought they would accept me for who I am, but somewhere along the line I fell in love with them and I'm happy to be here."

"To Bellingwood," Lydia said as the group raised their glasses.

Beryl stepped down, then sat on the table in front of Polly. She leaned forward and lifted her glass. "And to you, my friend. I know you will never acknowledge what you've done for us, but you are a catalyst. It's because of you that wonderful things have happened for each of us here. I know that crazy things happen around you and your life seems out of control sometimes, but to me, you are the woman who brought joy and excitement and dreaming back to our lives. I love you so much." Beryl blinked back tears and then let them flow. "I don't know where we'd be without you. Each one of us in this room has been changed for the better because you showed up."

She reached out and pulled Polly into a hug. "You are such a good friend. I will always be thankful for you." When Beryl sat back up, she gestured down at her dress. "I wore this dress for you, you know."

"What?" Polly asked.

"It's purple. Those purple panties were only the beginning of the fun times we have had. We aren't finished yet."

Polly looked around and then smiled in acknowledgment of Judy and Reuben's confusion. "That's a story we'll tell after a few more drinks." Then she put her hand on Beryl's knee. "Thank you, but the truth is, you've all done this by yourselves. I just hang around with incredible people."

"Before you get too weepy on us, maybe we should pour more wine all around," Lydia said, her eyes filled with tears again.

When Polly looked around at her friends, both old and new, she saw tears in everyone's eyes. These people had invested their lives in hers and she in theirs. "From the very beginning," Polly said. "You've been here for me. I love you."

BREAK THROUGH
THE CLOUDS

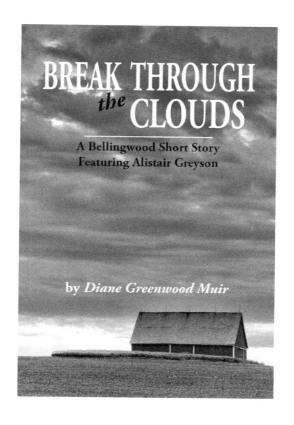

CHAPTER ONE

"Good morning, Grey."

He looked up from the file he was reading and smiled at the office manager. "Good morning, Nan. You're in early today."

"I saw you had an early patient. Thought I'd better get here in time to check him in. Did you make coffee?"

He shook his head. "I'm sorry. Didn't even think about it. This one's got me stumped."

"Anything I can do to help?"

"No. Thanks anyway." Grey smiled at her. "I just wish I could convince his parents that they need to be more involved."

"Want me to yell at them?" Nan clenched her fists and lifted them into a fighting stance. "I could punch 'em out, hogtie 'em and bring 'em in. Punched a calf once, you know."

He laughed out loud. That was one of her favorite stories. He couldn't help but feel sorry for the calf. Her father ran a ranch in Montana and Nan looked forward to going home every spring and fall to help with cattle drives. Evidently, when Nan was in junior high, a calf got stubborn and refused to go where the girl wanted it to … until she clocked the poor thing. From then on, that cow had a new level of respect for Nan. Her father wasn't necessarily pleased with her behavior, but she remembered him laughing when he thought she wasn't looking.

You'd never know that she was a rough and tumble cowboy by looking at her. After college and life in the city, the rough edges had worn off, leaving behind a beautiful young woman, filled with confidence. She worked as the office administrator for the group of therapists where Grey practiced, while studying to get her Master's degree in business. He had no doubt that she'd make a success of whatever she did with her life.

"I think we'll try to do it without punching and hogtying," Grey said. "But thanks. I'll remember your offer."

"Doctor Wagner just came in," Nan said with a sigh. "I'd better get the coffee started." She leaned forward. "He's coming your way."

"Thanks," Grey said, looking back down at his notes. Maybe Bill Wagner would notice that he was busy and leave him alone.

"Glad you're here early," the man said to Nan, his rough, boisterous voice booming through the office. "Gonna need lots of coffee today — patients are stacked a mile high. Somebody around here has to keep us in business, eh?" He rapped on Grey's door.

"What can I do for you?" Grey asked.

"I got double-booked this afternoon. Can you take the druggie?"

Grey frowned. "Joe Lacey?"

"Yeah. I don't have time for his whining today. He likes you better anyway."

"What time is he coming in?"

Bill shrugged. "Doesn't matter. He'll wait as long as he needs to wait. Not like he's got anything better to do."

"What time, Bill?" Grey asked again.

"Ask the girl." Wagner tilted his head toward Nan's desk. "It's sometime this afternoon. She has it on my calendar. If you'd just let her know to transfer it to yours, that would be great. In fact, why don't you take the case. She'll get the case notes. I don't like those charity cases, anyway. No money in it for us." He rapped on the door sill again. "Someone around here has to pay for this high-priced office space."

Grey bit his tongue while he wrote Joe Lacey's name down on a piece of notepaper. The poor kid didn't need to spend any more time with Bill Wagner. "I'll take care of it. Anything else?"

"That's all I need. Probably won't see much more of you today. Much too busy, you know. Get 'em in and get 'em out. I've got a tee time this afternoon — golfing with the mayor and Joe Leadenton. They want to talk about the in-patient clinic at the hospital. Wouldn't mind getting in on the ground floor of that one. Easy money, you know." Bill spun and strode away, leaving Grey shaking his head.

For some reason, the patients who came to Bill Wagner liked him and he seemed to be successful with them. He worked with youth and young adults whose parents had plenty of money. They ended up in his office after coming through the court system. Bill knew many of the judges in town quite well. If a lawyer could produce Bill's name, the judges usually let the young person go, knowing that would probably be the last time they saw the stupid kid.

Grey had been surprised when Bill allowed Joe Lacey to be assigned to him. He rarely took kids who came into the office on their own. Grey was curious about Lacey's family background. There had to be money there, otherwise why would Bill have agreed to take him in the first place?

"Doctor Greyson?"

He looked up at Nan and cocked his head. She never called him by his title.

"What's up?"

"Your eight o'clock isn't coming in." She walked into his office and dropped into the chair in front of his desk.

"Did he call?"

"No, his mother did. Ron killed himself last night."

Grey jumped up, then sat back down. "She didn't want to talk to me?"

"I asked, but she said it wouldn't do any good. They found him an hour ago and the police are there."

"I should go over to the house."

"She told me to tell you no. They don't want to see you."

He dropped his head into his hands. "I didn't see this coming. Last week things were getting better. He was putting together his own plan for the next steps. We were going to …" He looked up as Nan sat back down. She'd shut the door to his office and was sliding a cup of coffee across the desk to him.

Grey shook his head and pushed the coffee away. "We talked about suicide. He wasn't anywhere near wanting to take his life. Why would he do this?" He looked up. "Did she say how he did it?"

"Pills. She didn't say what, though."

"He's not on any medication that he could overdose on." Grey scratched the back of his head as he leaned back in the chair. "I need to go over there — I don't care what she says. They're in crisis right now. Can you rearrange my morning?" Then he saw the note with Joe Lacey's name on it. "This is one of Bill's clients. What time was he supposed to come in? It looks like I'm taking him on."

Nan picked it up. "After school. Three thirty. You have time."

"What about my morning?" Grey usually knew what his schedule looked like for a day, but right now he couldn't think straight.

"Nothing that can't be shifted around."

"I hate doing that," he said, reaching into his desk drawer for the keys to his car.

Nan nodded. "I know you do." She picked up a piece of paper from her lap and put it on his desk. "This is their address and directions."

"You knew."

She chuckled. "Of course I did. But I need you to do me a favor."

"What's that?"

"You'll be there all morning, right?"

Grey nodded. "Unless they kick me out."

"Would you bring back a salad for me? Just a quick one from a fast food place. Ranch dressing. Yeah?"

He creased his brow. "You didn't make plans for lunch today?"

"Working through it. I have a paper to finish. Thought I'd work on it while I ate. You'll bring lunch?"

He nodded absently and headed for the door.

"Grey?"

He turned to look at her.

"Pick up two salads, please."

"Two?"

Nan stood and joined him at the door. "Can you remember to do that for me? Two salads?"

"You're going to eat two salads?" He was so confused.

"Sure. We'll call it that. But be sure to bring two back with you. If you forget, I'll starve to death and be grumpy all afternoon. You don't want that, do you?"

"No," he said. "I hate it when you're grumpy. You're mean to me."

"You won't forget?"

"No. I promise. But two?"

"Two."

Grey opened his door and waited for her to go through first, then headed down the hallway to the back entrance and parking lot. By the time he got to his car, he was laughing out loud. "Oh," he said. "One of those is for me."

When he had his most stressful days in the office, Grey forgot to eat. One day Nan discovered that he had gone two days eating nothing but a couple of granola bars that she'd dropped on his desk. That had been a particularly horrific time for him. The start of the school year was always stressful for the kids he worked with. One boy had ended up in the hospital after passing out from cutting himself so badly. Another young girl was pulling so much hair out of her head, her mother finally recognized there was a problem. The number of kids that hated themselves because of bullies grew every year. It was almost more than Grey could handle some days.

At least he had Nan there to make sure he ate and drank regularly.

CHAPTER TWO

Resting her hands on Grey's desk, Mavis Tennys smiled at him. "How ya holding up?"

He looked down and shook his head. "It's been a long day."

"I'll bet. It's never good when we lose one. How is the family doing?"

"When I left them this morning, they were hanging on," Grey said. "Her pastor was there. That seemed to give her comfort."

"What about the dad?"

"Strong silent type. He's not talking."

"Did they have any idea what triggered this?"

Grey looked up at her, his eyes flat. "The kid got into his mom's pills last night. He told them he needed something to sleep. She just let him have access to her medicine cabinet. Evidently, he thought it would be interesting to combine some of them." He shook his head again. "I really don't know what he was thinking, but I can't be sure it was suicide. He may have just been experimenting. Nothing in any of our conversations pointed to this outcome."

"So you're not going to beat yourself up?"

"I can't be sure it *wasn't* suicide," Grey replied. "I've been going over the notes from our sessions, trying to find something I missed."

"And?"

"I haven't found anything yet, but I'm not giving up."

She sat forward and rapped on his desk, drawing his attention away from the computer screen. "You don't have time to wallow and I don't want you to spend the evening here. Go home and walk beside that lake you love. Call your pretty girlfriend and take her out for a nice dinner in an Italian restaurant, where there's too much noise, pasta, and life."

Dr. Mavis Tennys was one of the founding partners of the practice and a force to be reckoned with. The woman thrived on digging into the root of mental illnesses in her patients, knowing that once they arrived at an understanding, they could begin returning to some sense of normalcy. She was afraid of no one. He was certain that physically, she could destroy any person that threatened her. They'd installed a gymnasium on the ground floor and Mavis insisted that everyone spend time there during the week, but she haunted the place, bringing in trainers from many different disciplines — everything from Jujitsu to Krav Maga and kickboxing. Her latest trainer was a former MMA fighter. Mavis didn't mind taking punches, but she wanted to be sure she gave as good as she took. She scared Grey a little, and he'd been a beast on the ice back in the day.

The car accident that destroyed his hockey career had wrecked Grey's leg. No amount of surgery could put it back together completely, so he'd committed himself to physical therapy, hoping to regain as much mobility as possible. Because of Dr. Tennys's insistence on workouts and the fact that her trainers were available for anyone who wanted to participate, Grey had gotten to a point where his limp was barely noticeable. The leg still ached following a long day of patient sessions sitting in his chair, but after sleepless nights wondering whether he'd walk again, this was more than acceptable.

"Do you ever disappoint yourself?" he asked Mavis.

She sat back, crossed her legs and then her arms. He smiled at her deliberate move to close herself off from him. Both of them recognized what she was doing.

"A better question is whether I worry that I've made an error in judgment — either with how I perceive a patient or what I perceive to be the issue they're dealing with," she said. "Yes?"

"Do you?"

Mavis nodded. "Sure. I wouldn't be human if I didn't. I believe that to be healthy, we should always question our motives *and* our work. It keeps us humble enough to learn. But we can't let those questions control us; we can only allow them to guide us to look more deeply at the problem."

"That's really not answering my question."

"You want to know if you are justified in worrying that you made a mistake. My answer to you is yes ..." She paused and turned her steely gaze on him. "... and no. If your first instinct is that you saw no hint of suicide, then I trust your judgment and you should too. At the same time, it will never hurt for you to critically review the work you did with that young man."

Mavis took a deep breath. "Now for the question you don't want me to ask."

"I don't have an answer," he said. "Neither of the parents could look at me. They both knew that I had been asking for them to come in for a session with their son and it was their choice to avoid it. Do I think that they might sue me for missing this diagnosis? I just don't know. If an ambulance chaser shows up and tempts them with talk of easy money, he might convince them to proceed with a lawsuit."

"Then forward all of your files to me," Mavis said. "I'll review them myself. But I have faith in you. I won't find anything that you missed."

Grey squeezed the bridge of his nose and rubbed it, closing his eyes.

"What about Joe Lacey?" Mavis asked. "Nan tells me that Bill passed him off on you."

"It was a good session. I'd like to string up that little girlfriend

311

of his for introducing him to drugs, but he's done with rehab, his parents are moving him to another school, and he wants to be clean." Grey smiled at her. "We talked about hockey." He pointed at the trophies on his shelf. "He saw those and asked. I'm going to take him to the rink next week. We'll have our session there."

"Give him something else to think about?"

"Yeah."

"Is that what helped you get clean?"

Grey shook his head. "No. I was injured when I started drinking. I couldn't skate. That was most of my problem. I was bored, had nothing to do to keep myself occupied, and felt like my life was over. If I'd been able to skate, things would have probably been different."

"You won't hurt yourself on the ice now?"

"No," Grey said, rubbing his knee. "I skate all the time now. What with your workouts and my physical therapy, I'm in pretty good shape these days."

Mavis stood up suddenly and Grey responded by standing with her. He came around from behind his desk and walked her to the door.

"You're going home soon, right?" she asked.

"As soon as I compile the files and email them to you."

"I'm going downstairs at six-thirty. I don't want to see your light on in here, got it? You can finish your paperwork tomorrow."

"Got it." Grey started to push his door closed after she walked away, but Nan showed up and put her hand on the door.

"How are you doing?" she asked.

"You people need to quit worrying about me. I'm fine."

Nan glared at him. "You didn't look fine when you came back with lunch." She smiled. "Thanks, by the way."

"You're welcome. It was a stressful morning, but I have too many things going on to let it take over."

"That's horse crap and you know it. You haven't stopped thinking about that boy for a single minute today and don't try to tell me any different."

"Did Lynn call?" It was easier to just give in to Nan. If he argued, she'd continue pressing. He didn't have the energy for that this afternoon.

Nan handed him three notes. "Those are all in your email inbox, but I figure you've probably been distracted. What did Mavis want?"

"Same as you." Grey sat back down at his desk and pointed to the chair.

Nan didn't need the invitation. She was already halfway down.

"Just checking on me. I need to send her the files before I go home tonight."

"Worried that you're going to get sued?"

"Do you listen to everything in here?" He patted around the desk, picking up his phone and the few desk accessories he had, making a show of looking underneath them. "Do you bug our offices?"

"I'll never tell. Do *you* think the parents will sue us?"

"I don't know what to think. Anything can happen. People respond to death in many different ways, especially an unexpected death like young Ron's. They'll be looking for someone to blame."

"It's not your fault," Nan said decisively. "Can't be. If anything, it's their fault. They could have been more involved in his care."

"We do *not* lay blame in this office," Grey replied. "And you don't have to protect me." He flipped through the notes she'd given him, slipping one on top. Lynn *had* called. He needed to return that one before he left tonight. He wasn't sure if he wanted to be social this evening, but Mavis was right. He shouldn't stay in the office. If he went home, he'd just turn the television on and fall asleep in his recliner.

Nan pointed to the notes she'd given to him. "Your first appointment tomorrow morning canceled. Don't come in early. You need to sleep tonight. I'll let everybody know where you are."

"Thanks," Grey said. "I'll be in on time. I have paperwork that needs to be taken care of from today's sessions. I'm under orders to get out of here early tonight."

"Oh, good." Nan stood up and headed for the door before turning around. "Wish me luck. I have a blind date tonight. We're meeting at Blind Man's Bluff for a little steak and some dancing. We'll see if he's up to it."

"Good luck," Grey said. "Don't scare him too badly."

"I'll be good," she said, winking at him.

CHAPTER THREE

Ending the day this early was not how he liked to work. Grey sent the email off to Mavis and dropped his head into his hands. Opening one eye, he glanced at the stack of file folders on his desk. There was so much paperwork to deal with. On a normal day, he'd stay until it was finished. But he didn't want to cross the woman. Not tonight. He didn't have the energy and she was probably right. Even if he didn't like it, she was right.

The note from Lynn said to call her any time. He wondered if Nan had gotten involved. He wouldn't put it past her.

He opened the desk drawer and took out his cell phone, checking for any messages.

Lynn had left him a voice mail, so he listened to that first.

"Hello Grey. I had a great time in Chicago. The conference was good and it was nice to be able to spend time with my sister and her family. I can't wait to tell you all about it. Dinner tonight? Call me any time."

This might be just the thing for him. Lynn was a masterful story teller. She could have him laughing, crying, and laughing again within a span of minutes. Whenever she spent time with her sister, she came back with tales of motherhood and life with children that only an aunt could tell. The COO of a medical software firm, Lynn traveled all over the country. She worked long hours which gave them very few opportunities to spend time together.

When he was much younger, he assumed that by this point in his life, he'd be settled with children of his own. There had been short-term and long-term relationships, but he had yet to meet someone he wanted to spend a lifetime with. He was pretty sure that Lynn wasn't the woman of his dreams either, but they enjoyed each other's company when they were together. It didn't help that she thought hockey was a ridiculous sport — too violent and with way too much padding on the men skating around the rink. He'd taken her to several live matches and she'd watched everything in the arena except what was happening on the ice. He'd finally given up trying to explain things to her — she just wasn't interested.

She *was* interested in monster music festivals. She could stand in the middle of a wild, raucous crowd on a hot summer afternoon and sing along with every band that played. He didn't mind the music, but hours of standing in one place was harder on his leg than an evening playing hockey with his buddies. On the other hand, she would leave one of those concerts so energized and excited that she was a wild woman when they returned to her place. He just iced his knee and smiled the rest of the night.

If Lynn wanted to go out to dinner tonight, that probably meant she'd not only had a good time at the conference, but had also found success in connecting with clients. That also energized the woman. He smiled in spite of his stress. Yeah. He'd make this work.

Shaking his head, he chuckled and muttered. "You're a pig, Greyson." At least he was honest about it.

He swiped the call to her and waited.

"You called," Lynn said. "And you're early. What's up?"

"I'm taking off in a few minutes. Where would you like to go for dinner?"

"What do you mean you're taking off in a few minutes? How are you?"

"It's been a rough day, but I can tell you about that later. What about dinner?"

She let out a small sound and he could see her face while she did it. The corners of her lips turned up in a smile and her green eyes sparkled. Her nostrils flared as she gently tossed her brown hair back, away from her face. This was her "I've got a plan" face.

"What are you thinking?" he asked.

"I think you should pick dinner up and come to my house. I'll chill wine for me and Perrier for you. I bought a cheesecake. Maybe you can cover me with it for dessert."

"You had a good conference, didn't you," he said, the smile on his face growing.

"It was a *very* good conference. Three new clients are coming on board next month. Contracts signed and everything. I need to celebrate. You should probably pack a bag. Can you go in late tomorrow morning?"

Grey pursed his lips. She never asked him to do that.

"Have you talked to Nan today?"

"About what?" Lynn asked coyly.

"Just answer the question. Did you talk to Nan?"

"Well, I did call and she took my message, if that's what you mean."

"You know that's not what I mean."

"Does it matter?"

Grey thought for a moment. Other than the fact that those two women had manipulated him, he guessed it really didn't. Mavis had probably been in on the plan as well. He loved women and respected the hell out of them, but sometimes they just wore him out.

"I guess not," he said. "We'll see about tomorrow morning. I have work. Do you have a preference for dinner?"

"Pasta," Lynn said, "and bread — lots and lots of bread. You'd better order a couple of salads, too. I haven't eaten all day."

Now he was sure that she'd spoken with Nan. He shook his

head in defeat. "Got it. Do I need to pick up candles, too?"

"I know where I've hidden those." Lynn had dropped into a husky seductive voice. "I might have bought you a present when I was in Chicago."

"What's that?"

"I went shopping with my sister. She's looking to spice up her marriage. I'm just looking to entertain you."

Grey closed his eyes and gritted his teeth. He needed to end this call now. He knew his face was flushed with embarrassment. Nan would see that immediately. He didn't dare imagine what Lynn had purchased. He needed to focus for just a bit longer.

"Are you still there?" Lynn asked.

"You have to stop teasing me like this. I'll be over soon."

"Yeah. You're going to want to hurry."

"I'm on it."

"Don't forget. Your bag and dinner. We don't want to go anywhere else tonight."

"I won't forget. See you soon."

A smooth laugh preceded her ending the call. He put his phone down on his desk, blinked and rubbed his hands together. "Get up, you foolish man. You'd better hurry."

"Grey?"

He looked up to see Nan standing at his door, a smirk on her face.

"What did you do?" he asked.

"Just made sure you have a diversion." She held out a piece of paper. "Can I come in?"

"You might as well. You've had your hands in my business all day long. What's that?"

"There's a new Italian restaurant over on Dogwood. I ate there last weekend with Angel. It has the best food. They do takeout. Just give them a half hours' notice." She put the menu on the desk in front of him.

"I'm really not in control of my own life, am I?"

"Why sir, I don't know what you mean." Nan put a hand on her hip as she drawled out the words.

"How much did you tell Lynn?"

Nan sat down. "I didn't tell her much, just that you'd had a rough morning." She put her hands up, palms forward. "But don't be mad at me. She asked."

"How did she know to ask?"

"Got me," Nan said. "Maybe it was because you hadn't returned any of her calls."

Grey glanced at his phone and checked the time of Lynn's message. She'd called this morning while he'd been with the family. He couldn't believe he hadn't paid any attention to his phone. When he was in a session, it always sat in his drawer, muted and silent, so she was used to waiting up to an hour or so for him to call back. At least her question to Nan made sense now. He'd done it to himself. "Did you tell her I didn't have to be in early tomorrow morning?"

Nan winked. "I might have said something."

"Don't do that to me," he said.

Her brows creased and she flinched. "I'm sorry, Grey. I didn't mean to overstep."

"It's okay and I know you're trying to help me deal with this, but …" he let the words trail off.

"But you two aren't at that place and I assumed you were," she said. "I'm really sorry. That was my mistake. I should know better than to assume anything around here."

"What do you mean by that?"

"Nothing." She shook her head. "Nothing at all. I'll be more careful. Will you forgive me? I'm so sorry."

"Of course."

Nan stood up and headed for the door. Before she crossed the threshold, Grey caught up to her.

He put his hand on her arm. "Please don't worry, Nan. It's fine."

A tear leaked from her eye. "I can't believe I did that to you. I'm supposed to take care of you and I was thoughtless. And look at me. Now I'm trying to make it about me. I'm really okay, I just feel bad. Don't take care of me."

"Okay I won't," he said with a chuckle. "I'll deal with Lynn and see you in the morning."

She nodded and headed for her desk. He felt bad for being cross with her. The girl was usually right on target with the way she managed his business. Today had been strange for her as well.

Grey went back to his desk, opened the drawer again and took out his keys. Picking up his phone, he took one more glance at the stack of folders, clicked the button to shut of his monitor and left the office. Tonight had great potential.

CHAPTER FOUR

"You're amazing," Grey whispered at the woman lying in the bed. She didn't hear him. He bent over and picked up scarlet red panties from where they'd been dropped, then tossed them back on the bed. He went into the bathroom, turned on the shower and peered at himself in the mirror. Brushing his hair back and forth with his fingers, he chuckled. He wasn't getting any younger. There were more gray hairs these days. His father had been completely white by this age and Grey always wondered if he'd follow suit. No ... it was just enough to alert the world that he was no longer twenty years old.

"Thank God," he said out loud.

"Want some company?" Lynn asked from the doorway. "What are you looking at?"

"Just laughing at my gray hair. I'm getting old, you know."

She slipped the satin robe off and dropped it to the floor. "Not so old that you can't make me happy."

"I live for it." He pushed the sliding door open and gestured for her to go first. "Are we showering or not?" he asked, patting her bottom.

She laughed. "Maybe we should save our energy."

"Are you sure?"

Lynn turned to face him and wrapped her wet body around him, using him to block the spray of water into her face. "If you promise to make the rest of my night as wonderful as the first part, then I'm sure."

"Good thing," he said with a laugh. "You're wearing me out."

"I believe I've only just begun to tap into your inner reserves." She giggled wickedly and turned around again, presenting her back.

Grey responded by squirting some of her favorite coconut lime bath soap onto his hands. He rubbed them together to create lather and washed her back, shaking his head at his composure as she arched and moaned. The woman loved massages and adored having her back scratched. One touch and she was in ecstasy. When he wanted to wake her in the middle of the night, all it took was one finger, trailing down her spine. She came to life like a fire-breathing dragon.

"Let me do yours," she said, turning back to spin him around.

Long after the tips of his fingers had begun to wrinkle, they turned the water off and stepped out.

Lynn tossed him a bath towel from the linen closet. "I'm starving. I hope you brought plenty of food."

"I bought two extra orders of bread," he said.

"If it's not enough, I'm eating yours."

Grey finished drying himself and wrapped the towel around his waist. "I'll start heating the pasta. You finish in here." He tried to slip past her, but she grabbed the towel and flung it at her hamper.

"Like I haven't seen, touched and tasted it all," Lynn said, grinning at him. "You're a lot of fun when you're trying to set the stress of the day aside."

He'd finally stopped thinking about what happened earlier today and it all came rushing back. He opened the bathroom door and stepped back into her bedroom.

"Hey," Lynn said, catching his arm. "I'm sorry. I didn't mean to remind you. It's just that this evening has been really great. You aren't usually this adventurous. I like this Alistair Greyson. Don't let him run away."

He gave her a small smile. "He'll find his way back." Grey unzipped the travel bag he'd brought with him and took out a pair of shorts. "Shirt or no shirt?" he asked, trying to regain some of the levity they'd had.

"No shirt if I have a say in it." Lynn ran her hands up his chest, brushing her fingertips across the dark hair.

He looked down, grabbed her hands with his and held her close to him, then kissed the tip of her nose. "No shirt it is, then." He let her go, then caught her hand. "But I might have to wear a bib."

She giggled and went on back into the bathroom.

~~~

"Do you feel like talking about what happened this morning?" Lynn asked.

Grey reached across the peninsula and brushed at a drip of marinara sauce on her chin. "What do you want to know?"

"I guess I just want to know that you are okay with everything — that you don't feel guilty."

"Of course I feel a little guilt. If it was a deliberate suicide, I should have seen it coming. If it wasn't and he really was just messing around with his mother's medications, why would he do that? He knows better. Something made him dig into her stash."

"Why would she leave those kinds of drugs lying around anyway?"

"People get lazy. She should feel safe in her own house."

Lynn huffed. "Not likely. If your kid is in therapy, you keep your dangerous pharmaceuticals safe. Who knows what a kid will attempt?"

"I agree," Grey said, nodding, "but you can't blame her. This isn't about blame."

"Like hell."

He looked up, confused.

"You're blaming yourself. Don't tell me it isn't about blame. You think you should have been able to stop it and because you didn't, it's somehow your fault. It's not your fault." She took another bite of spaghetti and left some of it dangling from her mouth, a silly grin on her face. Gulping it in, she chuckled. "Sorry. Couldn't resist. I can't get all firm with you when you've just been all firm with me."

Grey shook his head. "I always feel so off-balance with you."

Lynn tipped her wine glass at him. "You like it and you know it. Otherwise you wouldn't keep coming back for more." She took a drink, smiled at him and said, "And more and more and more. You are a ravaging beast, sir. That's what you are."

"You bring out the worst in me."

"Oh, it's not the worst … it's really the best. The best I've ever had."

He felt his face flush again. She could embarrass him like no one else. Some days he felt like a silly teenage boy in love with a woman twice his age. But Lynn was several years younger than him and he was no longer a teenager. Wait. Did the word love just go through his mind?

"What are you thinking about over there, pretty boy?" Lynn asked, taking another drink from her wine glass.

"Nothing. It was nothing."

"Oh, it was something. I watched it happen all over your face."

"Do you ever think about us?"

She gestured back and forth between them. "Us — us?"

"Yeah, us."

"What about us?"

"I'm not getting any younger." He brushed his hand through his hair again. "You might be, but I'm not. Wouldn't you ever like to have a family? Someone who was at home when you got there after work?"

"Like you? You work longer hours than I do some days. And I like my house just the way it is."

"You're never lonely?"

Lynn shrugged. "If I'm lonely, I call you. Isn't this enough right now?"

"It is," he said, nodding. "But what about next year or the year after that. Are we still going to be doing this?"

"Why are you asking about the future?"

"Because it's coming our way and there's nothing we can do to stop it. Do you still want to be making booty calls in five years?"

"I haven't given it much thought." Lynn frowned at him and pushed her plate away. "When we started dating, I told you I wasn't looking for a family. I thought you were fine with that. You've always said that was how you felt too. What's changed?"

"I don't know that anything has changed. It's just that this ..." he mimicked her back and forth gesture, "... is pretty great. I have so much fun with you. I'd like these evenings to happen more often. Maybe someday we'll discover that we don't want them to end."

Lynn swallowed the last of the wine in her glass and picked up the bottle to refill it. While it was poised over her glass, she looked at him. "How long have you been thinking about this or is it a symptom of what happened this morning?"

"It's more about what happened this evening," he said. "I relax when I'm with you." Grey reached across and trailed his fingertips up and then back down her forearm, intertwining their fingers when he reached her hand. "I've never met a woman who is as brilliant and intriguing and exciting and glorious as you are."

"I am all that," she said. Lynn took her hand back, held the glass while she filled it and put the bottle back on the counter top. "But I'm not ready to settle down with you, no matter how much I enjoy spending time together."

"So ... too soon," he said.

"Much too soon." She nodded. "Okay, I get it that two years isn't too soon, but we've never talked about this before and I'm not ready to talk about it now."

He had to change this up. The evening was still much too young for them to have gotten to this point. "It's your fault, you know."

"What do you mean?"

"If you hadn't met me at the door in that filmy red lacy nothing bit of thing, I wouldn't have been spurred to think these less than honorable thoughts about you."

"Oh. I guess I do have to take the blame for that, don't I?" Lynn untied the knot on the belt that held her robe together and let it fall off her shoulders, revealing only the red panties that he'd removed earlier. "Maybe I shouldn't tempt you into having those types of thoughts again. What do you think?"

He took a deep, audible breath. "No more thinking. I believe you require action."

CHAPTER FIVE

Three weeks later

"Something happened to them," Grey said to Nan. "I keep them right there beside my phone in the desk drawer."

"You've been through everything in your office and now the whole car." She shook her head. "That was an expensive service call just to open your car."

"I don't know what to think. I don't lose things."

She laughed. "Apparently you do. What else could have happened to them?"

Grey looked at her and gritted his teeth. "Have you ever known me to be absent-minded?"

"You have another set of keys at home, don't you?"

"Good thing." He gave his head a quick shake. "At least I hid a house key in the yard so I can get in."

"What? Because you aren't ever absent-minded? You planned to lose your house key but not your car key?"

"Let's not go down that path. When I hid the key, I didn't know why I might need it. What if a woman wanted to meet me there or what if …" he paused and looked at her, "… something happened to me and you needed to get into the house and rescue me."

"A lot of good that would do." Nan sauntered over to her car. The horn beeped as the doors unlocked. "I didn't even know you'd hidden a key, much less where you put it. How could I get in?"

"If I called for help, I'd tell you."

She laughed at him. "You aren't going to win, sir. Not tonight."

"I'm sorry about making you take me home. I'll get a cab in the morning."

"No you won't. I'll be sitting outside your house bright and early. You can buy me coffee and a donut on the way to work."

"I should buy you dinner tonight."

"No fancy date with your girlfriend?"

Grey pulled his seatbelt on and shook his head. "I haven't seen much of Lynn lately."

"Did you break up? I thought things were going so well."

"They're fine," he said. "But lately, I've been thinking about the future. That scared her."

Nan swatted at his arm. "A future with you is sooooo frightening."

"I guess it is. We're just taking it one day at a time. When we get a chance to spend time together, we take it, but …" He didn't know how to finish the sentence. There were so many 'buts' surrounding the relationship with Lynn. But things had changed since the night they spent together three weeks ago … but he wanted to love someone and that frightened her … but she wasn't prepared to share her life with anyone else … but … but … but.

"But you two are on separate paths?" Nan asked.

"Yeah. That's as good a way to put it as any."

"You've been with her a couple of years now, haven't you?"

He leaned his head against the car window and slowly nodded.

"It's my fault," he said softly.

"What did you do?"

"I asked if she'd ever be interested in moving things along."

Nan tapped her fingers in a rhythm on the steering wheel. "If I remember right, you really did come into work late the next morning. Didn't you spend the rest of that night with her?"

"Yeah, and it was good, but both of us were thinking about our responses to the question. Even though we blew it off and tried to move past it, now it's out there. I said it out loud. I should never have said it out loud."

"After two years in a relationship, you have a right to say some things out loud. It shouldn't destroy the relationship. If you can't be honest with each other …"

Grey interrupted her by putting his hand up. "You trying to shrink *me* now?"

Nan stopped at a red light and looked at him, a silly smile on her face. "Even the big, bad therapist needs to hear the truth sometimes." She pointed at a burger joint. "Do you want something?"

"You really know how to show a guy a good time," Grey said.

"Unless you want to go somewhere nice, this is as good as it gets on your drive home."

"Fine," he said. "I'll take you to a nice restaurant."

She turned to him, her face alight with happiness. "Really? I've never gone to dinner with you." She frowned. "And you owe me, too. After all I do to take care of you, it's about time."

"If you weren't fifteen years younger than me, I'd marry you, Nan."

"My daddy would kill you dead," she drawled. "Deader than a rattlesnake under old Brownie's hooves. Kill. You. Dead." Nan aimed her index finger at him and snapped her thumb like a trigger. "Not that it wouldn't be fun up until he found out about it, but he'd hunt you down and shoot you right between the eyes."

"I get it, I get it," Grey said, laughing. The girl could make him laugh. "What's he got against older men?"

"If they haven't found themselves a wife to cook and clean for them by your age, there's got to be something wrong with 'em. That's what Daddy would say."

"Maybe there is."

"Oh stop it." Nan turned a corner too fast and he held on to the dash as her tires squealed on the pavement. "Oops. Sorry."

"That's okay. If you get pulled over, I'll just tell the officer I'm your father and you're learning how to drive."

"You're my grandfather," she said.

~~~

Nan turned onto the street leading to Grey's home. "Is that a police car in your driveway?" she asked.

"It looks like it. I wonder what's going on?"

"We're about to find out." She pulled in beside the police car.

Grey jumped out as a young policewoman stepped out of her car. "Alistair Greyson?" she asked.

"That's me. What's going on?"

"Where have you been this evening?"

"At dinner with a co-worker." He pointed at Nan. "She gave me a ride home."

"Did you lend your car to someone?"

Grey shook his head, starting to become concerned. "No. I lost my keys today. Nan offered to bring me home. I was going to get my second set and take them to work with me in the morning."

"I'd like to come inside with you, if you don't mind."

"What happened with my car?" he asked. He peered at her nameplate. "Officer Delgado?"

The officer nodded and gestured to his front door. "Shall we go inside?"

"I'm a little embarrassed to do this in front of you," he said. "But I need to retrieve a second house key." He counted the paving stones and when he got to the eighth stone, stopped and knelt down to dig in the dirt. He came up with a small box and took out a key.

"Clever." The officer smiled at him. "I'm pretty sure a thief would never know to look there."

"Came up with it on my own. I haven't had time to put a

keyless entry in the garage yet, so I had to do something just in case I lost my keys."

"You've been here for six years," Nan said, following them to the front door. "You still haven't replaced that garage door system?"

Grey glanced at her. Evidently, she was going to be part of this tonight.

He unlocked the front door and held it for the two women. Once inside, he pointed to the sofa and chairs. "Can you tell me now why you're here?"

Officer Delgado took a small notepad and pen out of her breast pocket and flipped to a blank page. "When did you notice that your keys were missing?"

"Not until I was ready to leave. That was about five thirty, right, Nan?"

She nodded in agreement. "We searched his office and had to call a locksmith to unlock the car so he could search in there, too. Nada."

"Where do you keep your keys? In plain sight?"

Grey shook his head. "In my top desk drawer with my phone."

"Does everyone in the office know that your keys are there?"

"Probably." He lifted a shoulder. "I don't hide them, if that's what you're asking."

"Does everyone in the office have access to your office?"

"I suppose. My door isn't locked." He looked at Nan. "None of the offices are locked, are they?"

"Just the main door when the last person leaves. The cleaning crew comes in four days a week. They need access."

"And you didn't see anyone go into your office that shouldn't be in there?" the officer asked.

"No." Grey tried to think. "I was in and out today. There was a staff meeting this morning in the conference room and I went to lunch."

"Did you drive?"

"I walked to the coffee shop across the street."

"I sit in the center of all the offices," Nan said. "I never saw anyone on the floor that didn't belong there."

The officer referred to her notebook. "Do you know a Joseph Lacey?"

Nan and Grey both looked at each other.

"He had an appointment today," Grey said, feeling as if the air had been sucked out of the room. "What did Joe do?"

"Did you leave him alone in your office?"

Grey swallowed, his mouth suddenly filled with saliva. He knew something awful had happened. "Just for a minute. We were in the middle of a particularly tough conversation and … well, he needed some water. I only stepped out to ask Nan to bring him a bottle of water from the staff room." He nodded. "And then I went to the door when she knocked and gave it to me."

"So he could have gotten into your desk drawer at that time."

"I guess. But why would he do that? What has he done? Please tell me what happened."

"Joseph Lacey drove your car into the front doors of the high school. His blood alcohol was very high."

Grey couldn't breathe. "Is he dead? Was he alone?"

"He's alive and no, he wasn't alone. There were three others in the vehicle with him. The passenger in the front seat was not wearing a seatbelt. When the car hit a post in the center of the school foyer, he flew out and was killed when his head impacted a glass trophy case."

"And the other two?" Grey asked.

"They were both wearing seat belts and will live. In fact, they probably won't even spend the night in the hospital. They were very lucky. Mr. Lacey, on the other hand, has severe internal injuries and is in critical condition."

Nan had come over to stand beside Grey and put her hand on his shoulder.

"I should go to the hospital," he said. "Joe is my patient."

"You need to take a breath," Nan said. "I'll call Mavis."

"No, don't. I'll call her." Grey turned back to Officer Delgado. "What else do you need from me?"

"There will be some paperwork with this." She took a business card from her pocket and handed it to him. "Contact me tomorrow and we'll discuss when you can meet with me again."

"Thank you," Grey said.

Nan tapped his arm. "Give her one of your business cards, Grey."

"Oh. Sure." He took out his wallet and drew a card from its pocket. "My numbers are all on there."

The officer gave him a brisk nod and stood, heading for the door. "The family is at the hospital with their son. Maybe you ought to give yourself and them the night to figure this all out. Your friend is right. You should take a breath first."

"Thank you," he said following her to the front door.

After she left, he turned back to Nan. "What in the hell?"

"I don't know what to tell you, Grey."

"How am I missing cues from these kids? I'm failing them all. Joe has been working so hard at his sobriety. He didn't want to go back into rehab. Why would he steal my car? He planned that, Nan. He planned it! He waited until I left the room and then he stole my keys. Then he waited until we left tonight and came back to take my car. He planned this!"

"Probably with the help of his buddies. What has he told you about his friends?"

"Not much. We haven't had enough time to dig into everyone he knows. We've been focusing on his family, his school work and finding healthy outlets for him. When I've asked about his friends, he just says they're good guys." Grey dropped down on the sofa and put his head in his hands. "What am I doing wrong?"

CHAPTER SIX

This last week had been highly stressful and Grey still didn't feel as if things were back to normal. He'd spent time with the Lacey family at the hospital, doing his best to help them through this crisis. Joe was in trouble. The kids insisted that they'd been in on it together, but the police continued to investigate the death of their friend and the accident. Until there were concrete decisions made regarding Joe's future, Grey was focused on helping the family stay together. It was a difficult situation all around. Fortunately, the parents of the young man who died chose not to make the situation worse, doing their best to understand that their son had been part of the planning for that horrible evening.

Grey hadn't replaced his car yet, choosing instead to drive the old beat-up pickup truck that he'd owned for years. It had been parked in the second bay of his garage. He thought that one day he'd either sell it or even restore it. The pickup had been his first purchase out of college and he just couldn't part with it. There was a lot of history in that truck. It felt like a comfortable pair of blue jeans.

Last week he took it in to his favorite garage. The bill looked as if they had replaced every ounce of fluid and all of the moving parts in the engine, but at least it was running smoothly again. Insurance companies were working to decide who was going to pay what to him for his car. He didn't care — he just didn't want to be involved in it.

Grey walked to the front window and looked at the sunset off in the distance. He was unsettled. Work no longer felt like the haven it had been most of his life. He'd lost patients before. He'd dealt with suicides and kids who went so far off the deep end they had to be hospitalized. This felt different. He approached every session these days with trepidation, concerned that his patient might make a choice Grey hadn't prepared for. He looked at everyone through the lens of failure and spent hours poring over his notes in order to ensure that he hadn't missed a hint or clue. He no longer trusted himself, and that wasn't a good place for him to be.

Mavis had spent time with him trying to help him work through it, but he found it more and more difficult to explain exactly what was going on inside his mind and his heart.

As the deep reds of the night sky turned darker, Grey let the curtain fall back into place and returned to his chair. He picked up the book he'd borrowed from the practice's library.

Cervantes' *Don Quixote* was one of Grey's favorite stories and he'd seen the movie too many times to count. Sophia Loren had been one of his first loves. There were times he felt like the main character — tilting at windmills. In his world, monsters were often disguised as something else. Poor Don Quixote. He wanted nothing more than to be a classical hero, but in reality, the character's mind was broken, caught up in the beautiful and ornate language of his favorite stories. It wasn't difficult to identify with Quixote's desire to be a chivalrous and honorable hero when the world was falling apart around you.

Only Mavis Tennys would fill shelves with classic fiction alongside the medical tomes they used regularly. She expected her partners and staff to read. He smiled. She expected a lot from the group that she surrounded herself with and they were willing to give it to her.

Grey's phone rang and when he picked it up to answer it, Mavis's name flashed across the screen.

"I was just thinking about you," he said as he answered.

"Come to the hospital," Mavis said, her voice filled with stress and grief.

Grey dropped the book on the recliner and headed for the front door, scooping up his keys as he opened the door. "What's going on?"

"It's Nan."

"What's wrong?" Grey's heart sank. What could have happened? She was going out with friends tonight — people she'd known for years. "Was there a car accident?"

"Grey, she's been raped and beaten."

"Ohhh," Grey moaned, his heart leaping into his throat. "No. Not Nan. Is she awake? Can she tell you who did this to her?"

The sound behind Mavis changed. "I had to leave the floor," she said. "I'm in the stairway. Grey, the beating was brutal and she hasn't come awake yet. They have her pretty well drugged up, but she said your name a couple of times. I think she wants you here."

"I'm on my way, but I can barely think, so I shouldn't talk to you while I drive."

"Got it. Drive carefully, but get here."

He tossed the phone onto the passenger seat of his truck, remembered to pull his seatbelt on, and backed up. He slammed his foot on the brakes as the lights of an oncoming car went past him on the street. Taking a deep breath, he admonished himself. "Nan needs you. If you're in an accident because you're being an idiot, you can't get to her. Slow down, think straight, and drive carefully."

Taking another long breath, he focused on calming himself, then backed out of the driveway and headed for the hospital. When thoughts of what Nan must have gone through this evening threatened to take over, he shut them down and concentrated on the cars around him.

The drive to the hospital seemed to take forever. He refused to honk his horn at drivers who swerved in front of him or drove too slowly or remained in place long after the light had turned green. He contained himself when a young man walking his dog ignored the lights and walked in front of him. By the time he pulled into the hospital parking lot, he was shaking. Grey got out of the truck, slammed the door, and took off at a run across the lot into the emergency room entrance. As he patiently waited for an orderly who was pushing an empty gurney to cross in front of him, he patted his pocket to make sure he had remembered his keys. They were right where they belonged.

"Grey! There you are!" Mavis pushed past a cluster of people and grabbed his arm. "Come with me. They'll try to stop you from going in, but I'm not afraid of them. Are you?"

He allowed her to drag him through the waiting room and stuck close when she pushed through a swinging set of double doors. Two nurses stepped out, then realized they knew who Mavis was and allowed her to proceed.

"Have you called her parents?" Grey asked.

"They're coming as fast as they can, but it might not be until tomorrow morning. I told her mother that we wouldn't leave her alone tonight."

A nurse pushed open a curtain and Grey felt his entire being clench in horror. He barely recognized Nan. She had a tube down her throat and IVs in her arm. Her tiny body was covered in bruises and her face was swollen, leaving only slits for her eyes. Nan's beautiful hair was matted with blood.

"She's not breathing on her own?" he asked.

"She wasn't when the ambulance brought her in," a nurse said.

Grey turned to Mavis. "I thought you said she was asking for me."

Mavis patted his arm. "She would have. When they called me, they said that your name was the first one she spoke to the EMT. She said your name several times. I'm pretty sure they were asking if you were involved in this, but I assured them that you were her friend and she wanted you to help her. You might have to talk to an officer later, but they have a pretty good idea who did this to her."

"She was with friends," Grey said. "Surely not one of them."

"No." Mavis shook her head. "A young man at the bar. Her friends are talking to the police about what happened before Nan left to go home."

Nan moaned. Her eyes fluttered open, then immediately closed again. All Grey saw in them was pain and fear.

"I'm here, Nan," he said and took the girl's hand, careful not to dislodge the tube that had been taped down. "I'm right here."

A tear leaked from her eye and she tried to speak, but couldn't with the tube down her throat. That caused her to panic and the nurse pressed a button.

"Talk to her," the nurse said.

"Calm down, Nan. You weren't breathing on your own, so there's a tube in place to help you. Please calm yourself," Grey said.

More tears flowed from her eyes and Mavis stepped forward. "You're taking it out now, aren't you? She's awake."

The nurse nodded and stepped back as a young woman came in and stood beside her.

"Nan," she said. "You must remain calm for just a few minutes as I draw this tube out. You woke up faster than I thought you would. That's really great. I'm proud of you. You are a very strong young woman. Now can you hold still for me?"

Nan gave her a slight nod, still unable to open her eyes for more than a blink.

In a flash, the tube was out and the nurse rushed to put an oxygen mask on Nan's face. "This will help you breathe for now, honey," the nurse said. "Okay?"

Nan nodded again and tried to say something.

The nurse bent in closer and pulled the mask back to hear her, then looked up at Grey. "Are you Grey?"

He nodded.

"He's right here, Nan. He's holding your hand. Can you feel it?"

Grey squeezed Nan's hand. "I won't leave you."

The girl relaxed, her head lolling to the side as she dropped back to sleep.

Her nurse replaced the oxygen mask and checked the monitors. "She's been through hell. He brutalized her. I'm surprised she wants you here. You must be a very special friend."

"They've been through a lot together," Mavis said, stepping back into Grey's line of sight. "If there's one person Nan trusts, it's this man."

Those weren't easy words for Grey to hear. He had no idea that Nan felt that way about him. He thought the world of her, but even though they saw each other every work day, he just assumed she treated him like she treated everyone else in the office. There was no way that Nan saw him in a romantic way. They'd hinted around that a couple of times long ago, just to make sure. That wasn't how she responded to him. She loved her father dearly, so he knew better than to think that she was looking for a daddy-figure in her life. If what she wanted was for him to be her closest friend, then he was happy to do that. It was a perfect relationship for him, in fact. At this point, he didn't know what to think of his relationship with Lynn, but that didn't matter right now. The girl lying on the bed in front of him was all that mattered. She had to be okay. The world needed this girl's vibrant life.

"You have to come back to us," Grey whispered.

Mavis put her hand on his shoulder. "I'm glad you're here."

CHAPTER SEVEN

Running himself ragged wasn't helping anyone, but Grey couldn't see any other option. He sat in the corner of the steak house by himself, too exhausted to think. He'd spent the last two weeks either at work or with Nan and her family.

Jonah Stallings and his wife, Louisa, were exactly as he imagined them. Jonah was a big, tall man with a ruddy face and graying reddish hair that grew thinner with every year; his wife, Louisa, was medium height, with eyes that flashed when she got angry. Her grip was like a vise, though she did her best to restrain her strength. Both Jonah and Louisa had spent their lives outdoors, their tanned skin no longer soft and supple. They were hard workers who were broken at seeing their daughter lying in the hospital bed, battered and bruised. The first time Jonah saw her, he spent just a few moments with his daughter, assuring her of his love for her before rushing from the room.

Grey had followed the man down the hall and waited outside the restroom while that immense strong man vomited up everything that he'd eaten in the last twenty-four hours. He came back out, red-faced and sweating, grief and anger vying for prominence on his face.

Last week, Nan was released from the hospital. Her parents moved into her apartment and they'd purchased a bed that they set up in the living room. There was no way Nan would be left by herself until she was strong enough to kick them to the curb. The police arrested the young man who had brutalized her. The idiot had recorded the entire thing on his phone. There was no need for Nan to see him face to face until the trial.

She was a shell of her former self. The slightest noise startled her and she flinched when anyone got too close, relaxing only by sheer force of will. Grey still didn't know how it was that she trusted him so implicitly, but it didn't matter. If he was who she needed to be around in order to feel safe, he would be there as much as possible.

He'd seen Lynn socially a couple of times the last two weeks. She was preoccupied with a million other things and between work and spending time with Nan, he didn't have the energy to question what was going on. She knew what he was dealing with right now and assured him that when his life returned to normal, she'd spend whatever time they could find together. Their last date had gone better than he expected and after dinner they'd returned to her apartment. The relief of having someone close to him who didn't need him to do anything except make love was extraordinary. He'd gone back to his own house that night to sleep, feeling like maybe things might get better.

Work was still difficult. Grey was beginning to wonder if burnout had finally hit him. Mavis didn't push; she knew how much time he was spending with Nan. She had assigned herself as Nan's therapist, meeting with the girl at her home and was taking her through the unimaginable course of therapy that would help Nan face what had happened, and find strength to move forward. Mavis Tennys was a terrific therapist and Grey was glad she could be there for Nan.

Today had been another rough day in the office. When two of his appointments canceled, Bill Wagner couldn't resist taunting him about losing clients. That arrogant bastard didn't know when to shut up.

Another young patient, a boy whose uncle had sexually abused him for years, and who was showing signs of sexual aggression in school, had attempted to cut his genitals off. While Grey knew that the boy was in deep trouble, this behavior came from out of the blue. Kids were so unpredictable sometimes based on what they experienced during their days — at school and at home. After two female classmates accused him of exposing himself to them, three male classmates beat him up when he returned to school, calling him names and telling him that he should kill himself. He'd done what he could to combat the intense emotions he faced. He and his mother hadn't had time to get to Grey before it all fell apart.

Grey wasn't sure how much more he could take. There was so much darkness around him right now. Other than a few stolen moments with Lynn, he felt himself falling into a morass of despair. If he weren't being held here right now by Nan, he would be gone. Whether it was a sabbatical, a vacation, or a new life, he needed to consider something different. But his needs didn't matter as long as Nan needed him. Her life was what was important.

The waiter refilled his water glass. "Your meal will be right out."

"Thanks." Grey looked up, realizing that he'd had his eyes closed. He needed to get out of his head. Thinking that a good meal would help, he'd left Nan with her parents and promised to bring something back for them to eat.

He looked at the couples and families at tables around the restaurant. Children's voices and low tones filled his ears until the sound of a familiar laugh caught his attention. He turned toward it and saw a man holding Lynn's chair as she sat down. He leaned in and the two kissed, as intimately as any kiss Grey had experienced with her. They lingered over the kiss and Grey turned away, sickened at himself for watching. They had no idea he was back here.

He couldn't bear it any longer and turned back. The man had

taken the seat next to Lynn rather than across from her. Grey watched as she took his hand and held it at the table, laughing up at the waiter who presented them with a wine list. Lynn handed the list to her date and smiled as he nodded and placed the order. With Grey, Lynn was always in charge. He was disgusted at them, and at the fact that he couldn't keep his eyes off the scene unfolding before him.

The two looked as if they were comfortable together, making him wonder just how long they'd been dating. Lynn leaned in when he spoke. Watching her caress the man's face was almost more than Grey could handle.

Flinging his napkin on the table, Grey pushed his chair back just as the waiter approached with his dinner.

"Can I help you with something?" the waiter asked.

"An emergency just arose," Grey responded as he took out his wallet. "How much do I owe you?"

"If you'll give me a minute, I can ring up a receipt and package your meal so you can eat it later."

Grey looked at the steak, unable to comprehend how he could possibly eat a bite of it. His entire life was collapsing around him and this kid wanted him to eat a steak? He slipped two twenty dollar bills from his wallet, closed his eyes to see the prices on the pages of the menu in his mind, then took a third twenty out. "That should cover it. Take it home and give it to your dog."

"But sir ...," the waiter said.

It felt as if the room were closing in on him as Grey wove his way through the tables for the front door. Then the worst thing that could happen, did happen. Lynn pushed her seat back and stood, nearly tripping over Grey.

She jumped back, catching herself on her chair, horrified at seeing him.

"Grey! What are you doing here?"

"I was just grabbing some dinner before heading over to Nan's place. Excuse me." He tried to push away, but couldn't seem to get his feet under him.

"This looks bad," she said.

He shook his head. "No. It looks like what it is. I don't understand why you didn't just tell me. Why did you …? It doesn't matter. You always do what you want to do."

"But Grey. I didn't want to hurt you. You've been hurting so much this last month. I didn't want to add to it."

He let out a groan. "Honesty. All I wanted was honesty." Frustrated with her and with himself, he leaned in and spoke softly. "Why did you sleep with me last weekend? How cruel are you?"

Lynn took his arm and turned to her date. "Excuse us. I'll be right back." Pushing Grey toward the front door, she waited until they got outside. "Because you needed me. That's why I slept with you. You needed to relax. I was going to tell you at dinner that night that we should break up, but you were already such a wreck."

He yanked his arm away from her. "I get it that you didn't want to break up because I've been a wreck, but why would you sleep with me? Damn it, Lynn. It's so much worse now. What must you think of me to do this? If you didn't want to be with me, you should have told me long ago. How long have you been dating that man?"

She looked at the ground.

"How long, Lynn? Be honest with me for once in your life."

"It's been a couple of months."

"A couple of months?" Grey threw his hands up in the air. "Does he know that you've been sleeping with someone else?"

She shook her head, then looked up and sighed. "He probably does now. I'm sure he heard you. Thanks for that."

"I don't believe you. It's my fault that your date knows you were sleeping with me? You aren't going to take any responsibility for this?"

"I was just trying to help," Lynn said flatly. "I figured that our relationship was winding down and you would just kind of go away."

"Well, I'm going away now. If I've left anything at your house, please just toss it in the trash. I never want to see you again." Grey stalked through the parking lot to his truck. He got the door open, sat in the driver's seat and slumped forward, his head making contact with the steering wheel.

When he finally regained some sense of stability, he put the key in the ignition and started the truck. Lynn had gone back inside. She would land on her feet. She always did. As he drove aimlessly through the city, his eyes caught sight of a liquor store, its neon sign in the window flashing that it was open. He pulled into a parking space in front of the building. Just as he reached to open the door, his phone rang. He pulled it out and swiped open the call from Nan.

"Hello?"

"Hello, Grey," her mother said. "Nan says she wants pizza instead of steak. Can we place an order and have you pick it up instead? It will be paid for when you get there."

He smiled in spite of all that had happened. Where would he ever be without Nan? Even when she didn't realize it, she was taking care of him. Damn, he wished she was fifteen years older.

"I'd be glad to. Call in whatever she wants and I'll bring it with me."

"You've been a godsend to us. Thank you for being her friend."

CHAPTER EIGHT

After work, Grey sat in his pickup truck in the parking lot. He didn't know how much more of this he was going to be able to take. He knew it was his own problem. This afternoon, he'd had an introductory session with a girl and her mother. The mother had just found out that her daughter was stealing muscle relaxers and pain pills from the medicine cabinet at home and at an aunt's house. They lived in the same general area and the families were always in and out of each other's houses. The aunt had discovered the theft, after it had been going on for quite some time. When confronted, the girl admitted everything. She was selling the pills to her friends and using the money to buy birth control pills from another classmate so she could have sex with her fifteen-year-old boyfriend.

By the time they got through the entire story, Grey was exhausted. He felt no compassion for the girl and wanted to call the mother out for her complete lack of attention to her daughter's actions. The girl sat through the entire session sullen and angry, never once opening her mouth to speak. Her mother, on the other hand, went back and forth between sobbing about how her life had been destroyed by this behavior and screaming at her daughter about how she could never trust her to be alone again. When he'd finally calmed the woman, he attempted to ask questions to find a way to help the daughter understand that what she did was wrong. That only spun the mother up again. He'd sent them on their way after an hour and a half of listening to the woman rant and rave, then packed paperwork and his laptop into a briefcase and fled from the building. He didn't care what that family did. As he thought back through the patients he'd met with today, he realized that he didn't care about a single one of them.

It hit him like a punch in the gut that he cared about nothing. He didn't want to know about the lives of any of his co-workers any longer. He was worn out by his patients and he didn't even care if he made it home tonight. Were it not for Nan and her parents, he'd have nothing in the world that was important to him.

He dialed Nan's number and waited for someone to pick up, surprised when it was Nan herself.

"Hello?" she asked.

"Hello, Nan. I'm just leaving work. Can I bring supper over tonight?"

"I don't know. You should probably ask Mom. Just a minute."

He opened his mouth to stop her, but soon, her mother came on the line. "Is this you, Grey?"

"It is. I was wondering if I could bring dinner over. If you and Jonah would like to go out for dinner, I'd be glad to stay with Nan. You all have been cooped up in that apartment far too long."

"That's so nice," she said. "But we'll be fine here this evening. Nan would like to see you, though."

"What about dinner?"

"Whatever you bring will be fine. We aren't choosy. Thank you, son."

"I'll be there after a while. Tell Nan I missed her today."

"I will." The woman ended the call. She sounded as exhausted as he felt. Nan wasn't getting any better. Mavis was concerned for her. Nan refused to leave the apartment and her parents didn't know how to change her mind about that. They'd tried taking her outside to walk in a local park, but Nan had panicked and run back inside, locking herself in her bedroom. It had taken them hours to talk her back out.

The young man who had beaten and raped her was in jail, so she didn't need to worry about him breaking out to get to her. Several of Nan's friends had stopped by to see her, but even those attempts were fading away. Nan couldn't bring herself to be interested in their lives. Everything that made that girl who she was had been destroyed by one young man who couldn't control himself.

Grey thought about the children he saw during the year. Some of them really worked to become more than they were, but he knew there was a percentage of those children who would become like the young man who beat up Nan. Their need for power and control far outweighed their sense of compassion for others. No amount of counseling would change that and no drug existed that would make someone care about another person. All he could do was teach them methods to learn how the rest of the world worked and how to be a healthy human being.

Grey pulled into the parking lot of a Chinese restaurant that they'd ordered from before and went inside. He told the host that he wanted to order takeout and was escorted into the bar with a menu. A waiter approached him after a few minutes to take his order and told him it would be several minutes. The waiter gestured to the bartender who came down to where Grey was seated, plopped a cocktail napkin on the counter and asked if he would like something to drink while he waited.

Staring at the cocktail napkin, Grey's vision blurred. He refocused as he looked at the bottles of liquor on glass shelves behind the bartender.

"Sir?" the bartender asked. "Would you like a drink?"

"Just a glass of water," Grey said. "Thanks." He nodded at the bartender when the glass was set down on the napkin that had been taunting him. Pushing aside the destructive thoughts, Grey leaned back in the seat. What was he going to do with his life? He couldn't go back to hockey — that was out of the question. He'd spent time and energy getting to where he was with the life he was presently living. He had respect, a good position, a great salary, a home of his own and ... that was it. Everything that he'd thought would lead to a future had been stripped away. He hadn't heard from Lynn again after that awful night last week. He wanted to hate her, but all he could do was hope that she would find a good life for herself.

The waiter brought two bags to the counter and presented him with the receipt. "Anything else I can do for you?"

"Thanks," Grey said. He took cash from his wallet and handed it to the young man. "Keep the change."

"Thank you, sir." The waiter smiled at him and Grey nodded toward the bartender, leaving a single on the counter.

Once he was back in the car, he took a deep breath. He needed to find an AA meeting soon. It felt like alcohol was presenting itself to him more and more these days and he was finding it difficult to walk away. The other night in front of the liquor store had been frightening. Grey started his truck. This couldn't be how his life would look for the next fifty years. It wouldn't be worth it.

The lights were all on in Nan's apartment. At least that was good news. That meant she was up and moving around. When things were bad, she wanted the lights turned down low. He didn't know how he would handle her if tonight was a bad night. He'd do what he needed to do, of course, but he was certainly glad to see the place lit up.

When the door to her apartment opened for him, Grey was shocked at the chaos in the living room.

"What's going on?" he asked.

Nan's mother took the two bags from him. "Come on in, Grey. Nan needs to talk to you. We have news."

He looked around for Nan and found her on the sofa with boxes and packing paper all around. "Nan?"

"Come here, Grey." She patted an empty spot at the end of the sofa.

He walked over and sat down. "What are you doing?"

Nan looked at her father. She started to speak, choked, and started to cry.

Jonah Stallings took the recliner next to Grey. "She's not getting any better here," he said. "We're taking our baby girl home. I have to get back to the ranch. Louisa thinks that if we can get Nan away from this city and back to a simpler life, she'll start to heal. She's got a lot of family there that will take care of her."

Grey turned to his friend. "You're leaving?"

"I'm sorry," she wailed. "I'm so, so sorry."

He put his hand out, then gently moved it back when she flinched. "Don't be sorry. Does this feel right to you?"

She nodded and dropped her eyes. "I think so."

"Have you talked to Mavis?"

Louisa came out from the kitchen with two plates in her hands. She put one on the table in front of Nan and handed the other to Grey. "Mrs. Tennys was here earlier today and she agrees. Nan needs a change. We'll come back for the trial, but she needs to get out of here. Jonah and I would stay as long as she needs us, but it's time to go home."

Grey didn't dare speak for fear that he would lose control of his emotions. He couldn't tell Nan what had been going on in his life the last few weeks. Before this all fell apart, they would have talked about it at the office and she would have given him a million reasons to get over himself. But that Nan was buried deep within the grief and pain she bore right now and he didn't know if she would ever return.

"Are you mad?" Nan whispered.

He snapped his head toward her. "Mad? At you? Absolutely not. You have to go where you can find yourself again. We all know that won't happen here. I'm proud of you for making this decision."

"You are?" She started to cry again. "Really?"

"Really. When are you leaving?"

Jonah looked up when his wife re-entered the room with a plate for him. He took it and leaned forward. "Joseph is on his way down right now with a truck. We'll leave before the weekend is over."

Grey did his best to not let anyone in the room see him sag. "This weekend," he said. "Is there anything I can do?"

"Just keep coming over until I leave," Nan said. "I'm going to miss you."

"Oh, Nan, I'll miss you, too. This place won't be the same without you."

CHAPTER NINE

Grey knocked on the door, then held his breath, waiting for permission to enter.

"Come in," Mavis said. She was typing at her computer when he walked into her office.

"Mavis," Grey said, standing in front of her desk.

She turned her chair toward him. "Grey. You're in early this morning."

"Today, I must formally resign my position with this practice." He placed his resignation letter on the desk and remained standing.

Mavis slowly nodded while she reached for the letter. As she pulled it toward her, she turned it in order to read what he'd written. "I see." She continued to read through the letter. "I see," she repeated. "Is this the only path you see ahead for yourself?"

"I believe it is. With all that has occurred in these last weeks, I find that I am no longer able to meet my own high standards, much less those set forth by you and the other partners."

"Relax, Grey." Mavis pointed at a chair. "Sit down. I'm not going to bite your head off. If this is what you believe should happen, then I support you — you know that. I'm incredibly saddened by your decision, though. You've been a wonderful asset and a good friend. I'm going to only ask you once — is there anything I can say or do to make you change your mind?"

"I regret to say that there is no possibility of my remaining in your employment." Grey remained standing in place.

"Seriously, Grey, I mean it — loosen up. Sit down and talk to me. What was the last straw for you?"

He took a deep breath, forced his muscles to unclench and sat stiffly in the chair she'd offered. "I don't know that there was a last straw. My decision comes as a result of the culmination of many different failures and catastrophes, both personal and professional."

"I know it's been rough, but it's hard for me to believe that you're giving up. That's not who you are."

"I prefer to look at this as a redirection of my life, Mavis. There comes a time when each person must face the truth that they are unable to continue as they have."

Mavis furrowed her brow as she looked at him. "You sound different today. Are you okay? I mean, really okay?"

"No," he said. "I do not believe that I am. Every step that I take these days is fraught with dangers I am unable to predict. With every turn, a new peril threatens my stability. If I don't remove myself from the things that surround me, I am concerned that it will overtake me to the point that I can no longer find a return to normalcy."

"Nan's gone, isn't she?"

"She and her family left last night. I don't expect to ever hear from her again. It's for the best. The child needs to heal. I am a link to the life that broke her spirit. It will fall to her mother and father, the animals she loves so much, and friends who remember her as a whole and healthy young woman to bring her back from this brokenness. I am confident in their ability to do so. Her father is a formidable man and her mother has the soul of a lioness. They love their daughter very much. She's fortunate to find herself within their care."

"Oh Grey." Mavis stood and came around the desk, coming to rest on its edge in front of him. "Your spirit has taken a beating in ways that I didn't realize were happening, hasn't it?"

"I'm sorry?" he asked, confused.

She reached down and took his hand in hers, then held it in her lap. "How did I miss this? You are such a strong man and you internalized all of the hits that have come at you until they eroded your foundation. Tell me you haven't been drinking."

He shook his head as he looked away. "Not yet."

"But you've wanted to, right?"

He gave her a barely perceptible nod.

"Have you been to any meetings lately?"

Grey looked up at her. "Yes."

"Good. Every night if necessary and if you need to leave the office, just go. If you need to talk to someone, find me." She turned, picked up his resignation letter and scanned it again. "Two weeks is plenty of time. At our staff meeting this morning, we'll begin assigning your clients to other members of the staff. If you believe that you should do introductions with any of them, we will make that happen. Take time to say goodbye, pack your office …"

He put his hand up to interrupt her. "I won't take much from my office. My books should remain with the practice. As there are very few items in there that mean anything to me personally, it will require no more than a paper bag."

"Are you sure?" She was still looking at him quizzically — he couldn't imagine why.

"Of that I am certain." Grey pushed his chair back. "If you will excuse me, I'll take my leave of you."

Mavis grabbed his arm and pulled him into a tight hug.

He responded easily. This woman was such a good friend.

"I hope you find yourself, my friend. Something happened in these last few weeks that changed you drastically. You are a treasure and it hurts me that somehow, I've been part of what wounded you. Are you leaving town?"

He nodded.

"Where will you go?"

"I'm unsure of my destination, but believe it will present itself when I arrive."

~~~

The next two weeks passed with a swiftness that Grey hadn't imagined. The partners and staff had taken on his clients with no discussion; even Bill Wagner took two. There were only a few questions regarding techniques and methods he'd used so they could ensure a smooth transition. He'd met with five of his clients in order to introduce them to their new therapist, but that left plenty of time for him to close out his home. He'd found a real estate agent, Deborah — actually, a good friend of Mavis's — to sell his home. The first week, he'd gone through it with her and they'd made a list of things that needed to be repaired, repainted, and re-carpeted. During that time, he'd emptied most of the furniture, taking it to thrift stores. He'd filled a dumpster with the worst of the junk and negotiated with the agent those things that could be sold as part of the house.

There wasn't a single item that he'd accumulated in the last seven years that meant anything to him personally.

He'd come across a few items that belonged to Lynn — a scarf, several pieces of lingerie, a pair of earrings, and a couple of books that she'd brought over during the years. It struck him that he felt dispassionate about each item and he wondered if his emotions might be fooling him. He set that aside, packed her things into a box, slapped a label on it and mailed it to her. She was out of his life completely now.

He'd taken his business clothes and good shoes to a local men's shelter that he knew prepared their clients to return to the workplace; the rest he packed into a duffel bag.

As the days passed and the house emptied, Grey found that he anticipated leaving more than he expected. He signed paperwork that needed to be signed, and finally found himself with nothing to do but leave for parts unknown. He carried very little away with him. His clothes fit into a suitcase and a duffel; a second duffel bag was filled with books and things that had held importance to him in the past. He also took two white five-gallon pails, one of which he hadn't looked inside since his parents died. His father had saved very few things from Grey's childhood and he'd stuck them into the bucket before pressing the lid closed.

Grey's childhood hadn't been easy. His mother was an alcoholic, bitter at how her life had been destroyed by her husband and children. Grey's two younger siblings had been placed in foster care and then adopted along the way. He'd lost of track of them during his own years of alcoholism. He hoped they were happy and healthy. He'd stayed at home because of his age. He was sixteen and she could no longer hurt him. His father traveled and was never home. There had been an expectation that Grey would remain home with his mother, but after she threw a pan of boiling pasta at him, he didn't care. It had mostly missed him, but he still had scars on his back from the burns. Hockey had allowed him to escape, and once he was gone, he never looked back. The team became his family and was there for him when he hurt himself in the car accident. If he hadn't become a drunk, they would have still been part of his life, but even the best guys on the team couldn't overcome Grey's alcohol-based depression. He could never let that happen again.

The day finally came when he met his real estate agent at the front door. They walked through the house once more; her taking notes, Grey nodding in agreement. He just wanted to be finished. He finally handed her the keys to the house, got in his truck, put the key in the ignition and then sat in his driveway. This was a good move. He could feel it. Every time he moved on, his life got better.

CHAPTER TEN

In only minutes after leaving the city limits, Grey felt freer than he had in months. He pulled off at the first rest area, got out of his truck and took in a deep breath. He didn't know where he was going and he didn't care. Something would come up. Even after all he'd been through, he knew in his heart that people were basically good — all he had to do was take time to invest in them and they would respond in kind. He smiled at a couple walking past with their small terrier. Maybe he'd get a dog. It would be fun to drive across the country with a dog sitting beside him in the truck.

Grey got back on the highway and continued to head east. There was no limit to what he could do. He could stop whenever he wanted to stop and go wherever his heart directed. This was his life now. He owed no one.

He caught himself humming and realized that the tune was *The Impossible Dream*. He wasn't dressed in armor and riding a beaten down old donkey, though this old truck was pretty close. Maybe this was the beginning of his quest.

Passing through Reno, Grey considered stopping. During the

bright light of day, it didn't hold quite the fascination as it did when neon lights called visitors into its casinos. He'd been here many times over the years. Today was not a day to return to past memories. Today was a day to make new ones. He couldn't remember the last time he'd been on this highway. He drove for hours, passing Nevada mountain ranges. Nothing called out to him to stop, so he continued to drive.

Toward the end of the day, he stopped in Elko, Nevada. These wide-open spaces took a long time to pass through, but that was okay. He hadn't thought about much of anything today.

That was one of those things that neither Lynn nor Nan could understand. When they'd been together, Lynn incessantly asked what it was he was thinking about. She refused to understand that there had been nothing traveling through his synapses. He'd just zoned out. Nan had difficulty with the concept as well, though she'd laughed about it. Her parents had the same argument all the time. After forty years of marriage, her mother still refused to accept that the man she'd lived with all those years wasn't considering the important news of the day. All the women Grey had ever known well was unable to turn their minds off, even for a short period of time.

Today had been quite relaxing. The only decisions he'd made were when to stop for gas — he made sure to fill up often — and when to stop for a snack and a break. After seven years of working to understand the inner psyches of severely broken people, this freedom was something that Grey could almost reach out and touch, it was so real to him.

He pulled up in front of an old strip hotel after leaving the interstate. Rooms were inexpensive and when he put the key in the door, he was pleasantly surprised at the size and cleanliness of the room. He'd asked for a room at the far end, not wanting to be disturbed tonight by the sounds of trucks coming and going as their drivers stopped for the night. The clerk at the counter pointed him to a diner down the road and Grey had dinner before returning to his room.

When he took his phone out of the duffel where he'd stuffed it, he found only one call and it was from Mavis. He listened to the voice mail she left for him.

"Grey, I just spoke with Deborah and she says that you are gone. I want you to know that you will be missed. If you ever need anything, please let me know. I will always be there for you. Thanks for your friendship and I'm going to miss you." She paused, then spoke again. "I really will miss you, Grey. Take care of yourself. Let me know when you settle down somewhere. Have a good life."

He looked at the floor and played the message again as a sigh shuddered through his body. It was over. He could hardly believe that it was finished. He hoped that he hadn't made the worst decision in his life, but he couldn't go back now.

~~~

Two days later, he was still driving. He'd taken it easy, not wanting to rush anywhere. He'd made a quick pass through Salt Lake City, just enough to see the Mormon temple and then out to the lake. He didn't want to talk to people or get caught up in crowds of tourists. The solitude of his truck was enough.

The drive through Wyoming had taken longer than he expected, but now he was in Nebraska. The different landscapes had been beautiful and he was grateful to have the opportunity to watch them transform as he traveled. With each mile, he felt peace restoring his soul. This country, with all of its problems, was filled with beauty and with wonderful people.

Grey stopped for a break and wandered across the road from the gas station to a stand where a family was selling rugs and fluttering kites. His leg was giving him more trouble than usual — something he attributed to the long days he spent in the truck. He tried to stretch his legs whenever he stopped, but he wasn't used to spending this much time in one position.

"Howdy," the man behind a table said as Grey approached. "Looking for something?"

"Just taking a walk. Your rugs are very attractive."

The man stood, and leaning on a cane, limped over to Grey. "We have more colors. If you don't see something that you like right off, just let me know. I might have it."

"I'm not looking to purchase a rug," Grey said. "My home is the road today and I have no floor on which to lay it."

"That's not a good place to be," the man said. "Are you okay? Do you need some help?" Before Grey could respond, the man called out to someone in the small RV. "Stella. Bring out that pitcher of lemonade and some of those cookies you made last night."

"You misunderstood," Grey said. "It isn't that I am lost, I just haven't found my home. When I do find it, I will know."

The man tapped a lawn chair with his cane. "Take a seat, young man. Join me. We haven't had many visitors yet today."

His wife, a pleasantly plump woman in shorts she shouldn't be wearing and a tank top that showed too much skin for Grey's taste, came out with a plastic pitcher hooked on two fingers, a container of cookies and three glasses tucked in her elbow. Grey was glad the pitcher had a lid, but he assumed she'd done this before.

"Hi there," she said, beaming at him. "Where you from?"

"California. I'm sorry. I didn't mean to intrude."

"Roy here doesn't get too many men who stop and chat with him. He's glad of the company. Where you going?"

Grey shook his head. "I must admit that I do not yet have the answer to that question. Wherever the road takes me, I will follow."

"One of those," she said.

"One of those?"

"You know, those nomads who are out to find themselves. Are you looking for yourself?" She put the pitcher and glasses down on a wooden box, then handed the container of cookies to her husband. "Go ahead and sit. If you're following the road, you're in no hurry. Right?"

Grey dropped into the chair, surprised at how much his leg hurt. He stretched it out in front of him.

"Saw you limping there," Roy said. "Football injury?"

"No," Grey said. "I was in an unfortunate accident. Long days of driving have aggravated the injury."

Stella poked at her husband. "You should show him. Want me to get them?"

Roy nodded. He didn't look as if he wanted to get up out of his chair again either.

She went over to the trailer parked beside their RV and returned with five beautifully carved walking sticks. "Roy carves these in his spare time." Stella handed them to her husband before going back inside the RV.

Grey leaned forward and put his hand out. Roy offered one and Grey ran his fingers across the carved head. It was smooth and had an easy grip around the vines and flowers. Using it as leverage, he stood, then walked back and forth with it. "This is lovely workmanship. Would you consider parting with it for a fair price?"

The deal took the last cash that Grey was carrying. He was thankful that he'd had enough. After finishing his glass of lemonade, he used the walking stick to help him stand upright again and put out his hand. "You've offered me joyful hospitality today and I am grateful, but it is time for me to press onward."

Roy pulled himself to his feet, leaning on his own cane. "Thankee for stopping by. Me and the wife wish you the best in your travels. Maybe we'll run into you again someday."

"Please offer your wife my gratitude." Grey nodded, and using his new walking stick for added support, crossed back to his truck. People were really good. He needed to find more of them on this trip.

CHAPTER ELEVEN

Crossing the Missouri River bridge into Iowa, Grey decided it was time to see more of the countryside than he could while driving on the interstate. He remembered that one of his buddies from his days of playing hockey together spoke fondly of his home in north central Iowa. On long bus trips, he would wax poetic on the beauty of lush green fields of corn and beans that had been planted in thick, dark black soil. He talked of white farmhouses and red barns, along with black cows and white sheep that dotted the rolling hills of the state.

Grey pulled off into the parking lot of an ice cream shop and took his phone out, thankful that there were still no calls waiting for his response. He really had left everything behind. His finger hesitated over the phone app, considering a call to Nan. She hadn't tried to contact him since the day she left and he'd been so busy these last two weeks that whenever he thought about calling her, he was able to push it aside and think about something else. She'd have hated this drive. The girl could barely sit still at her desk during the day.

He shook his head. It wasn't her desk any longer. He hadn't

bothered to learn the new office manager's name, but she wasn't going to last long. Bill Wagner had started in on her the first time he met the young woman and she'd been immediately cowed. Mavis wouldn't put up with that very long.

Shaking his head, he chuckled. Why did he care about any of that? Never again would he see those people. It was strange to realize that another chapter in his life had closed so dramatically … or not terribly dramatically, as it was. What was the quote about not with a bang, but a whimper? That's how he felt about how he'd left this part of his life. He'd whimpered and taken off, hoping that now that he'd turned this next page, it would be better.

He programmed in a route using state and county highways that would take him to a small town named Jewell. The map tried to return him to the interstate, but he gave it a few taps and committed several of the highways and cities to memory. He'd check it again if he got lost. After arriving in Jewell, he wasn't sure what his next steps would be. His buddy no longer lived there, but the name of the town was intriguing. If there was nothing there, he'd move on. There was an entire country to see and he'd barely scratched the surface. It had taken three days, but he finally felt like seeing something beyond the gray paved interstates.

Heading north, his first destination was Highway 30. It paralleled the interstate through Iowa and passed through quite a few small towns. Signs in Denison alerted him to the fact that Donna Reed had been born there. He'd only ever seen black and white re-runs of her television show. When he saw signs calling the road the 'Lincoln Highway,' he made a mental note to do more research. His memory of history didn't place automobiles on highways until long after Abraham Lincoln had been assassinated, but it was interesting to see something like this cutting through the center of Iowa.

By the time he arrived in Boone, Grey was hungry and drove into town to find something to eat. He'd driven most of the day consuming nothing more than a few snacks and coffee. He was fascinated as he drove through the main street into the downtown area. The homes along this drive were immense. Set far back from the road in large yards, they were clean and well-maintained, each unique and beautiful. What a pretty town. He parked in front of a pizza place and looked up and down the street at the shops, many of which were ending their work days.

Once inside, he placed his order and took a seat at a table, choosing to look around rather than shut himself away. He checked the map on his phone.

When the waitress arrived with his drink, he caught her attention. "If I were to travel north from here, what's the optimal route to Jewell?"

She bent over and tapped his phone, moving the map. "Just north of here, you can turn and go through Bellingwood." Smiling, she stood back up. "I'm from there. If you get on that road and keep going east, you'll get over to Story City. Just hop on the interstate and go north. You'll find Jewell."

"If I prefer not to travel via interstate?"

"Oh." She bent back over and pointed at the map again. "Take Highway 69 north before you get to Story City. That'll go right to it. It's just a slower drive. What's in Jewell?"

"I have yet to discover its beauty. Other than its name, I have no expectations."

"Bellingwood's pretty. It doesn't take very long to get through it, but it's a nice little town." She smiled and walked away.

Grey watched people come in and out, taking pizza orders with them, stopping to talk to folks they knew. He wondered at their stories. Had they had a stressful day? Were they going home to relax in front of the television? Was that man happy at home? He didn't seem to be in any hurry to leave, lingering over a last slice of pizza. The woman with four clamoring children just wanted to pick up her order and get everyone back into the car. After she paid, she handed a box to each of the two oldest and tried to move her horde back out the front door without tripping over the slow moving little ones.

The afternoon was fast escaping as Grey returned to his truck. He'd need to decide where he was staying tonight. Maybe the young girl was correct. There were options at the Story City exit on the interstate. He could spend the night there and explore the small town that had caught his attention. And maybe he needed to cease thinking about that town and focus on some others in the region. The waitress had expressed a love for her own community. If he arrived there and discovered that it was filled with interesting people, he could return to Boone and spend the night in a hotel. Signs pointed to Mamie Eisenhower's birthplace. He would enjoy exploring the smaller historical sites around the country. He'd been in such a rush to leave California. Now might be a good time to slow down and see what America had to offer him.

He followed the simple directions the waitress gave him and drove out of Boone, heading north. His buddy from hockey had been absolutely right — rolling hills, black dirt, and green cornfields. Small farmsteads dotted the landscape as he traveled. He was startled out of his reverie when he came upon a stop at an intersection with a sign pointing to Bellingwood. If she loved her hometown, he should take a moment to see what it had to offer.

Turning right, he watched the landscape give way to a small community. His eye was caught by an old schoolhouse to the south. There was quite a bit of activity there. Someone must have purchased it for renovation ...

The thought had barely entered his mind when out of the blue a small car cut in front of him, going so fast that he couldn't stop in time. He slammed on his brakes, but it was too late. The sound of metal crumpling rang in his ears as the impact threw him forward and then back again. He blinked several times, trying to take in what had just happened. Taking stock of his body, he realized that he wasn't badly hurt, but the small car was crushed. He pushed his door open and got out, heading for the other vehicle. Onlookers were moving toward him. Hopefully they'd call for help.

When he got to the mangled car, he bent in, saw the driver and stood back up. How could his life continue to fall apart like this? It was too much. He threw his head back, hoping for a sound to escape, but nothing came out.

"Are you hurt anywhere?" a young woman asked him.

"Don't bother with me," Grey said, pointing to the car. "Help him."

"I've called 9-1-1 and my husband is with him. I want to know if you've been hurt."

Grey couldn't make sense of this. He just wanted her to take care of that young man. "I don't know. I don't know," he said. "He came out of nowhere. I didn't mean to hit him. All of a sudden, he was right there in front of me and I couldn't stop in time."

"What's your name, sir?"

Grey tried to focus on her. Why was she asking him questions like this? "Why do you need my name?"

"Because I want to have a conversation with you. I'm Polly Giller and that's my husband, Henry. And you are?"

"Alistair Greyson." There was so much more he could tell her, but he just wanted this to be over. He kept looking back toward the car where the young man seemed to be losing too much blood, and was thankful when he heard emergency sirens coming.

The first vehicles on site were police cars and soon one of the men was standing in front of him.

"What happened here?"

Grey looked at the two vehicles. "I was just coming through town when all of a sudden, he was in front of me. I couldn't get stopped. He was right there."

"I need to see your driver's license and car registration." The officer moved him away from the young woman. "Have you been drinking this evening?"

If the man knew what Grey had been through lately, his assumption about Grey's drinking could have been right, but tonight that wasn't a consideration. "No, thank goodness."

"What does that mean?"

"Nothing, really. It's been a long, difficult several months."

The officer put his hand out. "I'm Police Chief Ken Wallers. It doesn't look like your truck is going anywhere. Do you have family around here?"

Grey shook his hand. "No. Nothing."

"We've got a hotel in town, but I want to send you down to the hospital and have you checked out first. We'll make sure you get to where you need to go. Why don't you sit in my squad car while they take care of young Denis, there?" He walked Grey to the car, opened the back door and waited for Grey to sit. "You'll be okay. I'm sorry this happened to you, but we've got you."

Grey sat back and the police chief walked away and over to the couple who had burst into action. They looked friendly, and the woman, though insistent, made him feel safe. It felt like he was talking to someone who was a lot like Nan. If he was going to be in town for a while, he ought to get to know these people. He did a quick self-check, hoping that there wasn't anything wrong with his body. His knee was giving him quite a bit of trouble, but nobody could help that.

He'd let them take him to the hospital, but he was okay. He craned his neck to watch as they put the young man in the ambulance. Why had he driven in front of Grey's truck? It had to have been deliberate, and he had heard people whispering about the kid's drug and alcohol problems. As much as he didn't want to, he knew he was going to get involved. He couldn't help himself. Maybe Bellingwood was where he could find his redemption.

~~~

The next chapter in Grey's story begins in *Look Always Forward* — Book 11 in the Bellingwood series.

THANK YOU FOR READING!

I'm so glad you enjoy these stories about Polly Giller and her friends. There are many ways to stay in touch with Diane and the Bellingwood community.

You can find more details about Sycamore House and Bellingwood at the website: http://nammynools.com/. Be sure to sign up for the monthly newsletter so you don't miss anything.

Join the Bellingwood Facebook page:
https://www.facebook.com/pollygiller
for news about upcoming books, conversations while I'm writing and you're reading, and a continued look at life in a small town.

Diane Greenwood Muir's Amazon Author Page is a great place to watch for new releases.

Follow Diane on Twitter at twitter.com/nammynools for regular updates and notifications.

Recipes and decorating ideas found in the books can often be found on Pinterest at: http://pinterest.com/nammynools/

And, if you are looking for Sycamore House swag, check out Polly's CafePress store: http://www.cafepress.com/sycamorehouse

CPSIA information can be obtained
at www.ICGtesting.com
Printed in the USA
LVHW08s1048141018
593523LV00008BA/405/P

9 781977 616739